A Love Like This

The Remembrance Trilogy—Book 3

by

Kahlen Aymes

TELEMACHUS PRESS

This book is a work of fiction. Names, characters, places and incidents are either the product of the author's imagination or are used fictitiously. Any resemblance to actual persons, living or dead, or to actual events or locales is entirely coincidental.

A Love Like This: The Remembrance Trilogy—Book 3

The publisher does not have any control over and does not assume any responsibility for author or third-party websites or their content.

Edited by Elizabeth Desmond, Sally Hopkinson and Kathryn Voskuil.

Cover Designed by Telemachus Press, LLC

Cover Art:
Copyright © iStockPhoto/Stockphoto4u
Copyright © iStockPhoto/ 19757859/ Sarah Neal Photography

Published by Telemachus Press, LLC
http://www.telemachuspress.com

Visit the author blog site:
http://www.kahlen-amyes.blogspot.com

ISBN: 978-1-939927-18-7 (eBook)
ISBN: 978-1-939927-19-4 (paperback)

Version 2013.07.17

Acknowledgments

For my readers… I appreciate and adore you and thank you for every moment you spend with my words. You are my inspiration.

Deepest appreciation to "Team Ryan." You know who you are and all that you do for me. I'm forever grateful for your dedication. XOXO

The book blogs are too many to mention, but I thank you for every post, tweet, share, and word of encouragement. I couldn't do it without your incredible support.

To my daughter, Olivia, for being understanding when I am chained to my keyboard. Thank you and I love you.

When love beckons to you, follow him,
Though his ways are hard and steep.
And when his wings enfold you,
yield to him,
Though the sword hidden among his
pinions may wound you.
And when he speaks to you, believe in him,
Though his voice may shatter your dreams
as the north wind lays waste the garden.

For even as love crowns you
so shall he crucify you.
Even as he is for your growth
so is he for your pruning.
Even as he ascends to your height
and caresses your tenderest branches
that quiver in the sun,
So shall he descend to your roots and shake
them in their clinging to the earth.

~From The Prophet by Kahlil Gibran

A Love Like This

The Remembrance Trilogy—Book 3

~1~

Julia ~

I waited outside the ER for my husband, Ryan, to come out at the end of his shift. Ryan was halfway through his first year of residency at St. Vincent's in Lower Manhattan. Later in the evening we'd be flying up to Boston where his brother, Aaron, and one of our best friends, Jenna, were getting married. I was very happy for Jenna. She waited almost nine years for Aaron to marry her, but the responsibilities of college and then medical school had been his priority. She supported his efforts without complaining and, after gentle nudging, Aaron finally bought a ring.

Ryan and Aaron fulfilled their childhood dream of attending Harvard Med together, but afterward, Ryan had chosen to do his residency in New York City so that he and I could be together. We'd gotten married on a spur of the moment decision at the same time that he and Aaron were graduating last June. Every minute since then had been heaven. At least, the moments we actually spent together.

I tapped nervously on the steering wheel of my Mazda and, as I looked around the parking lot, a mixture of impatience and uneasiness settled over me. The ER was generally busy with all kinds of cases, and Ryan regaled me with details on several occasions. Most were just what you'd expect, but, as in any major city, there were gangs in New York and Ryan was constantly dealing with shootings, beatings and stabbings. I shuddered as fear I tried to push back, resurfaced. It wasn't as if the many hours he spent away from me weren't bad enough without worrying about these types of people hanging out at the hospital while their 'homies' were treated for the latest fight or drive-by.

Take tonight. There were several rough young men hovering outside of the entrance, smoking, spouting trash-talk and generally harassing anyone who tried to go into or out of the hospital. No distinctive racial group, they were a mixture of white, black, Asian and Hispanic descent, but collectively, they were a scary bunch. Two or three of them looked particularly agitated during the conversation. I couldn't make out their words, but I could tell from their expressions and body language that they were arguing. One tough-looking thug, who was clearly the leader, shoved another of them with enough force to send him sprawling head first onto the pavement.

"Do that again and I'll kill you, man! I'll fucking kill you!"

I flushed and shrank down in the seat a little further, hoping they wouldn't take much notice of me while I waited for Ryan. My heart constricted in worry that he would have to walk through them on his way to where the car was parked across the lot.

An old man entering the hospital glanced in the group's direction and was rewarded with a bitter threat, which was loud enough so I could hear clearly.

"What are you looking at, motherfucker? Stay out of our business or I'll cut you!" he shouted. I jumped when he pulled out a switchblade and waved it at the old man.

I swallowed and made sure the doors to the car were locked. The gentleman put up both hands in a silent plea to be left alone as he hurried inside the double doors. It was no wonder Ryan didn't like me waiting here alone, though, I hardly found myself

in this sort of situation. My job at Vogue was on the Upper East
Side and our new apartment was in Midtown Manhattan and
rarely did Ryan allow me to visit him at work.

I glanced at my watch. Ryan would be out any minute and
we'd go straight to the airport. It was ten minutes past four and I
was grateful for the daylight that remained. It was cold and I
needed to keep the car running, and the defroster kept the windows from fogging over.

As I waited, I let my mind drift. Jenna planned a big affair
and was holding her reception at the same hotel where Ryan and
I were married. Our wedding was smaller and more intimate than
the one Jenna had planned, but it was a perfect reflection of our
relationship. Very close and tight, so, very intimate.

Guh! My heart still thudded within my chest at the memory
of the vows and the incredible night of lovemaking that followed. It didn't matter how much time passed, I was more and
more in love with my beautiful husband every day. Ryan was my
entire world and I looked forward to the time alone with him in
Boston. His work schedule was so frantic that our time together
was precious, and there were days when we wouldn't see each
other at all beyond a kiss as we passed each other coming and
going. I missed him like I hadn't seen him in years.

I grabbed my purse from the passenger seat and reached in
to retrieve my ringing phone.

"Yes, Jen!" I smiled as I answered. She was so anxious to
have us back in Boston, that I'd expected her call.

"When will you be here?"

"Soon. We will be! Relax."

"I'm relaxed. Aaron, on the other hand, is a basket case.
You'd think he was being led to the gallows," she mocked with a
chuckle. "I think he's more excited to see you and Ryan than he
is to marry me!"

"Nah. He's probably just yanking your chain. You know Aaron."

"I'm so happy, Julia! The dresses came today. Ellie's outdone herself again."

I looked cautiously at the group of men, now beginning to take notice of me sitting in my car, and I bristled in my seat. I was frightened but I didn't want it to come through in my voice. "I can't wait to see them. Jenna, were you able to get the suite for us?"

"Yes! It's a good thing the Four Seasons has more than one honeymoon suite or you would have been out of luck!"

Excitement raced through me as I anticipated Ryan's reaction to spending the weekend in the same suite we'd spent our wedding night in. I smiled a secret smile in retrospection, but then one of the unruly young men was making his way toward me, leaning down to glare into the front window of the car. I turned my back and faced the opposite direction, hoping he would leave me alone. *That's if we make it out of this stupid parking lot!*

I looked nervously at the door and wondered if I should pull closer. One of the smaller men was nudging the leader and pointing in my direction. I bristled in my seat.

"Thank you. I can't wait to see you! Will you be at the hotel tonight?" I ignored the men and concentrated on my call with Jenna but my pulse quickened and I shuddered.

"Yes. Gabe and Elyse are already here and my parents are arriving around the same time as you and Ryan."

"Ellie and Harris?"

"They're here already and Marin and Paul arrive on Saturday morning."

"Yes, Dad is busy with a case and can't be away too long, but I'm happy that they will be there. I never expected to have us all together this soon." This was going to be the first time I'd seen my parents together since their reunion and our wedding.

Ryan finally appeared behind the glass of the hospital entrance and was soon walking toward me across the parking lot. My heart stilled as he glanced in the direction of the men and nodded to them. It seemed to calm them slightly and they dropped back, letting him pass without incident. I breathed a sigh of relief and the heavy pounding of my heart reminded me how scared I really was.

"No shit. I'm excited to see everyone!" Jen said breathlessly.

"You deserve this, finally. Ryan is almost to the car, so I'll call you when we land. Love you."

"You, too! Bye!"

Ryan opened the passenger side door and slid into the black leather seat and I quickly relocked the doors. He looked worn out but leaned toward me after he was in the car and cupped the side of my face with his hand.

"What's the matter? Did those men bother you?" he asked, intently searching my face.

I shook my head.

"No, but they are frightening. Do they always hang out here?"

"No. Don't worry. We get some rough people here, but other times they're just idiots playing around. Tonight someone got pushed off a roof while they were sparring with friends. They don't understand how dangerous that kind of injury can be. The kid had a ruptured spleen and went to emergency surgery. If we didn't get it out, he would have died of internal bleeding. Stupid fuckers."

His scent enveloped me and I longed to melt into his arms and feel safe, to know he was safe. I searched his face for reassurance, but my heart constricted despite myself.

"Ryan, they look like a gang."

"Probably. Don't worry, baby. I'm just glad you work uptown."

My eyes searched his. The blue depths were intent despite the fatigue that lurked there.

"It's adorable how you worry so much, but there is no reason for it. I'm okay except I'm missing my wife so much it hurts," he said in his velvet voice. I pressed my face into his warm hand.

I smiled, taking in the dark circles beneath his deep blue eyes. "Ryan, you're so tired." I was more at ease now that he was here beside me, but the men were still watching us from a few yards away. Ryan didn't seem to notice, his focus was completely on me.

"I'm okay." His thumb brushed over my bottom lip and pulled it down slightly as his gaze dropped to my mouth. "Give me some of that." He smiled softly before his other hand closed around my forearm. He pulled me toward him and his mouth settled on mine in a gentle kiss.

I couldn't help it, my mouth opened and my own hands reached out to clutch at the front of his dark blue button-down between the opening of his black leather jacket. He'd changed out of his scrubs for the flight and was looking good enough to eat. He responded by increasing the pressure of his mouth on mine and the hand holding my head pulled me closer. His thumb brushed back and forth along my jaw as his tongue plundered my mouth. We kissed deeply for a minute before his mouth lifted and then returned to tease my lips in a series of sucking kisses.

"Jesus, you taste so good. Why does it feel like I never fucking see you?" he said and kissed me one more time.

"Maybe because you never fucking see me," I quipped in return and he groaned, his mouth reaching for mine again as his eyes slid closed, but I rested my forehead against his, denying him the kiss he was seeking.

"Baby, I could kiss you forever, but we're going to miss our plane. Besides, those goons are still eyeing us, and they scare me." I reached up and brushed my fingers along his jaw and then up to push the hair back off of his brow. "We should go." I moved more fully into my seat and put the car in gear.

"Don't be scared. I won't let anything hurt you, sweetheart."

"The only thing that hurts me lately is the lack of time with you."

His mouth twisted and he frowned, pulling the seatbelt down and buckling it.

"Um hmm, and here I thought getting married and moving in together was going to make things easier," he said apologetically. His hand reached out and his warm fingers closed around mine, lifting my hand to his mouth to brush his lips across the inside of my wrist. His touch always set my body on fire and my heart thudded in my chest.

"Mmm... well, I'm thankful for the time we do have together. This weekend will be hectic, but at least we'll be together for 72 hours. I want to make sure that you get some rest tonight."

"Well, I want to make sure I get some lovin' from my gorgeous wife," he said with a devilish grin. "Lots and lots of lovin'." He turned in his seat and looked at me seriously as I navigated my way through the city.

"Ryan, what is it?"

"I know this weekend is about Aaron and Jenna but I want some time for just us; if we can manage it. I really miss talking and just *being* with you. Alone."

I knew what he meant. He was my best friend in the world and we were closer than any couple I'd ever seen. Lately, on the rare occasion our schedules meshed we were so desperate for the physical connection; we devoured each other. Rarely did we go out and do anything together. Instead, we opted to closet ourselves away from the world and soak up as much love as we could in the few precious hours we had. His eyes were sad and I desperately wanted to see him smile again.

"Oh? I remember now, it's my *words* you can't live without. Not my body, right?" I cocked my head and raised my eyebrow. It worked.

Ryan laughed and squeezed my hand. I knew by his response that he remembered the conversation that I was referring to. "That's right. I'll be completely *miserable* making love all night if I can't talk to you first."

"Yeah, right. Okay, then I'll make sure to throw the new lingerie I bought for this weekend out when we get to the hotel."

Ryan sobered, his thumb rubbing back and forth over the hand that he held. "I love you, Julia," he said seriously. "I do want to talk to you. I want to find out what's going on... but I love that you think about me that way. You always know just what I need."

"Because you're everything to me. Even if I can't see you so much, I wouldn't trade one second of my life with you. I love you." I threw a glance and a small bittersweet smile at him before returning my focus back on the traffic.

Since my accident nine months before, there were times when he'd get deep and brooding, withdrawing into himself and I was sure he was remembering how painful it was. I was sometimes amazed by how much it still affected him, but I'd learned to recognize the look in his deep blue eyes and the silence that he would cloak himself in. The pain that still flitted across his perfect features from time to time ripped at my heart and I wished I could vanish it forever. As much as we loved each other, we no longer took any of our time together for granted, having seen how precarious life could be. We were both well aware of how much we needed each other.

My throat tightened up as I tried to speak. As usual, Ryan could read me like a book. My emotions and my thoughts all laid bare to him, despite my attempts to squash them.

"I never want to go through anything like that again." The ache in his voice was still so prevalent whenever he spoke of it and I wondered if he realized that had I not been in that accident, we'd have a one month old baby by now. Despite the happiness we shared and my memory being fully restored, he held his misery very close to him and we were both still suffering the loss. Ryan had endured so much when I didn't remember the past, the baby, or what he called our mad, mad love.

My heart thumped loudly in my chest remembering the night it all came rushing back when he poured out his pain as I poured out mine. Every precious moment and ounce of pain brought us closer. I still found it almost impossible that anyone could love this much. Almost, because the proof of it was sitting next to me.

"We won't. I love you so much," I said, my voice trembling and my eyes welling slightly. I blinked back the tears as we drove in silence for a few minutes, our hands laced together. I could feel his eyes boring into my profile so I turned my face toward him. "I have a surprise for you later," I said softly. His eyes locked with mine and the corner of his mouth lifted in the crooked smile that always took my breath away.

"In addition to the lingerie?" he asked. When I nodded, he smiled even bigger. "I have one for you as well."

"Really? Tell me what it is," I said anxiously, the mood suddenly lighter.

"Not a chance," Ryan said shortly but with a wide grin. "If I have to suffer, so do you."

"Mmm."

"Julia, do we have to meet up with the others tonight? I'd rather not. Not tonight."

"Ryan." I shook my head at him in exasperation. "*Yes.* Your parents are here and we're meeting them with Aaron and Jenna in the bar for drinks. We don't have to stay long, but we do have to go for a bit. Aren't you anxious to see them? It's been six months and you're the best man."

"I suppose I should be, but I just want to get you alone and wrap myself around you all night. I don't give a damn if it's selfish."

"We can get some wine. It will help you relax so you can sleep, and when we go back to the room, I'll run you a bath and give you a massage so you can relax. We'll have plenty of time to be alone."

"Okay," he said begrudgingly, his lower lip extending boyishly in a slight pout. My heart leapt at the adorable gesture, and the obvious emotions behind it. His desire to be alone with me echoed my need to have his arms around me. "But I disagree. There is never enough time with you. I feel like I haven't touched you in forever."

"You're touching me now."

"You know what I mean, Julia. I want to make love to you. I need to lose myself inside you." I drew in a deep breath as his voice reverberated in several waves of electricity. Yes, I knew what he meant. I craved his touch like air. "*I want you.* Every second." The tone of his voice lowered huskily.

"It's only been four days," I said in an attempt to offer comfort, and also communicate that I was aware of how long it'd been since we'd last been together. It was not lost on him and Ryan's hand tightened around mine.

His schedule was so erratic that we rarely were home together at the same time, and when he was he was beat and most of the time I had to insist that he sleep.

"Four days too long."

Ryan ~

I watched Julia from a few feet away, at the far end of our group. My parents reserved four tables along one side of the room near the band. She was laughing with Ellie and Jen, their faces full of animation and their eyes full of the type of light that was visible even in the dimly lit room. Thank God we were able to check in and take a quick shower before we'd been required to come down to socialize.

I cringed and inwardly chastised myself. *For Christ's sake!* It was my only brother's wedding. Even if we weren't related by blood, we were bound by life, love and experience. The least I could do was show up long enough to celebrate.

The girls' tinkling laughter filtered down from the end table that they were all huddled around. Jenna's younger sister, Anna, her parents and two other couples along with my family, and Ellie and Harris rounded out the numbers.

I squinted in the direction of the people I didn't recognize, trying to place them. While they were vaguely familiar, I couldn't put names with the faces, and tonight, I was too tired to try. I should have paid more attention when we first arrived. I rubbed a hand over my face from my temples down over my chin and scratched at the twenty-four hours worth of beard growth. I hadn't taken the time to shave after my shower and I was sorry now. I had no desire to chafe Julia's perfect alabaster skin, but there was no way I wouldn't be kissing all over her curves later. My fingers played along my jaw as I judged how harsh it would feel against her smooth flesh.

My mother's hand traced over the muscles of my back and brought me out of my personal thoughts and back into the room around me. She was sitting on my right and my dad was on the other side of Aaron. The two men were in deep conversation together, a concentrated frown on my brother's face and a look of wry amusement on my father's.

"Are you all right, Ryan? You look exhausted." Mom's voice floated around me. I turned toward her slightly and covered her hand with my own, trying to reassure the worry out of her voice and her expression.

"Sure, Mom. The hours are hellacious, but I'm fine. It's nothing that a few hours of sleep won't cure." I lifted the corners of my mouth in the start of a lazy smile.

"I remember when your father went through his residency. There were times when I barely saw him," Mom continued.

I groaned softly in protest. "Don't remind me." My eyes snapped back to the gorgeous picture of my own bride, giggling with her friends. Her voice sent little tingles through me and found me wishing that we'd have been smart enough to tell them that we couldn't get in until the morning and snuck off to some small hotel where we could be alone all night.

A good portion of porcelain skin on Julia's shoulders and back was open to view by the neckline of the deep pinkish-purple sweater she had on. The sleeves were long, but the design was meant to be provocative and it was. She must have felt my stare because her soft gaze landed on mine, followed by a half smile lifting her soft lips. It was an innocent gesture and full of love, but damn if my body didn't tighten immediately in response. Those pouty little lips, the lower one jutting out slightly before being captured by her top teeth, combined with those deep green pools would be my undoing. I was so fucking hungry for her; I could barely restrain myself from hauling her up to the room right then and there. My eyes narrowed and I smirked at her. Julia's eyes danced with mischief. She was well aware of the effect she had on me. She knew it well, and milked it for every last drop. I loved that shit. I chuckled softly to myself and reached for my drink.

"Julia looks beautiful. Married life agrees with her," Mom observed, her hand still moving lightly over my shirt.

"Mmmm. Uh, yes." I pulled myself out of my daze to answer her precisely and turned my head in her direction. "With both of us. We're very happy except we do wish we had more time together. Has Dad been very busy? Why don't you guys take a trip or something? Shit, if it were up to me, I'd be whisking Julia off to some remote part of the world at least once a month."

"I thought this was a trip, and once a month is a bit excessive. Even for you, darling."

Harris came back from the bar with three more bottles of wine and handed one to me with a corkscrew, followed by a waiter carrying the ice bucket for the bottle of Chardonnay.

"The money this place charges and I have to open the damn wine?" I grinned at him as I grabbed the bottle and sat up in my chair, causing my mom's hand to fall from my back. The waiter glanced at me apologetically and stood patiently beside the table until he could take the bottle, wrap it in a white linen napkin and place it inside the chiller.

"I didn't want to wait," Harris said shortly, his tone stilted as he threw a hard glance in the direction of the women. My eyes shot to Aaron's, who's widened. He shook his head just enough to communicate that I shouldn't go there.

The music coming from the band was a cover mixture of various artists; there were people dancing and the lights were low. The atmosphere was much the same as it'd been the night when I'd found that ass Moore here with my Julia. That night started out badly, but where it ended couldn't have been better.

I still thought about that night all the time. The kissing on the dance floor that finally connected Julia and I after months of denying the love and the lovemaking afterward had been so fucking profound the earth had moved. Jesus, the thought of it still rocked me to the core. Fuck, it had been hotter than hell. We didn't even have sex in the traditional sense, but it had been one of the most intimate nights of our lives. Every time we touched, I was still amazed at the intensity.

Harris poured another round of wine after I'd finished opening the bottles and then flopped back down on the other side of my mother. He seemed out of sorts so I took it as an opportunity to speak to Aaron.

"Aaron. Why aren't you on the dance floor with your bride? Get your ass out there and show me how it's done." I nodded my head in the direction of the girls. Jenna was talking to the group and using her hands in a flamboyant way to express her words. Julia threw her head back and let out a peal of laughter at whatever Jenna was saying. Aaron walked to Jenna and grabbed her hand, pulling her with him to the middle of the dance floor. Jenna was radiantly happy, her cheeks glowing and a brilliant smile dancing on her lips.

The music pulsed and my eyes moved from the couple on the dance floor to the woman walking toward our table. When Julia reached us, she leaned down and kissed my father on his cheek and moved around me to lean down to hug my mother. "I've missed you two."

"You look beautiful, sweetheart. How are you?" Dad asked.

"I'm fine, but Ryan is exhausted." Her hand found its way to the top of my head and her fingers threaded through the hair at my forehead, pushing it back. The sensation of her touch felt wonderful and my lids dropped over my eyes right before she leaned in to kiss my temple. Her perfume only added to the miracle of Julia and I reached for her free hand.

"Yes. He's been putting up a good front, but a mother knows these things."

"You're having a good time, so I can go up and you can stay with the girls, babe."

Her face twisted sardonically, clearly showing me the absurdity of my idea. "Don't be crazy. Of course I'll come up with you. It's late." Julia's eyes lifted from mine to glance between my parents and then to Harris; still brooding and staring in Ellie's direction without saying anything. "Do you mind if I steal my boy away?" she asked gently.

I rubbed her hand lightly with my thumb and leaned in toward Harris while Julia said goodnight to my parents. "Hey, man, what's up? You okay?"

"Huh?" He looked up at me while I stood from my chair, still holding my wife's hand.

"Oh, sure. I'm a little preoccupied, that's all. How have you been, Ryan?"

"Really good. Every second is occupied so it feels like the time since Julia and I have been in New York City has literally flown. How's the band doing? Julia mentioned you got a record deal a few months back, right?"

"Yes. We've just started promoting it and hopefully we'll have a tour in a couple of months."

"That's great, man. I'm looking forward to hearing all about it."

"Sounds good. We'll talk more tomorrow. Have a good night, dude."

Julia pulled her hand from mine and turned to hug Harris goodbye. "Bye, Harris. See you tomorrow." Her arms tightened around his neck and he hugged her back lightly. "Love you."

My hand slid automatically around her back and pulled her close to my side as we walked through the hotel and up in the elevators. I drew in a deep breath.

"What's going on with Ellie and Harris?" Ellie would have told her everything, and if I knew my wife, it was bugging her.

"They're struggling a little. He's asked her to marry him multiple times and she won't agree," she said softly. Her hand reached around my waist and she leaned her head on my shoulder.

"What? That's crazy. Isn't it? I thought she loved the guy." I felt her head nod against me and I turned mine to place a lingering kiss on her forehead as we walked together.

"She does. But they've distanced some due to his traveling with the band and the demands of her job. They'll work it out. You have enough to worry about," she said softly as we made our way though the hotel room door.

Finally alone. I reached out and grabbed her arm, pulling her roughly back into my arms while my eager mouth sought hers. "Julia, come here."

I gathered her close to my chest and her arms slid up over my chest and around my neck as we kissed hungrily and I turned her toward the bed. It hadn't escaped my notice that this was the same suite we stayed in on the night we were married. I was aware of it earlier as we showered and rushed out, but now I let my mind wrap around it. *My perfect girl must have conspired with Jenna.*

We kissed for a few minutes, each of us caressing and grasping, feasting on the other's mouth like we were starving. "God, you taste so good," I murmured as Julia turned her mouth away from mine to gasp for breath. I slid my hand up her back to twine in the hair at her nape. "This suite…" I murmured as my arm tightened around her waist to lift her onto the bed and follow her down, never letting go of her.

Julia nodded against my neck, her mouth kissing along the skin. "Yes," she answered breathlessly. "We have it all week-end."

I settled down on top of her, and she welcomed me into the cradle of her body, arching up to meet me. I pressed my erection into her softness and pushed my hips against hers in a slow rhythm. "Mmmm… Julia." I pushed up her sweater with eager hands and started to kiss her again but she pulled back slightly, her hands threading through the hair at both of my temples.

"Ryan, you need to rest, my love. I'll give you a back rub to relax you so you can sleep."

I growled in protest. "I need you. I want you. Right now."

She smiled and continued to stroke my hair. "Baby, we have all weekend." Her luscious mouth reached up for mine and she sucked the top lip between both of hers. "All weekend…"

My hand continued its quest upward underneath the soft cashmere toward the swelling flesh I wanted. My hand cupped around it gently and the pebbled nipple brushed my palm. Her breath rushed out causing even more blood to rush into my dick.

"I'll sleep when I'm dead. Make love with me, Julia. I'm so hard it hurts. Please." My free hand found her hip and I held her in place as I ground my hips into hers. "God, I've missed you."

"I'll take care of you, but I want you to relax. Lie back."

I sighed against the skin of her throat as I pulled the neckline of her sweater down. "Take this damn thing off," I commanded.

She lifted her arms for me and I pushed it up and over her head, exposing the delicate, black lace bra she wore underneath. I let my gaze roam over her, the sheer lace leaving her nipples visible underneath and the swells of creamy flesh gently spilling from the top edge.

"You're so beautiful. Julia…"

I kissed her hungrily again, my tongue thrusting into her mouth, demanding a response. Her mouth opened and her hands in my hair pulled me closer as she gave in, moaning softly into my mouth. Those sweet little sounds she made as I loved her drove me fucking insane.

We rolled around on the bed dry-humping and kissing until we were both panting. When she finally reached down between us and rubbed me through my slacks, I thought I'd explode. "Ryan, please lie back, baby."

I slowed my frantic movements and rolled over onto my back, pulling her with me. I couldn't bear to lose contact. "Okay, I'm on my back," I said against her mouth, licking her top lip and then kissing her softly beneath the curtain of her hair.

The room was dark and Julia moved up to turn on the lamp by the bed. "What the hell? Julia, are you stopping?" I groaned and used my hands around the back of her waist to pull her back.

She laughed softly. "No. I'm not stopping. You'll have your way, but I want mine, too."

"Don't you want to fuck your husband, Mrs. Matthews?" I smiled between kisses.

"Mmm… constantly. He's sooo hot."

"Is he?" I teased.

"Yes, irresistible."

She sat up, straddling my hips and went to work on the buttons of my shirt. She was smiling down at me, a devilish look on her beautiful features. I couldn't take my eyes off of her, roaming over the graceful curve of her neck and her collarbones, down her full breasts covered in the provocative black lace and down over her taut bare stomach.

Soon she was loosening my belt buckle and I was working on the button and zipper of her black pants. Before I could get the job done she was pulling my pants and boxer briefs down my legs, bending to kiss my stomach and run her tongue up my length as she moved down my body. I sucked in my breath.

She pulled off my socks and then moved off the bed to shed her pants, revealing a matching black lace string bikini. "Wow. Julia... that's amazing."

"I wanted to give you a massage tonight, but since you are determined to make love, who am I to deny you?"

She settled back on my lap and my hands roamed over her slender form as we started to kiss and move against each other. I could feel her heat against my groin and her hands on my body. It was too much to withstand. Soon I was pushing aside the lace and finding her entrance with my fingers.

"Oh, honey..." The breath rushed from my lungs as I parted the moist flesh and began a slow pulse against the swollen nub. I knew just how to touch her and I was anxious to see her fall apart. Her mouth hovered over mine until finally she bit down on my lower lip. *Oh, God.*

"Uh... Uh..." she was panting, pulling at my shoulders and pressing her pelvis into my hand and lap.

"Ryan, baby... Don't wait." Her knees curled around my hips. The want in her voice was my undoing. I pushed myself inside her, moaning as she sheathed me in her delicious heat.

"I love you. Uh, babe. Christ, I missed you."

After that, words were lost; as together we drowned in our love. We were frantic. Our hands moved over each other's bodies in the desperate need to get closer to each other, our mouths slanting over each other and tongues hungrily warring together. I felt my body tighten too soon and tried to slow down but she was insistent, her hips rocking into mine in a relentless rhythm. She knew she'd have me coming very soon.

I pulled my mouth away and slid my hands on both sides of her face, my thumbs running along her jaw as I looked into her eyes. She was beautiful. Breathtaking. That luscious mouth was wet and open and her heavy breathing was like music... a savage beat, exquisite evidence of the effect I had on her. Her jade eyes languid; the lids dropped and her head fell back.

"Julia. Slow down, baby. I'll come. I don't want to come yet. Stop. Stop!"

"No. I want you to let go," she whispered breathlessly. "Give it to me. I want it all." Her head lifted and she bent toward me to take my mouth with hers and her body kept moving in relentless pursuit. I could feel every curve of my erection rubbing in and out, back and forth and the pressure brought me to the point where I didn't want to stop it anymore. She felt so good and it had been too long.

I pulled the lace of her bra aside and gently squeezed, rolling her nipple between my fingers as my tongue plunged into her mouth. Julia started sucking on it at the same moment her body clenched in cadence around my body. She was coming and I could feel every tremor of it. It sent me over the edge and I exploded inside her with a groan, my body quaking and jerking against hers as my arms tightened around her and I filled her.

As our bodies came down we kept kissing, unwilling to lose the precious connection. Her fingers curled into the muscles on my shoulders and she moved her mouth along the side of my face in a series of soft caresses from my temple to my jaw. She pulled back slightly, still straddling my lap and I pulled her hips into mine tightly, still deeply imbedded inside her body.

I struggled to get control of my breathing and rested my forehead against hers, running my hands up and down her back in a light touch. I finally unclasped the bra and slid it from her body. I wanted to keep touching her. To never stop. I buried my face in her neck, kissing the slight sheen of saltiness from her skin and running my tongue along her collarbone to end with an open mouth kiss on the sweet skin below her ear. "My God. I love you, Julia."

Her fingers fisted into my hair and she pulled back to look into my face. She smiled softly, devilishly. "I know."

I would never get used to the effect she had on me. My throat tightened and I brushed her hair off her face.

"Thank you for getting this suite. I'm so lucky you're mine."

The smile went away and she shrugged softly. "You're all I want."

I swallowed and lifted the corner of my mouth. It was my turn to smile in the wonder of it. "Sweetheart, your pill cycle is up at the end of the week, isn't it?"

She nuzzled into the side of my face with her nose. "Yes. Don't worry. No period this weekend."

I chuckled softly. "That's good. I mean... wouldn't stop me. I miss you too much."

"Me, too."

"Julia. Look at me." I pulled her hand to my mouth and kissed the inside of her wrist as her eyes met mine. I could see the love behind the green depths and it never ceased to amaze me. "I think it's time, don't you?"

She didn't ask for me to elaborate. She knew. "Are you sure? You're working so much and I'm not sure if I want to go through that without you around."

"You always could read my mind."

"No." She shook her head with a smile. "I can read your heart."

Julia's eyes softened with tears and I kissed her cheekbones and then her eyelids, moving in a series of butterfly touches toward her mouth. I kissed her softly, tasting and ghosting my mouth over hers in a tender caress, tasting her like the finest wine.

"Mmm...yes. I'm sure. I'll have residency for another three years. I don't want to wait that long. Let's make our baby."

I rolled to my side and slid out of her, rising up on my elbow and letting my fingers splay out over her flat stomach. My eyes burned into hers and watched every emotion that crossed her face. She got a little crinkle between her eyebrows and her chin trembled slightly.

"But I don't want to lose this. I love this time with you." Two fat tears tumbled from her eyes. I bent to kiss them away. "It's never enough."

"Nothing will change between us."

"Uh huh! I'll get fat and ugly. Like a whale and you won't want me." Her face crumpled slightly as she tried not to cry.

Happiness burst up inside my chest and I chuckled softly. "No, you won't! You'll be carrying my baby. You'll be the most beautiful thing in the world to me. Don't you know that? You'll always be beautiful to me, and seeing you swell with the tangible evidence of our love," I had to stop as the words lodged in my throat. "There's nothing I want more." We looked at each other in awed silence for a few seconds and my chest tightened at the emotions flashing across her features. When she closed her eyes and more tears fell, I finally found my voice. "But if you don't want to have a baby now..." I began and my heart fell slightly.

She reached up and laid her fingers against my mouth. "No, I do. I do, Ryan. I want a little boy with big blue eyes and golden hair, who looks just like you."

I took her wrist in my hand and kissed the fingers against my mouth. "Are you sure? I don't want to rush you."

"As long as you promise things won't change."

"I promise. You make me so happy, Julia."

"Let's keep it a secret. That we're trying, okay?" Her voice quivered around the words and my heart swelled inside my chest. I was the luckiest bastard on the planet and I knew it. She was everything I could ever want and so much more.

I nodded as my vision blurred. "Yeah. This is the most intimate thing in the world and I don't want to share it with anyone but you. You're so perfect... you'll make a perfect baby. So beautiful."

"Because his daddy is so gorgeous."

I leaned back and reached out to turn off the light before pulling Julia gently onto my chest. She settled in with a sigh as we wrapped our arms and legs around each other. I sucked in a deep breath and stroked my fingers through her silky hair, spreading it out on her bare alabaster back.

"I love you," I said into the pitch darkness and felt her turn and place an open mouth kiss on my chest, then another. "We should use condoms for at least a month after you're off of the pill, babe."

"Yes, Dr. Matthews," she said, her voice laced with amusement.

"Well? I want that shit out of your body. He's been waiting all these months. The least we can do is make sure he's healthy when he finally gets here."

She laughed softly. I couldn't see her face, but she turned toward me and snuggled closer, resting her forehead into the curve of my neck. The warmth of her breaths rushed over my skin and I turned to kiss her forehead.

"Yes. But... we've never used condoms. How will you manage?" she teased.

"I'll manage."

"We could always abstain. Not have sex for the five weeks," she teased.

I smiled. "Like hell," I retorted with a huff, my fingers still tracing delicately over the skin of the arm she held across my body. "What should we name him?"

"We have months and months to figure that out. Something perfect, though." I yawned, exhaustion finally getting the better of me. Julia heard it. "Now hush and sleep."

Her breathing evened out and I closed my eyes.

~2~

Ryan ~

The reception was huge. Easily three times that of our wedding, Jenna must have invited all of Boston proper. She was beautiful in a huge tulle-skirted ball gown and Julia had loaned her Mom's diamond pins to wear in her hair, saying it was only fair that both of the Matthews brides share in the tradition. Jenna was very moved at the gesture and it fulfilled another tradition of something borrowed. She looked like a fairy princess, and completely luminous. Aaron was beaming and holding on to her for dear life. I smiled. *It's about Goddamn time.*

The party was winding down and my eyes searched for my own gorgeous wife. Julia, Ellie, and Jenna's sister were all in black, but like our wedding, the bridesmaid dresses were completely different styles. I noticed them briefly, but didn't register the differences all that much. All I knew was that Julia left me gasping in the black silk creation that skimmed her body and dipped low in back leaving her creamy skin completely bare to just below her waist. A smattering of sequins outlined the edging and followed around over the shoulders and to the neckline, leaving just a hint of the top swells of her breasts visible. It left little to the imagination the way it hugged her body. At least... *my imagination*, since I knew firsthand what lay underneath. It was sexy as hell and really a far cry from a traditional bridesmaid dress. Her hair was up loosely with tendrils falling free in front and one or two down the back. It gave her a soft, subtly ruffled look that screamed she'd just been made love to. I couldn't help the quirk of my lips.

I was sitting at the table we'd been assigned, next to the dance floor and talking casually to Tanner and a couple of my other Harvard friends. Aaron and Jenna were socializing with some of her family and Harris was at the bar getting drinks. I hadn't seen Julia or Ellie for a good half hour and my eyes were starting to search.

Tanner was talking about one of the cases he wanted me to consult on and I tried to keep my focus, but the alcohol and my preoccupation with my missing wife wasn't helping.

"I've run all types of pulmonary tests and pulled in specialists and none of us can seem to agree," Tanner said. "One says COPD, another says it's a heart issue. I can't find anything wrong with his lungs and his oxygen levels are normal."

"Have you done a coronary angiogram? Maybe it's a valve problem. If the lungs are clear and the patient still can't get enough oxygen, it seems logical that something is wrong with the heart. Maybe he isn't getting enough blood to or from his lungs. It may be congestive heart failure." I mumbled off the diagnosis' most obvious to me. "Might need a defibulator."

We continued our conversation and Harris came to join us, but as he was last night, he was preoccupied and distant. I noticed that he was drinking much more than he normally did.

"Hey, man." I looked up at him and followed his movements with my eyes as he sat down near me.

"Hi. Julia looks incredible tonight."

A grin broke out on my face. "Yes. Beautiful. Ellie is too. She did a beautiful job on the dresses."

Harris huffed. "This wedding has been all she's cared about for months. Honestly, I'm glad it's over. Now maybe we can get back to normal."

I turned my chair toward him so I could speak directly to him and not let the others at the table be privy to the conversation. "What's going on? Do you want to talk about it?"

He shrugged and shot me a glance before returning his attention to his almost empty glass. "It's just different. She's changed. We're both busy and she seems checked out. I come home from being on the road and there is a huge wall between us. I can't seem to knock it down and frankly, I'm sick of trying. She works like a dog on everyone else's wedding but won't marry me, and I'm not sure I even want to anymore."

"I sensed something was wrong between you two. I asked Julia about it, but all she said was that you were going through something tough, but you'd be able to work it out. I got the feeling Ellie didn't want her to share their conversations with me. Harris... I'm very sorry, man. I can't imagine going through anything like that with Julia. Is there anything I can do?"

His lips twitched in response, he closed his eyes and shook his head. "I'm not sure if even *I* can do anything about it."

"Maybe you two should get away together. It's hard to imagine that you'd be so at odds. Ellie has always been so crazy over you." I paused and he just seemed mesmerized by his drink. "How long has this been going on?"

"Four or five months; since before your wedding. Seeing you and Julia," Harris stopped and sighed, "has made me really face the abyss between Ellie and me. The two of you together... it's... well, it sort of puts my situation in perspective."

I was uncomfortable at his words and I looked down at my hands, clasped between my knees. My elbows were resting on my legs as I leaned over them. I hardly found the words. "Harris, you can't measure what you and Ellie have against my relationship with Julia. No two couples are the same. We're not perfect. We have our struggles, too."

"Yeah? Like what? I can see the love between you. Shit, I can feel it if I'm within fifty yards of either one of you. She's always touching you and the way you two look at each other. I envy you," he said, his voice deep.

I could hear the pain in his voice and I felt bad for him as I expelled my breath. "Well, our schedules are hellacious. We don't see each other much. Sometimes it's literally days apart."

"Yeah, but does Jules think you're fucking around? Ellie is distant and I can see it in her eyes that she doesn't trust me. Shit, she says she doesn't! Always accusing me of cheating on the road."

I sucked in a deep breath and filled my lungs up to capacity and blew it out before answering him, carefully considering my words.

"Julia trusts me. I trust her. It's not about that. She's very supportive of my residency, but there are times when she resents all the time I'm away from her. She didn't get married to be alone and I hate it as much, or maybe more, than she does."

"But you love what you do and the bottom line is, she backs you. She knew she was marrying a doctor. She'd never ask you to give it up, right?"

"No." I said without hesitation. If anything, it was me that wished I'd picked a less demanding profession, no matter how rewarding it was. "She'd never do that. Has Ellie... asked you to quit the band?"

"Not in so many words. But she's stopped coming to gigs and practices and then she bitches when we don't see each other. She yells at me about the fans, but that's all part of it. If we make it big, it will get even worse. I'm not sure she can handle it and

I'm not sure if I want to argue all the fucking time. I'm tired of defending myself for shit that isn't even happening."

"Damn. I didn't realize it was that bad. I can't imagine how I'd feel if my wife doubted me. I wouldn't wish that on anyone."

"That's just it. She married you when she didn't even remember everything about your relationship. That's *how much* she trusts you, Ryan. You're luckier than you know. Ellie doesn't even believe me when I say I'm not screwing the groupies and we hardly ever have sex. It's killing me."

Oh, I knew how rare the love Julia and I shared was, which made it difficult to sit here and try to convince Harris that his relationship with Ellie would be okay. I couldn't, because honestly, I wasn't sure.

"No, I know how lucky I am but I almost fucked it up good. Julia threatened to leave me to get me to trust how much she loved me, Harris. Maybe Ellie needs a wake-up call like that. I hate to suggest it because I love Ellie and I don't know her side, and I don't want to speak out of turn, but it's an idea. After it happened with us, I became even more aware that when I wake up with Julia close to me, I'm holding the world in my arms."

He huffed in exasperation. "Even when you speak about her... it's like poetry. As devastated as I am with this crap between me and Ellie, with you guys it would be worse. I hope nothing ever comes between you because it would literally knock you on your ass."

I nodded. "No shit," I said quietly. "I know. I've lived through almost losing her once and I don't think I could take it again." I reached out and put my hand on his shoulder. "It will work out if you love each other enough."

"Maybe."

"It will. Ellie totally lights up when you're around, so focus on that." I said the words, but I had to qualify it in my mind.

During the last couple of times we'd seen them, the strain between them was clear.

I sat back in my chair. The DJ had been playing some faster
music, but was finally starting a slower set. It was getting late,
almost eleven o'clock, and the talk with Harris made me want to
get my hands on Julia. My eyes continued to scan the room.

My parents and Julia's were on the dance floor along with
Aaron and Jen. I cringed when I noticed the familiar figure of
Liza across the room talking to Min and a man I didn't
recognize.

What the fuck was she doing here? Jenna detested the
woman and I couldn't see Aaron adding her to the guest list. She
must be here as a guest of someone who was invited. I prayed
she wouldn't try to talk to me and I'd been lucky so far.

"Do you want another drink, Harris? I'm going to see if can
find Julia. I can get you one on my way back."

"No, that's okay, Ryan. Go enjoy yourself. I need to find
Ellie, too. I want to leave if possible. I have an early flight and
this situation really wipes me out. I want to go to bed."

"If I see her, I'll send her to find you." I held out my hand
to him to shake it goodbye. "It'll work out, man. I wish you the
best, you know that."

"Thank you. It was good to see you and it's always a pleasure to see Jules. She's terrific."

"She'll want to say goodbye to you. Will you wait to leave
until I find her, please?"

"Sure. I'd bet money she and Ellie are together anyway."

I smiled apologetically. "Probably right."

I wandered through the crowd, acknowledging people I
knew and stopping only to chat briefly to Dr. Brighton's wife,
Cynthia, before finally finding Julia and Ellie in the hallway outside the ballroom. They were leaning against the wall with their

heads close together and Ellie was clearly upset, her face pinched and red, her cheeks damp with tears. Julia reached out to her friend and hugged her close, causing Ellie to sob into her shoulder.

I hesitated, wondering whether or not I should interrupt. Scenes like this were weird and I stopped a few feet away to consider it. Some of the other guests milling around on their way to the bathrooms or in and out of the hotel were casting curious glances in the women's direction.

Julia noticed and whispered something into Ellie's ear. She nodded and moved out of my wife's arms to begin wiping at her eyes with both hands. I moved forward and pulled a handkerchief out of my front right breast pocket and held it out to Ellie wordlessly, my left hand skirting down Julia's bare back to rest on her hip.

Ellie's expression was embarrassed but she took the hankie and dabbed at her eyes. "I'm sorry I'm such a mess. I should be inside with Aaron and Jenna and here I am blubbering like an idiot!" she sniffled.

Julia's arm was around my waist and she leaned into me slightly. I knew her heart was breaking for Ellie when her head tilted and rested on my shoulder. I resisted the urge to turn and place a kiss on her forehead, knowing I needed to focus on Ellie.

I released Julia and hugged the other girl close to me, but Julia's hand remained on my lower back, rubbing slightly and maintaining the connection between us.

"Ellie, what can I do? Can I get you a stiff drink? Do you need to go up to your room? Should we come with you?"

Ellie shook her head. "No. I can't take you away from your brother's wedding, Ryan, but thank you for being so sweet. Harris should be out here with me, but obviously, he doesn't care where I am."

I sighed. "I don't think that's true, honey. I just spoke with him. He's upset, too. You two should talk."

I glanced down at Julia, whose eyes met mine and she bit her lip. I could read the look I found there. This was bad.

"We have talked. What did he tell you?" Ellie asked, still trying not to cry.

"Uh... I think you should talk to him about it."

Ellie's face hardened and she pulled away abruptly. "Look, Ryan, I know he's been screwing those groupies. They all do it; the rest of the band, too. I'm not cut out for the life of a traveling rock star and Harris's solution is that I quit my job and follow him around the world. *My* job! Then, if he leaves me, where the fuck will I be? I can't do that. I won't," she snapped.

My hand slid down her arm and I took her hand. "I don't think he's cheating, Ellie. I really don't. I can see that you're hurt, but so is he. He's devastated that you won't marry him."

"I've seen those girls hanging on him. I surprised him on the road and I saw how they are with my own damn eyes! I can't possibly marry him after that."

I stiffened. Harris hadn't told me that part and maybe it was worse than I thought. I felt helpless to ease her pain. "I'm... Did you see him doing anything or just some woman hitting on him? Ellie, think about it."

"She was all over him, and he didn't stop her." Fresh tears filled her dark brown eyes and spilled over on to her cheeks. She used the handkerchief to dab at them.

"I see. I'm so sorry, Ellie." It seemed pointless to continue the conversation when the one she needed to have it with was Harris.

Julia was silent and I could see the resignation on her face. The deep sadness meant she'd tried to have this same talk with her friend and Ellie obviously wasn't in a place to listen. "Why don't we go say goodnight to the bride and groom and then I'll take you upstairs. If you don't feel like staying with Harris tonight, Ryan will stay with him and I'll stay with you." She looked up at me apologetically and I nodded shortly.

"Of course." I was disappointed to lose the last night of this time alone with Julia, but Ellie's situation was more important, so I agreed without hesitation.

"Thanks for being so sweet, but I wouldn't want to do that to you. I can deal with it one more night. He's flying out very early anyway."

"You're not even traveling together?" I asked incredulously.

She sensed my trepidation and rushed to clarify. "We're not going to the same place. He's meeting up with the band in Toronto and I'm going back to Los Angeles," Ellie explained.

I put one arm around Ellie and the other around Julia and turned them back toward the ballroom. "I see. Well, before you go upstairs, you owe me a dance, little bit."

"Yeah, my feet hurt anyway," Julia interjected with a smile.

I laughed and Ellie's lips lifted in a smile.

"Yeah, right. If you're trying to make it seem like I've stepped on your feet, wife, you're lying. She's the one who steps on my feet, Ellie," I teased.

"Shut up, Matthews. You know what they say; if your feet get stomped on while dancing, it's because you didn't move them out of the way fast enough."

Julia reached out the hand that was behind Ellie's back and squeezed my arm that was resting around Ellie's waist. It was more of our silent communication.

We all laughed softly as we made our way back to the table where Harris was waiting. He stood up as we approached. "Ellie, would you like to dance?"

"Uh... I was... sure, okay." She looked reluctant, but took Harris's proffered hand hesitantly. Harris's expression softened and I felt Julia relax next to me, a deep sigh expelling from her lungs.

As we watched them move off toward the center of the parquet dance floor, I turned Julia into my arms. "What about you, Mrs. Matthews? Would you care to dance with your husband? I promise not to step on your exquisite feet."

Her arms slid around my waist and she tilted her head up to look into my face. She had on ridiculously high heels, but I was still inches taller. I loved it. She seemed so fragile and perfect; so magnificent. Her skin was translucent and glowing and her full red mouth called to me in silence.

"Mmm... I only said that..."

Our bodies worked well together and dancing was no exception. I bent my head and took her mouth with mine, placing a gentle kiss on her luscious lips.

"I know, my love." I released her slightly and took her hand in mine, our fingers twining together as was our usual habit. Her head fell to my shoulder and her other hand clasped around my bicep as we made our way to the dance floor.

I pulled her close and sucked in the sweet scent of her perfume as she snuggled into my shoulder, her head coming to rest just below my chin. I rubbed it back and forth on the top of her hair a few times because I couldn't resist.

"You feel so good," I said softly as we swayed to the music. The lights were low and the dance floor was crowded. Paul and Marin had left earlier and Gabriel and Elyse were still dancing a few feet away. My mother smiled at me when she saw the way Julia and I were wrapped up together and I grinned at her over the top of Julia's head. She nudged my dad and had him glance in our direction. He shook his head at us and smirked.

I shrugged slightly and mouthed some words for their benefit, but so Julia wouldn't hear. *"I can't help it."* They both smiled
again before he twirled my mother around quickly at a tempo too
fast for the music, eliciting a high-pitched laugh.

I turned my attention to the soft woman in my arms and
bent my head to kiss the bare skin of her shoulder. She moaned
softly as my tongue pressed down between my open lips. The
sound caused an immediate reaction in my body. She had so
much control when she wasn't even trying. I still found it mind-
boggling.

"I'm sorry, baby. Being away from you tonight is the last
thing I want, but if Ellie needs me..." she said softly, one hand
running down the front of my shirt to fist in it.

I continued my trail of kisses and moved aside a small ten-
dril of hair so I could kiss the curve where her shoulder met her
neck. "Mmmm... I know. It's okay," I murmured against her
skin.

"Is it?" She pressed her body closer and slid the fingers of
both hands into the hair at my nape. I fucking loved it when she
did that and Julia was well aware of her affect on me.

"Not really, but I'll live. I understand, sweetheart."

She turned her head and kissed my jaw, her sweet breath
rushing hotly over my skin. She smelled of wine, perfume and
Julia. Utterly delicious.

"Kiss me, Ryan," she whispered softly and my arms pulled
her closer, sliding up over the bare skin exposed by the backless
dress.

"You don't have to ask me twice." I turned my mouth to
hers and it opened hotly underneath mine, both of us pulling the
other closer. The kiss was slow and hungry, probably more than
we should have allowed in the crowded room, but it was dark
and I hadn't kissed her like this for several hours.

"Mmmm," she moaned again as I lifted my head and stroked her cheek with the back of my knuckles. "I want you."

"Do you, now?" I said softly as I nuzzled her cheek with my nose. I pressed the evidence of my desire into the softness of her stomach. "You drive me crazy with it. It never goes away, Julia," I whispered against her skin as I dragged my mouth back toward hers.

"Uhhhh, Ryan. Always." We kissed again, a series of soft, open-mouth kisses that left me aching and hungry for more.

"I could swear you have a room, dude! Why the fuck aren't you using it?" Aaron's jubilant face suddenly appeared a few inches away from my wife's and mine, intruding on the intimacy. We both smiled as we abruptly broke apart. A beautiful blush flooded the apples of Julia's cheeks and I still held her close to my body. Aaron's arm was around Jenna's waist and she was laughing out loud, her face flushed with happiness. She looked every bit the radiant bride. "I thought I was the horn dog around here, and it's *my* wedding night!"

"Hey!" Julia moved out of my arms to hug my brother and his new wife, wrapping one arm around each of them, careful not to pull Jenna's very full veil from her head. She was beautiful, but *very, very fluffy.* So different from the glistening, simply elegant bridal gown that Julia had worn. My heart still skipped a beat whenever I thought about it. At times, I was even grateful for Mike Turner because of the breathtaking photos he'd taken of Julia and then of us together right after we were married. I loved looking at them and I enjoyed it immensely when I caught Julia doing so.

"Yeah? So what in the hell are you still doing here, then?" I teased. "Don't you have a plane to catch?"

"Yes! That's why we're interrupting," Jenna took Julia by the arm and started to pull her away.

"All the women are coming up to help me change and I want you to join, too. Will you?" Her eyes were sparkling when Julia nodded in the affirmative.

"Of course!" The two of them had become even closer since Julia's accident and I was happy to see it. They'd been friends a long time, but now they were more like sisters. "I wouldn't miss it!"

"Where's Ellie? She seemed upset earlier," Aaron observed.

"Yeah, she was," Julia's face fell slightly, before she tried to mask it; she wouldn't want to take the sparkle off of Aaron and Jenna's night. "She and Harris were dancing a minute ago. I'll get her and meet you upstairs, okay?" Jenna nodded as Julia took my hand and glanced at my face, an intimate smile meant only for me lifted the corners of her full lips. "I'll see you a little later, handsome." The fingers of her right hand reached up to brush along the now slightly scruffy line of my jaw and my own hand closed around them so I could kiss the tips.

"I'll miss you," I said softly and bent to kiss her mouth softly. "Love you."

When Julia left us to go find Ellie, I turned to find Jenna and Aaron watching me intently. Jen's expression was deadpan and Aaron was shaking his head.

"What?" I knew what he was thinking, but I pasted an incredulous expression on my face.

"*What?* Are you fucking kidding me?" Aaron shot back. "She's not going to the moon, dude. You're pathetic."

I chuckled in response, the rush of love I felt for my beautiful wife must have been very evident in our exchange. "We're still newlyweds, too, so shut it!" I retorted with a grin and pulled Jenna into a hug and twirled her around. "You're looking very stunning, sister. Good thing I'm already married or I'd have to steal you away."

Jenna's laughter tinkled through the air and Aaron joined in
with her. "As if!" she giggled. I sensed she was slightly tipsy and
was still holding a half full glass of champagne. She leaned in
and placed a chaste kiss on my mouth. "We're so glad you're
here, Ryan. We miss the shit out of you."

"Yeah, even though it is nice to have the apartment to ourselves," my brother nudged me and smiled before turning to Jen.
"Babe, get your sexy ass changed so we can get the hell out of
dodge." She nodded and left us to go up to her room. Anna and
my mother were waiting at the door to the ballroom to go with
her, and Mom wrapped a hand around Jenna's waist to lead her
from the room.

"You're still the consummate romantic, Aaron," I teased.
"Shit, where did I go wrong?"

"Not all of us can be sappy asses like you, Ryan."

"Whatever. Have you talked to Dad about Christmas yet?"

"Yes. He knows that we may not be able to make it since
we're taking time now to go to Hawaii. When are you taking
Julia on a honeymoon?"

We were sitting at a table and I glanced around the room.
Harris was speaking to my dad and he looked somber. He nodded his head in agreement to something Dad said and shook both
of their hands.

"Uh...I think I'll try to surprise her with a trip soon." I
longed to tell my brother that Julia and I had agreed to start a
family and so I needed to get her away before she got pregnant,
or maybe on a quest to get her that way, but couldn't since we'd
agreed to keep it between the two of us. "I could really use some
uninterrupted time with her. Don't get me wrong, this weekend
has been wonderful, but we don't have enough time to just focus
on each other these days."

"You deserve to get away, but will you be able to? It was almost impossible for me to get away and it was for my honeymoon. The hours are just ridiculous."

"We knew they would be," I agreed, "but it sucks more than I anticipated. It's worse than med school. I don't know if I'll be able to do it, but I'll try like hell. I'd sacrifice Christmas in Chicago for one-on-one time with Julia."

"Mom will be disappointed if neither of us can get there," he stated the obvious.

I shrugged slightly. "She'd understand. She knows we're both working like dogs. She lived through it with Dad."

I was watching Harris come toward us and both Aaron and I stood. Aaron threw his big arms around the smaller man in a light embrace. "Glad you could make it, dude. I hear you're heading to Canada tomorrow."

"Yes. Congratulations, Aaron. Jenna looks stunning. I have an early flight so I'm going to turn in, if you don't mind. Have a wonderful honeymoon."

"Thank you. We will," Aaron said goodbye to Harris and then turned back to me. "I should go change and say goodbye to the parents. We'll see you again as soon as we can get time off, but it might be a while."

After filling Aaron in on the conversation I'd had with Harris earlier in the evening, I said goodbye to him and wandered up to the room to wait for Julia, *or not wait for her*, whichever the case may be. If Ellie was still upset, there was a good chance I wouldn't see her before I fell asleep. Seeing everyone had been wonderful, but the late nights partying weren't helping my exhaustion. Julia was sad because her best girlfriend was in such emotional turmoil, so I wouldn't be surprised if she didn't reappear.

I loosened my tie as I entered the room and threw it on the suitcase along with the jacket of the tux. The room smelled like Julia's perfume and I inhaled the familiar scent, saddened slightly that tomorrow we were going back to the New York rat race.

Julia had a trip to Europe coming up in two weeks, the second in three months. She was usually only gone a week to ten days, but combined with my work schedule that racked up our time together right before and after, it would be more like fifteen days without each other. I ran my hand through my hair, then unbuttoned my shirt, pulling it from the waist of my pants at the same time. Julia's make-up and hair brushes were scattered all over the vanity in the bathroom—the mess left in her hurry to get ready. She did look amazing and I told myself once more how lucky I was.

My phone was on the table in the entryway where I'd left it with my keys and I heard it vibrate from the other room.

"Hey, babe," I answered on the third ring.

"Hi. Where are you?"

"I just got back to the room. Are Jenna and Aaron gone? I wasn't there to see them off, but Aaron isn't big on pomp and circumstance and I'm wiped."

"Mmm huh, they left a few minutes ago."

"Are you still with Ellie?"

"Yes. Although I think I've talked her into speaking with Harris, or at least letting him back in their room tonight. She just called him."

"It sounds like a fucked up mess to me. I talked to Harris but I'll tell you about it tomorrow on the plane."

"I'll try to get back before too long. Don't wait up, honey. Get some sleep."

"Will you wake me up when you get here?" I asked softly, not able to bear the loss of any time in her arms.

She sighed into the phone. "Ryan, you need sleep so badly. Tomorrow night you have to work and I want you to be rested."

"I can sleep when I'm dead and the flight isn't until two in the afternoon so we can sleep in a little. Even if it's just to talk to you or hold you, I want you to wake me up. Please don't argue. Fighting is the last thing on my mind tonight," I murmured and I could picture the soft smile lifting the sides of her luscious mouth. "I want to kiss you goodnight."

"Okay." She sighed softly.

"Promise?"

"Yes. I promise. Love you."

"Okay, babes. Love you."

Julia ~

Ellie was in the bathroom. I glanced at my watch, wondering when Harris would come up to the room. My friend was a disaster. There was no other way to put it. She'd worked hard to keep the problems to herself and not let Jen or Aaron in on the drama during this weekend, but Jenna could sense it as easily as I could. Both she and Harris had put on good game faces and got through it, but they were struggling and my heart was breaking for them.

Ellie was taking a bath in an attempt to calm down and I dug some Advil out of my purse and put it on the bedside table with a glass of water. I also had Tylenol PM, but since she'd had wine tonight, I decided the other would be best.

"Julia?" she called from the other room.

I stood up from the edge of the bed and went to the door. "Yes, Ellie? Do you need anything?"

"Thank you for being with me so much tonight. I get that Ryan is unhappy that you're with me instead of him."

I put a hand on the door. "He's okay. He understands and he loves you, too. He wants me to take care of you. You've done so much for us, so don't worry."

The sound clicking as the keycard was inserted on the other side of the door alerted me to Harris's arrival. "Harris is here, Ellie. I think I should go now, okay? Give you guys some privacy?"

"Okay, Julia. Thank you. Will I see you tomorrow?" Her voice held prevalent evidence from her tears, her nose clearly stuffed up.

"We don't leave until the early afternoon, so sure. Just call me when you get up."

"Okay." I heard the water slosh as she got out of the tub. I turned to see a weary Harris enter the room. My arms opened and his folded around me automatically. He buried his face in my neck.

"I'm so sorry for the both of you, sweetie," I said softly and stroked the back of his head. "I hate to see you suffering like this, but don't give up."

He nodded against me and then moved out of my arms to pour himself a drink from the refrigerator that was hidden in the armoire below the television. They didn't have a suite like Ryan and I did, but the room was still very nice.

"Thanks, Jules. You and Ryan are good friends."

"Ellie told me you're going to Canada early. What time is your flight?"

"Six AM," he said sadly. "Did she tell you that she thinks I fucked a groupie? Because, I didn't."

I sighed, my heart tightening in my chest. "I know you didn't. She said she saw…"

"Yes. I'm sure it looked bad, but I didn't start it, and I didn't encourage it. In this life that shit happens. There are always women around but I don't ask them to be there. Some don't even give a damn what band they follow around or even know who we are. There are some that think it's a status thing to screw a rocker. And, I won't lie. There are guys in my band that take full advantage of it, but not me."

I walked up to him and rubbed his back lightly. "I've told her the same thing, Harris. It's very hard for Ellie to be away from you so much."

"But she won't come with me. Believe me, I've asked."

I nodded. "I know. She told me, but to her it appears you think her job is disposable but it means a lot to her. She works hard. I wish I had a solution for you."

"How do you and Ryan..." he began, but the bathroom door opened and Ellie emerged in a fluffy pink robe with her hair wrapped in a towel. Her eyes were red and puffy and she looked stiff.

"Hey," he greeted her.

"Hey," she said in return, hanging in the doorway without really moving toward him.

I got up and gave her a hug. "Okay, I gotta go. I love you."

Ellie nodded, her eyes filling with tears.

"Have faith and listen to his words," I whispered into her ear. "He loves you, Ellie. Believe that."

Her arms tightened around me as she nodded without saying a word.

I turned and put my arms around Harris. "Thanks, Julia."

"I'm waiting patiently for a signed CD as soon as you get it off the presses."

There was an uncomfortable silence behind me as I left the room and I realized how tightly I was wound. The muscles in the back of my neck burned and my heart was sick for the both of them. *How in the hell does something like this happen to two people who love each other so much?*

It was almost ninety minutes since I'd spoken to my husband and I was hoping he was asleep. I worried about him so much. The residency was so demanding. He didn't get enough rest, didn't eat right and worked himself silly. It was his habit to worry more about me than himself.

I pulled the keycard out of my purse and inserted it in the door, carefully turning the handle so as not to make too much noise and then held it as it closed to keep it from slamming. He'd left a light in the sitting room on for me, but the light was off in the bedroom. The darkness was visible through the crack in the door and I could hear his even breathing. It was a comforting sound and the love I always felt filled my heart to the point of bursting. I couldn't wait to slide in between the sheets next to Ryan and be wrapped in the strong arms that would unconsciously come around me, even in deep sleep. I went and turned off the light and immediately; the entire suite was shrouded in darkness. I let my eyes adjust for a moment so I wouldn't knock into anything and make noise that would wake my husband.

I kicked off my shoes and unzipped my dress, dropping it in a puddle of fabric at my feet. I continued to peel off my bra and panties, leaving a trail behind me like Hansel and Gretel in the forest. Once in the bedroom, I could see Ryan in the bed. He was lying on his stomach with the sheet dropping low on his waist, the strong expanse of his back and shoulders visible. His arms were curled under the pillow he held to his head and his left leg was bent out to his side.

I stopped to take off my earrings and necklace and place them softly on the nightstand before lifting the sheet on his right side. I slid in and curled up behind him, touching as much of his body with mine as I possibly could. This was the last night in a while when we'd get to sleep in each other's arms and I wanted to get as much of him as I could. He moaned slightly as my arm went around him and I nuzzled into the back of his neck.

"Hey, you." I tightened my arm around him as his came down to cover mine, the fingers of his hand threading through mine. I placed my open mouth on his shoulder blade and prepared to drift off to sleep, sucking in the musky scent of his skin and letting the heaven of his skin on mine wash over me and through me.

"You're supposed to be asleep. Are you asleep?" I smiled against his back.

"You're supposed to wake me up, wife," he said huskily, turning and taking me into the fullness of his embrace, almost pulling me completely on top of his body. His mouth found my forehead as I snuggled into him, my head coming to rest on his chest and my leg getting sandwiched between both of his. I started drawing circles on the skin of his chest and abdominal muscles, mostly because I couldn't keep myself from touching him. "Is Ellie okay?"

"Time will tell. Harris came to the room right before I left, so hopefully they're talking or making love right now."

"Mmmm..." he stirred underneath me. "Harris is quite upset, Julia. I think he's as miserable as she is. He said she doesn't trust him."

"I know," I said quietly into the darkness. "He told me his side while Ellie was in the bath."

Ryan's chest rose and fell underneath my cheek and I closed my eyes, so grateful that he was mine and everything was so perfect.

"I don't know what I'd do if something like that happened to us. It would kill me to have you doubt me." His voice was soft, but urgent in the silence

I lifted my head and rested my chin on his chest so I could look up at him. Even though it was dark, I could see his eyes sparkling as he looked down at me. "I wouldn't. I couldn't."

"Aaron teases me that I'm too in love with you. I know I tell you a hundred times a day, but I can't help it, Julia. I won't let anything come between us."

Yet again, his words moved me to the point where my throat ached and my eyes stung. "If it was a thousand times, I'd never get tired of hearing it. Aaron can bite me." I tried to laugh.

Ryan's breath rushed out in an amused huff. "Julia, the other night when we talked about the baby, you seemed hesitant. If you want to wait, I'm okay with it. It has to be right for both of us."

I swallowed at the reverent tone in his voice. It was like a caress that I could physically feel as it flowed over me, so loving and safe.

"I want to. More than anything, but I'm just worried about the timing. This..." I stopped and kissed his chest with an open mouth and his lungs filled beneath me as he sucked in his breath. "This... as you say, our *mad love*... it means everything. These moments between us are so, *so* precious to me." I shrugged slightly in his arms. "I want a baby, but I don't want to lose *us*. We're so incredible together. Nothing is more important than being with you right now."

His hand that had been stroking my back came up to thread through my hair and then his thumb brushed my chin. "Julia, you'll never lose me. Nothing could make this less than it is. Having a baby is the most intimate of bonds a man and a woman can share and nothing will make me happier than to be that close to you. Just you. It *is* mad love, you know. It drives me crazy. I sometimes wonder if I've imagined it and you. It's so intense."

Tears welled and I closed my eyes against them. His hand ran down my back and up again, his fingers curled and the nails scratched softly. Such an innocent touch, yet so arousing because it was Ryan. I knew what those hands and mouth were capable of and my body reacted of its own accord. He surged against me and I knew we wouldn't be sleeping anytime soon. The answering throbbing started deep within me and I sighed against him, giving in to the deep-seated need that never ebbed.

I should have known he could read me like a book. His eyes never left mine and his hands moved down around both of my upper arms to bring me up so his mouth could close hotly over mine. Lately, he was ruining my plans to take care of him, to give him a massage, let him sleep or to taste him. He'd been so hungry for my body under his and his mouth on mine that I couldn't deny him anything. His urgency echoed my own.

My hands slid into his hair as we kissed over and over, rolling around frantically on the bed until the covers were on the floor and my legs were curled around his waist. The air was cool on my bare skin wherever his body wasn't covering mine, but the tremors weren't caused by the cold.

"Uh....Juuuliiiaaa," he groaned, as his body finally came into mine and we moved together in the love dance that was so familiar but surprising in its magnificence at the same time. He whispered against the erratically beating pulse at the base of my neck before dragging his mouth up over my jaw and back to my lips, "Is it wrong to be this happy when other people are hurting so badly? God, baby," he grunted as I arched up to take him deeper into the warmth of my body.

I could feel every inch of him as we brought each other to depths of pleasure that transcend the physical, both of us panting love words and calling each other's names over and over again, fingertips gently digging at the other's flesh. Ryan loved hearing my sighs and moans, so I let them all out as he brought my body to fulfillment. Words weren't necessary between us as we worshiped each other with our bodies and our mouths. It was breathtaking and soul shattering every time. Tonight our love-making was laced with a bit of the desperation we felt for our friends' plight and the longing we would suffer in the coming days when we were apart; our kisses deepened and the touches became more clinging.

He filled me in every way. Heart, body and soul; I was bursting and I could feel the intense desperation that drove Ryan on as he made love to me as no one else ever could, touching me in places I didn't even know existed. It was everything; it was amazing.

I wanted every day of forever to spend in his arms, secure in the knowledge that he loved me in ways I couldn't comprehend and I loved him more than I could ever put into words.

"Julia…" he breathed as his body poured into mine.

The love between us was too much and yet… not enough. If we died drowning in each other's arms, it would never be enough.

~3~

Julia ~

I threw the photos down on my desk in disgust. This is what I get! This is what I get for letting go of a project even one little bit. *Fucking hell!*

"Andrea!" I let go of the button on my phone that buzzed the intercom in her office. "Get in here, *now*! Who the hell is responsible for this?"

In fifteen seconds she was rushing into my office. "Julia, what is it? Do you mean Mike Turner? Kent? Me? What are you talking about?"

I was too pissed to sit so I stood behind my desk, glaring down at the photos that now represented hours and hours of extra work for me, Andrea, sales, layout and editorial. Time and, literally, tens of thousands of dollars down the fucking drain.

I glanced up at her and huffed. "Can't I even be gone for five days? *Five damn days*?" I asked angrily and ran my hand through my hair. "This layout is not what I asked for. The storyboards I left were very clear. Everything was in-house, so how in the hell did this happen? I mean... *shit!*"

"Uh... I guess I don't know what you mean, Julia," Andrea answered. Her hesitation was clear and she moved closer to the desk to get a better look. "What did he do? The pictures are amazing."

If it were possible, my back stiffened even more. "Andrea, he knows better, but I thought you were watching him? I rushed back from Spain as it was. And now...!" I threw my hands in the air. "There better be a good explanation why this happened. I mean, couldn't Editorial get the story? Did Meredith change the directive?"

She stood looking at me as if I were insane. "What? Is this for the *New Yorker* project? The AIDS benefit?"

I shook my head. "No. It's for the January issue of Vogue; the fashion feature. Hasn't anyone noticed that the clothes on these models are the wrong damn designer? I mean, Jesus! Get Mike in here and call Kent Jared. Find out if the cover's been printed yet and let Denise know what's going on so she doesn't waste time working on the page lay-outs until we know where we stand. If we've caught it in time, maybe we can shift cover stories between the two months. Dior will be pissed, but that's the best case scenario we can get. If the cover is done, we are even more screwed. We'll have to re-do the shoot in fast forward."

Andrea stood frozen as I flopped down at my desk and put both hands in my hair. I looked up at her and stopped in my tracks. "What are you waiting for? Go!"

She scrambled out of my office and I stared as the door closed with a heavy thud. I sighed deeply.

The last week in Spain and dealing with Ellie's fragile emotional state had been hard enough. I hadn't even been home yet. Ryan was working so I came straight to the office and right away I was faced with this bullshit. I picked up the phone to call Meredith. She answered on the third ring.

"Hey, babe, didn't think you'd be back in the office today." She paused a second or two. "Didn't your plane just land? I thought you'd be rushing home to that gorgeous man and humping his brains out."

I frowned. "Well, Ryan is working all day and it's a damn good thing I didn't go home first. Are you aware what's going on with the January feature?"

"I know the shoot was last Wednesday, but I haven't seen the pics yet. Why?"

"Oh, nothing." I leaned back and pushed my sandaled feet on the edge of my mahogany desk. I was in ratty jeans, a t-shirt and flip flops. Slip-on shoes were mandatory for the airport security, albeit if all wrong for the New York winter. "Just the shoot was on the *wrong designer*. Not really a big deal. It could just fuck the whole issue," I said with mock casualness that I wasn't feeling. My heart was pounding and I was freaking out, perspiration was dotting my forehead.

She gasped and I could see her almost jump up from her chair in a frenzy. "How in the hell did that happen?" she burst out. "More importantly, can you save it, Julia?"

"How should I know at this point? I just found out ten minutes ago! I'm taking inventory of what's been done and I'll know more when I find out if the cover printed. Jesus, I'm glad I didn't wait until Monday to come in here. Then there would've been no chance to salvage it."

She sighed on the phone. "Well, fuck!"

"I couldn't have said it better myself," I retorted.

"What can you do?"

I loved how the messes always landed in my lap. No matter who caused it, I was expected to clean it up. I rolled my eyes and shook my head.

"I'm going to concentrate on the fix and then I'll figure out how this happened. I'm so pissed right now I'd like to fire whoever is responsible. I may have to order a reshoot or we may have to beg Dior to let us switch months. It won't be easy because they have their show in January. Not fucking *February*!

We'll be lucky if they don't pull all together. Either way, I'm left doing a completely new shoot and it's gonna cost the magazine a bunch of money. If the cover is printed, we'll have to reshoot with the correct material this weekend." I wondered if the disgust I felt was obvious in my voice. Ryan was supposed to be off on Sunday and now I had to work. "Ahhhhhh!" I almost yelled into the phone. "This is not how I was planning on spending the weekend, Mere. Far from it."

"Yes, I can imagine."

I huffed. *No, you really can't.*

My eyes sought out the wedding photo on my desk. Ryan was so handsome and the way he was looking at me melted my heart.

When I finished the call on my office phone, I pulled my cell phone out and sent a page to Ryan, letting him know that I was back in New York safely. Due to all of the equipment in the ER, the staff wasn't allowed to have cell phones on during their shifts so I had to content myself with hearing from him during his breaks.

He wasn't going to be happy. Now our plans on Sunday were screwed. We'd planned to do early Christmas shopping and he wanted me to make the cranberry and white chocolate cookies he loved. Then there would have been the hours lying in each other's arms in front of the fireplace. Ryan had been so happy when I called him yesterday and told him I'd be coming home a few days early. I wanted to surprise him, but I couldn't keep it to myself. Now it was pretty much ruined.

My heart dropped into my stomach in a sickening sort of way. *Don't be mad at me, baby,* I silently begged him in my mind. But, of course, I knew he'd be livid.

Mike stormed into my office without knocking, loudly banging through the door and I jumped in my chair. "What the hell, Julia? Andrea called and said I had to get in here immediately, but wouldn't say why. What's going on?" he said impatiently. "It's a good thing I was already in Manhattan having lunch with a friend."

"Hmmm... yes." He was dressed casually, but always trendy. He certainly looked the part of a swank, fashion photographer, his hair in a modern cut that he managed with gel. "Well, the shoot last Wednesday? Did you look at the program I left?"

His face creased. "What? I did." He shook his head. "The models were from Ford, I let the make-up people do their thing per your instructions. I didn't do shit but take pictures. What was wrong with it?"

"Only the wrong wardrobe, wrong designer."

He was incredulous and his surprise showed on his face. "Holy fuck! No way!"

"Yeah. No big deal, right? This is a hot mess."

Mike fell down into one of the leather chairs opposite my desk. "Crap, Julia. I'm... sorry."

I shrugged. "Let's just get it fixed and then we can try to find out how it happened."

My phone rang and I could see from the caller ID it was Andrea. "Hey, what'd you find out?" I said the minute I picked up the phone.

"Bad news. Kent said the cover is printed and already been shipped to bindery to wait for the pages. You know the drill. We're stuck with the features and the page count now."

"Crap." I leaned forward on my elbows and inhaled until I thought my lungs might burst. "Okay, get on the phone and see if we can get the same models back for the weekend. Whatever day, it doesn't matter. I've got Mike with me so I can deliver the happy news to him, but line up the make-up, set and lighting people for the day you can get the models confirmed."

Andrea groaned. "They're gonna complain because it's so close to Thanksgiving. I can hear it all now."

"It can't be helped. I'm not happy about it either. It will be expensive, but at least we don't have to tell the designer. Just get on the phone to Paris and tell the house that we're having some delays getting the garments back to them, but we will send them on Monday. Apologize profusely for that, but don't tell them what happened."

"Okay, will do," she answered.

"Thanks. You rock, girl." I hung up the phone and looked back at the man sitting across from me. He was running a thumb across his lower lip, his eyes raking over me. I looked very different than he was used to seeing me.

"Cancel your plans, lover-boy. Your new honey will have to cool her jets this weekend."

"I gathered. How was Spain?"

"Gorgeous. It's beautiful there. I really want to take Ryan back if I ever get a vacation from this place."

"What about the work?" He raised his eyebrows in question.

"Are you still mad at me because you didn't get to go? I needed you here."

"And look how well that turned out," Mike stated the obvious with a smirk and incredulous expression.

Smart ass.

"Yes," I answered, sarcasm lacing my tone. "The settings at Gibraltar were amazing, but the photographer wasn't you. Satisfied?" I bit my lip and tried not to smile.

"No! But that helped a little. What are you doing here, anyway? Trouble in paradise?" Mike asked sardonically.

"No." I shook my head and smiled brightly. "No trouble at all. Bliss, just not enough time. It's not bad enough that Ryan lives at the hospital, but then I have this type of shit to deal with! Any ideas on what caused it?"

Mike's brow dropped slightly as he considered the question and he shook his head. "Ah... nothing. I followed the logs. Who was in charge of them? Andrea?"

I shoved my chair back from my desk and picked up one of his photos. They really were incredible. Too bad they couldn't be used. "Not Andrea. I'd trust her with anything. Look how well she did when I had the accident. Nothing went wrong at all during those months, right?"

"Nothing to this magnitude; but it wasn't perfect. I'm sure Meredith didn't want to bog you down with the details."

"Hmmm. I guess. I'll let you know if it's Saturday or Sunday for the shoot. Thanks for coming in."

"Julia, it's good to have you back." His eyes roamed over my body suggestively. "You look good."

"Happiness will do that for you!" I shot back. "See you this weekend."

I decided that I might as well leave the office, so after one last check-in with Andrea and I'd answered all of the pressing emails, I was out the door. The wind was brisk as I hailed a cab that would take me home, hoping that I'd find my luggage waiting for me with the concierge.

I pulled my phone out and looked at it longingly. No word from my husband yet. He must be incredibly busy or he would have called by now. *Ugh.*

I watched the people rush over the crosswalks in droves as the cab stopped at the light. The buildings, cars and people melted into a blur as I lost myself in my thoughts. I missed Ryan and ached to get my arms around him, to feel his body cover mine. I closed my eyes and rested my head against the back of the seat, silently wishing it was the middle of the night and Ryan was finally joining me in our big bed. The hours would drag until then.

At home, I busied myself with calling my parents and Ellie to check in. My parents still required I call at the end of a journey to let them know I was safe and I wanted to see how Ellie was doing. She seemed a little better, but rattled about a new celebrity client. The woman was a big name, so she should have been ecstatic, but her voice was decidedly flat. My heart was still aching for her, but part of me wanted to yell at her to get her head out of her ass.

In my heart, I knew Harris was loyal to her. *So why didn't she?*

I'd just spent every non-working moment in Spain trying to convince her. I felt bad for both of them, but they were both so stubborn. There was a real chance that they would break up for good if neither of them were willing to compromise. The situation made me sad and long for Ryan's arms around me. I could think of nothing more important to me than him. Nothing I wouldn't sacrifice to be with him.

I sighed as the doorbell rang. It was the bellman with my luggage and I took it from him gratefully, then went to my purse for a tip.

"Thank you, Brian." I smiled at the teenager. He smiled shyly and nodded but didn't say anything.

I needed to unpack and do the laundry and then make myself a light dinner. *Alone. Again.*

The emptiness of the apartment screamed Ryan's absence like a banshee. Ryan left the bed unmade and after I toted the bag in and dropped it on the floor, I fell upon it, wrapping my arms around the pillow and filling my lungs with his familiar scent. *Yum.*

I was tired and I could fall asleep immersed in the bed he'd vacated pretending he was with me, wound up with my body. My eyes were heavy, as I rolled further into the pillows and let them drift shut, my breathing getting deeper. It was six hours later in Barcelona and so the jet lag was bound to be an issue. If I slept now I would be awake when Ryan finally came home around two in the morning. Yes... this was a good idea.

Ryan ~

I peeled the latex gloves off as I left the examining room. It had been a hellaciously busy day and it was only dinner time. I looked longingly at the clock. I'd been on for almost twelve hours and still had eight more to go.

I was excited when Julia told me that she was coming home three days early, but I'd carefully arranged my schedule with the other residents and the attending so that I'd be off on Sunday, the day after she was supposed to arrive.

"Jane," I spoke to one of the nurses, "I'm going to take a break for a few minutes. My wife is getting back from Spain and I need to see if she called. I'll be right back."

"Sure, Ryan." The pretty blonde smiled at me. She was a very good nurse, competent and efficient; two traits extremely important to work in emergency medicine. I could count on her to be steady and focused. She didn't get rattled like some of the others. A few were so scattered, I wondered how in the hell they ever made it through school.

"Page me if I'm needed." She nodded and I rushed to the physician's lounge so I could retrieve my phone from my locker. I rubbed the back of my neck as I walked down the sterile hallway, the white floor shining in the bright florescent light. "Uhhh…" I sighed as I pushed the door open.

It was a large room with lockers on one wall and a few tables with counters, a refrigerator, cupboards and a microwave on the opposite side. There was a television and a few recliners on one end and a door leading into a couple of small rooms with cots where the residents could rest when we were on call. I sometimes felt like I spent more time in these rooms than in my own apartment.

Caleb Montgomery, one of the other residents, was coming out of a sleeping room. He was a small kid, almost scrawny with red-rimmed eyes and hunched shoulders, easily six inches shorter than me. He was third year, and even though two years my senior, he seemed younger, somehow. He was a genuinely nice guy and we became fast friends when I offered to share some of Julia's cheesecake a couple of months back.

"Hey, Ryan. How long you been on?"

I continued my walk to my locker. "A little more than twelve hours. You?"

"Just ten. I have a couple more then I'm outta here. Do you have any of Julia's deliciousness with you?" Caleb asked with a smirk.

I smiled as I fumbled with the padlock. "Not today. She's been in Spain all week. I haven't seen her."

"Spain, huh?"

I flipped my phone open and saw a text from her. She'd paged me earlier, but I couldn't get to my phone to call her back.

I'm back in town. Cluster at the office. AGAIN. Going straight there from JFK. Home later. Can't wait to see your handsome face. Love you, BB. XXOOXX!

I sighed and then registered Caleb's words. "Yeah. She was working on a shoot in Gibraltar and Barcelona."

"Sounds like a rough gig."

"It can be. Coordinating our schedules can be murder." He made no move to leave so I decided to go into one of the sleeping rooms to call her. "Hey, man, I need to call Julia. Will you excuse me?"

He smirked at me. "Sure, I understand. Does she look as good as she cooks?" I laughed and went back to the locker. I pulled out my wallet, flipping it open to the photo just on the inside and handed it to him. It was the close up of her outside of Harvard that Mike had taken of just her face, veil and flowers. Caleb's appreciation was apparent in the low whistle that came out.

"Wow. She's a beauty."

I just smiled and took the wallet back when he was finished. "Thanks, I have to agree." He moved past me to leave the room and I continued toward one of the sleeping rooms to place the call. The light was low, only a small built-in fixture strip at the top of the shortest wall. It was designed to give enough light to get around, but dark enough to sleep easily. The doors were heavy and the space small, only slightly wider than the single cot along one wall. I sat down and hit the speed dial to reach Julia.

It rang several times and then went to voicemail. I sank down on the cot and leaned back slightly. I was disappointed. I wanted to hear her voice. I missed her and longed to hear more about her trip. It was bad enough when I couldn't see her, but I absolutely hated it when I couldn't talk to her. My eyes burned from tiredness and my stomach grumbled. I'd hoped that Julia would be able to pop in for dinner with me, even though I hated when she came down here alone in the evenings. I needed to set eyes on her. I pressed redial and this time when it went to voicemail I left a message.

"Hey, sweets. I'm sorry I couldn't call before. It's been so busy, but hopefully it will settle down now. I'm going to grab some dinner and then I'll try to call again. I'm beat, but if I can, I'll try to catch a couple hours of sleep here later so I can be up with you when I get home. I love you, baby."

I rubbed my stomach as it grumbled again wondering what delicacies they'd managed to dredge up in the cafeteria tonight. The food at St. Vincent's wasn't horrible, but I was sick of it; the same things over and over, week after week. Ugh. When Julia was traveling, I was left at its mercy.

I couldn't wait for Sunday. We had the whole day together and I knew she'd spoil me with something delicious. *And lots of sex.* I grinned to myself as I imagined her warm and soft in my arms, murmuring my name in that enticing, guttural moan I loved. Suddenly I was hungry for more than just food.

I longed for the days when I could just walk across campus to her dorm or the few blocks between our apartments in the last two years at Stanford. I took her presence for granted then, never realizing how much I would miss it. I huffed in self-annoyance. I was married to the woman of my dreams and I was whining like a baby. "Stupid ass," I muttered.

I pushed off of the cot to head back to the ER. It wasn't busy. The nurses were hanging out at the nurse's station and Caleb was leaning against it with his hip, leisurely sipping coffee, listening to them with interest. He had a crush on Jane. I recognized the way he looked at her as the same way I used to drool over Julia before she knew how I really felt about her.

I didn't wait to be invited into their conversation. I was tired and I really wanted the time alone. "Do we have anything inbound that we know about?"

"Nope." Beth, a young nursing assistant, piped up. "Thank goodness."

The ambulance dispatch or the public services, police and fire departments, usually alerted the hospital if they had any critical issues on the way in. "Okay then. Since it's slow right now, I'm going to run down to the cafeteria. I haven't eaten all day."

"Sure, Ryan," Caleb nodded in acknowledgement.

I made eye contact so he knew that I heard him and then turned around and walked out the double doors that separated the emergency department from the rest of the hospital.

The cafeteria was several floors down and in the opposite wing of the hospital. It took a good ten minutes to walk there. The hospital halls were quiet and the lobbies empty with only one or two visitors roaming the halls. Visiting hours were over and only the more critical care patients or emergency patients were allowed to have visitors. The administration staff was gone and only one admissions clerk remained in the department for emergencies to be admitted as needed.

"Ryan..." I heard some footsteps behind me and Jane's voice calling after me. I stopped and glanced over my shoulder.

"Yes? Do they need me in ER?" I asked anxiously as I paused in the hallway.

"No. But I haven't eaten either. Want some company?" She was half running down the long corridor toward me, her long ponytail wagging behind her.

"Sure, that's fine."

Jane smiled and I resumed walking when she reached me, but truthfully, I didn't feel much like conversation or company. I could tell she wanted to talk. We knew each other a little bit, talked a little over coffee or hanging out in the ER between patients, but it had been pretty impersonal. Except for the day I lost my first patient. Jane was working on the little girl with me and had been the one to call time of death, practically pulling me off as I continued to work on her. It still hurt to think about it. Especially after what happened later when Julia remembered losing our baby.

"Rough day, huh?" she asked, and it was clear that I wasn't the only one who felt uncomfortable. She'd arrived at work several hours after I did. The nurses worked three twelve-hour days, but the residents practically lived at the damn hospital. *Someday you'll make the big bucks*, I reminded myself.

"Not terrible. Surprisingly, no trauma. Usually we have three or four really bad cases a day." I ran my hand through my hair as we entered the cafeteria. It smelled good, even if the flavor of it was less than appetizing. I smiled weakly. "Of course, you know that right? You've been here longer than I have."

"Yes. Almost five years."

I looked at the menu for the day. Standard hospital fare: Meatloaf, hot turkey sandwiches, lasagna, some sort of Mexican glop that was supposed to be enchiladas, burgers, chicken sandwiches and then the sandwich and salad bar. I ordered a grilled chicken sandwich, and to my surprise, Jane got the glop.

I didn't realize it, but my face must have reflected my horror because she laughed. "You don't like enchiladas?"

"Is that what that is?" I joked lightly. "It looks like barf."

"I'll let you know in a minute." She chuckled lightly.

We each paid for our own meals and then found a table near one of the windows. I pulled my pager off of my belt and sat it on the table next to my tray. No word from Julia yet. This was weird and I was starting to worry slightly. I sighed loudly as I picked up the top half of the bun and opened one of those little packets of mayonnaise.

"What's the matter?"

"I'm expecting a call. Julia was out of town all week and got back today. She has some issue at her job and so I'm not sure if she's home yet."

"Julia's your wife?" She glanced at the platinum and diamond band on my left hand.

My face split into a huge grin as I reassembled my sandwich with lettuce and tomatoes. "Yes. Are you married?"

"No, but I have a boyfriend. We've been dating for four years. I wonder if he's ever going to get around to asking me to marry him."

"Four years is a long time. That's how long Julia and I were technically a couple before we got married as well... but we were best friends for another four before that."

"Holy cow!" Jane's eyes widened incredulously. "That's forever!"

I watched her take a bite of the glop and waited for her reaction. Her nose wrinkled a little bit and I laughed out loud.

"See? If it looks like barf, don't eat it," I teased. Jane nodded, but took another bite.

She smiled. "I don't see you in the cafeteria much. You get used to the barf over time."

"I bring my lunch most of the time. Julia rocks in the kitchen, so I'm spoiled. Puts this shit to shame. When she travels on short notice, I'm stuck with it, however."

"She travels? What does she do?"

"She's a fashion editor at Vogue and is working her way up the ranks. Sometimes she needs certain settings or a certain designer for a layout but other times, someone else can't go as scheduled and they send Julia instead. Those are the times my stomach pays. When she knows she's leaving, she sets me up in advance." I was talking more to myself than to Jane, wistful in my thoughts.

"She *does* spoil you. I can't cook to save my life."

"That explains your open attitude toward this shit, then," I quipped and we both laughed.

We passed the rest of dinner in easy camaraderie and soon went back upstairs.

I stopped by the lounge once more and tried Julia again. Still no answer, which made the next two hours pass by at a snail's pace. I was clock watching. We had a heart attack victim and a minor car accident to deal with, but we were way over-staffed for the amount of work we had to do. More snail's pace clock watching. Finally, at midnight, my pager went off from Julia and when I had stabilized the heart attack victim and we'd gotten him admitted, I was finally able to call her from one of the phones in the department.

Julia answered on the first ring and my heart lifted at the sound of her voice. "Hi, sweetheart. I'm sorry I didn't get back to you earlier. I fell asleep."

"I forgot about the time difference and the jet lag." There were too many people around to speak to her in the intimate way I wanted. She sounded sleepy and I could imagine her all warm and rumpled in our bed. "Are you feeling okay?"

"Yeah, babe. I'm just a little sleepy, still. I woke up with a start knowing that you'd probably be freaking out that you hadn't heard from me."

"I was a little worried. I knew your work wouldn't go until midnight. Did you get it fixed?"

"Um... not completely. I know what has to be done, but um... baby, just don't be upset, okay?" I could hear the trepidation in her voice which told me I wasn't going to like what was coming.

"What now?" I couldn't help the defeat that flowed through the words.

"We have a re-shoot and…"

My muscles tightened and I sucked in my breath in preparation for an angry retort. "What did that little fucker screw up this time, Julia?" I shot out.

"*Nothing.*" Her voice was soft. "It wasn't Mike's mistake this time. He went to the set, he used the models and clothes that were there, but someone screwed up the production instructions. The wrong designer's line was brought in. So now I have very good photos, but I don't have shots for the clothes I need for the issue I'm working on. The cover is printed so I'm screwed. I have no choice but to re-shoot."

I relaxed a little as I listened to her. She sounded soothing even if her words meant the weekend was royally fucked.

"When?" I asked, already knowing the answer.

"Sunday. I couldn't get it together in time for tomorrow. I tried."

I didn't say anything because the nurses were looking at me, clearly wondering what I found so upsetting. My face felt flushed and I turned my back on them, lowered my tone and leaned on the counter. "I know. I just… *shit!* I was looking forward to spending the time with you," I rasped out roughly.

"Me, too. I was really mad about it, but now I'm just sad. I'm so sorry, Ryan. You know where I want to be."

I could hear it in her voice and I didn't want to make it worse. I sighed deeply. "I love you, Julia. I'm not mad at you. I'm just… *pissed* at the situation. We can't get a fucking break."

I could hear her breathing on the other end of the phone and my heart melted. This was my baby and I had no right to be irritable over something she couldn't control anymore than I could control my own God damn schedule.

"I'll keep the bed warm. When will you be home?" she said softly.

Love flooded through me until I felt like my chest would burst. "I don't know. It's up in the air. It's not busy but I don't think they'll let me leave early, just in case something happens, but it's boring as hell. Most of tonight we've been doing nothing. Don't wait up, honey."

"Did you eat?" My lips lifted at the corners. She was always worried about me. After all this time I didn't know why it still shook me to the core.

"Yes. I had a cardboard chicken sandwich two or three hours ago."

"Will you get time to rest if it's that quiet?"

"Probably. But I wish you were here. I'd sleep better with you next to me."

"Mmm... me, too. But lately, I don't recall much time sleeping when we're together. I've missed you."

"Oh, babe. God, I can't wait to see you. I think I'll chain you to the bed and tell Meredith to fuck off next time she wants to send you packing."

Julia chuckled softly and I had to join in. I couldn't help it.

"Mmmm... sure, you can chain me to the bed. Sounds sort of fun."

"Doesn't it? I want my hands on you."

"More with the torture, Matthews. If you're not too tired, maybe you can come with me to the shoot on Sunday. It won't last all day. Will you?"

Hell, yeah. "Seriously? I'd love to watch you work."

"I won't be doing much other than making sure nothing else gets screwed up."

Jane and Beth were watching me and Caleb was in one of the curtain partitioned examining rooms with a patient and another nurse. "Baby, I have to go. They're all looking at me like vultures waiting for their last meal. The only thing going on is that the other doctor is digging a marble out of a kid's nose." I huffed and laughed softly when Julia giggled in my ear. The kid's mother was screaming louder than the kid and I found the whole situation beyond hysterical.

"Wow. So promise to get some rest?"

"Yes, *Mrs.* Matthews. Just promise we'll teach our kids not to shove stuff up any of their orifices? It gets damn embarrassing!"

The sound of another burst of tinkling laughter filtered through the phone and I smiled again. "Love you. Um... are you planning on shoving something up any of my orifices later? 'Cause they are missing your probing parts... *Bad.*"

I burst out laughing in response, the sound of it filling the empty ER and bouncing off the walls. The girls glanced at me again, looks of puzzled amusement twisting their faces.

I struggled to contain the unadulterated pleasure that Julia's words brought to me. The laughter continued to fall from my lips around my next words.

"Oh, you can count on it. I remember why I love you so much. See you soon, babe."

Julia ~

I was still smiling when I hung up the phone. He was so funny! I loved our little moments of lighthearted banter. Leave it to my perfect husband to turn what could have been a tense conversation into one that ended in fits of laughter.

I missed him. I wanted to touch him, hold him, tangle my fingers through his hair and kiss him until we were both breathless. I just wanted to feel him next to me, and his strong arms around me; to smell his breath and hear his passionate whispers and moans while he made love to me.

Ugh... traitor body. Traitor mind. Delicious torture.

I toppled back onto the pillows, the brilliant red numbers on the digital clock mocking me as it shone in the darkness. It was screaming: *Ryan isn't coming home for several more hours!*

"Oh, shut the hell up, already!" I took one of the pillows and flung it in the general direction, knocking the lamp and the clock off of the nightstand and onto the floor. They landed with a loud thud and I rolled back onto my stomach, spread-eagled on the bed.

"I hated that stupid thing anyway," I groaned in disgust. It wasn't good for anything but counting down the minutes until one of us had to leave, reminding us how few minutes we had left together.

If I never saw another fucking clock again, it would be too soon. Especially in our bedroom. In this room, I didn't want to be reminded of the time. This room was sacred. All I wanted was my husband, his arms, his body, his glorious mouth all over me. This was our sanctuary, so no more clocks-or thinking about how short our time together always seemed.

I was wide awake now and had no hope in hell of going back to sleep. I got up on my hands and knees, pushing off of the bed to stand in the dark, contemplating what to do. I could go bake something, I could draw, or I could do laundry. Or... I could go see my man. Couldn't I?

I hesitated only seconds before I was ripping the clothes from my body on the way into the bathroom, turning on the light, and then the water in the shower. I rushed into the water, my mind spinning and my heart racing because of my decision. *Why the hell not?* It wasn't busy and what was the worst thing that could happen? He'd be busy by the time I got there but I'd at least get to look at him, maybe hold him close for a minute.

I didn't bother with make-up, only a little lip gloss and a touch of mascara, and threw on the first clothes I could grab. It was November, so leggings and the Aran sweater that Ryan's parents had brought back for him from Ireland our junior year at Stanford. It was heavy and long, landing just above my knees. I scrambled around the apartment getting my phone, purse and finally shoving my feet into some black boots. I grabbed Ryan's down parka off of the rack in the entryway and rushed out the door of the apartment.

Should I take a cab or my car? The decision made, I pushed the down button for the elevator and glanced at the lights at the top of the door. Why did the damn thing always take so long when I was in a hurry? *I mean, who is using the elevator at one in the morning?*

I got my answer when it opened up and Lisa and Stan, our neighbors from down the hall stumbled out of the elevator, both clearly inebriated. She was giggling and he was trying to suck on her neck. I smiled as I watched them move past me. "Oh, hey, Julia," Lisa mumbled as she tried to push Stan's face away in embarrassment. "Stan, stop it."

"Hi. See ya later."

When I got to the street I hailed a cab and quickly hopped in the back.

"Where to lady?"

The cab driver was a scruffy older man wearing a Yankee's cap.

"St. Vincent's. ER."

"Oh, are you okay? Are you hurt?" he asked anxiously, glancing over his shoulder to check me out.

"I'm fine. But this is sort of an emergency." I laughed out loud. It was crazy going halfway across Manhattan but I couldn't wait. "I haven't seen my husband in six days."

"Lady, I still don't get what that has to do with the hospital." He pulled out into traffic and started heading south. "But whatever floats your boat."

"He's a doctor. A resident."

"Oh. I see. Got any kids?"

"Not yet. We've only been married a few months. Ryan is first year so he works all the time."

"That's got to be tough. Pretty young thing like you; I bet he's chomping at the bit to get home."

"About as much as I'm *chomping* to have him there, yeah." I smiled and sat back in the seat, willing the drive to be over as quickly as possible.

During the course of the remainder of the drive, I found out that the driver's name was Marvin and he had three children. One was in dental school in Michigan, one was an artist and the youngest was a waitress in a fancy restaurant on 5th Avenue. He and his wife had a small house in Queens and he'd been driving a cab his whole adult life. He seemed happy, but I could only imagine how tough his life must have been.

The parking lot outside the emergency entrance was relatively quiet. Only three cars and no emergency vehicles. The other two times I'd been here, it was much busier. This gave me hope that Ryan would either have time to take a break or he might be able to leave early. The second option was probably wishing on the moon, but one never knew.

I leaned up and handed him the money. "It was nice to meet you, Marvin."

"Will you need a ride home? Should I wait?"

"It's nice of you to offer, but um, I'm hoping my husband will be off soon and I can ride home with him. Do you have a card? Then I can call you directly next time I need a cab, yes?" I flashed him a big smile as I readied to exit the vehicle.

A large smile spread across his gentle face in happiness at the gesture. "Yes, miss. Thank you."

"Julia. My name is Julia, okay?"

I took the card he proffered and opened the door, his words following me as I got out. "Thank you, Julia. You are one classy babe. Your husband is a lucky man. I'll wait until you get inside before I drive off."

My heart warmed and I leaned toward him to put my hand on his shoulder through the window he'd rolled down to speak to me. "Thank you, Marvin. Have a great night." I gave him one last smile before turning and walking quickly into the hospital.

It was quiet but there was a small group of nurses and two doctors standing at the counter in the middle. A tall man in his late twenties turned toward me. He was thin, and his face was plain with a shock of dark hair that fell over his high forehead and light grey eyes. "Hello. How can we help you? Are you ill or injured?" He took the four or five steps necessary to cover the distance between us.

One of the nurses walked past us and into one of the curtained rooms behind the doctor.

"Um, no, thank you. I was wondering if I could... is er..."

Something dawned on the man in front of me because his face split into a smile and he reached out his right hand to me. "I'm Caleb; I work with your husband. You're Julia, right?"

My face twisted slightly as I tried to figure out how he knew who I was. I glanced around the ER looking for any sign of Ryan.

"Yeah, but how did you know?"

He chuckled. "I've seen the picture in Ryan's wallet. No mistaking that face."

I felt myself blush and I took his hand. "It's nice to meet you, Doctor."

He shook his head and frowned. "Caleb, please."

"Caleb it is. Thank you." He didn't seem to notice my anx-iousness despite the way I was fidgeting and bouncing up and down, or the fact that I kept trying to get a glance into the room where the nurse had disappeared. Surely, Ryan had to be in there. "I know I shouldn't have come, but I've been out of town. I haven't seen him in several days. I couldn't sleep, so," I ram-bled on and on.

Caleb looked at me and nodded. "He told me earlier. I think he's taking a break in the doctor's lounge. I can't let him leave the hospital until his replacement shows up, but he was beat and I sent him to rest."

I sighed. "Yes, he sounded tired when I spoke to him. I don't want to wake him if he's sleeping, so I guess..." Disap-pointment washed over me. I looked at the white and black clock on the wall. He still had several hours until he would be home. "Is there someplace that I can wait for him?"

"You can go down there. If you want?"

Bingo. I grinned up at him. "Really? If you really don't mind then, yes, please."

"I get it. Newlyweds," he teased.

I shrugged and shoved my hands in the pockets of Ryan's coat. "We've always kind of been this way. Married or not."

I noticed two of the nurses nearby. One of them was work-ing on a laptop computer, connected to a hand scanner that I as-sumed held some records of one of the patients and the other was leaning on the counter, openly listening. My eyes drifted be-tween her and Caleb.

"I see. Jane, can you show Mrs. Matthews to the doctor's lounge?"

The blonde that was checking me out smiled slightly. "Sure. Be glad to. This way…" She used her arm to indicate which direction we'd need to go.

I took a couple of steps in the direction she lead me and then turned back to Caleb. "Thank you."

My heart was racing as we walked down the hall but the silence was a little awkward. "Jane, Ryan told me what a good nurse you are." I struggled to find something to say. She seemed shy and extremely reserved.

"He's a good man. A brilliant doctor, actually."

I nodded and glanced at her as she walked beside me. "Yes. But he works hard. He pushes himself. Sometimes I think he's too critical of his work. He wants to be perfect."

"Uh huh. I know. I've seen that side of him; the one that won't give up even when he should." She sighed.

Ryan had mentioned Jane on a few occasions. I recognized her name and remembered that she was one of the nurses with him the night he lost the baby with the bee sting. That sad, heartbreaking, *beautiful* night… the night my memory came back. The night I got Ryan back, but realized the loss of our baby. Hearing her speak with such respect for Ryan, my heart swelled with pride. He was amazing and not just to me.

"Yes," I agreed quietly. I wasn't going to tell her how incredible my husband was or how he had taken care of me and made me fall in love with him twice. The memory was so real. I smiled a secret smile and the other woman watched.

"What is it?" Jane asked me, reaching out to place a gentle hand on my shoulder.

"I'm fine, just a little overwhelmed. I've been away for a few days and I'm just anxious," I explained.

She stopped in front of a closed white door. "He should be in here. If he's not in the lounge, there are a couple of sleeping rooms near the back."

Jane turned to leave.

"Wait. I'm sorry. How will I know which one? I'd hate to barge in on someone."

"Ryan's the only one in there. Everyone else is in the department."

My heart pounded in my chest. We would be completely alone and I couldn't wait a minute longer. "Thank you, Jane. He'll be very surprised." I pushed the door open and my eyes quickly scanned the room, entering as she turned to leave.

A television was on but no one was watching it, all of the chairs and couches vacant. I walked to the back of the room and leaned my ear to first one door and then the other. There was no sound coming from either one. Ryan was probably getting some much needed sleep.

I turned the knob carefully on the door to my right and pushed it open just enough to see inside. The light was very low, almost dark, and the room was very small. He was lying on the small cot with one arm thrown over his eyes and one leg hanging off of the edge, his foot flat on the floor. I couldn't help my smile. I was so damn happy to see him and now I could hear him breathing.

I let the door close but held it with the knob turned so I could latch it without a sound, and then tiptoed the few feet to the cot and slid down the wall opposite Ryan. His scent surrounded me and I saw the 24 hours worth of stubble that had accumulated on his jaw and chin. My body quickened. It still amazed me how moved I was just looking at him. I ran a finger along his forearm to see if a tickle would make him move it. He moaned softly and like magic, his arm moved to his side and his head turned in my direction. I wanted to touch him. I scooted closer to the edge of the bed and leaned on it so I could look into his face, brushing his unruly hair off of his forehead. My eyes drank him in. Jesus, he was so gorgeous. Exhausted and unshaven but still beautiful.

Ryan drew in a deep breath. "Julia..." he whispered softly but his eyes were still closed. "Baby, you smell so good."

My breath stopped and my features softened, biting my lower lip. I felt like he'd reached right inside my chest and squeezed my heart. I pushed the parka from my shoulders and left it on the floor where it fell, sitting up on my knees so that I could lean over him. I let my lower lip nudge his upper one and then my open mouth hovered over his, breathing in his delicious breath, and then I used my teeth to gently tug on his lower lip. My hand roamed lower, under the hem of his shirt, tracing the happy trail down to the tied band of his pants. He was so fucking sexy.

Instantly, his mouth came to life beneath mine and his arms closed around me, one hand sliding into the hair at the back of my head. "Julia... Am I dreaming?"

His tongue slid inside my mouth in a desperate kiss and he pulled me on top of his body. When I pulled my mouth from his, his eyes were open. His mouth split into a big smile and his arms tightened in a huge bear hug. "Oh, my God! I missed you, babe! What are you doing here? Did you sneak in?" He pushed my hair off of the left side of my face and kissed my lips gently. "Hmmm?" He kissed me again and then the side of my face at the temple.

"No sneaking, yet. Jane and Caleb showed me where to find you."

"Mmmm..." His nose nuzzled the side of my cheek and his tongue licked at the corner of my mouth and I moaned. "Remind me to thank them later. Jesus, Julia. You feel so good."

I straddled his hips and his hands were wild as they roamed over my body on top of my clothes and then under the hem of his sweater that I wore. When they encountered the bare skin of my back and found no bra strap he paused and then sat up beneath me.

"You naughty, naughty girl," he said softly as his mouth came back to mine for some slow, sucking kisses and his hands moved around the front to cup my breasts. Both of my nipples puckered beneath his palms and I felt his erection, steel hard and pressing against me. I arched into him and he groaned before his hands moved down to the waistband of the leggings I wore.

"Ugh... Why?" He pulled on the stretchy material in exaggeration. "Get rid of this shit. I want you naked." He laughed quietly, but his hands slid into the offending garment and cupped my bare ass cheeks. "Mmm... more naked Julia." His hands moved lower and he slid a finger into me. "You're so hot and wet. Uhh... honey, I want to taste you."

My head fell back as he moved his fingers deeper until I was gasping. The sweater wasn't a great choice after all since the collar was interfering with Ryan's mouth on the skin of my neck and chest. I raised my arms and threw it off, finally rewarded with his low groan and that glorious mouth sucking and kissing along the cord of my neck. He was frantic in his movements, yet somehow measured and deliberate. Slow and deep.

Ryan pulled his hand free and put his fingers in my mouth. "God, Julia, let me..." he rasped out. "Fuck... I need more. I want you to come in my mouth." His hands started to peel off the leggings, baring my stomach and hip bones, which he clasped and stood me up next to the cot, pulling at the material as his mouth moved over my rib cage and lower, his tongue leaving a hot trail in its wake.

Jesus, that was hot and I felt the wetness rush between my thighs, my body opening internally in anticipation.

"As much as I want that right now, you can't go back to work smelling like sex."

"I don't care..."

"Ryan," I groaned and his hand forced me down so he could capture my willing mouth with his. He kissed me hungrily, again and again, our breathing along with our moans getting louder. I wanted to get him off, but we needed to be quiet about it.

"Baby... Remember where we are. What if they page you in the middle of all this," I gasped softly, before sucking his earlobe into my mouth. "I can't be completely naked and neither can you."

"Okay, not completely... but I want you. I'll apologize in advance in case I get paged and we have to end in a hurry, my love."

I pushed him down and then moved lower on his body, one hand sliding up his chest under his shirt and the other working the tie of his pants free. His cock was engorged, huge and hard. Ryan was panting as I pushed the material down just enough so it sprung free and then ran my tongue up the length of it.

"Uhhh..." His breath left him. "Julia, are you sure?"

"Completely. I want this inside of me. In any way I can get it." I said before I took him fully into my mouth. I moaned, letting the vibrations on my lips and tongue, pleasure him.

Ryan tried to watch me as I worked over him, but eventually his head fell back against the pillows at the same time as his hips surged forward, pushing himself further into my mouth. "Baby... you're so good. God, it feels amazing, Julia." Love surged through me like a river. I wanted and needed to give him everything within my power. I wanted him to let go, proof of how much he wanted me and the depth of our love. I raked my nails down over his hips and the tops of his thighs, concentrating on keeping my teeth from hurting him. My hand closed around the base as my tongue circled, sucked and bobbed on him, the head was enough to fill my mouth. He was breathing hard in a short time and I could tell by the sour and salty taste of pre-cum that he was close.

"Julia, don't make me come yet. If you make me come like this, I won't be able to walk, let alone work."

"I want to. I want you to come."

"Uhh... uhhh... Juliaaaa... please. Not yet."

I sat up and looked at him, unable to deny him, but I knew he was left aching, as was I. My body was screaming for his. His blue eyes were on fire and intent as they roamed over me. "You are so fucking beautiful. Come here."

He sat up and threw his legs over the side, leaning the short distance back against the wall. I stood up and he turned me around, yanking the offending material that covered me down to my knees and reaching around to slide his fingers down over my stomach, through my pubic hair until his fingers were parting the slick flesh. "Ugnnnn..." Ryan moaned softly in response, his mouth beginning to burn trails over my back and shoulder, his other hand grasping my left hip and pulling me backward toward him. "Baby, Julia... I want to feel you around me. Sit on my lap; take me inside."

The leggings around my knees prevented me from turning to straddle him. I knew what he wanted and I gave it to him by reaching behind me and guiding his cock to my entrance. I rubbed the head in the wetness and he moaned, thrusting his hips in need. He used both hands to lift me until I was sitting on his lap and then he was pulling me down and filling me inch by delicious inch.

"Ah, yeah. God, that's it."

My hands on his knees allowed me to move over him and his hands roamed the front of my body as I rode him. The room was silent except for the heavy breathing and soft moans we brought from each other. I was moving on him in long, slow strokes, not wanting it to end too soon, but feeling the tension building in my own body. I clenched on him involuntarily. He moved his hand down and touched my clitoris, applying pressure in slow pulses that matched the rhythm in which we were moving together and I knew I was gone.

"Uhhhh…" I gasped for breath as my orgasm rocked me and my insides hugged around him as spasm after spasm of pleasure washed through me.

"Jesus…" Ryan groaned and his arms tightened around me to hold me down on his lap as he released deep inside me. "Fuck, Julia." His forehead rested between my shoulder blades and his breath rushed hotly over my skin as he jerked again and again against me. "I love you."

When he was kissing my back and his breathing regulated slightly, I pulled off of him and turned in his arms in my need to hold him. Instantly, his hungry mouth was on mine in a series of deep kisses. "I love you, more," I whispered against his mouth.

Ryan leaned his forehead in the curve of my neck and I could feel the light sheen of perspiration there. "This was the best damn break I've ever had, Jules. If I don't get fired, we'll have to do this again."

"I wasn't planning on seducing you. Only seeing you. I couldn't wait another minute."

He pushed the hair off the side of my face and placed a kiss on my temple and then one on my cheekbone. "You're my baby. Right?"

"Mmmm... always. I want more." I pushed my fingers through his hair and he leaned into my hand.

"Me, too, but I should get back before they send a search party." Ryan's hands rubbed circles on my back.

"Okay," I said reluctantly. "Should I take a cab home or wait for you?"

"Get a cab. It will be a couple of hours, probably."

"Ugh. I don't want to let go of you now that I have you."

I got up off of his lap and pulled up the leggings and re-trieved the sweater from the floor and quickly got redressed while he adjusted his clothes and checked for telltale wet spots.

I laughed softly as I watched him. "Don't worry; I think I got most of the glop."

"Do I smell like sex?" he asked, a grin spreading out on his face.

I leaned in and sniffed. "Nope."

"You can't tell because it's on you too, silly." He gathered me up and lifted me off the floor so he could kiss me hard on the mouth. "Thank you for *coming* to see me."

I giggled and kissed him back.

*****

The sun was coming up when I heard the door open. Finally, Ryan was home. I had showered and tried to sleep but all I could do was lay awake and wait for him, reliving the glorious half hour in the doctor's lounge. I pretended to sleep so that he would shower and climb into bed with the intention to sleep and not make love.

He didn't take long and was soon sliding his muscled, na-ked self in bed behind me. He curled up next to me and pulled me back against him. I was naked as well and he murmured a soft sigh. His strong hand closed around my forearm and his face settled in the curve of my neck.

"I know you're awake, Julia. You aren't breathing hard enough to be sleeping. You can't fake me out," he whispered.

"I guess next time I'll breathe heavier, then."

"Jesus, I'm tired," he sighed against me.

I felt content. Safe. Whole.

"I know." I looked over my shoulder toward him. "Sleep, my love."

"You feel so good against me like this. My whole world exists right here in this bed."

My hand traced over his forearm that was wrapped around me. Over and over I lightly traced his warm skin, the muscles and sinew strong beneath my fingers "It's nice to have you home. You work too hard."

"I'm sorry you have to work tomorrow, sweets. It's too bad we can't goof off all day, but thank you for asking me to come along. Can I ask for something?"

"Anything."

"Will you make lemon muffins for breakfast? Before my day shift?"

I smiled and pulled his hand up to kiss it, dragging my mouth over it lightly. I loved this man so much. I'd give him the world and all he wanted was lemon muffins. "Of course. Anything you want."

"I knew you would. I don't care about anything else. Take my job. Take it all. I just want you. I want to hold you forever and never let go," his voice was starting to slur as he drifted quickly to sleep.

I snuggled in closer and breathed in his breath as my eyes closed. "Okay, then don't. Don't let go."

~4~

Julia ~

"I'm sorry, babe," I said in hushed tones. "I'm gonna miss my flight. It can't be helped."

Ellie was crying in the other room, her relationship with Harris in shambles. It was impossible to leave L.A. and head back to New York as I'd planned.

Ryan sighed heavily on the other end of the line. I could picture the disappointment on his handsome face.

"Julia, the timing sucks!" he said harshly.

I flushed guiltily. Ryan had been monitoring the most optimal time to conceive even more diligently than I had, and he'd only agreed to my impromptu trip to L.A. on the understanding I'd be home in time for the weekend. It was rare he had two days off in a row and we'd both looked forward to a weekend sequestered in bed in our quest to make a baby. But mostly, to just soak each other up.

"I know!" I said adamantly then lowered my voice. "I'm disappointed, too. I'm sorry! But Ellie's a mess, Ryan." I cringed when my friend burst into a fresh bout of sobbing in the other room. Surely Ryan could hear her wailing. "She's devastated. Harris broke up with her last night. I just can't leave right now."

"Christ! Why now? I can't get a *fucking* break!" Ryan's tone became harder. "I knew this was coming! She brought this on herself."

"She's my best friend! I can't believe you're being so selfish!"

"I'm selfish? I let you run off across the Goddamn country on a moment's notice! It isn't like we can afford this type of shit, anyway! Ellie needs to grow the fuck up."

"You have no idea what it's like to be dumped by someone you love! It's never happened to you, so you can't understand what she's going through! You're being a dick, Ryan!"

"She doesn't trust the guy! He might as well screw around if he gets accused regardless of what he does! Jesus Christ!"

"I'm sorry if I can't make it home in time for the freaking schedule! You're acting like a spoiled brat!"

"I'm acting like a man who works eighty hours a week and never sees his wife!" he spat angrily.

"There's always next month."

"That's beside the point, and it wasn't what I said! Just forget it!"

"Ryan... I..."

Ellie came out of the bathroom, her face swollen and blotchy, letting her cell phone drop, unbidden, from her hand before she landed on the couch next to me and started to sob quietly, shaking her head. I reached out to take her hand in mine. Ryan would just have to understand.

I was heartbroken for her and trembling in the wake of the angry exchange with my husband when he sighed heavily on the other end of the line.

"When do you think you'll be home, then?" His voice was quieter, defeated in response to the sound of Ellie's misery in the background.

My heart ached at the tone in his voice. He missed me which was the crux of his anger. He was always generous with others, but he was over-worked, impatient and probably horny as hell.

"I'm not sure. But, I love you."

He didn't respond right away and I turned my back to Ellie so she wouldn't read my expression.

"Ryan, I said *I love you.*"

"Yeah."

"Please don't make me feel guilty for being here."

"I gotta go." He ended the call before I could respond and I glanced up at my friend.

"Shit!" I sighed as I threw the phone down next to me.

"I'm sorry, Julia. I'm ruining your relationship as well as my own."

"He'll get over it. He's exhausted and not himself." My words didn't sound convincing, even to me. "What did Harris have to say?"

"He won't take my calls," she said miserably before another torrent of tears began. I put my arms around her and stroked her hair as she sobbed against my shoulder.

Ryan ~

"Jane!" I shouted as I ran in with the paramedics. We were wheeling the patient in from the ambulance bay.

"Room 5." I pointed in the direction I needed them to go. Barry and Neil were the best paramedics around. I'd seen their skills many times in the months I'd been at St. Vincent's, and as far as I knew, none of the others could touch them. Many patients made it to the hospital alive that might have died with others attending them.

"Gunshot to the upper left chest, close range 22 through the upper lobe and possibly out the back. We didn't have time to check for an exit wound, but there is a chance of spinal injury.

Reflexes are dead in the legs. The lung is punctured, we've aspirated, and started saline," Barry rattled off the details, while Neil gave the task of bagging over to Jane. "BP: seventy over thirty, pulse is weak, pupils are fixed and dilated. He's in shock and crashed on the way in. We managed to resuscitate, but it's a bad one, Ryan."

The patient was gurgling, literally drowning in his own blood, and I took over pressing the gauze into the wound. It was quickly saturating.

"How long?" I asked as we wheeled him into the room.

"20:13," Neil responded, hanging the IV bag on the hook above the gurney. I glanced at the clock. Time was short. Fucking Golden Hour; survival was more likely if we could stabilize the patient within an hour of the injury, and already 23 minutes of that was history. Adrenaline coursed through my veins and my team launched into action as Barry and Neil left the room.

I looked down at the kid. He wasn't more than 16 or 17 years old, wearing gang colors, and now if his life wasn't over, he might wish it was. Jane began slicing off his shirt and jeans, moving calmly and confidently, while another nurse stood hooking up the monitors. I had to stop the bleeding or he'd die within minutes. "Start a transfusion. Push two units of O negative." Usually the attending resident would make that call, but he'd left the ER for his dinner break not ten minutes earlier. "Then page Wagner."

The wound was a sucking wound—air wheezing sickeningly in and out of the hole in the kid's chest. I stuck my gloved finger in the wound, trying to ascertain the extent of the damage. It felt contained, mostly penetration trauma with little cavitation. Jane pulled the fabric free of the boy's body and began examining it. His lungs began to fill more easily, his breathing less labored with my finger sealing the wound.

"It appears to be a single exit wound, right shoulder blade, Ryan, so there should be no fragmentation. It looks clean." It was too dangerous to turn him over to see what we were dealing with, but there was just a fraction of blood on the back of the shirt, so the majority of the damage appeared to be in the left lung. "Blood pressure is dropping, pulse is weak."

"Push the fluids," I began, suctioning as much blood as I could from the wound. Jane appeared at my side with the clotting medication. She set it on the tray next to me and then went to adjust the IVs.

Screams from the reception area warned us mere seconds before the door burst open. Everyone inside was startled as three young men rushed in. They were all banged up, one of them—a bulky black kid with his head shaved—was bleeding profusely. He had one hand holding the gash in his side as he fell weakly up against the wall near the door for support.

A smaller white kid's face was bruised and swollen. He was nervous, tattoos covering both of his bare arms and neck, while a large Hispanic man wearing a black and white bandana pushed in front of the other two, waving a large butcher knife.

"Get away from that motherfucker, Doc! He deserves to die, and we're gonna make sure he does. He dies, or you die!" The voice was brutally deep, cold as ice and unmoving; without remorse.

The surface of my skin ran cold and I paused for a split second, glancing briefly over my shoulder to assess the situation. The smaller man had a gun and was waving it around. My eyes met Jane's across the patient's body. She continued to squeeze the bag with barely a second's hesitation in her rhythm and I grabbed the packet of Celox, preparing to continue with my job. Her face was pinched, I could see she was horrified at the young age of the patient; he couldn't be more than 16. And she was terrified; it showed in the shaking of her hands. Still, she kept working.

"Please put the gun down," I said. My gloved hands, covered in blood, had a difficult time opening the cellophane packet of medication.

Kari, one of the other nurses, moved forward to the boy by the door of the examination room, who was now close to falling to the floor. He was weak, blood seeping out of his wound to spread eerily over his shirt, a dark trail starting down his right thigh. His eyes were glassy and started to roll back in his head. *Stupid fuckers! Such a waste. And for what?*

"Get him on a gurney, Kari!" I instructed. "Take him into another examining room!"

There was shuffling outside the room and I could only assume that the staff was moving the other patients out of the ER. At least, I prayed they were.

"No! He ain't going no where!" The gang leader shouted. He moved around the table where my patient lay, like a predator ready to pounce.

"He'll bleed out in a few minutes if we don't attend to him." My eyes met his without flinching.

"He's dead already." The man dismissed his friend with deadly calm. "This little cocksucker stuck him in the gut. Killed my little brother, too, so he has to pay."

My chest filled painfully as I sucked air hard into my lungs. The smaller kid bounced back and forth on his feet, a small handgun dangling from his hand. I recognized his jittery demeanor and glazed over eyes. He was definitely high. The last thing we needed was for the gun to be dropped and go off with an errant bullet ricocheting around the room. "We might be able to save your friend but you have to let us try."

"I said! He's already dead!" The larger man shouted. The fifteen seconds that it took for all of it to go down seemed like a decade. I glanced at Kari, who was kneeling next to the frightened, wounded boy, trying to part his blood-soaked clothes with gloved hands, murmuring softly that he'd be okay. We all knew he wasn't, even if they did let us treat him.

"What are your names?" I asked, trying to distract the men long enough to figure out what the fuck I was going to do. The kid on the table might live if I could finish what I'd started.

The barrel of the gun painfully nudged the base of my neck, pushing into my flesh and making it burn.

"I'm the Grim Reaper," the smaller kid said over my shoulder with a cackling laugh. He was so close that his sour breath whizzed past my nostrils. He smelled of whiskey, sweat and blood. His voice was whiney and high-pitched. "If you know what's fucking good for you, asshole, you'll stop trying to save that worthless piece of shit. We ain't fucking around! I'll shoot you!" He jabbed the gun into my flesh again, harder this time. I couldn't help but cringe, pain shooting sharply down my neck and shoulder. The leader's eyes narrowed and his thin lips lifted in an evil grin.

"The doctor is just doing his job!" Jane said. The bravery she showed was admirable, but I could see the horror in her blue eyes, her brow pinched with immense strain. My own heart was thumping sickeningly in my chest as if counting down to my own death. I tried to focus on the kid in front of me, and getting the powder in the wound without attracting too much attention.

"And I'm just doing mine, bitch!" The leader moved forward and shoved her roughly to the floor. She screamed, then fell against the table with a grunt, sending some of the steel instruments clattering to the floor.

"Do you really think you can get away with this?" Jane asked, looking up at the man as she slowly rose to her feet with a wince and positioned herself back at my side. "This is a hospital. There are hundreds of people here. You can't kill everyone!"

The man laughed, sneering maniacally, his tone sinister and his rotten teeth showing the black discoloration of a meth addict. "I can kill you and everyone in this room, bitch! After that, will you give a flying fuck? Will your family care that you saved this dirt-bag? You'll be dead; lights out."

I tried to fill the wound with the medication as inconspicuously as I could but my mind was on one person. I closed my eyes for a brief second and my soul seized.

Julia. Would the last time I spoke to her be an argument on the phone? I never answered her when she told me she loved me. I fucking hated myself in that moment.

For the first time in this nightmare, her beautiful face flashed before my eyes. Our entire relationship passed in front of me in a rapid series of stills. My heart thudded so loudly I thought it would burst from my chest, and my throat tightened, bile rising up until I thought I was going to vomit. I coughed and wiped at my forehead on the sleeve of my scrubs. I realized that if I let this boy die, I'd be breaking my Hippocratic Oath, yet, if I saved him, we'd all probably get killed. We'd probably get killed anyway, I acknowledged. I felt like I was suffocating and wanted to be rid of the confining surgical mask and eye guard that was standard operating procedure when treating an open wound.

"Aren't you listening, motherfucker?" A single shot rang out as the small man fired into the ceiling and the women screamed, all of us flinching in unison. The menacing laugh of both men echoed through the stark room. I glanced at Kari, still next to the kid on the floor. His blood was seeping around his lifeless body in a puddle. She shook her head. He was dead. I moved my head toward the door, silently telling her to get out of the room while the criminals were somewhat distracted. She stayed low and quietly opened the door, slipping outside the room.

"We're listening," Jane said, more softly now, working to keep the focus on us. Her eyes searched my face and she let go of the bag and began moving around toward the man with the knife. I shook my head at her, but she ignored me. She was so brave, yet my mind was screaming for her to stop. What the fuck was she doing? *It's okay, Ryan,* her eyes pleaded with mine.

"Get out if you wanna keep breathing!" One of them said behind the handkerchief that covered the lower half of his face.

The other two nurses looked at me with wide eyes and I nodded. "Go. You, too, Jane."

She shook her head, her eyes wide and frightened, but determined, as she continued to move around behind me, while I kept my finger in the wound in the patient on the table.

"Come on, let's take it easy. You're right." Jane tried to reason with the unreasonable. "Is he worth any of our lives? What about you? Don't throw your lives away. You can leave. We won't call the police."

I kept my movements to a minimum, trying to thwart any attention to myself so I could continue to work, but it was difficult with no help.

The man laughed bitterly. "Jack, she says she won't call the cops. I think she wants to be our friend. Maybe she wants to party."

He grabbed her roughly by the arm and pulled her mask from her face, grabbing her chin roughly and tilting her face. She winced in pain but didn't make a sound. I paused for a split second but didn't turn around. "Leave her alone," I commanded softly.

The man named Jack shoved me roughly and I stumbled and fell hard against the wall. "My boy said stop working, Doctor Do-gooder! Are you fucking deaf?"

I stopped what I was doing and whipped around, knocking the gun away from my neck. The rest of the instruments fell with a clatter on the floor and the gun went off when it clattered to the floor. My heart seized. I was unsure, at first, if I'd been shot or not, as adrenaline raced through my veins.

The young man staggered back and away from me, and the air whooshed from my lungs as the other man put a fist in my kidney, doubling me over. I grunted as intense pain shot through my torso. I fell to my knees, shaking in agony.

"Ryan, stay down. He's not worth it," Jane pleaded softly. "Please." I could see her chest rising and falling with the effort of her breathing, her arms at her side, palms face up as her eyes begged me to do as she asked. I couldn't. These men were insane with hatred. They didn't value the life of their friend who bled to death in front of them. They sure as hell weren't going to listen to reason.

It was all a blur after that as I stumbled to my feet and a flash of steel appeared before me. Jane yelled my name and ran forward, shoving me away with all her might, making me fall off balance and fall backward.

Jane's scream pierced the air just as pain sliced through my shoulder and right arm. I slammed heavily into the wall with a loud bang.

My vision blurred as resentment and anger welled up inside me. Who the fuck did these bastards think they were? What gave them the right to decide whether any of us would ever see anything outside of these walls? If Jane, now lying on the cold tile floor, her lower abdomen ripped open and pouring out blood, would survive more than this minute or the next? Who the hell were they to decide if I would ever lay eyes on Julia again or if she'd be made a widow on this night?

Sirens screamed outside in the ambulance bay as I crawled over to Jane. Her body jerked and her eyes glassed over, starring up into nothing, blood quickly saturating her scrubs.

"Jane!" I moved over her and lifted the material away. The shirt of her scrubs was slit open and a large cut was made in her pants below her waist. "Jane, you're gonna make it. Look into my eyes. Stay focused on me, Jane!"

She blinked and opened her mouth but nothing came out. Her pupils were huge and dilated. I knew they'd be unresponsive if I tested them. I pulled off my gloves and reached for a box of gauze bandages from one of the counters and pulled out handfuls of it to press to her wound. She was cut on her lower torso, below her belly button; the huge, gaping slash full of blood that seeped in again as soon as I could mop it up, gushing in time with her heartbeat. Fuck, it was bad. It had to be the abdominal aorta or the uterine or common iliac artery for that kind of pulsing rhythm. There was no time for new gloves, but I didn't concern myself with the risks. She needed surgery and stat. Sweat was starting to bead on my brow and drip down into my eyes. I wiped at the sting with my sleeve but it did nothing to alleviate the problem and only succeeded in smearing my own blood across my face.

I struggled to keep my voice from shaking. "C'mon, Jane, stay with me." My heart stopped, her eyes that were staring up at me were fading fast. She wouldn't make it to the OR at this rate. I had no access to instruments and even if I did, blood was filling the cavity too quickly to see where the artery was cut so I could get a clamp on it. She was bleeding out, her blood seeping down her body and onto the floor, into the knees of my scrubs.

If I wanted to save her, I had one choice. I reached inside her, using my fingers to search for the flow of blood and when I found it, I used my fingers to pinch it off. I needed both hands to secure the artery on both sides of the wound. It was a fumbling remedy. At best, blind and slippery, but it was all I had.

"Jack, let's go! The cops are coming. Kill that fucker so we can get out of here!"

Somewhere in the back of my mind my subconscious reminded me that the police were already on the scene and that the boy on the table was close to death as well. Worse, that I could be the 'fucker' they were planning on killing. In the split second it took for the two men to move around me and plunge the knife into the chest of the kid on the table, I prayed. Prayed I'd be alive. Alive to try to save Jane and to make sure Julia knew how much I loved her.

The kid jerked violently, and I did, too. My first instinct was to jump up and try to stop them, but given my current circumstance at Jane's side, it was impossible. Jack pulled the knife brutally from the boy's chest and the air wheezed out of my lungs like I'd been the one stuck. I was helpless. All I could do was listen to them leave and then pray that someone would come through the door. I couldn't move. To do so would mean Jane would die for sure. My own blood was soaking the sleeve on my right shoulder and running in streams down my arm and mingling with hers. I barely noticed.

"Kari! Kari, get in here! Bring a gurney and get Caleb and Dr. Wagner! Stat! Jane is hurt badly!" I shouted. Kari and Jared burst into the room, followed by three other nurses and the attending.

"Holy shit, Ryan. Have you been stabbed?" Caleb asked as he and a wide-eyed Kari ran forward.

"Forget about me. Jane is critical. Kari, grab some clamps! Tell Dr. Wagner we'll need Jameson. She needs emergency surgery." The madness of a scuffle and several gun shots that popped just outside the doors reminded me that it was not over as the police dealt with the gang. My heart felt like it would fly from my chest. I wasn't sure if the pulse in my hands was mine or Jane's. This wasn't some stranger whose life I held, literally, in my hands.

Caleb frantically pulled on some gloves and moved to my side, ripping open the sterile package containing the surgical tools which would contain the clamps, as another group of nurses and doctors rushed in and Dr. Wagner got on his phone and assembled Dr. Jameson and the surgical team. "Oh, my God!" he said.

"Clamp just above the fingers on my left hand and below them on the right." I was breathless. "A little higher." He pushed the open clamp into Jane's wound. "Higher! Got it? Now the other."

My colleague clamped off the other side and the others lifted her to a gurney and began working on stabilizing her.

I sighed heavily. I was covered in blood, not sure if it was Jane's, the kid's, or my own. My knees felt weak and Kari helped me to a chair, while the others scrambled around Jane.

Caleb ordered fluids and blood, the nurses were rushing around hooking up the equipment and doing CPR. They were in overdrive, and if Jane had a chance, I was confident our team would make the most of it.

"Fuck! Fuck! Fuck!" Guilt crashed over me. Was it my fault that kid was dead? Or that Jane was barely alive? My head tried to wrap around what happened. She moved in front of me just after my shoulder was sliced. No doubt, without her intervention, it would be me fighting for my life.

"Call time of death." I flushed, thanking God it had come from the other side of the room. It was a hollow, wooden echo that got lost behind the din of the discussion over Jane. Jane would be prepped as soon as they had her stable and rushed in for emergency surgery.

I glanced to my left. The boy didn't make it; they were pulling a sheet up over his body. Somewhere he had a mother who had just lost her sixteen year-old son to a senseless tragedy.

"Caleb, how bad is she?" I asked hoarsely, but loud enough for him to hear me. I winced. My shoulder was on fire as I gingerly tried to move it. It felt sticky, the blood beginning to clot and crust in the streams down my arm. It was a sign it wasn't too deep. I'd need stitches, but no major arteries or veins were struck and the muscle, though protesting, worked. I grunted in pain.

"Not good, Ryan. She'll probably need a hysterectomy. Her insides are like hamburger."

I had no words. In light of my own weekend quest to make a baby with Julia, and the miscarriage we suffered, I felt Jane's loss and felt it hard.

"Come with me, Ryan," Kari said. "Let's head into another room so I can get this cleaned and stitched up."

"I'm fine," I protested. I'd gotten the least of it.

"Stop being stubborn. There's nothing more you can do. She's still alive because of you."

"It should be me on that table."

"Hush. You're being silly. You were amazing. You knew what to do to help her and you did it without hesitation. All that blood is a dangerous situation. Some people wouldn't have been so selfless, Ryan. If I ever get hurt, I hope you'll be the one working on me." Her eyes filled with understanding and compassion. "Come on. We'll only be in the way and they'll be transporting her soon."

"Okay." I nodded as she helped me up and nodded to the wheelchair she had waiting. "But I don't need that damn thing."

Julia ~

I glanced at my watch and sighed, impatient and anxious to get home to Ryan. Even though I'd been annoyed as hell with his insensitivity to Ellie's broken heart, I couldn't stay mad at him. He was tired, working his ass off and all he wanted was to see me. How could I hold that against him? It only reminded me how perfect he was and I found myself aching to put my arms around him.

This weekend had been something we'd both been looking forward to, and if I was honest, I was annoyed with my friend, too. Why couldn't she see how she alienated Harris? Every time she questioned and mistrusted, he closed off more and more, which only fed her suspicions.

I sighed in resignation. I was tired of listening to the same thing over and over when she clearly wasn't hearing my advice and she wasn't listening to the man she loved. I reminded myself how I used to feel when Ryan went out on dates; I was devastated, even though we weren't even dating. Ellie had to be feeling even worse, except it was all in her head. That was the infuriating part and it made it all a huge waste.

Somehow I managed to get on a plane, but it was much later than I'd originally planned. Witnessing the state of Ellie's relationship with Harris, made me sick at how I'd left things with Ryan. I hated any sort of distance between us, and more than the 3000 miles that had separated us, the emotional chasm, however temporary, left me bereft and itching to fix it.

I called Ellie's mother, who'd always coddled her daughter as long as I'd known her and was only too happy to come be with her only child. Ellie cringed at her mother's meddling, sometimes feeling smothered, but in this case, she ran into her arms like a small child. After the older woman arrived, I made a hasty exit, inviting my friend to come to New York as soon as she could manage it. A change of scenery was just what she needed to get her head and heart around her own situation and the New York Fashion District was just the distraction to help.

Despite Ellie's adamant posturing that Harris was sleeping with a different woman every night, I knew in my heart he wasn't. Harris's sorrow had turned to anger after multiple attempts to convince Ellie to the contrary failed. Who could blame the poor guy?

Finally on the tarmac in New York, I pulled my phone out of my purse and checked it for message from Ryan. I frowned at the blank screen. That was weird. He had to be really mad if he hadn't responded yet. We usually made up within hours.

"Where you going, miss?" the driver asked as he loaded my bags in the trunk of his cab. He had olive skin and a heavy European accent, flashing me a pleasant smile when he held the back door open. I gave him the address to our apartment and climbed into the backseat. As we made our way through town, the radio played as the concrete jungle that was Manhattan, now lit up and glowing, passed by in a mirage of brilliant colors. I leaned my head back on the seat and closed my burning eyes. I was exhausted, even though my internal clock was three hours earlier than the 12:13 my watch showed.

"It's nice they're finally playing music. The past hour's been nothing but that incident at the other end of town. What a

shame kids have to go all crazy like that." The old man
readjusted the Yankee's baseball cap on his head as he shook it. I
barely noticed. I was watching a couple nuzzling each other on
the corner as we waited at a red light.

"Hmmm?" I smiled and looked at the man's face in the
rearview mirror. "Don't you have Sirius?"

"In this old hack?" He laughed. "Good thing I don't, too.
Need to know what's going on around here. I like oldies and talk
radio. This thing at St. Vincent's tonight. Stupid kids," he huffed
gruffly.

I quickly tuned in to what he was saying. "What?" I asked
anxiously. "What about St. Vincent's?"

I dug the phone out of my purse and pushed Ryan's speed
dial, holding the phone to my ear at the same time waiting for the
driver's answer.

"Some gang thing. A shooting, and then a fight in the
Emergency Room. Several people were injured, I think a few
died, and several others injured, from what I hear. I hope they
get those bastards."

My breath left my body. "Oh, my God!" I blinked as my
eyes started to sting. "When? When was it?" Panic seized my
chest. Ryan was working tonight and maybe that was why he
wasn't answering his phone!

"Just tonight."

"Oh, my God! Please take me there! I have to get down
there! Now!"

"It might not be safe, or the cops might not let anyone in.
According to the news, they've been deflecting emergencies to
other hospitals."

"Please! I have to get down there!" I reached up and ur-
gently grabbed the back of his seat. "Please! My husband is a
first year resident and he was working tonight! I have to go!"

Two tears plopped onto my cheeks and I hastily brushed them away and returned the unanswered phone to my purse. "Please!"

I was shaking so badly that when I tried to find Gabriel and Elyse's number, it fell completely from my hands and landed with a thud on the floorboards. All I could think about was getting in touch with someone that knew something. Since Ryan wasn't answering his phone, maybe his parents knew something. I scrambled to pick it up as the driver made a U-turn at a light and headed toward St. Vincent's.

"The hospital was unaffected. It was only the ER."

"Ryan works in the ER! Please!"

"Okay. But, I doubt they'll let us in."

It seemed like years until Elyse picked up the phone and the time it took the cab driver to navigate through the Manhattan traffic was excruciating.

"Hello?"

"Oh, thank God! Elyse, have you heard from Ryan tonight?"

"I haven't spoken with him since Wednesday. Why? What's wrong, Julia?"

"I don't know. Maybe nothing. Have you watched the news? Maybe it's not national news." I was rambling and my voice trembled. "There was some sort of gang warfare at the hospital. I don't know the details, I just got in from L.A. I'd hoped you'd know if Ryan was safe."

I could hear Ryan's mother audibly gasp on the other end of the phone. "Oh, no! Gabe! Turn on the news! We've been out to dinner with friends all evening, so I haven't heard anything! What do you know?"

"Not much. I'm on my way to the hospital, now."

"Julia, is that wise? If it's dangerous, Ryan wouldn't want you to go down there."

"I have to!" I almost screamed. "I'm sorry," my voice was softer now. "I just... I have to make sure he's okay. He's not answering his phone!"

"Ryan never answers his phone at the hospital, honey."

"I know, but he should be home now. I tried his pager, too. I'm..." my voice cracked and I brushed a stray tear from my cheek. "Oh, God, I'm so scared!"

"Julia, no news is good news." Elyse tried to calm me down, but I could hear that her fear echoed my own. "I won't believe anything has happened to my son. Just calm down."

I almost told her two people had been killed but decided to wait until I knew more. "I'll call you back when I know more. I'm just getting to the hospital."

There were flashing lights from half a dozen police cars and four news vans at the Emergency entrance. The parking lot wasn't blocked off, though, and the lane for ambulances delivering patients was clear. "I gotta go, Elyse. I love you."

"You, too, sweetheart. Call us as soon as you know something."

"I will." I hung up the phone and dug out thirty dollars to give to the cabbie. "Thank you," I said as I rushed from the car.

"Miss! What about your bags?"

"I can't worry about that now!"

"But..." he called after me as I rushed up to the police officers standing at the entrance.

"Ma'am, are you in need of medical attention?"

"No." I was breathless, my chest tight as I tried to move around the officers. One of them put his hand up and the other grabbed my arm. "Please, I have to get in there."

"This is a crime scene. We're only letting critical emergency patients through."

"Please!" I knew the panic showed on my face as I looked up into the officer's face. "My husband works here! I just need to know he's safe!"

"I'm sorry. No can do. You have to leave, ma' am. We have to keep this area clear while the investigators do their job."

I stood there ringing my hands, unable or unwilling to do as he asked. I looked away, trying to stem the panic and thickening in my throat, but my eyes welled. When I looked back, his burly face was a watery blur. "Please." I reached out and grabbed his arm frantically, my voice shaking. "Are you married? Wouldn't you want to know if your wife was safe?"

"I'd want her safe, and I'm sure your husband wouldn't want you in the middle of this. We can't let you in. We're just flat feet. We don't get to make these decisions. I'm very sorry. You'll have to leave."

I could see behind him through the glass doors. The waiting room was filled with more police milling around, and one woman was screaming hysterically. Sobbing and falling to her knees as one of the officers caught her. I closed my eyes. *Please, God.*

"You let that woman in! Please! I have to make sure he's okay!" I was openly crying, clutching at his arm. "I'm begging you."

"She was already in there when it all went down, ma'am." The officer put his arm around me and physically pulled me back toward the cab. The driver, leaning down and over to look anxiously up through the window watched it all in silence. The policeman opened the rear passenger door and pushed me inside. "Take her home. This is no place for her."

I felt helpless and angry, frustration threatened to explode in my chest. "This is bullshit! Tell me he's okay and I'll leave!" I screamed at the man as he closed the door behind me. The cab driver rolled the electric window down and regret crossed the features of the two officers. "Can't you at least do that?"

The one who wasn't saying much finally stepped forward. He was shorter with gray hair and gentle features, sympathy written all over his face.

"What's his name?" the second policeman asked.

"Ryan Matthews. He's a resident." I put my hand to cover my mouth as a sob rose up in my chest. My nose was running. I was a snotty mess and I wiped at the tip of my nose with the back of my hand and blinked up at him.

"Okay, I'll go in and find out. We can't let you in, but I'll have someone call you, okay?"

I nodded and dug in my purse for my business card to quickly hand to the man. "Thank you. My cell number is on my card."

"Now, get out of here," he said with a soft smile and then turned and walked past the other officer. The glass doors parted and he disappeared inside. The other officer waved to the driver and the car started to move away from the entrance.

I closed my eyes, and wiped at my wet cheeks. "Can you pull around to the front of the hospital, please?"

I watched through the back window as the cab pulled out of the driveway.

"He said to take you home. Aren't you going?"

"No. I can't leave until I know. Just take me around to the front and drop me off, please. I'll pay you. Can you take my bags to my apartment?" I gave him the address and a hundred dollar bill as I got out of the car and ran into the front entrance as fast as my feet would carry me. I knew my way around the hospital and hurried through the halls toward the back of the hospital where the Emergency Room was located. As I got closer, there were policemen, more staff and several men in suits were wandering around. The doors were off the hinges and leaning up against the wall, plaster and debris littered the floor. Two armed guards put up their hands to stop me. One was a huge black man, and the other a younger and much smaller white man, both in hospital security uniforms. I inhaled, ready to fight my way in.

"Sorry." The big officer crossed his arms in front of him and shook his head. "No one gets in."

My head fell back and I gasped as I looked at the ceiling. My eyes felt swollen and I knew my face was red and pinched. "I have get in there. Please." Determination laced my voice.

He shook his head again and his partner spoke up. "You got someone in there?" he asked.

"Yes. My husband is a resident. He was working tonight. I just need to know he's okay."

Dark eyes scanned my face and he frowned.

"Please?"

"What's his name?"

"Ryan Matthews."

"Oh, Ryan. He's a good dude. Julia, right?" I nodded quickly, a tiny ray of hope beginning to flicker. "He's not one of the casualties, but he was injured. We'll take you in."

Ryan was alive. I was relieved, but still panicked because I didn't know how badly he was hurt. I wanted to bolt through the doors, and once we got into the ER, I glanced around quickly, my eyes desperately seeking those of my husband. I recognized some of the nurses and Caleb, whose scrubs and lab coat were covered in blood. He looked up from the clipboard he was holding, acknowledgment filling his expression. He nodded at the guards. "I've got this. Julia, come with me."

The officers remained where they were as I walked beside the other doctor. "Just please tell me he's okay."

"He's okay. He has a pretty nasty slice on his shoulder and he'll be sore, but he's going to be fine. They're stitching him up."

At that moment, we came to an open doorway and I saw Ryan, shirtless, with an older woman in a white lab coat, sewing up his shoulder. He was hunched over with his back to me. All I could see was the blood. His arm was stained red with it, and his pants were saturated, his scrub shirt and lab coat were sitting on the table next to him, all covered in large bloody splotches. They looked like they'd been used to mop up a murder scene.

"Ryan?" I called softly. His head snapped around instantly and his eyes met mine. Relief flooded through me. I was so grateful for the light in those beautiful blue eyes. He held out his good arm and I rushed to his side, and he wound it tightly around my waist. I buried my face in the crook of his neck and clung to him, trying hard not to let the torrent of tears break free. He smelled like Ryan, but the scent of his cologne and skin was masked by the salty rank of blood.

"What are you doing here? I thought you were still in L.A."

"Oh, my God!" I said, unable to answer.

"This isn't all my blood, baby," he soothed. My hand moved to his face and I kissed his jaw and cheek. "I'm fine. Really, Jules, I'm okay," Ryan soothed. His eyes softened at the fear in my own. When the nurse asked me to wait in the chair against the wall, Ryan shook his head in refusal, so she continued working as Ryan held me with his good arm. It felt so good to be held closely to him, his warm breath reassuring me he was still alive, rushing over my face and neck. "I'm so glad to see you." His arm tightened and his lips found my temple. "You're all I thought about. I was so worried I'd never see you again."

I clutched around him harder, as the dam burst and I closed my eyes. "Don't ever say that to me. Ever!"

"I'm okay, babe. You're stuck with me."

"Can you go home tonight, or will you have to be admitted?"

"Pfft! For this little scratch," he joked, trying to make me feel better. I knew it was much worse than he was letting on. It looked deep and would leave an angry scar on his perfect skin.

"Let's go home when you're done. You can tell me what happened, but I want to get out of here and I need to call your parents."

He rolled his eyes. "You called my parents?"

"You wouldn't answer my texts!" I exclaimed, thankful for the amused look on his face.

"I need to check on Jane, before we leave."

I remembered the pretty blonde nurse. "She was hurt pretty badly. She stepped in front of me when the bastard with the knife came at me. She got the worst of it. I might be dead if it weren't for her. She's in surgery, now. I'd like to stay until she's in recovery. Okay?"

"What happened to her?"

Ryan briefly explained and I nodded. "Okay." Gratitude was an understatement. Tears blurred his beautiful face before my eyes. He looked so tired. "Can I stay with you? I can't bear to have you out of my sight."

His lips quirked in a soft smile. "Yeah. I'd like that."

"Does it hurt?"

"Yep. Like a son-of-a-bitch. They gave me some Vicodin, but I can't take it until we get home. It'll put me to sleep."

"I remember how that is." I said softly as he leaned over and placed a soft, open-mouthed kiss on my lips. "I hated taking it."

It was only a few minutes more and Ryan was bandaged up and we went to the doctor's lounge so he could change into clean scrubs. He was quiet as he took my hand and walked with me down the hall to the elevators. We found a couch in the waiting room of the surgery floor and he pulled me down onto his lap. I went without protest and curled into him, resting my forehead on his jaw, content to be held by him.

After he called Elyse and promised to call again with more details the following day, Ryan unloaded about the horrible happenings of the evening. I was frightened just hearing about the cold-blooded murder that happened right in front of their eyes and how Jane saved my husband by sacrificing herself. I had no way to show her how grateful I was. She'd saved my life, too.

"I'm so thankful, Ryan. I'll never be able to repay her."

"I know. Me either. She was so selfless. I owe her everything." His arms tightened and he kissed my forehead. "I owe her *this*."

~5~

Ryan ~

My shoulder burned like a son-of-a-bitch and the other one was aching where it had slammed into the wall and floor. It was pitch black and 3 a. m. when Julia and I finally pushed through the door of our apartment. Jane came out of surgery an hour earlier and was in recovery. She wouldn't be lucid for hours, so I decided to take Julia home. The artery was so badly damaged, along with her uterus being almost sliced in half, the surgeons had to perform a complete hysterectomy to curtail the bleeding and save her life. I felt horrible; immersed in guilt and decided it was my responsibility to deliver the devastating news. I was going to grab a few hours rest and then get back to the hospital early in the morning.

Julia padded softly around the bedroom and bathroom as we both brushed our teeth and got ready for bed. She silently rubbed my bare back and kissed my shoulder, standing there, watching me in the mirror with her soulful eyes. My chest filled. I'd never been so happy to see anyone in my life as I was when she walked through that door in the ER.

I put down the toothbrush and gingerly slid an arm around her waist and tugged her close to my side. The familiar scent of her, the warmth and love I found in her face when she looked at me, was as life-giving as a bonfire in Antarctica. My lips found her forehead and then moved down the side of her face. Her skin was warm beneath my mouth; *alive*. I breathed in deeply, suck-ing in her life-giving breath for my own.

Julia's arms wound around my waist and she kissed my jaw before our lips met in a gentle kiss. I could feel the remnants of her fear and sensed the ache in her heart at the prospect of losing me. It was a feeling I remembered all too well.

She drew a shuddering breath as I forced my arms to wrap around her despite the pain that knifed through me with the movement. "I was so scared. I couldn't bear to lose you. I don't know what I'd do without you."

My hands framed her face as she looked up at me, her fea-tures gentled by sadness and love, my thumbs brushing along her cheekbones. She seemed so small, so fragile... so luminous. Emotion flooded through me and my heart constricted. It was so real—the possibility of the end of everything—and losing just one second with her was something I couldn't contemplate. Even these quiet moments were so precious. It would've been easier being the one who died, rather than the one left behind. My brow knitted and I closed my eyes, nodding, pulling her little body closer into mine. "You won't lose me, baby, but I know what you mean."

Julia buried her face in my bare chest and held onto me for dear life, her fingers splayed out on my back and curled sharply into my flesh. I could feel the desperation in her touch; the mag-nitude of her terror and overwhelming love, as if her feelings were my own; because they were. We were two halves of one person.

"Does it hurt if I hold you this tight? I can't seem to let go."

"Even if it did, I want you to touch me. Come on, sweet-heart. Let's go to bed."

She nodded, pulling out of my arms and retreating to the other room as I moved to follow her. The bed wasn't made. I flushed, wondering if she was silently berating me because I hadn't bothered tidying up the prior morning. Normally, Julia would scowl at me, but she silently pulled back the covers, straightening them as she went. I slid under, grimacing as I eased my upper body down. Everything fucking hurt.

Julia left the room, returning with a crystal glass full of ice water and a small white pill in her hand. She smiled gently as she held it out to me and I took it from her.

"Nighty-night." She smirked and I couldn't help but smile back. She was so cute.

I paused before I put it in my mouth and reached for the water. I was propped up on four pillows and she began to rearrange them, putting one under my injured right arm. "What am I, an invalid?"

"Yes. Shut up and take your medicine, Matthews."

"What if I don't want to go nighty-night, Mommy?" I wagged my eyebrows at her.

Her eyes widened as did her smile. She sat on the edge of the bed watching me until her brows rose. "I don't care what you want. You need sleep." When she bit her lip, I laughed.

"Since when don't you care what I want?" I reached out and ran a finger down her arm to her hand. "Even if you didn't, I can make you," I said suggestively. My voice was teasing, but we both knew the truth in my words. I grabbed her hand in mine and stared at her with an intensity we could both feel. "We were supposed to make a baby tonight."

Her doe eyes softened, jade green turning darker. "Ryan, you need to rest. It's so late. Let's just sleep."

"I know," I admitted. "But I'd rather make love. You can be on top. I'm an invalid, remember? Maybe if I come, I won't need these damn pills."

"You know you'll still need them. Do you still have tomorrow off?"

"Yes. But I'm going in to check on Jane. I want to be the one to tell her about the hysterectomy." Julia nodded sadly. I obligingly took the Vicodin and then handed the glass back to her.

She shut off the lamp and then walked around to crawl in next to me, curling on her side and wrapping a hand around my bicep. Her lips were warm and soft as they caressed the skin just below the bandage on the curve of my shoulder. "I'd like to go with you. I'll never be able to fully thank her, but I'd like to try. I know it's not the same, exactly, but I can empathize."

It was true. We'd lost a baby, but we at least could look forward to having more. Jane wouldn't ever know that joy. I sensed Julia's sadness and wanted to hold her close to me; to wrap her up in my arms, but the dull throb in my shoulder reminded me of the sharp pain I'd feel if I moved. I nodded into the dark, turning my face toward hers. It was an awkward position—forced as I was to lie on my back. I couldn't reach out to her like I wanted.

"That would be nice, baby. I'm sure Jane would appreciate seeing you."

In the waiting room and on the way home, I'd told Julia all about the gang storming the hospital, how they demanded I stop working; how we'd tried to save the boy in the middle of it all, the fight, the thug with the knife, and finally Jane getting slashed and the kid on the table murdered. Julia visibly shuddered, clearly painting the picture in her mind from my words. I sighed heavily. The kid died anyway, so was it worth it? I had to believe I'd done the right thing. I was certain Jane would say that I did, despite her loss.

"You did the best you could." Julia read my mind, as usual, as her fingers gently stroked the hair back off of my forehead again and again. It was soothing and I closed my eyes at the comfort and normalcy in her touch. All of this... could've been lost. "You risked your life, Ryan. What more is there?"

"I don't know. *More*," I said miserably. Her hand cupped the side of my face, her fingers lightly caressing the skin of my cheek.

"It's so horrible. The woman in the ER—the one sobbing—who was that?"

"The dead boy's mother. I'll never get used to that shit. He was so young." My eyes were getting heavy, my words becoming a mumble. Julia's hand slid to my chest and my fingers curled around hers, pressing then flat into my flesh. "What a fucking waste..."

"Does Jane have any family? Anyone to help her recover?"

"She has a boyfriend, but I've never met him. He doesn't come to the hospital and I don't think she has much of a family. We've never discussed it, beyond that her parents live in Michigan."

"That seems sad. I know what it's like to move to New York alone."

I turned toward Julia despite the searing pain, to search the darkness for her expression. I reached out and smoothed a finger along the crinkle between her brows. "Was it that bad?" I asked quietly.

She shook her head. "No, because at the end of it, I have you." Julia grabbed my hand and pulled it to her mouth, lingeringly kissing my fingers. The love seeped from her into me and I was grateful. She was my calm, my home and I was reminded of the many nights we lay in bed just talking for hours. The passion was always so magnificent, but her words, the way she always understood what I needed, even just a simple touch. She took my breath away.

"Were you scared? Really?" I asked quietly.

She shrugged softly, still holding my hand. "A little in the beginning. At least I was used to a bigger city. Jane must have been terrified. Do you know where in Michigan?"

My eyes began to droop, the painkiller finally starting to dull the burn and aches. "I barely know her outside of work. We've shared a couple of lunches and small talk. Somewhere north, I think? She's nice; a good person."

"She'd have to be to sacrifice herself like that."

"I'm sure it was adrenaline. Sometimes, it's pure instinct to act."

I stared through the darkness, her eyes glistened black; and I was fighting to keep mine open.

"How is Ellie?"

"Not great. Her mom is staying with her for a while. I may need to invite her to stay with us for a bit. A change of scene might be good for her."

"I'm sorry I was such a prick. But, it did get you home and I need you tonight."

Julia's soft sigh filled the silence. "Yes. I'm glad I'm here."

"Is Harris out of the picture? I feel for the dude."

"I'm not sure. Maybe." The bed moved with her shrug. "He's so hurt. I'll tell you more tomorrow. Please rest, Ryan."

She turned on her opposite side and I pulled her back against me. I wanted nothing more than to be close to her. She was warm, and her sweet scent floated around me as I began to slip from consciousness. "I know it would kill me if you didn't trust me. I really am sorry. About being such a moody ass before, on the phone."

"Hush." She pulled my hand up and laced her fingers through mine, leaned over and brushed my lips with hers. "I love your moody ass and I'm right where I want to be."

Julia ~

I woke with a start. The light was streaming in, the bright rays of the late September morning breaking through the cracks in the blinds. The bed was empty next to me, the covers pushed back and the indent of Ryan's head still on the pillow.

"Ryan?" I called into the empty apartment, already knowing I'd get no answer. I crawled out of bed and walked out of the bedroom. The phone in my purse was conspicuously absent of calls. Not even one from Andrea telling me we had some fire to put out at the magazine. "Oh," I mumbled. Realizing she, and everyone else at Vogue, thought I was still in California. Still, being out of town never stopped them before.

My stomach rumbled and I rubbed it, walking into the kitchen to find something to eat. The smell of freshly brewed coffee was welcoming as was the note propped up against the wall next to it.

Hey, Babe,

I wanted to get to the hospital before Jane wakes up. Meet me there? Take a cab, I have the car. I love you,

~R

P.S. I didn't want to wake you. You looked so beautiful.

I lifted the note to my nose and inhaled softly. Just the slightest whiff of his cologne laced the paper. I was sure Ryan hadn't eaten. I looked at the clock and decided a few more minutes wouldn't matter. I pulled out a bowl and quickly whipped up some lemon poppy seed muffins and popped them in the oven before rushing through a short shower and dressing quickly in old jeans and Ryan's Harvard sweatshirt. It was overly large and hung loosely off of one shoulder, leaving the straps of my dark blue, knit cami showing. I shoved the burgundy sweatshirt back into place but it was a useless effort. The material was worn and soft from overuse, the gold letters faded on the front, but I loved wearing his things.

After the muffins were cooled and nestled in linen in our picnic basket, I pulled my hair into a messy knot at the back of my head, and shoved my feet into my old Chuck Taylors. Far from glamorous, for sure, but I didn't care.

The air was cool, the wind blowing in from the east was brisk and had me wishing I'd grabbed a jacket, but it wasn't long before I was nestled in the back of a cab and on the way to the hospital. I felt anxious; unsure what I'd say to the woman who had saved my husband's life. My throat tightened and my eyes began to burn. How do you thank someone for that? I sighed; at a loss to find the words in my mind. The reality hit me that it was more than a possibility that I could've been a widow today if it weren't for her. I quickly brushed the two fat tears that escaped down my cheeks away and wiped at my eyes with the back of my hand. Ryan and I had faced so much, but this? I physically shuddered and my throat constricted. It was silly. Ryan was fine, but if I let myself, I'd start sobbing like a baby.

The cab driver made a comment about the picnic basket and how good whatever was in it smelled, so I left him with two of the muffins with the cab fare. He thanked me with a smile, his eyes suspicious at the glassiness of mine.

"Miss, are you all right?"

I smiled tremulously. "Yes! I'm happy, that's all. It's missus. I'm married!" I jumped out of the car and hurried into the hospital's main entrance without a backward glance. It occurred to me that I didn't know Jane's last name and I'd have to figure out what floor she was on.

I stopped and glanced around. An older woman with short, bluish hair in a light pink hospital smock sat at the information desk. She watched me as I floundered in the lobby.

"May I help you, young lady?"

"Yes, my name is Julia Matthews. Last night in the ER..." I began.

"Oh, yes, dear. That was just dreadful! I mean, to think of those hoodlums rushing in here like that! It was all over the news this morning. I suppose it will be a media circus around here now... the state of the world is in shambles..." she rambled on and waved her hands about.

"Yes, ma'am. My husband works in Emergency and he was here..."

"Oh, goodness! I hope he's all right?" she interrupted me again.

"He was injured, but not seriously."

"Thank the Lord for that!"

"There was a nurse injured and I'd like to check on her. Unfortunately, I don't remember her last name. I guess I can go to the ER and ask someone."

"Her name is Jane Cooper, dear. Is your husband that dear Dr. Ryan?"

I smiled brightly. "Yes! Do you know him?"

"He's a sweetie. He buys Vogue every month at the gift shop and gives it to me. Of course, I thought it strange, such a virile young man reading a woman's magazine, but he explained that his wife works there." Acknowledgement dawned on her face, pale with too much powder than punctuated with too much blush. "You?" She pointed a long, bony finger at me, and smiled.

I nodded, my cheeks infused with heat. "Guilty. I didn't know he bought it, though. It may be because I don't bring copies home. Work intrudes enough."

The woman smiled, her bright red, Marilyn Monroe-esque lipstick a stark contrast to her pale skin. "She's been moved out of critical care; in room 511 dear. You go right on up." She waved me toward the steel doors of the elevators to our left. "Say hello to your handsome husband for me, if he's here."

"I expect that he is. It was very nice to meet you..." I hesitated.

"Oh, Louise. But Ryan calls me Louie. Now, don't be jealous, honey." Her light blue eyes sparkled from her jovial expression.

I couldn't help but giggle. "I won't. It's so nice to meet you, Louie!"

The ride to the 5th floor was fast and I quickly found Jane's room. The door was partially closed but I could see Ryan sitting on a chair he'd pulled close to the edge of the bed. There was no one else in the room and their voices were hushed. Uncharacteristically dressed in jeans and a hooded sweatshirt, his hair messier; he looked like he hadn't showered. I expected as much in his rush to get here.

Ryan leaned toward Jane, hunched over and brushing her hair back, though I could tell from the stiff way he moved, his shoulder was killing him. My heart constricted in pain for them both and suddenly hatred for those responsible filled my chest in a suffocating way. Last night, I was scared and just glad Ryan and Jane were okay, but now, I was angry at the men responsible. My lips thinned and I leaned my head on the door, taking a deep breath before tapping on it softly.

Ryan sat up and turned around, acknowledgment settled on his features as he waved me in. My eyes searched his, and the sadness behind them told me all I needed to know. Jane hadn't taken the news well. How could she? I'd be devastated if I were in her position.

For the first time, I saw Jane's face. There were tears running down her cheeks and she was trying to wipe at them with the back of the hand that wasn't laden down with IVs.

"Jane, I hope you don't mind. Julia wanted to stop by." Ryan stood and came to me as I walked into the room, sliding his arm around my waist and placing a light kiss on my temple. "Morning, babe."

My hand flattened on Ryan's stomach as his arm tightened around me. I wanted to melt into him and rest my head on his chest, to hold on for dear life, but resisted the urge out of respect for Jane. I smiled at Jane and handed Ryan the basket of muffins. "I brought breakfast. Can Jane have one?"

"Oh, I'm not very hungry," Jane said weakly. She looked pale and very sad. I couldn't help but wonder where her family and boyfriend were. Jane tried to smile at me as I moved toward her.

"Is it okay if I sit down for a minute?" When Jane nodded, I took Ryan's place on the chair and reached for her hand. I felt the familiar sting behind my eyes and my throat tightened as emotion filled my chest at the poor girl's plight.

"Jane," I began, her face beginning to blur behind the tears filling my eyes. "I can't even begin to thank you for what you've done." My voice cracked and Ryan's hand came down on my shoulder and squeezed gently and I blinked back the tears. "To risk yourself like that to save Ryan… I don't know what I would have done if I'd lost him. I'll never be able to repay you." I squeezed her hand. Jane's pale blue eyes also welled as her face crumpled.

"You don't have to repay me. Ryan would have done the same for me."

I nodded, wiping at my tears and reaching for one, then another tissue. "I know he would, but it still doesn't lessen my gratitude. I'm so sorry this happened to you."

She looked away and the struggle to keep from sobbing was clear on her face. She closed her eyes and bit her lip with the effort.

"Jane, you should try to calm down. You won't recover properly if you don't rest," Ryan warned.

I tried to smile at the woman in the bed and nodded in Ryan's direction. "Always a doctor." Jane nodded as I handed her a tissue.

"A hungry one!" He laughed uncomfortably and patted his stomach. I smiled weakly at my husband, understanding that the brilliant smile split across his face was superficial and designed to lighten the mood. "Starving! I'm going to get some coffee to have with these muffins! I'll be right back."

It was obvious to me that he was giving me some time alone with Jane. When Ryan walked out of the room, I was a little lost for words, with Jane staring blankly at me. I knew that pain. "I'm sorry if Ryan seemed uncomfortable, Jane. He's just glad you're alive, and believe it or not, he does empathize. He feels responsible."

"He's a good man. Very good," she whispered weakly, tears still dripping from her eyes. She sniffed and weakly lifted her left arm to wipe at her face with the tissue I'd given her. "One of the best I know."

Emotion erupted and I struggled to keep my voice even, despite the thickening in my throat. "Yes. He's very concerned for you and couldn't wait to get here to see you." Jane's chin began to quiver and I reached out for her hand. "Jane, I'm so sorry." I felt helpless. What could I say to ease her pain?

"I always wanted a little baby," she cried through the words.

My hand squeezed around hers, my heart breaking for her. "I don't know if this will help you, but Ryan and I lost a baby. I understand how much it hurts." Silent tears tumbled from my eyes onto my cheeks.

Her light blue eyes widened and then squeezed shut as another sob broke free of her chest. "But now, I'll never have one! I'll never be able to hold my baby in my arms! Ever!" Her shoulders shook as she sobbed, and even as she grimaced in pain, there was nothing to stop her misery. "You can still have one!"

I closed my eyes and held tightly to her hand in silence. Words didn't seem like enough. What could anyone say to ease her pain? She was right; she wouldn't ever know the joy of holding her own child in her arms. I ached to speak of adoption and the many unwanted children that needed someone wonderful to care for them, but couldn't insult her with patronizing clichés. I knew I'd be pissed if someone said something so trite while I was still reeling in shock from such a tragedy. There would be plenty of time for those conversations when she was stronger. I looked around the room wondering where her boyfriend was, imagining how alone I would have been without Ryan by my side when I'd remembered our baby. And when I'd lost my memory and wasn't able to remember him, he was always with me. I felt sick for Jane that the one person she needed the most wasn't there.

When Ryan returned, his handsome face twisted in concern and he quickly set the coffee he'd brought on the tray table next to Jane's bed. Rushing around to the opposite side of the bed, he sat down and put his good arm around her shoulders, careful not to jostle her, but wanting to offer comfort. She turned her face into his neck and cried harder.

"Shhh, Jane. I'm sorry." He rocked her and I bit my lip and looked away, struggling to hold back my own emotions and feeling like I was intruding somehow. It was so horrible what Jane had lost and the evidence of what I had gained because of her sacrifice, sat there, trying to comfort his friend. Ryan's sad blue eyes rose to mine and I folded my arms across my stomach and raised the tissue in my hand to stem my tears. I wanted to hug them both.

"I'm sorry. It's going to be okay" Guilt, compassion, sadness and empathy, I could read it all on Ryan's face as he said the words. He was in hell. He didn't know if it would be okay. He knew time deadens the sharp, evil twist of pain, but it doesn't erase it. This would leave scars, but there was little else either of us could do to offer comfort.

"I'm still glad it was me and not you, Ryan," Jane sobbed. "I'm still glad."

He didn't respond, just held her until her sobs lessened as I fought off my own tears.

"Are you hungry?" I stood and went to gather the basket where Ryan had placed it on the window seat. "I hope you don't mind the muffins. I thought you might feel up to eating a little something, and from what Ryan tells me, hospital food sucks."

"Ryan calls it barf," Jane stated simply, a weak smile finally lifting her pale lips as she sniffled back the last of her tears. She was still getting blood, but her complexion was ghostly, her blonde hair fell in fine wispy strands around her head to her shoulders.

I smiled wider and shook my head with an amused huff. "Well, he would. He's spoiled."

Ryan chuckled. "Don't listen to a word Julia says," he teased but threw a wink in my direction. He was trying. I was trying. But still, Jane was alone in this room with two people who weren't her family or even close friends.

"He's amazing." Jane studied my face as the silence began to expand between us. What could I say? I'd always felt that way about him.

I nodded slowly. "I wish I'd get to see him in action. I'd love to watch him work."

"He's so sure of himself, even though he's a first year resident. He was born for medicine."

It felt weird, another woman saying those words about my husband, and with such conviction and familiarity; like she was telling me something I didn't already know. I found myself a little uneasy at the thought there were some things about Ryan that Jane might know better than me.

"You're going to give him a big head, Jane. Trust me, when you're on the other side of his stethoscope, he's less appealing. He can be bossy as hell."

"Hey! *Now* you're complaining?" he scoffed and opened the basket, pulling out the paper plates and placing a yellow muffin with crumb topping on one for Jane. He elevated the head of her bed slightly and pushed the tray table into position over the bed so she could reach it. "Eat. I'll get you some juice."

I rolled my eyes and smiled as Jane's eyes met mine. "See what I mean?"

For the first time, her eyes brightened.

Ryan ~

After I'd consumed four of Julia's muffins and Jane managed to get half of one down, my wife packed up the basket. I was sitting on the foot of Jane's bed, as I watched her neatly stow the cloth napkins and forks back into the basket and throw the plates and coffee cups in the trashcan that was below the window. She was always so giving in subtle ways.

"Thanks for making the muffins, babe." Julia's eyes shot up and she smiled. "They hit the spot."

"Yes, they were delicious," Jane murmured. I saw her watching Julia intently and wondered what she was thinking.

Julia hadn't bothered with make-up and looked younger. Dressed in my sweatshirt, she absent-mindedly shoved the neckline back in place when it fell off her shoulder.

Julia nodded and smiled at Jane. "It was my pleasure."

"Jane, is there anyone we should call for you? Your parents or boyfriend?" I asked, hesitantly. It might be a sticky subject since whoever the mystery man was hadn't made an appearance.

She nodded. "I think Caleb called Daniel and my mother last night. He mentioned it this morning."

Caleb had a thing for Jane and was disappointed when he found out she was dating. He'd asked me what I knew about the relationship, and the truth was, not much. Julia moved to my side and we looped an arm around each other without thinking. I could see the sadness on Jane's face and words died in my throat.

"Did Caleb say when you could expect them?" Julia asked.

"Daniel is so busy at work, we don't see each other like we'd like to." Her voice was hollow and distant.

"Boy, do we know how that is," Julia added softly. "I'm sure he'll be here, though. Ryan, why don't I go to the office for a bit and you can wait with Jane for Daniel? Maybe give him another call?" Her eyebrows raised, communicating to me her disapproval of Daniel's absence. Her fingers scratched into the hair at my nape and it sent little tingles through me. I longed to spend every minute of the day with Julia, but circumstances required a change of plans.

"Okay." My hand curled around her hip and I pulled her close as she placed a chaste kiss on my mouth. I found my chin lifting to reclaim her lips but she was already moving away. I flushed, guiltily glancing at Jane. "Good idea."

"Don't overdo it. Go home and rest and I'll stop by the store and pick something up for dinner."

In her covert way, Julia was telling me that this evening, she'd make up for the missed time today. My heart leapt at the loving expression on her face. Her fingers lingered on my cheek before she leaned down and kissed Jane's cheek. "Be well, Jane. I'll visit again, if that's all right with you?"

Jane nodded. "I'd like that."

"Take good care of Ryan for me, but don't let him bully you."

The other woman smiled, amusement filling her eyes. "Sure."

"Will you make those medallion thingies?" I asked with a smirk. "With the apples and mashed potatoes?"

Julia smiled brightly. "Sure. Take care, Jane. See you to-night, babe." Julia gathered up her things, but left the basket of muffins, leaving Jane and I alone.

"What's the deal, Jane? I expected your man to be here. He should be with you today. Fuck his job." I realized as the words left my mouth how insensitive I sounded and Jane's face fell. "I'm sorry, I shouldn't have said that. I just mean that his place is with you."

"Not every man is as perfect as you, Ryan. You hold every-one to your standard and few can measure up."

I rolled my eyes. "That's bullshit. There's no excuse for him not being here."

She shrugged. "He's not like you."

I moved to sit in the recliner near the window thinking he must be a narcissistic prick. "What's he like then?"

"I guess you'd call him a nerd. He's really into computers and books. He's very focused and doesn't get into frivolous things. He doesn't even like the Yankees."

I huffed. He sounded like a first-class asshole. "I'm a Cubs fan. I can't help it. I grew up in Chicago."

"I love baseball. Is Julia into it?"

"She has fun when we go to games, but she's not a hardcore fan." I smiled, remembering many of the baseball and football games we'd attended over the years. She used to roll her eyes at Jenna, Aaron and myself when we'd scream obscenities when the opposing teams did better than our own. "My brother's wife is huge Red Sox fan. Julia is more into music and art."

"She must be very talented."

"She is," I said without hesitation. "I'm very proud of her. At the magazine, she takes on the jobs of her colleagues and even her boss. Basically, when something goes in the shitter, she's the one called in to solve the problem. Believe me, it's been a thorn in my side, more than once, but she's very ambitious."

"Like, you, Ryan. Sounds like the two of you are perfect." Jane's face seemed sad and I was again reminded that it was me with her and not this faceless Daniel. I already disliked the fucker. I wanted to make her feel better, but struggled for the words. Julia was damn near perfect, and though we had our spats, I wouldn't trade a minute of our life together. I was well aware of how insanely lucky we were, but it didn't help to have a reminder dropped in our laps now and again.

"Eh, we've had our struggles."

"Yes, Julia told me. About the baby."

My eyes widened in surprise. "She did?"

"Uh huh."

"Wow. No one knows except our family and best friends. It's so... Well, it's just something that we keep between the two of us."

"She probably told me because of..." her words fell off as her voice thickened again.

I ran my hand through my hair and nodded, wondering how much of it Julia shared. I didn't want to make Jane feel worse, nor did I want to expose too much of something so close and intimate. Losing our baby was raw because we lost a part of us. Just us. "Yes."

"When did it happen?" Jane's eyes searched mine and I winced at the memory.

"Several months ago." It wasn't really that long ago when I stopped to consider it. I hated the way it still ate away at my gut.

"You'll make an amazing father, Ryan."

I didn't know how to answer, because it wasn't something I talked about and the pain was a reminder of why I didn't like to wallow in the past. On top of that, Jane had her own misery to deal with.

Still, she pressed me. "So, it happened before you were married?"

"Yes. It wasn't planned. Julia had been sick and was on antibiotics. I was still at Harvard and made a trip to New York over Valentine's Day. I'd planned on proposing and took a few extra days off to surprise her. We didn't see each other enough, and when we got together, we just didn't think about the effects of the meds on her birth control." I stared out the window of the hospital room and into the concrete jungle that was Manhattan as I talked. I huffed. "Julia was getting promoted and I was mad that we'd continue to be apart after graduation. We had a huge fight."

"Why would you be apart?"

"Vogue was sending her to Paris for several months. We'd been separated for so long at that point, the prospect of more... well, I sort of lost it." I cleared my throat.

"Oh, I see. Make-up sex."

I shrugged. "Yeah, well, then she was packing up to leave a few weeks later, she discovered she was pregnant."

"That must have made you happy, Ryan."

"I didn't have time to be happy. I didn't find out until after it was already over." Even I could hear the sadness and disappointment that flooded my words.

Jane let out a soft gasp. "What?"

"Julia decided not to go to Paris after all and came to Boston to tell me about the baby, but there was a car accident between the train station and my apartment. It was really bad. She had a severe head injury and I really thought I was going to lose her." I stood and faced the window, away from Jane, as the memory of it sliced through me like it was yesterday. I didn't want her to see the pain of remembering on my face. "Anyway, thankfully, Julia recovered, but no baby."

"I'm sorry, Ryan. But at least Julia is okay and you'll be able to have more children." But, you won't. The unspoken words hung like a storm over us.

I nodded and turned back to my friend. "I know." I couldn't tell Jane that Julia and I were on the verge of trying to get pregnant again. My heart constricted for her. "But, we're both so busy, who knows when that might happen. You just concentrate on getting better and don't worry about us. Has Caleb been in to see you?"

"Not yet."

My body was aching and the slice on my shoulder tight, reminding me of my own injury. "He will. So will Daniel and your mother. So, uh, I'm going to head out. You'll be out of here in a few days. You'll see."

"I want to get back to the ER. I need to concentrate on that, and forget about last night."

"I know. Me, too." I smiled, but inwardly I felt bad that Jane didn't have more in her life beyond her job. I loved my job, but I loved my life with Julia more. This thing with Jane made me realize I'd been unfair in my insistence that it was time to get Julia pregnant again. I was ready. But, was she? I decided then and there that I needed to talk to my wife. "I'm going to check the orders and see when you're allowed to have pain meds again then leave you to get some rest."

Jane reached out for my hand and she looked up at me be-seechingly. "Will you come back, Ryan?"

"I'll call you later and I'll see you tomorrow, for sure. Okay?"

Jane's face fell slightly.

"You'll have your family here. I'll just be in the way. Don't let them wear you out. Doctor's orders." My lips twitched in the start of a smile.

"I've told my mother about you. Working with you, I mean." Jane stammered slightly, still holding my hand. "I'm sure she'll want to meet you." I squeezed her fingers gently and then placed her hand beside her on the bed.

"There's plenty of time for that." I walked toward the door and turned. "Thank you, again, Jane. I'll never forget the sacri-fice you made for me."

"I'd do it again, Ryan. I'd… do it again."

I patted the door frame once and left the room, trying to ig-nore the implication of a deeper meaning in her words. I rubbed the back of my neck as I rushed out of the hospital, anxious to find my wife.

Julia ~

It was a rare moment. My husband's arms were wound tightly around me, and his chest rose and fell steadily beneath my chest. His even breathing a sure sign of his slumber and his heartbeat, strong beneath my ear, was comforting. I listened to it thud and closed my eyes in prayer. He was here and he was mine. Forever. Nothing would ever mean more. I felt safe and I didn't care if I ever moved from this spot.

The rain pattered on the widows, and the grayness of the late fall day made the apartment dark. We were lying on the couch all tangled up together and it was nothing short of heaven. I tilted my head back to glance up into Ryan's face and was surprised to find his bright blue eyes open and a small smile curving his perfect mouth. My fingers slid beneath the hem of his navy blue t-shirt to curl into the solid muscles beneath it. I smiled up into his amused expression.

"This feels damn good," he murmured. His fingers brushed my chin just before his open mouth took mine in a soft kiss. "Mmmm… tastes damn good, too."

"Let's stay here forever."

"Sounds amazing. I'm in."

I laughed softly as his arms tightened slightly.

Ryan turned toward me, grunting slightly as his injured shoulder moved. His arm slid beneath me, his other hand on my hip pulled me close and over him until my knees rested beside his hips. Both of his hands moved to hold my face, his thumbs running along my cheek and jaw. His face turned serious and the smile on my face faded in response. "Ryan, are you hurt? Be careful, honey."

"I'm fine."

I bent to run a path of kisses along his jaw and up to his earlobe, which I pulled between my teeth. Ryan shuddered beneath me. Warm fingers ran lovingly down my arms and back again. "Baby, I want to talk."

I sat up at the serious tone in his voice and remained straddling his lap, Ryan holding both of my hands in his. "What is it?"

Ryan's brow was furrowed as he studied me, and I pulled one hand free to reach out and touch his face. "Ryan, what is it?" I asked again.

"Last night..." he paused, "It has me thinking. Maybe we need to talk more about trying to conceive."

My lips pressed together as I struggled for words. I frowned and shook my head. "But, I thought we decided. I'm off the pill. Are you having second thoughts because of Jane?"

He shook his head. "Not because of Jane. It's always about you. Is this what you really want? I know I want it, but are you just doing it for me?"

I huffed under my breath and plowed both hands through my hair, clutching at my scalp. "No, Ryan. I want a baby, too. I didn't think this was the best time, but I've always wanted it."

"Don't get your panties in a bunch. That's my job." He teased, smiling all the way up into his eyes and my heart melted as the back of Ryan's fingers brushed down my cheek. "I just want to make sure. You're right. We both work like crazy and I don't want to be unfair to you."

Our fingers threaded together, his eyes intensely searching for each subtle emotion on my face. I'd never be able to hide from him, even if I wanted to.

"I wish I was already pregnant. After last night, my perspective has changed."

"In what way?" He knew what I was saying and still he was going to make me say it.

"Life is short and you never know what could happen. What if something happened to one of us? We'd at least have part of each other to hold on to..." My words dropped off, emotion cracking my voice as my eyes welled. "What if I'd lost you?" I felt the grief at the possibility as strongly as if it had happened and the tears tumbled down my face uncontrollably as a sob broke free against my will.

"Hey." Ryan immediately sat up to enfold me in his strong embrace. His hand tangled in my hair at the back of my head. I buried my face in his good shoulder and pulled him closer to me. Ryan kissed the side of my face, following the tracks of my tears to my mouth. "Hey," he soothed again. "Oh, baby. Jules, you know you're my whole world. I love you, so much."

"I love you, too," I croaked out. My fingers curled into his nape and I hung on for dear life.

"We'll make our baby, but I was unfair this weekend. I shouldn't have been such a prick when Ellie needed you."

I pulled back and stared at his face, tears still clinging to my lashes, and sniffed. "Really?"

He nodded. "Really." His fingers stroked up and then dragged down my arms and back again; his touch so reverent. "Let's just be together. Make love when we want, with no pressure, but no precautions. It will happen when it's supposed to happen."

I bit my lip, his tenderness touching me at the very core, and I nodded. "Okay. Remember what you told me?"

"Yeah." Ryan pushed my hair off my face and behind my ear. "The baby will choose when. He's waiting."

"He?" I asked, pushing up his navy blue t-shirt to expose his hard stomach and the happy trail that disappeared into his old faded jeans. "What if it's a girl?"

"Then I'll suffer through, I suppose!" Ryan laughed softly and I leaned down to kiss him and he responded with ardent hunger, signaling he wanted to get down to baby-making pronto. "You know I'd love to have a little girl that looks just like her mom," he whispered against my lips. I wasn't sure why, but those words were a huge turn on, like he'd just made my ovaries explode and I couldn't wait to get pregnant by him.

"What's in your Kool-Aid?" I teased, going in for another kiss.

"What?" Ryan laughed against my lips.

"You always know what to say. It's like you weave some magic spell to turn me to goo."

Ryan's hands ran down the side of my body, from the sides of my breasts down over my hips until they cupped my butt. His long fingers wound around the back half of my thighs and he massaged gently, his blue eyes intent on mine. "I like you gooey." He grinned.

"I know you do." I giggled. I loved every minute with him. "I can get you all gooey, too, you know."

"Mmmm, huh." His eyes lidded and his chin lifted so he could take my mouth again.

The timer beeping in the kitchen put the kibosh to our love play.

"Awww, hell!"

I kissed his mouth lightly and then dusted my lips over his cheekbone and then pressed them into his temple. The scent of his skin mixed in with his cologne and I silently cursed the confection in the oven.

"Something smells good."

My nose traced his cheek before I sat up. "You can say that again."

"What's in the oven, sweet?"

"I made butterscotch cake for dessert." I jumped up and rushed into the kitchen, not wanting to let it over-bake. I'd already lingered long enough.

"Oh, my God. Really? Do you need help?"

"No, baby, you rest. It will be at least an hour and fifteen until dinner is ready, so go back to your nap."

"That long?"

"You asked for Pork Medallions and glazed apples, Ryan. You know that takes a while." I threw the words over my shoulder as I removed the two cake pans from the oven with potholders.

"I'll help," Ryan said from just behind me.

"Did you ever consider that I won't have as much time to lavish on food once we have a baby?" I set the pans on a wire rack to cool and moved to the refrigerator to take out the pork tenderloin I'd purchased earlier. Ryan sat on one of the kitchen stools as I removed the packaging and began to slice the meat.

"It's a sacrifice I'm willing to make."

I could feel his eyes running down my body and lingering on my ass. I glanced in his direction and he smiled guiltily.

"You say that now. But we'll also lose time in bed."

"We'll see."

I lined the meat up on a wooden cutting board and Ryan rummaged around in a drawer for the metal meat mallet.

I sighed softly and he came up behind me and wrapped his arms around me, his warm breath rushing over my neck just as his lips pressed to the skin below my ear. I trembled in his arms. "We'll still be us, Julia. We won't lose the mad love."

"Promise?"

His arms tightened. "You know that's impossible. Don't you?" His lips continued their sweet torture down the cord of my neck and suddenly I wanted to scrap making the meal and head to bed. Instead, I layered my arms on his and leaned back into my husband.

"Yes."

"I understand that's what you're worried about, but don't be. After eight and a half years, I'm still crazy for you. Six or seven pounds of baby isn't going to change that."

"What about fifty or sixty pounds of Julia?" I asked sardonically.

Ryan laughed out loud.

"Well? We're newlyweds. What if I turn into a whale?"

"You'll be gorgeous and I'll still want you. I already told you."

"Hmmm."

Ryan's phone buzzed on the counter, he went to answer it while I pulled the flour canister open to begin the dredge for the meat.

He frowned at his phone.

"What is it?"

"It's a text from Jane. She wants me to call her."

"Okay," I agreed. I figured he must have left his number with her before he came home.

"You're sure?"

"Ryan, please. The poor girl is in the hospital and she just went through a horrid ordeal with you. She probably needs to talk about it and you're the natural choice. I got this."

"You're amazing. It won't take long." Ryan hesitated at the edge of the kitchen. "I wanted to help you pound the meat."

I laughed. "You're so funny, but I did it already." I lifted one piece of flour-dredged meat up for his inspection. "See?"

"Really, it was an excuse to be with you."

"Awww!" I went over and touched his cheek, standing on my tiptoes to kiss his mouth. His lips opened under mine, sucking my lower lip into his mouth. It was always so sexy the way he did that and it encouraged me to give similar treatment to his upper lip. The familiar warmth began to spread but I forced myself out of his arms. "We have all night. Go on."

Ryan started to dial the number and exited the kitchen, leaving me to giggle at the flour fingerprints I'd intentionally left on his cheek.

~6~

Ryan ~

I glanced at the round clock on the wall of the examining room. It was noon and my stomach was rumbling. The last patient was resting comfortably after we'd gotten her stabilized and she would soon be moved to the cardiac unit. She was elderly and suffered a moderate heart attack and was admitted with chest pain, shortness of breath and sweating. We gave oxygen and nitroglycerin and after the attending physician approved my recommendations, she was scheduled for an EKG, and ultrasounds of her heart and coronary arteries. The tests would be done and a diagnosis made by the cardiologist on duty upstairs, so my job was done. I nodded back at Kari, indicating my exit and that she would be left to monitor things until the patient was moved upstairs.

I assured the patient, "We're just going to see what caused the heart attack and the cardiologists will decide the best course of treatment, okay? You'll have a few tests."

"Thank you, young man. You surely saved my life." Her arthritic hands reached out to grab one of mine. I smiled warmly at her.

"Naw! You aren't going anywhere for quite some time." I was pleased to see color returning to her weathered cheeks.

"I bet you'd like my granddaughter, Aimee. Did you see her? She's pretty, isn't she? And, she's very smart. She'll be

back in to see me later." The old woman's blue eyes sparkled
hopefully, her breath fogging up the oxygen mask when she
spoke.

I couldn't help but grin. "She is very pretty," I agreed about
the dark haired girl who'd brought the woman in to the hospital.
I lifted my left hand and pointed to the ring with my right index
finger. "But, I'm married. If you speak too much right now,
you'll inhale the carbon dioxide you've just exhaled and it makes
the blood vessels in your lungs constrict. You'll get short of
breath so you should refrain from talking as long as you need
oxygen, okay? If you need it upstairs, they'll use a cannula." She
started to speak again. "No!" I stopped her with a wry look and
patted her hand. I was rewarded with a resigned nod before I left
the room.

I glanced around the ER looking for Jane. More and more, it
had become my habit. She was back to work and physically fine,
but she visibly jumped at any loud noises or shouting that sometimes occurred when the paramedics brought in a critical patient.
I'd seen her earlier and she was in a good mood, so I prayed to
God that my evening wouldn't be interrupted. Again. That had
become another habit. Jane was recovering well physically;
mentally and emotionally, she was fragile with little or no support from her asshole boyfriend or her family. I let the desk personnel know I was grabbing some lunch and checked my pager
to see what messages came in while I was with my last patient,
expecting a page from Jane. There seemed to always be a page
from Jane, but, thankfully, there wasn't one.

I didn't know how to refer to that hideous night in my head.
Incident seemed so "CSI", but it sure as hell wasn't an accident.
My shoulder, now fully healed, was left with its angry red scar as
the only reminder; except for Jane. When she talked about it, she
always called it 'that night'. Well, *that night*, had fucked us all.

I felt guilty every Goddamn time I looked at her and guiltier still that I was so damned happy because Julia and I would probably be pregnant within a few months. Whenever I thought about it, I could literally feel my face soften. I didn't want to feel guilty about something so damn beautiful. Julia certainly didn't deserve that and I didn't want to think about Jane every time I touched my wife, always concerned what affect a pregnancy would have on her fragile psyche. Having a baby would be like rubbing salt in Jane's wound, but from a personal standpoint, I was happy that we'd agreed to let it happen. Hell, I was more than happy about it, but every time I looked at Jane, I felt so damn selfish that I wanted something she could never have. And worse, I felt responsible. I could see similar guilt mirrored in Julia's deep green eyes. I didn't want to think about it anymore.

Tonight was to be spent with my wife and my anticipation made the day crawl. I longed to lose myself in those soulful eyes; to allow her touch to erase everything but her. I wanted the comfort of just being in the same room with her. There was no way in hell I was going to let Jane invade my thoughts tonight. Tonight was all about my beautiful Julia. I inhaled deeply, filling my lungs to capacity. The break and the chance to check my messages would make time pass more quickly.

I stopped by the lounge to get my phone before I went to the cafeteria and couldn't help grinning when I saw the text waiting for me.

Making all your favorites tonight. Try not to be late. ~xo~

I decided to call instead of text because all these thoughts of baby-making created the need to hear her voice. She picked up on the first ring.

"Hey, handsome."

My heart surged at the happiness in her voice. "Hey, *you're my favorite*. You're all I want tonight. Don't make a mess that takes hours to clean up. I'm looking forward to holding you for hours."

I could hear her soft breaths. "Mmmm, sounds good. I promise no dishes tonight. We'll make a different kind of mess."

A huge grin split my face. "Mrs. Matthews, you are a naughty girl and I love it!"

"Are you on break? Have you eaten?"

"I'll get something light. Don't want to overeat before to-night."

She didn't contradict me, which told me my intuition was right; she was making something big. "Dinner is hours from now, so eat, Ryan," she commanded.

"What are you making?"

"You ask way too many questions. It's a surprise." She giggled softly through the phone and my heart filled. I was waiting for the newlywed giddiness to wear off, but it never had. A surprise meant it would be amazing.

"I love you."

"I know." She laughed again, softly. "Now go eat and stop bothering me! I have to go to the grocery store."

"Okay. See you tonight."

I tucked my phone back into the locker and turned to leave, stopped by the sound of someone quietly crying behind me. I did a one-eighty, my eyes scanning the room. Jane huddled on the couch on the far side of the room, her back to me. I could see her shoulders shaking and her hands covered her face as she wept. *Fuck.*

I moved closer, unsure of whether to let her know I was there. Part of me wanted to comfort her, but another part of me said to keep on walking. I wondered whether she'd want to talk or would rather be left to her misery. After a moment's hesitation, I sat next to her on the couch.

"Jane." I said softly, my hand reaching out to rest gently on her back. "I thought you were off today."

She didn't answer, so I pressed. "Are you okay?"

She only cried harder and shook her head, her face still hidden by her hands. "No! Daniel doesn't understand what I'm going through. My mom left 3 days ago... and he's... mad because I'm still such a mess. He expects too much!"

My head dropped, my arm resting on my knee while I sat there and listened to her misery. I could feel my skin flush as anger welled in my chest. *How could he be such an insensitive prick?* I'd only met the guy once—the day she was in the hospital—and he was only interested in his fucking smart phone; he'd kept pounding away on the keys, his eyes intent on the screen. I'd wanted to rip the motherfucking thing from his fingers and throw it out the window, all the while screaming for him to stop being a dick. I just didn't get why Jane would be with such a douche. I wracked my brain for the right thing to say so I wouldn't let how I really felt about the guy show through. "He is probably still working through it, too, Jane. He almost lost you. Believe me, he was probably reeling and unsure how to help you."

She straightened her shoulders and finally looked at me, wiping at her nose with a tissue she dug out of the pocket of her scrubs. "He doesn't care about anything but his job and his stupid computers! He yelled at me because I can't have sex yet. The only time he touches me is when he fucks me."

The air left my lungs in a huff and I was sure I flushed. I was shocked. I'd cussed enough around Jane, but I'd never heard her utter one crass word. Ever.

"Jesus, Jane! That's screwed up. How are you even with this guy?"

"I love him, I guess." Her sorrowful eyes beseeched mine while my brain ripped him limb from limb. "I just can't seem to get him to take an interest in me outside of sex. He said I was damaged now." Her face crumpled and she sobbed. My arms automatically surrounded her and she leaned into me, crying hard onto my shoulder. I could feel her hot tears soaking through the material of my shirt. "My body is... so ugly and scarred!" she wailed.

Oh my God! I pushed her back to take hold of her shoulders with both hands. "Listen to me, Jane. You're a beautiful, desirable woman and he's damn lucky to have you. He's no prize, for Christ's sake!" Her eyes widened and snapped to my face. "Well? He needs to get his head out of his ass. You have so much to offer; you're kind and giving. Any man would be lucky to be with you. He doesn't deserve you."

Her only answer was a sniffle and blink at me.

"Hey, are you listening?"

She smiled, two more tears running down her face. "Thank you, Ryan." Her hand reached out to my face and I quickly pulled it down with one of mine. She shifted uncomfortably and pulled her hand from my grasp. "If I could just get him to spend some time with me. But when we do, it's always in a group of friends. I mean, if he takes me anywhere, it's because someone else makes the plans."

I listened and I watched her expression then I did the thing I didn't want to do. If that fucker required a group, so be it.

"Listen, Julia is making dinner tonight. Why don't you bring Daniel? Maybe he'll forget about work."

Her features lit up. "Really? Won't Julia mind?"

Yeah, Julia would probably kill me, but she knew Jane needed our support right now. "I'm sure she'd love to see you."

She leaned in and hugged me tight. "Thank you, Ryan! That would be wonderful."

When she pulled away, I leaned over, pulled another tissue from the box on the table in front of the TV and handed it to her. I needed to get to the cafeteria, grab something and get back to work. "Why are you here today?"

"Sally's kid was sick and she needed someone to cover the first half of her shift until her husband could leave work."

"I see. Well, I need to grab a quick sandwich and get back to work. Call Daniel," I said, getting up to leave.

"I will. Didn't Julia pack your lunch today?"

I paused by the lockers, pulling out the phone and quickly texting Julia.

I invited Jane and Daniel for dinner.
I'll tell them around 8.
Don't be mad. Not a good day for Jane.
I'll make it up to you.

Jane's eyes were still swollen, but at least she had a smile on her face. "Nope. She was working on some promotional stuff for a fundraiser her magazine is doing on New Year's Eve. No leftovers for me. Besides, when I'm working, she doesn't make a big meal. Tonight, she's probably making something amazing." I looked down at my phone, but no response before I shoved the phone back and walked toward the door of the lounge.

"What time?" Jane asked.

I pondered for a moment. I got off at six, which meant dinner Julia would normally have dinner around 7:15, but something told me I'd better be home before Jane and Daniel showed up, so I could have time to talk with my wife. I figured telling them eight would give us some time alone before they arrived.

"Eight-ish? I'll text you the address."

So now I had to wolf down a burger and get back to the ER without knowing if Jules got my message. She understood that Jane needed friends' support right now.

Julia ~

Jane's first phone call with Ryan started a pattern. Ryan's devotion while visiting her at the hospital and his availability whenever his phone or pager went off only reinforced her access. Jane was back to work after a week in the hospital and another week to recuperate at home. Her ever-absent boyfriend, Daniel, made only one appearance at the hospital. Apparently, he was the IT administrator for Chase and constantly on-call. I wasn't ignorant enough to believe the excuses he piled on Jane. I was starting to believe his importance was more in his head than reality if his responsibility to his girlfriend was a sign of his commitment to other things, but it was only Jane's opinion that mattered. Daniel's lack of involvement with Jane's recovery only fueled Ryan's natural protective tendencies. I should be proud and understanding and I was, to a point, but I was pissed at myself because Ryan's concern for Jane was starting to wear on me.

I pushed open the door to our apartment, juggling two bags of groceries. Ryan invited Jane and Daniel to dinner at the last minute and I was scrambling to get the apartment cleaned up before they were set to arrive three hours from now. I always kept the makings of a cheesecake on hand and one was chilling in the refrigerator. I purchased the ingredients for the fresh strawberry topping along with an expensive cut of prime rib, wine, potatoes, fresh horseradish, asparagus, sour cream and herbs for the rest of the meal. Ryan loved everything I was making for dinner. I felt flustered and disappointed as I stared at the label on the wine in my hand and thought of the new negligée hiding in the top drawer of my dresser. We really couldn't afford this expensive meal or the little tidbits of satin and lace.

It was Saturday and it was rare that Ryan had the evening off. I'd planned on cheesecake and prime rib, but selfishly, hoped it would be one of our rare evenings alone. I sighed in regret. Well, I might as well buck up. My plans were flushed the minute I read Ryan's text. Jane was having a bad day. So what else is new? I cringed at my own lack of compassion, but damn if I could stop myself from allowing the unfairness of the situation to creep into my thoughts.

I cranked the oven to 475 and leaned down to pull a skillet and the roasting rack from the cupboard. I seasoned and seared the meat before tucking it into the hot oven with the foil wrapped potatoes and set the timer for one hour. I wanted a bath, internally reminding myself that it was wrong to feel sorry for myself. *Fuck it.* I did feel sorry for myself. *Whatever.*

I passed the boxes of new Christmas ornaments next to the half a dozen that each of our mother's had sent, and the naked tree waiting patiently for attention. This was our first Christmas together as a married couple, and Ryan wanted to decorate the tree after dinner with a roaring fire in the fireplace. I planned to meet him at the door in nothing but the sheer red babydoll trimmed in white fluff and a Santa hat and tease him mercilessly all evening; maybe even follow it up with a good game of Truth or Dare. Now that was all shot to hell, and if I had my way, the tree wouldn't get decorated until Jane and Daniel had gone home.

The small amount of time I'd spent in Jane and Ryan's presence taught me that I'd be completely left out of the conversations as they discussed medical procedures or emergency cases. Ryan was passionate about his work and Jane appeared completely captivated by every word that came out of his mouth. Naturally, he couldn't help his enthusiasm for his work and her interest in it. The fact that she knew the medical jargon and details about the running of the ER made it easy for her to interject what I couldn't. Ryan shared with me about his work as I shared mine with him, but obviously, it was on a different level. With Jane, he could talk 'shop' and he seemed to enjoy it a lot. Between that and the shared near-death experience, they had a lot to talk about. Hopefully, with Daniel invited, too, it might be less all-engrossing. I was looking forward to finally putting a face with Jane's description of her beau. Ryan was angry that the man had been so absent when Jane needed him most, and if I knew my husband, he'd find a way to make the other man squirm during dinner conversation. Yay. I was so looking forward to that since it would only make Jane more googly-eyed for Ryan. I huffed at the direction of my thoughts and did my best to push them away as I stripped off my clothes and added my favorite bath salts to the water. I had an hour to lounge in the tub and it was just what I needed.

With my phone safely on the vanity, I sank thankfully into the warmth of the soothing water. I closed my eyes; trying desperately to push any resentment toward Jane away. It wasn't fair to be angry with her. Her intrusion was a small price to pay for what she had done and soon it would all fade into the background. I would be gracious to our guests and not torment Ryan by telling him of my Santa plans. I just wish he would've asked me first and that it didn't have to be tonight of all nights.

I rubbed wearily at my temples. Work was hectic, and with plans for the New Year's Eve bash at Lincoln Center, there would be no possible way that Ryan and I could get away to

Chicago for Christmas as his parents had hoped. We should have known that his schedule and my obligations at the magazine would make it impossible this year. I longed to invite them to New York, but our apartment was small and Ryan would probably be working at least part of Christmas Eve or Day. I'd pestered him six weeks ago to put in an early request for New Year's Eve so he could accompany me to the gala and I suspected he'd be required on the other holiday. We'd talked about it and decided that it was more important that he attend, however, I didn't look forward to Christmas Eve without him. I didn't know what my problem was, I'd known he'd be working like a dog for the next four or five years, and it was better than being separated by two hundred miles, but I still missed him like crazy. Sometimes, I felt silly how much.

When the intercom buzzed and the phone rang simultaneously, I was startled, sitting up in the tub and splashing water on the floor.

"Shit!" I ranted as I hopped out and grabbed the phone and a towel and slipped on a puddle next to the tub. I flailed and grabbed the sink just in time to catch myself, but the phone went clattering to the floor and I winced as pain shot through my lower back. Ugh. The buzzer sounded again as I scrambled to answer the phone. It was Ryan.

"Hi, sweetie." I tried to keep the pain still ricocheting through me out of my voice as I struggled into the white robe I'd left hanging on the bathroom door and hurried to the front door of the apartment. "I need to call you back. Someone's here and the doorman is buzzing."

"Go see who it is. I'll hold on."

I didn't argue. "Okay. Just a second." I pushed down on the intercom, still holding the phone to my head. "Yes, Adam?"

"Miss Cooper is here, ma'am. Should I send her up?"

Are you fucking kidding me? She was two hours early! I was dripping wet and not prepared to entertain her until Ryan arrived home, but what could I do?

"Sure. Just give me five minutes, Adam."

"Yes, ma'am."

"Damn! I'm sorry, Jules," Ryan muttered on the phone.

"It's fine, but I don't have much time to talk." I hoped my irritation wasn't coming through on the phone. "I'm not dressed, I don't have make-up on... and dinner isn't to a place where I can sit and socialize. I was not prepared for guests tonight."

Ryan sighed. "They weren't supposed to show up until 8 o'clock."

"I wish they weren't showing up at all." The words were out before I could stop them; the phone perched between my ear and shoulder as I struggled to pull on panties and jeans over my wet legs. I jumped up and down a couple of times as I yanked them on over my wet legs.

"Julia," Ryan began. "I was trying to give Daniel a reason to show his face."

I pulled a white cable knit sweater from bottom drawer of the dresser and a bra from the top one, slamming it when I was done and then shoving the red negligee' carelessly into another one. *Screw it if it got rumpled.* I didn't fucking care.

"Honestly, Ryan? If Jane isn't enough incentive to show up, I doubt an evening with us will be. In any case, Adam didn't mention Daniel. Apparently, he's not with her."

I inhaled deeply, trying to wash the anger away. The man probably wouldn't show up at all and I was beginning to wonder if he even existed. I felt flustered and pissed at Ryan and I couldn't help if it showed in my voice. "Is her relationship your responsibility now, too?" I didn't wait for his answer and rushed on. "I gotta go, Ryan. She's ringing the doorbell." I shut my phone off and threw it on the bed, ran into the bathroom and quickly brushed my hair off my face and tied it up in a messy knot. My face was pale except for the angry flush on my cheeks. I shrugged ambivalently at my reflection; my plans to take extra time with my appearance impossible, now, too. *Whatever. If Ryan thinks I look like a hag, it's his own damn fault.*

I hurried down the hall to the door and stopped, pushing a lose strand of hair out of my eyes and pasting a bright smile on my face before I opened the door.

"Hi, Jane! Come in, please." I tried to sound happy to see her. She looked amazing and I felt hideous. Her hair was curled and hung in soft waves to her shoulders, her eyes were bright, lined perfectly and she smelled flowery as she walked past me into the apartment.

"Hi, Julia. I'm sorry I'm early. I went to meet up with Daniel, thinking he and I could have drinks first because I live so far out. I took the subway in," she was rambling. I took her coat and groaned internally at her pretty dark blue cocktail dress. Coupled with her expensive high heels, it left me feeling like Little Orphan Annie. Jane turned to watch me go into the kitchen and I motioned for her to follow. "Well, he didn't want to leave work yet, and I had nothing to do. I hope you don't mind."

"Of course not," I lied, gushing as much as I could manage. "I'm happy to have you! You can keep me company while I finish dinner, though I might sneak away to freshen up a little when we're done." I smiled again and ushered her onto a stool. When she was sitting at the counter, I pulled the baked potatoes out of the oven with oven mitts and left them to cool on the wire rack.

I went toward the refrigerator and my eyes found the Merlot sitting on the counter that I'd planned to share with Ryan. I'd bought two bottles, one for dinner and one for Truth or Dare. I prayed my aggravation wasn't showing on my face. "Would you like a drink, Jane? I have Ryan's favorite wine for dinner, but I can open it now, if you wish." I opened the refrigerator and rummaged through it.

She hovered and I glanced over my shoulder. "Do you like red wine?" I asked. Her unease was plain and I felt terrible that I was resenting her presence. "I can get you something else. Soda, tea, Perrier?"

"I like it, but let's save the wine for Ryan. I'll have Perrier, please." Jane glanced around the small apartment; taking in the art table and the keyboard sitting next to each other in the small living room, then back around the kitchen. "What's his favorite?" she asked as I pulled the bottle out.

"Well, we're saving for a house, so his favorite *at the moment* is Charles Shaw. It's cheap." My smile was genuine. "Do you want ice?" When she shook her head, I poured the Perrier into two glasses after adding ice to one.

"Is the art table yours?"

"Uh huh. Guilty."

"I figured. Because of your job." Her conversation felt forced and I wanted to make her feel more at ease.

"Yes, I use pencil and other mediums. Soft pastels, charcoal..." I switched on the stereo and the strains of Pink's "Trouble" flowed into the room from one of the Top 40 stations. "I've always been artsy. My dad called me artsy-fartsy when I was young. It was so embarrassing! Ryan tried it once, but I smacked him good." Jane laughed as I removed the potatoes from the foil, sliced the tops off of each and then switched off the oven. The meat would remain inside for two more hours without added heat: very hot at first then slowly finishing to assure that the ends of the roast would be more medium-well but the center would remain a perfect medium-rare.

"What are you making, Julia? It smells delicious. I wish I could cook as well as you."

"Everyone has their own special talents but cooking is easy. If you can read, you can cook." I shrugged then realized I hadn't answered her question. "Prime rib, twice-baked potatoes and roasted asparagus."

Jane's eyebrows shot up. "Wow. It will be delicious, but that's expensive, isn't it?"

"Tonight was a splurge. I wanted to do something special, plus, it would make a couple of lunches for Ryan, and I usually make stew out of the leftovers." I scooped the insides of the potatoes into a bowl and added all the yummy stuff you normally pile on top of the potatoes and mashed it all together before piling the mixture back inside the shells. Jane watched in silence as I sprinkled the tops with more cheese and set them aside in a baking dish. I felt awkward and at a loss for words, which was weird considering I spoke with huge fashion designers and bigwigs at major ad agencies almost daily. *Shit.* I told myself to find something—anything—to say, but all that came to mind was my aching back and my fucked up evening. I arranged the cleaned asparagus on a baking sheet with olive oil, sea salt, and pepper. I wouldn't make her feel bad even if I was upset, refusing to allow myself to act like a pouty child.

"It's very nice of you, Julia. You've been so wonderful, and Ryan has been an incredible support since the stabbing."

I sat down with the other woman when Jane reminded me of all she'd suffered. I felt like a heel for even thinking what I'd been thinking. *Could I be a bigger bitch?*

"Ryan's been worried about you. We both have, and we'll do whatever we can to help you." My earlier chagrin toward the woman vanished. "I assume Daniel will arrive in time for dinner? Ryan and I are both looking forward to having him."

Jane pulled her hand free, and her eyes wouldn't meet mine. "Mmm... no. He said he won't be able to get away from work."

"Surely there are others who can be available for a few hours?"

She shook her head and got up to roam around the living room. "Nope. Just Daniel."

"For such a big corporation?" I was doubtful. Either this guy was the biggest asshole on the planet or he was a figment of Jane's imagination. "I mean, isn't there a whole team of IT people?"

Jane's fingers ran along the keyboard, almost in a caress. "Sure, but he's in charge. Ryan plays?" She dismissed the discussion of her boyfriend.

I wondered why she would assume it was Ryan? Obviously, he hadn't told her. "Yes, he's amazing."

"I can see he would be. He has such amazing hands; I can imagine his long fingers caressing the keys so gently. Maybe he'll play later?"

The hair on the back of my arms stood up. Either I was oversensitive or Jane showed way too much interest in Ryan's hands. "He's usually pretty beat, but you can ask him."

She sank down on the sofa, staring up at the portrait I'd done of Ryan which was hanging over the fireplace mantle. "Wow. He's so handsome. Did you do that? It's incredible."

"Yes. A few years ago." Jealousy reared its ugly head, and I tried to push it away, but there was no way I was willing to share the details around that drawing from the first Thanksgiving in Los Angeles. I'd drawn that portrait the night we'd first made love and it meant the world to both of us. "It's..." I began and then stopped.

"Why isn't it finished? I mean, it's cool the way it fades out like that, but is there a reason?" Jane probed.

My mind rushed back to that moment and a soft smile curved my mouth. "He woke up." I had no clue what to say, so I told the truth. "It was a special time for us. Ryan said I stole his soul that night." I got up and pulled out a cutting board and knife to begin slicing the strawberries for the cheesecake. *Let's get some perspective, shall we?*

A soft huff left the other woman's mouth. "Wow. He's so..."

I swallowed and forced my hands to keep slicing the strawberries, waiting for her next words, while a sick feeling of dread washed over me. It wasn't easy watching another woman fall in love with your husband. I'd have to be an idiot not to see it. I must have been an idiot not to expect it after his devotion to her at the hospital. Not even a year ago, I was the one in a hospital bed with Ryan by my side. It took me all of five minutes to fall in love with him again.

"He's so romantic and special. Daniel hasn't ever said anything like that to me."

I swallowed and forced myself to keep slicing the strawberries. What could I say? *Yes, Ryan is very romantic and special.* Those were the words racing through my head, and the dreamy look in her eyes had them followed up with: *but he's mine.* I felt bad for Jane on one hand, but very territorial when it came to Ryan. I couldn't help the way her words made my entire demeanor stiffen. I didn't want to hurt her, and I was compassionate to her situation, but I didn't want her building romantic dreams around my husband. I decided the best course of action would be to reverse the conversation. "Yes, I'm very lucky. How long have you been seeing Daniel?"

Methodically, I went through the motions of making the dessert. It was a good thing my back was to her, because my face burned as Jane told me about Daniel, her voice lacking the awe and enthusiasm it held when she'd just talked about Ryan. I was proud of him, but the familiar way in which she spoke of him had me wishing he wasn't quite so damn giving. I was used to women wanting him; I'd had years of practice. He'd always been indifferent to other women before, and I never felt threatened. Even with Liza Nash; that twit from Harvard, Ryan's disinterest had been obvious. However, he respected Jane, and he liked working with her and it was clear he was letting her in. My heart thudded sickeningly in my chest. So Daniel wasn't coming, and I'd be forced to endure an evening packed with Jane's awe of Ryan.

"Julia?" Jane's question brought me out of my thoughts and I looked up from what I was doing and quickly glanced over my shoulder.

"Yes?"

"I asked what you're getting Ryan for Christmas."

"Well," I began as I returned the now beautifully dressed cheesecake to the fridge. I didn't want to tell her because it was so personal. I was working on a composite portrait of both of our baby pictures. I hadn't told anyone, not even my family. I certainly didn't want anyone spoiling it by telling Ryan prematurely... plus our baby-making was a secret. "I'm not sure yet. Maybe some better shoes for work, but he doesn't want anything. As I said, we're on a budget, so we've agreed to keep it minimal. Do you have something special in mind for Daniel?"

Jane fidgeted on her chair. "Um, he's a gamer. I'll probably get him a new game he's been wanting."

How romantic. "Wow, he really is a computer nerd, huh?" I tried to lighten the awkward tension hanging between us. Other than the time when she'd shown me to the doctor's lounge, Ryan had always been there when I'd seen Jane and she was pushing me. I knew it. She knew it.

My eyes narrowed and hers got wider when she nodded. "Yeah. I hate video games because he's always got his head in them. Do you have an Xbox?"

I poured us each a refill of the sparkling water and glanced at the clock. Ryan should be home in thirty minutes, and I wanted to freshen up. Despite my lack of enthusiasm for having Ryan in the same room with this woman, I was longing for him to hurry the fuck home.

"No. We don't. We spend our time with movies and music when one of us isn't working on something or other. Life is busy, so we tend to concentrate on each other when we're together."

Jane pushed a strand of hair back and her cheeks flushed uncomfortably. I could see her visibly swallow. This was a good place to make my exit since it was all I could do not to tell her that friendship was fine but she needed to remember Ryan was mine.

"I'm just going to put on a little make-up, if you don't mind? Ryan should be home soon. You're welcome to watch TV and make yourself at home."

The other woman nodded. "Yes, he's scheduled off at six."

I inhaled until my lungs wouldn't fill any further and tried to smile as I left the room. "Yep."

Ryan ~

I was so pissed at myself. I'd wanted to get home before Jane arrived to soothe Julia's ruffled feathers, but no, Jane had to show up early. I sighed as I walked through the lobby of our building to the elevators, silently berating myself for being pissed that I'd cheated myself out of time alone with my wife.

Jane needed my support and she'd earned it. A fact which I reminded myself of at least five times a day. Every time my pager
went off.

When the elevator doors opened, I was inundated with the
wonderful smells I knew originated from our apartment. I ran a
hand through my hair. Obviously, Julia had something planned
for us, or she wouldn't have sounded so upset on the phone. I'd
probably fucked myself big time. I was confident that Julia
would be gracious to our guests. No doubt in my mind, but she
might not be so agreeable after they left.

There was music playing softly in the apartment and my
eyes searched in the low light. I could see Jane sitting on the
couch, looking out the window. I'd never seen her dressed in
anything other than her scrubs, and I was slightly shocked at how
pretty she looked. I glanced toward the kitchen, hoping I'd get a
minute alone with Julia to test the waters, but there was no sign
of her.

"Hey, Jane," I offered in greeting as I kicked my shoes off
and shoved them in the entryway closet along with my parka.
"Where's Julia?"

A wide smile spread across Jane's face. "I think she wanted
to freshen up a bit. How was work after I left?"

"Pretty slow. We had four cases of the flu, one broken arm,
and a heart attack." I glanced down the hall. "Would you excuse
me, Jane? I'd like to check on Jules."

"I'm sure she's fine, Ryan. She made a beautiful dinner and
just needed a minute. Let her be and pour me some wine."

"Where's Daniel?" I asked, walking to the kitchen and taking three wine glasses from the top shelf of the cupboard nearest
the sink.

"Working. Same story, different day." Her voice was flat.

The cork creaked as the corkscrew pulled it from the bottle. I noted the extra bottle sitting on the counter and looked forward to sharing it with Julia, alone. I didn't get why Jane put up with the bullshit this guy doled out. "Jane, forgive me," I began as the blood red wine filled two of the glasses, leaving the other waiting for Julia. "But, I don't get it."

I wanted to say more, to tell her the dude was a total loser, but in light of the deluge of tears earlier and her comments about being disfigured and not being wanted, I didn't want to open that can of worms. Maybe she felt no one else would want her. I felt bad for her.

I turned, a glass in each hand, prepared to make my way back into the living room, but Jane was standing two feet from me. "Shit!" I exclaimed, startled. A little of the wine sloshed over the rim of one of the glasses, and Jane took it from me. "You surprised me."

"Sorry, Ryan," she said, holding up her glass and licking the spilled wine from the edge. "What should we toast to?"

I leaned back against the counter and touched the rim of my glass to hers. "Good friends."

"To friends," she agreed, and we both lifted our glasses to our lips to drink.

"Well, it looks like you started without me." The coolness in Julia's voice snapped my head in her direction. Her green eyes glanced from me to Jane, noticing the glasses in our hands. I set mine down and reached for her hand. Her fingers were stiff as I pulled her nearer, wanting to lean in and kiss her. To my surprise, she turned her face so my lips landed on her cheek. My jaw set. Obviously, she was pissed at me, but I refused to let go of her hand and started to rub small circles on top with my thumb.

She looked beautiful, but casual, in jeans and a vibrant moss green sweater. It was modest, but the neckline was low enough to offer up the creamy skin of her neck to just below her collarbones, her hair flowing in a wavy mass down to the middle of her back. Her dark hair and wine-colored lips were a striking contrast to the sweater, which matched her eyes. Eyes that right now told me she wasn't pleased. "Dinner smells delicious." I smiled softly at her. "I'm starving."

Julia pulled her hand away and walked behind me to pour wine into the waiting glass. "Thanks," she said caustically, taking a large drink and refilling it.

Disappointment was written all over her face. She refused to meet my eyes, and I was practically freezing from the cold shoulder she was presenting me with. Jane might not notice, but I knew her too well to be fooled by the stiff façade. I'd have to work hard to soften her up. I put up a finger to Jane, silently asking for moment. Jane nodded and turned into the living room as I turned toward my wife, gently nudging her shoulder with mine. I felt her soften, if only slightly.

"Hey," I said softly, lifting the curtain of hair to press my lips on the warm skin of her neck. She smelled so sweet. Like coconut shampoo and her perfume, mixed with the scent of her skin. I could feel her pulse beneath my lips and I opened them to flick my tongue across her skin.

"Ryan. We have a guest. Stow the PDA." She twisted in my arms, trying to move away, but I refused to allow it. Her eyes flashed anger and hurt, and instantly, I felt guilty for trying to make light of our lost evening.

"Jules, don't be mad at me, baby. I'll make it up to you, I promise," I whispered in her ear and moved to place a soft, lingering kiss across her cheekbone. I closed my eyes as I breathed her in, suddenly as regretful as she that we weren't alone. "Don't pull away from me. At least let me touch you." I slid my hand down her arm and entwined my fingers with hers, my eyes beseeching for her understanding. "I still want to touch you."

She looked at me then, setting the glass on the counter and facing me, letting me hold her hand. "Then you shouldn't have invited guests," she sulked. "What pisses me off the most is that I'm full of resentment and I don't want to be! I can't seem to help it. But I feel like slime."

Her large green eyes, made even more striking by the shade of her sweater, locked with mine. I felt my heart slam into my chest wall. "I know, honey. Our time is precious. I get it." I reached out to cup the side of her face and let my thumb pull at her bottom lip. "I want to kiss you so damn bad."

"Just a little one," she smiled, her full lips curving up just a fraction. I didn't need to hear it twice; my head swooped so my mouth could gently taste hers in a soft caress. Julia responded, then pulled her lips from mine and pressed her petal soft cheek against my scruffy one, her fingers caressing the opposite jaw.

We stood there, barely touching, but I was reluctant to move. "We have a guest," Julia whispered. "Go on. I'll get dinner on the table."

During the meal, my gaze was drawn to the barren tree in the entryway, bereft of ornaments and looking as sad as the mood. Jane was upset that Daniel didn't show despite the conversation about work and a Master's in Nursing course she had decided to take. I encouraged the course. It would keep her mind off her problems and help her move past it. I'd told her twice already today that Daniel didn't deserve her, so I didn't bring it up again. The food was amazing, the table was set with Julia's grandmother's antique bone china that we'd gotten for a wedding gift from her mother, and the Waterford crystal wine and water glasses sparkled with the votive candles at each place setting. The crystal vase holding a small, budget-conscious arrangement of white poinsettias and the cheap wine were the only telltale signs that we were on a tight budget.

I rubbed the back of my neck, feeling stiff after the twelve-hour shift in the ER. Julia was quiet for most of the evening. Sitting to my right and across from Jane. The position made it hard to look at her while Jane talked on and on, but I reached underneath the table to touch her hand or squeeze her knee several times. Her hand covering mine, assured me that she'd forgiven me for changing the evening plans.

"That was incredible." My stomach was so full I thought I'd burst. I reached out to brush the back of my knuckles across Julia's cheek because I couldn't help myself. She was so good to me. I grinned. "What's for lunch tomorrow? No cafeteria crap, huh?" I asked hopefully.

Julia laughed and rose to begin clearing the table. "No. I thought I'd make a cheesesteak sandwich and there's an extra potato for you to take."

"I may have to make you share, Ryan," Jane interjected. "You're a wonderful hostess, Julia. Thank you."

"My pleasure. Who wants cheesecake?"

Dinner wound down with the delicious dessert and coffee. I glanced at my watch. Jane was still chattering on, but as I rubbed a hand over my jaw, I hoped she'd take the hint. It was ten and I was anxious to have the evening end. Julia was busying herself putting things away in the kitchen and I assumed making my lunch for the next day. I longed to be alone with her, to explain why I invited Jane and Daniel last minute, to hold her and make sure she knew I was feeling as shitty about the change of events as she did.

"Is Daniel picking you up, Jane?" Daniel; that *asshole*. Jane didn't seem as upset as I was that the fucker didn't show up.

She looked pensive and shook her head. "Oh, no. I'm taking the subway."

I scrubbed a hand down my face in barely concealed exasperation. The twenty-four hours of beard growth had begun to itch. I needed a shower and a shave before I crawled under the sheets with Julia, but now, I had to take Jane home. I couldn't let her ride the subway alone at this time of night. "Can you call him?"

She rose from the table, looking down at me. "It's fine. I'm fine on the subway."

Without my knowing, sometime during the conversation, Julia had walked up behind me, and she now slid a hand over my shoulder. I reached up and grabbed it.

"Nonsense, Jane. We'll take you, won't we, Ryan?"

I pulled gently on her hand as I rose from my chair, then sliding my arm around her waist. She leaned into me and I glanced down into her face. I could read her like a book, but I was thankful she said we would take Jane home; we, as in both of us. At least I'd get to spend time with her in the car.

"I'll drive, if you're too tired, hon."

"I don't want to put you both out." Jane scrambled to interject, looking flustered.

Julia's eyes narrowed slightly but then she moved to the hall and began putting on her coat. "It's no bother, but we should get going. Ryan has an early shift, tomorrow."

*****

The drive back was quiet. I held Julia's hand the entire way and quietly explained why I'd invited Jane and Daniel and how it had backfired in a big way. She was silent, turned toward me in the passenger seat, her head resting back, her eyes drooping as sleep tried to claim her. It took more than an hour to get Jane back to Queens and I was about ready to pass out myself.

"I need a shower," I mumbled and brought the hand that I was holding to my lips as we navigated our way through the streets. Her skin was soft. "Dinner was amazing. Thank you for making it for me."

"It was for you, you know," she said softly. Her sleepy eyes were soft, love radiating out of them. "Always for you."

I kissed her hand again, my lips brushing reverently over and over. "I know. I really wanted to be alone with you tonight."

She could have berated me. She had every right, but she didn't. Instead; she ran a finger on the hand that I was holding, down the line of my jaw. "We're alone now. It's okay."

"Yes, but most of tonight is over," I said regretfully. I felt the loss, big time.

"It's okay. See, the thing is, you're stuck with me forever, so there will be other evenings."

My heart filled. She was fucking perfect. I ruined our plans and she was still so fucking perfect.

My breath left in a small huff, and I flashed a smile. "I love you."

"I know."

We were silent the rest of the drive, but I never let go of her hand.

When the door of the apartment opened, the wonderful smells of the meal still lingered. We both kicked off our shoes, and I hung Julia's coat up after my own. Her hand ran down the front of my shirt to linger on my abdomen. "Go take your shower."

I kissed the top of her head and then her temple. "Okay. It's going to be short."

When I left her and went into the bedroom, I walked through it to the bathroom and flipped on the light and the water. In a matter of seconds, my clothes had been whipped off, and I was standing under the comforting spray of the warm shower. The water felt good. I was tired, but I wanted to be with Julia. I wasn't thinking of the baby we were trying to conceive; I only wanted my hands on her, the silk of her skin next to mine, and her breath rushing across my skin.

I was so tired. Exhausted was a better word, and there were only six hours until I'd be back at it again. When I'd decided to become a doctor, I hadn't considered the physical toll it would take. I needed to work out at least three more times this week. Thank God for the fitness room at the hospital that we were able to use when the ER was slow. And thank God for the showers, too.

I squeezed shampoo into my hand and was scrubbing it briskly through my hair when the bathroom door opened. "Hey, sweets," I called. The light flipped off but a soft glow remained in the room. The steam parted when the shower door opened and Julia stepped inside. I paused rinsing my hair. "Hey…" I said again, taking in the glorious site of her naked body in the golden glow of the candles she'd set on the vanity. It didn't take a single touch for my cock to stiffen. She was so beautiful, her curves were a delicious combination of glowing skin offset by the shadow wrapping around her from behind and the green eyes, luminous, as she looked up at me. Her intent was clear and my heart sped up. I reached for her at the same time as her hands slid up my shoulders, the remnants of the shampoo leaving my skin slick under her fingers. Electricity shot through me.

My hands moved from the sides of her breasts, gently cupping and brushing her already puckered nipples, down the concave slope of her waist and back, over the voluptuous curves of her delicious ass. Her fingers curled into my wet hair, the water running over both of us now. She tilted her head, lifting her mouth in offering as my throbbing cock pressed into her stomach, and her eyes slid closed.

I kissed her jaw and down her neck, my mouth open, tongue laving her delicious skin. I never got tired of touching her; of feeling her come alive next to me. My body hungered the sweet-salty taste of her, the feel of her tightness around me, her heat... and my heart craved her incredible love. There was nothing like making love to Julia and never would be.

Her fingers yanked at the hair at my nape and she moaned, deep in her throat, urging me to pick up the pace. It was so fucking sexy. I bent slightly, enough to part her legs from behind and lift her against the back wall of the shower. Julia wrapped her legs around me and I slid one hand up to cup the side of her face so I could claim her mouth, the very moment I pushed into her, hard.

"Uhhh..." her breath rushed out as we began kissing; deep, needy kisses that I wanted to go on for days, so good I almost forgot I was buried deep inside her. She clenched around me at the same time as she sucked on my tongue. It was so hot, and I went into overdrive, thrusting deeper, harder. Julia's hips met mine, both of us moving together in our urgent need for release. I never wanted it to end. We didn't talk, but hands teased, mouths worshiped and skin slid over skin and the small space filled with steam and moans of pleasure.

I was having trouble breathing; I couldn't decide if it was the heat and thickness of the air or the fact that I loved this woman so Goddamn much. I pulled my mouth from hers and opened my eyes, needing to see her expression while we both got closer to the edge. I could feel my body tighten and I wanted to see the pleasure I was giving her; I needed her to see mine. Her eyes opened, half-lidded and she looked at me. I changed to slow, long thrusts, but kept the pressure hard. Her body pushed up on the wall each time I slammed into her. I loved watching her pouty lips drop open at the same time she kept here eyes trained on mine until the pleasure got too much.

"Uhhhh," she sighed and shut her eyes, turning her head when I reached between us and found her clit. I moved in slow circles, wanting her climax to be long and hard, slow building. My body was screaming; each time she clenched around me, it was all I could do not to let myself go. "Uhhhh, Ryan…" She bit her lip. "I want…" she panted.

"I'm there baby…" I groaned as she tensed and shuddered around me. Julia's head fell back and I latched onto her mouth, thrusting my tongue inside to meet hers. She clutched the hair on both sides of my head as she kissed me back deeply, riding out her orgasm as I gave in to mine.

My head fell to her shoulder as our breathing evened out, the water still pelting my back and the steam so thick it was like we were inside a cloud.

I kissed her lips again; soft and gently caressing. Needing her to know with just my lips how much she meant to me. I ran my nose along hers and kissed her one more time before I opened the shower door and I walked out holding her to me, still connected. I pulled two fluffy white towels from the rack and wrapped one around her, sliding out and setting her on the floor. We dried each other off as if we were still making love. It was soft and thorough and reverent.

Her eyes got glassy. I could see the emotion there, and it was all the same for me. *Jesus Christ*! I'd never get used to how much we loved each other. She lopped another towel over my head and rubbed as I softly dried the water from her hair with one of my own. When I was done, I ran the pad of my thumb across her cheek. I wanted to touch and keep touching.

The bedroom was several degrees cooler than the bathroom, and we quickly slid beneath the covers. I pulled Julia to me, and she came easily into my arms. We fit like a glove, curled around each other, both content while the warmth between our bodies seeped out to slowly warm the sheets. I was satisfied, yet unsatisfied at the same time; always wanting more of her.

"I never want to leave this bed," I said into the darkness, my lips pressed to her forehead, her damp hair tickling my chin.

"I never want to leave your arms," she murmured sleepily.

My arms tightened around her as her hot breath fanned my chest.

Fucking perfect.

~7~

Julia ~

My pencil tapped against the hard surface of my desk as my tired eyes stared out across Manhattan and Central Park. The sky was grey, winter robbing the trees of leaves and the buildings on the other side of the park blurring into lifeless oblivion as thoughts of the morning flooded my mind.

I rushed out of bed when a loud clatter from the kitchen, followed by a grumpy expletive, jolted me out of sleep. I ran down the hall, pulling one of Ryan's discarded t-shirts over my head and pushing my arms through the sleeves.

Ryan was already dressed in black scrubs and bent down picking up the pieces of a broken coffee cup. My hand slid slowly over his back, unable to resist even the slightest opportunity to touch him before I grabbed some paper towels to soak up the coffee. The aroma was pungent, much stronger than I would make it, but Ryan was working nearly 80 hours a week and needed the reviving effects of heavy caffeine.

His head snapped around at the touch of my hand. "Baby, don't step in this. You might cut your feet." Ryan dumped the broken cup in the trash and lifted me up to sit on the counter in one smooth motion, his right arm wrapped around my waist as if I weighed nothing. I loved how strong and capable he was, his muscles flexing only slightly with the movement. When his arm began to slide from around me and his left hand reached to take the towels from me, I couldn't help but cage him in with my arms and legs. An overwhelming feeling rushed over me, and I just needed a moment to hold him close. I missed him as if we still lived two hundred miles apart, and I hated that he was leaving me again.

Instantly, his arms enfolded me in a tight embrace, one hand threading through the hair at the back of my head to press my face deeper into the curve of his neck and shoulder.

Silently we just held each other and he kissed me long and deep, forgetting the wet mess on the floor. I wanted the whole fucking world to go away. "I wish we could just lie on the couch, all wound up in each other, for the whole day," I'd murmured into his neck. He was warm and smelled of fresh soap and Ryan.

"Sharing the iPod?" he asked.

I could only nod against him as a lump in my throat swelled painfully. I tried to content myself with the briefest of moments, like this. I could feel his pulse against my forehead as I wound my arms tighter around his waist.

"Me, too, baby."

My heart tightened and my eyes stung. I could still feel the urgency of his embrace; my body remembering his hard contours pressing into my softness, as much as my mind remembered his words. Remembering should leave me fulfilled, but it left me hungry and aching. I didn't know if I was blinking back tears or trying to rid the burning caused from lack of sleep. The few minutes this morning would have been perfect if it weren't for that stupid hospital phone going off and ruining the moment. That phone was just a more efficient version of a pager. He'd glanced at it briefly before clipping it back on his waist, his eyes touching mine then looking away. Ryan left after gulping down another cup of coffee and shoving the lunch I'd made the night before into a bag. The call had to be from Jane. Before she got hurt, that phone never went off at home, and I was far from stupid. The single benefit to working in the ER was that someone else was on call when Ryan was off-duty. If it were a medical emergency, they would have paged someone on site. I could tell by the guilty look in his eyes that he knew I was well aware of who originated that call and that it had nothing to do with work. I guess I should be thankful she wasn't calling his personal phone. I huffed in disgust.

I blinked at the layout on my desk next to the final guest list for the gala that Andrea had mocked for me. It was just after two, and I groaned. The end of the day couldn't come soon enough to suit me. Even though I faced another evening without Ryan, I wasn't concentrating and couldn't wait to get the hell out of here. Other than a check-in with Ellie earlier that morning, I hadn't accomplished a single thing. Even that was unproductive. I regretted calling considering that the call ended with her bawling her eyes out and me unable to comfort her at all. I sighed deeply. I'd told her over and over that Harris loved her and wasn't cheating. He'd told her the same thing, but she didn't believe either one of us, and we were both at the end of our respective ropes. I loved Ellie; I felt sad for her, but she was being an idiot. I felt even sadder for Harris.

A light tap on the door startled me out of my thoughts, though I welcomed the distraction. All this wallowing wasn't getting me anywhere, and it sure as hell wasn't constructive.

"Come in!" I called, hoping I managed to inject a little enthusiasm into my tone.

Andrea's bright smile and brighter red head popped around the corner of the half open door. "Want some company?" I wondered what she was so happy about when I was so miserable.

I threw the pen down on my desk and sat up straighter in my chair. "Sure," I said blandly.

"Gee, thanks, boss," Andrea admonished with a wrinkle of her nose, still not coming in and half-hiding behind the door. "I love you, too."

I guiltily waved her in. "I'm sorry. I'm just not here today. What's up?"

The door flew open wide, and to my surprise, Jenna rushed in, laughing happily. Her cheeks were flushed a pretty pink from the cold New York air, and she was dressed in a thick blue parka and jeans.

"I'm what's up!" she laughed as I jumped from my chair in surprise, flashing a big smile as I rushed into her embrace. "Or down, as the case may be."

"Jenna! Why didn't you tell me you were coming?" We hugged each other tight. The familiar scent of her perfume wafted gently around the room. "I'm so happy to see you!"

"I wanted to surprise you!" She hugged me again. "You look amazing..." She eyed me curiously, taking in the finely tailored suit and mauve silk blouse I wore. "Aside from those god-awful bags under your eyes."

I laughed and grimaced simultaneously. I could always count on Jenna's brutal honesty to slap me in the face. "Thanks. You look great, too; sans bags, of course. What are you doing in New York?"

She plopped down in one of the upholstered chairs opposite my desk, quickly undoing her coat and shoving it off her shoulders to reveal a heavy, cream-colored turtleneck sweater over dark jeans. "I need to shop. Aaron and I are staying in Boston for Christmas and I have to get things shipped to the families. You, too, right? Obviously, when Elyse and Gabe were arranging it at the wedding, we should have known better."

I wasn't buying her excuse for making the trek down to New York, but it didn't matter, I was just glad she was here.

"I guess." My response was lackluster. This Christmas didn't feel much like I'd hope it would, considering this would be Ryan's and my first Christmas as a married couple; the first Christmas one of us didn't have to travel to be with the other. I'd been looking forward to decorating, preparing and shopping with him, but it wasn't working out that way. I wanted it to be so special, but our lack of time together along with added crap like my derailed plans last night were putting a serious crimp in things.

I shook myself out of my thoughts and smiled at Jenna's expectant face. "And there are no shops in Boston; none what-so-ever. I remember now," I teased, my brows lifted mockingly.

Jenna rolled her eyes and screwed her face up. "Whatever. I wanted to see you, so shoot me. I miss you and I *suh-pose* I miss that moody man of yours, but don't you dare tell him I said that! Is he working today?"

"Yes. Always working. Do you want some coffee?"

"No, I want you to get you and your Gucci-clad ass out of here!" Jenna grinned. "The day's almost over anyway, right?"

I looked guiltily at the work piled on my desk. "Uh, yeah. It was pretty much a wash today, anyway." I flushed as I realized I'd just moved the conversation to a place that it didn't need to go.

She studied my face as I sat back down behind my desk. "What's going on?" she asked seriously.

"Probably nothing." I offered a half-assed shrug before continuing. "I don't know."

"Is Ryan okay? He's fully recovered from his injury, isn't he? That was almost a month ago."

Was it only a month ago? It seemed like longer. "He has a scar and sometimes that shoulder gets stiff, but I think that's just an excuse to get me to give him a massage." I tried to joke, but Jenna saw right through me.

She leaned forward in her chair. "Okay, I never thought I'd ask this, but are you and Ryan okay?"

I slowly rose from my chair, taking the layout back to the easel as I tried to look busy. "Yes. Of course, we're fine."

Jenna wasn't convinced. "Really," she stated flatly. Somehow it wasn't a question.

"Yes. These bags under my eyes are because we made love most of the night."

She leaned back, her eyes scrutinizing. "Uh huh," she said, clearly disbelieving.

I wanted to word vomit all over the place about Jane, but I knew Jenna would spill to Aaron, and I didn't want Ryan to know I was upset. He had enough to worry about, and I felt petty and silly for even feeling the way I did.

"What?" I asked, trying to make it sound as incredulous as possible. "We did! I'm tired."

"Look, Julia, I thought we were closer now. Ever since your car accident, I've thought of you as my sister."

"Me, too."

"Right, so you can spill more than Ryan's and your bang-a-thon!"

I couldn't help bursting out laughing at her words. "Oh my God! Only you, Jenna! How romantic you make it seem!"

"Okay, how's this? All night hump-session? Ryan poke-fest?" We both fell into fits of giggles for at least sixty seconds. "Peen-o-rama?" Jenna continued without mercy.

Peals of more laughter ripped through me as I planted my forehead down on my desk, my shoulders shaking. I was laughing so hard, my sides ached, my face hurt, and my eyes were beginning to tear. "Stop!" I managed to choke out.

Jenna was grinning from ear to ear when I finally lifted my head.

"Really. What's up?"

I sobered almost instantly and inhaled deeply. Not only was I going to regret telling her, I was probably going to sound insane.

"It's probably all in my head." I threw my hands up and began to pace around the room. "I don't want Ryan to think I'm upset, and Aaron will tell him whatever I say, so I should just zip it before I even get started."

"I won't tell Aaron, I promise, but I will bet my ass that if you're worried or upset about anything, Ryan already knows. He is way too in tune with you, girl."

"Lately, he's so tired, he may be a little tuned out. And, as I said, it's really nothing."

"Oh my God! Are you going to tell me or *what*?"

I bit my lip, hesitating, but I really did need to talk it out. It was eating me alive. "Only if you promise never to say a word to either one of the guys."

"Oh, Jesus, Julia!" Her exasperation at my stalling was barely kept in check. "I said I promise, didn't I?"

I ran a hand through my hair and sat down again.

"And stop bouncing around! You're giving me a headache!"

"After that night in the ER, the woman who got stabbed? She calls and texts Ryan constantly… last night I had this big romantic dinner planned, but he called in the middle of the afternoon informing me he'd invited Jane—her name's Jane—" I rambled, "and her invisible boyfriend to dinner." I stood up again, my nerves making it impossible to sit still, despite Jenna's disapproving look. "Sorry! I can't help it! Then the boyfriend bailed. God, I feel so guilty for even talking about her like this after everything she's been through."

Jenna was silent, letting me ramble as she took it all in. She didn't tell me I was crazy, which was unexpected.

"Invisible?"

"I've never met him. I wonder if he's just made up."

"Ryan feels responsible, and like you, he is probably full of guilt. You, of all people, know how compassionate he is. He told Aaron how extensive her injuries were," she stated simply. "If you want to put it into perspective, she didn't save his life any more than he saved hers."

"I know, but she wouldn't have needed saving if she hadn't done what she did. That's why I feel so horrible! I should be bending over backwards for her, but I'm just so... damn jealous! I'm married to him, and I know you're right about everything you just said," I looked down at her, wringing my hands, "but, I'm still so freaking jealous, I can't see straight."

Jenna smirked at me. "Jules, Ryan is so Goddamn charming he can't even help himself, and when he's really trying to be nice, any female within 100 yards falls down panting. That poor thing doesn't stand a chance in hell. You should feel doubly sorry for her," she said in her best deadpan.

Logically, I knew Jen was right, so why did my heart feel like it was on fire? I folded one arm across my body as I absently chewed the thumbnail of my other hand.

"Maybe she saved his life; maybe not. You don't know what would have happened."

I looked away from the window, over my shoulder at Jenna. "Oh, come on. I know that those thugs threatened Ryan when he refused to stop trying to save that kid. There was a scuffle, and one of them came at Ryan and Jane stepped in the way and took the knife full in her gut." I shivered just thinking about it. "She had to have a hysterectomy. And, she's young, Jenna. I can't imagine being faced without the prospect of babies."

Jenna was leaning nonchalantly back in her chair, but my words made her straighten up and her face to turn serious.

"Yeah, it sucks, Jules, but it wasn't your fault and it wasn't Ryan's, either. She made the choice to intercede."

"I know, but Jenna, if I'd lost him…" I could feel the burning as my eyes began to tear. "I *am* grateful, but I'm beginning to resent her, and I'm so pissed at myself for that. This morning, just before Ryan left, she paged him at six o'clock in the morning. Paged him! I just… I can't help it! We haven't gone for coffee in a month," I ranted, once again pacing the room. "Our time together is so short, I don't want to miss out on a second of it. When we do see each other, most of our time is spent in bed. I'm selfish, I guess."

"You're complaining because he's making love to you too much?"

"Of course not. I mean, it's amazing, and we're so close in those moments, but I want to hear about his day, spend time just being with him. I miss the best friend part of us."

"I guess you did spend four years *just talking*. I can see that you'd be feeling like that. Have you told Ryan any of this?" Jenna's voice and eyes were rock steady.

I huffed. "No. We don't talk, as I said, plus I feel like an idiot."

"This is what I know. One: Ryan would want to know how you feel; two: it's not the first time some twit has woven some baseless romantic fantasy around him which, by the way, he never even *notices*; and, three: your ass is coming with me! Nothing like some retail therapy to make you stop feeling sorry for yourself." She stood and began to shrug back into her coat. When I didn't move, she paused and looked at me. "What the hell are you still standing there for? Get your coat and let's go!"

I rubbed roughly at my right temple. "I can't. I have to work. I have too much to do."

"Wrong answer."

I stared blankly at her, the prospect of shopping didn't sound like a lot of fun since Ryan and I had decided to take it easy on Christmas gifts, but if I was being honest, there was no work getting done today. I shook my head, shrugging. "Andrea!" I called.

"Yeah, boss?" Her perky red head popped around the corner within seconds; a cheeky grin spread across her face.

The door was still halfway open and she must have been hovering just outside.

"That was fast." I glared at her. "This feels like an ambush."

Jenna's partner-in-crime bounced into the room. "Yep. Your schedule's been freed up. And, um…" she cleared her throat, "I was hoping I could tag along?" she suggested hopefully, tongue in cheek. I just stared at her, waiting for the explanation I felt would soon tumble from her lips. I cocked an eyebrow when she hemmed and hawed around. "When Jenna called, I made sure to get everything finished. The guest list has been approved, and I've placed the invitation order with the engravers. The art department is expecting the layout on Monday. We can finish it up tomorrow. So can we go?" Mischief sparkled in her dark blue eyes as she retrieved the jacket to my black wool crepe suit and passed it to me. Obediently, I shrugged my long cashmere coat on without a word.

Ryan ~

It was midnight when I finally dragged my ass through the door to our apartment. My stomach rumbled uncomfortably, and I hoped I'd find something to eat without making too much noise. Surely, Julia would be asleep by now. It was Thursday. I had Saturday off, and I'd taken an early shift tomorrow so I could surprise Julia. I hoped to hell Jane wouldn't find out. I had pangs of guilt on both fronts. The past month, I'd barely spoken to my wife.

My stomach made another angry grumble. The leftovers that Julia packed should have been enough for both lunch and dinner, but I couldn't say no when Jane asked to share the delicious steak sandwiches. When she sat with cafeteria lasagna in front of her and looked longingly at the pile of deliciousness in front of me, I couldn't refuse. It was self-preservation as well, I told myself, as I carried Jane's meal to the trash before getting a clean plate and filling it with half of my food. That lasagna smelled like shit, which could ruin my enjoyment of my lunch. However, when dinner rolled around, I was left with nothing more than a bag of Oreos from the vending machine. I needed to work out badly and had every intention of spending thirty minutes at the building gym before showering and falling into bed. If only I wasn't so fucking exhausted, and my shoulder didn't ache so much.

I was glad to get Julia's call that Jenna was in town and thankful she would have company over dinner. Truth be told, I missed Jenna's smartass remarks and Aaron's presence at work. Caleb, Kari and Jane were my friends, but it wasn't the same as Aaron and Jenna. The time in Boston when Julia was recovering brought us all even closer, and I missed having them around.

The apartment was dark, except for the glow from the TV. Jenna's head popped up from where she was lying on the coach. I was surprised to see her awake when Julia wasn't.

"Hey, pretty boy."

I smiled tiredly and went to hug her after throwing my keys and stethoscope on the entryway table. "Hey, you snarky bitch," I answered as my arms went around her. Jenna's laugher joined my own. "Is Jules in bed?"

My stomach rumbled again.

"Yes. I dragged her ass all over Manhattan today. I think I wore her out. You look like shit."

"Thanks," I mumbled, retreating into the kitchen to begin my forage.

"Jules mentioned your all-nighter."

I ignored her comment and went to dig through the refrigerator. "The hours are killing me. I'm sure Aaron is suffering from it, too."

"Yes, but Dr. Brighton is easy to work with. How's it going for you here?"

"I'm doing well. If I didn't know better, I'm getting much more responsibility than most first year residents."

"You always were a rock star."

"Don't you mean, I work my ass off?" I pulled a Styrofoam takeout container from the refrigerator and looked inside, sniffing the contents. It was filled with some sort of chicken dish with a mushroom sauce and linguine that smelled divine. "Julia didn't eat much dinner, huh? Where'd you guys go?"

"Some Italian joint. I can't remember the name. That's not her dinner; she ordered that for you, dipshit." Jenna plopped down at the table with a grin and pointed to a brown bag on the counter. "Breadsticks?"

My lips lifted slightly at the jab as I opened the microwave and set the box inside to warm up the pasta. "Did you snarf all of the cheesecake, Miss Piggy?" I teased, taking the bag and pulling out the bread and, not bothering to heat it, I took a huge bite. My eyes danced with laughter. I'd seen half of the cake still sitting on the shelf in the refrigerator, but I had to give her shit anyway.

"What was that? I can't understand you with your mouth full, porky," she mocked.

I laughed quietly, sitting down next to her with the bag of bread and the now steaming pasta. I loaded my fork. "I'm starving."

"Julia said that was for you to take tomorrow. Didn't you eat tonight?"

"No. I shared my lunch with a co-worker, so didn't have anything left for tonight."

Jenna eyed me skeptically, like she knew something I didn't. "Hmmm…" was all she said as she watched me eat. The expression on her face had me ready to ask what she was thinking, but we were interrupted when a sleepy Julia padded down the hall wrapped in her fuzzy white robe. She looked all soft and beautifully rumpled, and I longed to pull her down on my lap and kiss her senseless. She leaned down to place a soft, lingering kiss on my temple.

"Hi, babe," she murmured, pushing the hair back from my forehead and bending to place another brief kiss; this time on my mouth. "Missed you today."

I wrapped my left arm around her waist, drawing her closer to my side while her fingers scratched my scalp gently. It felt so good to have her next to me. "You didn't need to get up."

"I wanted to." She left me to get a bottle of water, took a drink and then set it down in front of me. "Can I get you anything, Jen?"

"I'm good. I just wanted to wait up long enough to say hello to this butthead, but I think I'm off to bed." She shoved my shoulder with her fingertips and then rose from the table.

"Can you stay a few days?" I asked. I wouldn't be around much, but it would be nice for Julia to have Jena around.

She shook her head. "I wish I could, but I have to work the day after tomorrow. I just wanted to check up on you two. Slow down a little. It's okay to be number two, Ryan."

"Pfft!" I dismissed. "That's the life of a resident." I finished the pasta, and Julia took the empty box and disposed of it, setting the fork in the sink. "It makes it hard to play newlyweds, right?"

"For sure. No rest for any of us wicked. Aaron worked a 12-hour day on Thanksgiving."

"Isn't it weird how time flies and drags at the same time? I can't believe Christmas is less than two weeks away." Julia said, tiredly. She yawned, her French manicured fingers covering her mouth. "Sorry, I can't seem to keep my eyes open."

"Go back to bed, honey. I'm going to eat, rinse off and then I'll join you."

"Are you hurting? Do you need me to rub something on your shoulder?"

Jenna disappeared quietly into the small spare room next to ours. "No, I'm okay, but I am beat." I grabbed the front of the robe, deliberately pulling it slightly loose so it gaped, and I could run my finger along the inside edge of one breast. She was warm and softly swelling against my fingertips. I pulled her down toward me with the other hand and kissed her lips, dragging my mouth down her neck to her collarbone. "I missed you today, too."

Her hand slid up the side of my face, pulling me in for another brief kiss.

"I'll see you in bed." Her voice was low and soft; always so seductive when it was laced with sleep. When she left me to wander back down the hall, I followed; quickly pulling the shirt to my scrubs off before I'd even hit the doorway to the bedroom. A small sliver of light infiltrated the room from the cracked door to the bathroom. Julia dropped the robe and crawled into bed, lying on her side, away from me, and my eyes couldn't help but trace the curve of her waist and hip on my way past, the comforter doing little to disguise her shape.

I missed her so fucking much. The scent of her shampoo and perfume lingered lightly in the air, my body stirred, and despite my exhaustion and her steady breathing, I was still aroused. With no intent to make love to her, I was still moved to it. I smiled and shut the bathroom door as quietly as I could, quickly jumping into water colder than I wanted it to be. It had the desired effect, and I turned it to hot and let it beat down on my injured shoulder, my fingers tracing over the ugly red scar now marring the smooth skin. I began kneading the muscles, hoping some of the stiffness would be relieved. I rotated the joint a few times before shampooing my hair and soaping down in record time. It must be almost one and I'd be out the door at six again; only tomorrow, I was done no later than seven. I couldn't wait. I dried off quickly and briskly rubbed my hair. No doubt it would be a mess in the morning, but I didn't give it more than a quick comb with my fingers.

I switched off the light and felt my way to the bed in the pitch darkness, looking forward to feeling Julia's warm skin against mine. I'd find her naked beneath the sheets, and we'd wind around each other, as always. I pulled back the covers and slid in beside her, wrapping my arm around her and pulling her close. She sighed, her legs—smooth as silk—slid between mine, her fingers locking around my wrist and pulling my arm tight against her breasts. I hesitated, inhaling her and then left a soft, hot blaze of kisses over her shoulder that ended with my lips buried in the curve of her neck, hungry for her mouth. I rubbed the stubble on my chin gently against her skin. "I'll make it up to you for yesterday. Tomorrow night is all us. I'm off at seven."

"Really?" She half turned and I kissed the corner of her mouth, knowing if I did more than that it would be at least an hour before we slept.

"Yeah," I whispered. "I love you."

Her fingers tightened and then laced through mine. She kissed my knuckles. "Love you, more," she said, her lips moving against my hand and her breath rushing hotly. I smiled and pulled her back, flush against me, until very inch of skin was touching. It felt amazing.

This was it. All that mattered was right here. My heart was full as I closed my eyes, knowing that tomorrow night we had precious hours of just the two of us. The warmth of our bodies seeped into the blankets and love wrapped us up in each other. I was content.

*****

"Ryan!" Jane called after me. I was on my way down to the lounge and glanced at the cheap watch on my wrist. It was the one my dad bought me before med school because I needed the second hand. He'd given Aaron one, too. The clasp was wearing out and the crystal was badly scratched. I was already twenty minutes past when I should have left. "Ryan!"

I stopped and quickly turned, irritated at another delay. "Yeah, Jane?" I worked to hide my impatience.

"What are your orders for Mrs. Williams?"

"Caleb has the chart. He'll answer your questions. Have a great night." I turned and started back down the hallway.

"Where are you going?" I ignored the anxious tone in her voice. I was just thankful I was leaving, and she was just arriving.

"I gotta get home!" I called over my shoulder.

"I thought you were working swing?"

"Traded with Caleb. See ya!"

I disappeared into the lounge without giving her another chance to speak to me. I rushed to change out of my scrubs and into dark jeans and a burgundy button down, leaving the scrubs, along with my hospital shoes, in a pile on the bottom of my locker. I had vague memories of how Julia told me to leave my stinky clothes and scrubs at school after Gross Anatomy. I ran my hand roughly through my hair and then over the rough surface of stubble on my jaw. There was nothing for it; I didn't have the time to shave. Julia liked the scruff anyway. I only wished it was twelve hours older so it would be softer against her skin.

I felt giddy and ridiculous because I had a date with my wife! A big ass grin split my face, and I almost laughed out loud. We weren't even going out, but she was making Pad Thai, we were decorating the tree, and if I had my way, we'd have a long talk and then round out the evening with a little game of Truth or Dare. Hell, it'd probably be morning by then.

I was still smiling as I climbed into my old CRV and the engine roared to life. I hated the New York traffic, and it wasn't often I drove to work, but I wanted to stop and pick up the Christmas gift I planned to give Julia. We agreed nothing extravagant, and I'd been struggling with what I could get her. I noticed her perfume was getting low last night before I jumped in the shower, and I wasn't sure if I was getting it for her or me. I gave her a bottle of that perfume for her birthday the first year we knew each other, and it was still her favorite; and mine. I couldn't exactly describe it, but it was like spring and sex; Julia and familiar.

My fingers banged out a text before I threw the phone on the seat and slammed the truck into gear.

Running a little late. Be home soon.
I'll help with dinner. Do we need wine?

I needed a good excuse to be later still. My phone vibrated and I grabbed it.

No. Come home. I'm hungry. Are you hungry? ☺

I chuckled and changed my plan. Hell, yes! I was starving and for more than curried rice noodles. The perfume would have to wait. The cab drivers cutting me off had me slamming on my brakes and cursing every couple of blocks. It was crazy the way they didn't stay in lanes, pushing their way ahead while laying on their horns, often with mere millimeters to spare. It was a solid metal river on practically every street, the cars separated by mere inches and five rows of cars crowed into four lanes. It was a miracle that they weren't rubbing together. "This is why I take the subway," I grumbled, impatiently tapping on the steering wheel with my thumb.

My phone vibrated. Either Julia was as impatient as I was, or she'd forgotten an ingredient she needed me to pick up. I glanced at the screen, but it wasn't a number I recognized. I threw it back on the seat as another horn blared loudly followed by a squealing of brakes. "Jesus Christ! Fucking nightmare!" The person on the phone could call back or leave a message. I refused to risk an accident or another delay.

Forty minutes later, boxes of Christmas ornaments were strewn about the living room, and I was getting bark and pine needles all over the living room carpet as I put the base on the tree. The branches and needles dug into my bare forearms as I pushed it into an upright position. "Babe, bring in the water," I called. Julia was cleaning up the remnants of dinner while I worked on the tree. There was Christmas music softly filling the cooperating as large, white snowflakes drifted past the window, glistening in the glow of Manhattan. It was unlikely they'd stick, but the thought of it snowing while it was so cozy in the apartment was wonderful. The scent of pine wafted together with the burning wood.

"Coming!" Her voice was distant, coming from down the hall and not the kitchen. I stood back; eyeing the tree to make sure it wasn't lopsided and did some slight adjusting. I smiled to myself. This was the first time we had the entire holiday together since college. In the past four years, I'd only been able to help her decorate the tree one other time, but now it would be always. The feeling went deeper than contentment or mere joy, it was more deep-seated and solid; a sort of elated wonder that we were finally together for good. Despite the feeling that our time spent in the same room was never enough, we were together. I was always dumbfounded by my thoughts. It never ceased to amaze me how much I loved her, how I looked forward to seeing her and how every picture of the future had her in it. Only one thing would make it more perfect. My smile widened as I started organizing the strands of lights. Maybe next Christmas, we'd have a baby.

I sat down with the two boxes of lights and began to separate and untangle them one by one. Some bigger white ones and others the little colored LED type. Julia liked hundreds of colored lights on the tree, but it was my guess from looking at the boxes of stuff from both of our mothers, there would be significantly more ornaments. My fingers worked through the intricate loops, the bulbs making them difficult to untangle without breaking the blubs and frustration made me impatient, which only made it worse. Screw this! There had to be a better way to organize them before packing them away, and I would sure as hell figure it out when we took them down.

Julia was taking her time doing whatever she was doing. I huffed. "Hey! Are you leaving me all of the hard part? These lights are a mess!"

She laughed lightly, her voice soft but closer, just behind me as I huddled over the lights.

"Stop being a moody ass." I couldn't help the smile tugging slightly on my lips. "It might help if you turned on some more lights. We have all night."

I was sitting on the carpet in front of the fire, and besides a light over the kitchen sink, I'd turned them all off. I was trying to be romantic, and she was telling me to turn on the fucking lights, I mused. We'd rushed through dinner because we had this to accomplish, and I found myself yearning for firelight, low music, and the feel of her skin against mine.

I huffed again, my fingers still pulling at the electric cords. "Well, maybe I didn't plan on spending the entire evening on the stupid tree," I complained.

I glanced over my shoulder at her and stopped dead in my tracks. Julia was gathering up the other end of the lights and arranging the ones I'd already straightened into a straight line, bending over to plug one end into the wall, but she was doing it dressed in a sheer red baby doll and a white fur-trimmed Santa hat. A small spattering of sequins glistened in the firelight and the glow given off by the now lit strand of lights.

She was so gorgeous. The shape of her body; the soft swell of her hips and full breasts, the soft shadow of her navel, all completely visible through the sheer fabric, made my cock swell. I couldn't tear my eyes away as she nonchalantly worked with the lights, as if she were wearing jeans and a T-shirt or sweats.

Obviously, she planned on teasing me to death. I wanted to grin so bad my face hurt with the effort of keeping it at bay.

"Just what in the hell do you think you're doing?" I tried to keep the amusement out of my voice as I stood up. Her eyes ran over me, clearly checking out the bulge in my pants. I tried to keep my expression hard when her eyes finally met mine. They were dancing with amusement.

"Checking to make sure these lights work," she said with mock innocence. My fingers curled into fists and released at my sides, aching to reach out and touch her, but damned if I'd let her get away with it. Two could play at this game, as long as I could keep from laughing.

"Well, you're doing it all wrong." I took the lights from her hands, while trying hard to ignore how she'd made her hair all wild and the intoxicating scent of her perfume.

"I am not." She bent to take them back, letting her full breast brush against my bicep and her breath rush across my neck.

"Are too."

The next hour was spent with delicate touches and provocative looks, but I gave as good as I got. When the lights were finally wound around the tree and we were ready to start decorating, I finally pulled her back against me, letting my hands roam her body, cupping both breasts as my mouth feasted on the cord of her neck. She shivered, breaking out in goose bumps. She pushed her little ass into my hard groin and I groaned, my arms tightening as she gave me more access to her neck and her hand snaked up to wind in my hair.

"You're gonna get it." My tone was low and guttural.

A soft, almost nonexistent laugh left her mouth, but it was more like a desperate sigh. "Okay, give it to me. Now."

She turned in my arms and our mouths crashed together, sucking and pulling, our tongues doing an intimate dance inside each other's mouth. I pulled her closer and up until she was fully in my embrace. Julia wrapped her legs around my waist and her hands clutched in my hair and at my shoulders, pulling me closer, encouraging and begging for deeper kisses. For a minute, I gave in, letting the want take over, but just when we were both panting, I walked to the couch, untangled her from me and plopped her unceremoniously down on the cushions.

"No."

The confused look on her face told me what a million words couldn't. She never expected me to beat her at her own game. Damn if I wasn't in physical pain from wanting her so much, but maybe a little anticipation was good for the soul.

"No?"

"We aren't finished decorating the tree."

"You're serious?"

"Pay back is hell." My erection pressed painfully against the denim and zipper on my jeans, and I adjusted myself in her full view. She knew what she did to me, and I knew if I let my fingers graze her panties, she'd be hot and damp. I wanted to keep touching her so fucking bad, but that would make it impossible not to throw her down and make love to her right there, like I was dying to do. I wanted to make love to her slow, in the glow of the freshly decorated tree, worshiping her with every touch, not screwing frantically amid a bunch of ornament boxes.

She scowled at me.

"I love you in lingerie, and—" I spread my hands out in front of me, while she still sat where I'd placed her, frowning, "You know how much I want you. It's obvious," I indicated the giant hard-on still raging in my pants, "but, I have plans for later."

"I just thought…"

I nodded. "You thought right. You're gorgeous and I'm dying to make love to you, but, trust me, baby." The back of my knuckles traced the line of her face, and her hand came up to grasp my wrist. "Later, when we get the tree done. I don't want to rush."

She read my mind, her scowl faded and her expression softened; her luminous green eyes shimmering with love. "Making love slowly doesn't slow down time, Ryan. Sometimes, it might make it go even faster."

"It goes too fast when we're together," I murmured, my arms going around her and pulling her gently into my arms again. "I remember the minutes better if we don't rush through it," I admitted.

Her hand traced my jaw, and my breath stopped at the look in her eyes and the subtle smile on her lips. "Why are you so amazing?"

I kissed her briefly, an open-mouth kiss that could have escalated if I let it, but I slid my hand inside the ass of her panties and gave her a playful squeeze. "I'm not," I say wryly. "I just love you. Now, get busy, Mrs. Matthews, so we can get to the good stuff." I released her reluctantly and picked up a box of ornaments.

We worked together, filling the tree with the childhood memories, telling each other the stories behind each ornament our mothers had sent and adding the new ones that Julia had purchased at the end. The evening was magical, filled with soft, sexy touches, entwined fingers and lingering kisses that promised the amazing lovemaking that would follow. Her half naked body was driving me mad.

The tree was turning out beautifully, and I watched Julia carefully placing the baubles evenly on it; the style was eclectic, blending nostalgia with new, and I realized it was so like us. Eight years of memories, some sparkling and some not so much, a solid base for the precious new ones that would adorn our future. I shook my head. When did I become such a sentimental sap?

We were almost finished, only the garland and tinsel remaining, when my phone rang. It was just after eleven. Julia began picking up the empty ornament boxes and put them away in a bigger cardboard box for storage.

"Maybe it's your mother," Julia suggested. "She knew we were decorating tonight. She probably wants you to send a picture."

"Should I send her one of your hot ass in that get-up?" I teased, walking to get the phone from the table in the hall.

I answered without checking the number. "Hello?"

"Ryyyaaannn!" Jane sobbed on the other end of the phone. "I'm so... sorry to call, but I didn't have anyone else I could talk to!"

My jaw hardened instantly as I glanced at Julia, who was still straightening up the living room. This was not going to go well. I didn't want to say anything, reluctant to ruin the amazing evening that we had going.

"Can we talk tomorrow or on Sunday?" I would be back at work on Sunday. Julia's back straightened and she turned to look at me. I could see it in her face, she knew who it was. Surely, she could tell I wasn't happy about it.

"Noooooo!" Jane cried. "Daniel left! I can't believe he did this to me right before Christmas!"

Fuck! The fucker was a first class dick. "I'm really sorry that happened, but maybe you're better off. He didn't appreciate you." The words rushed out of my mouth before I could think. "I told you that before."

She hiccupped on the other end of the phone. Instinct told me to turn away from Julia so maybe she wouldn't hear the conversation, and maybe I could get off the phone before too long. "I know. He doesn't want me because I can't have kids."

I could feel myself flush, the blood rushing hotly beneath the skin of my face. I'd be an insensitive ass if I tried to cut her off, but damn if that wasn't what I wanted to do. Julia's expression told me she was upset, and I was helpless as I watched her throw the garland angrily into the box and storm off down the hall, closing the door loudly behind her.

"I'm sorry, Jane. Maybe he'll come around, if that's what you want."

"I don't know what I want anymore..."

She continued to ramble on, and I could find little words to comfort her. I knew if I tried to get off the phone I'd come off like an insensitive prick, but now I had my own mess to clean up.

*****

Almost an hour later, I was finally able to end the call, promising Jane we'd talk more, and she'd feel better after a good night's sleep. I was feeling like hell, knowing that what I'd face in the bedroom would not be the loving, sex-kitten Julia that a few hours ago was teasing the shit out of me. I was an asshole, no matter what I did. I ran a hand through my hair and prepared to take my medicine. Maybe she'd understand.

Whenever I worked late, it was Julia's custom to leave the bathroom light on and the door cracked so I could find my way to the bed, but tonight the room was awash in total darkness. I pulled back the covers and listened for her breathing to see if she was asleep. She was on her side, turned away and curled into the fetal position, her hands clutched around the covers across her chest. I knew she wasn't asleep. The sleeve of her T-shirt made me pause. *She was wearing clothes to bed...* something we just didn't do—not since we'd been married. Not unless it was sexy lingerie that didn't make it through the night. The hope that the night wasn't completely fucked was dashed at the absence of the baby-doll she was wearing earlier. I tensed and prepared myself to do whatever necessary to rip down the invisible wall that felt tangible between the two of us.

I fumbled in the dark, shedding my clothes into a pile on the floor before sliding in next to her. It had been another long day and I was exhausted. I was anticipating this bed so damn much before that phone call screwed it all up. I felt guilty on both fronts. I resented the interruption even though it was clear Jane needed my support, and guilty, because even if Julia didn't say anything, I knew the continued interruptions from Jane were wearing on her. It was getting more and more obvious that something was going to have to give. I wasn't fucking blind but I didn't exactly know how to get myself out of the quagmire without hurting Jane. *How did I get in this fucking mess?*

I rolled onto my side toward Julia, longing to curl up next to her and feel her against me, trying find a way to heal the damage that had been done. I'd wanted so much for tonight, but now it was late, the evening lost. I sighed in regret. It was my own damn fault. I needed to grow a pair with Jane. I reached out to Julia even though it seemed like she was asleep already.

The minute my hand touched her back, she recoiled sharply, and my breath caught in my throat. Never in the whole time we'd known each other had she pulled away from me like my touch burned her skin, and not since we'd been married had there been a night she wasn't wrapped up, naked, in my arms. My chest tightened painfully. It was worse than I thought.

"Julia..." I began, but the words fell away. I knew she was pissed. Hell, *I* was pissed, but I felt a responsibility to this poor girl who was stabbed and mutilated in my stead.

What a damn nightmare! And now, it was screwing up my life as well. I reached out to Julia once more, and she flinched again.

"Julia," I said more forcefully. "I'm sorry. Don't pull away from me."

My words just made matters worse. She curled into a tighter ball away from me, scooting to the very edge of the bed, so I moved in closer, propping my head up on my hand. I was as close as I could get without touching her. I felt the heat radiating off of her body onto mine, and she must surely feel my breath on her shoulder. I leaned in to kiss it softly. The sweet coconut scent of her shampoo engulfed me, but she stiffened even more when my lips touched her skin. My heart fell. Her hair was still damp from her shower, and I wanted to hold her and feel her body yielding to mine. Soft, warm and wanting... my Julia. I closed my eyes in the dark and inhaled deeply when I was met with her silence.

"Babe, will you talk to me?"

"I'm tired, Ryan, okay? Just go to sleep."

If her stiff posture wasn't enough, the tremble in her voice showed her internal battle, and her words were like a slap in the face. We never went to bed without kissing goodnight, which usually ended up in the glorious lovemaking I craved. We couldn't keep our hands off of each other, so we had a huge problem.

"Not until you kiss me," I said softly, my hand stroking her wet hair. "I love you."

"I know. But I'm tired. I don't want to talk right now." Her voice was quiet, but with a heavy thickness to it. I hated that she was hurting.

"I didn't ask you to talk. I asked you to kiss me," I said softly, still stroking her hair, threading my fingers through it in a way that I knew weakened her resolve. Usually.

"Well, I don't want to kiss you right now, either!" Her tone hardened and my hand stilled instantly.

I rolled on to my back with a sigh and ran both hands through my hair. *Fuck!*

"Julia. I know you're upset about the phone call, and I'm sorry, okay?" I said in frustration. "You know the situation."

"I said, I don't want to talk about it, Ryan! That woman is everywhere, so can we please keep her out of our damn bed, at least?" she asked angrily.

"Well, *I want* to talk about it. I can't stand it when you pull away from me. Just... *quit it*!" I turned toward her and reached for her again quickly, but she reacted just as fast by jumping out of the bed, grabbing her pillow and racing around to the end of it. "What are you doing?" I asked in surprise as I sat up. It never occurred to me that she would walk out.

"I'm sleeping in the other room. I don't want..." her voice cracked slightly as she moved toward the door. "I can't be with you right now. I need to be alone."

I watched in disbelief as Julia exited the room and then jumped from the bed and rushed after her, not even caring that I was naked. By the time I'd made it to the hallway, she'd already reached the spare room and closed the door with a heavy bang behind her.

"Julia, don't do this. Come on." My hand closed around the doorknob, only to find it locked, and anger welled up within me. "You fucking *locked* the door?" I rattled the knob loudly as I stood there, unsure of what to do next. This was new territory. She never shut me out like this. "Julia!" I yelled and slammed my open hand on the door several times. "Goddamn it! Open up this door right *now*!"

"Just stop it, Ryan! It's midnight for God's sake! Just leave me alone!" I could hear the thickness of her voice and knew she was crying. Suddenly, my anger dissipated into thin air.

I leaned my head on the door and ran my hand over the wood. "Baby, I'm sorry. Please don't cry. I can't stand it when you cry."

She didn't answer in words, but I could hear her sobbing softly behind the door. "I love you, and I want to finish what we started earlier. I'm sorry. I wouldn't have taken the call, but I didn't check who it was. Please come back to bed with me. Julia!"

Again, she didn't answer. I wasn't sure how long I stood there waiting and listening with my hand and forehead on the door. Her crying finally stopped, and I realized she must have fallen asleep. My heart ached. I knew we'd get past this and talk it out tomorrow. I was grateful for my day off, but it hurt that we were going to bed angry enough to sleep separately. It never happened before. Not *once*. Even before we were married, even on the night she told me she was going to Paris before her damned accident. In almost five years, I'd never slept under the same roof with her when she wasn't in my arms, except for the few months she'd lost her memory.

I couldn't breathe as I walked back to our room and fell heavily on the bed. I flung my arm over my eyes as my throat started to ache. *Jesus, what was I thinking?* How could I think that this shit wasn't going to eventually come back to bite me in the ass? How could I think that Julia would be left untouched, no matter how badly she felt for Jane? I knew how I'd feel if the situation was reversed. Devastated. Insane. I'd want to kill something.

This was going to be one long fucking night.

~8~

Ryan ~

I couldn't sleep. I tossed. I turned. I got up for water and wandered around the apartment to stand at the window in the living room to watch the twinkling lights of Manhattan. I wasn't sure what the right move would be. Should I go to Julia or wait until she came to me? I had to be straight with Jane. I wasn't an idiot. I could see her growing more attached to me, more reliant, and to offset it, I talked about Julia even more; hoping to God, Jane would get the hint. If only Daniel wasn't such a fucking pussy, I wouldn't be having this problem. If only *I* wasn't such a fucking pussy I wouldn't be in this mess. I sighed and ran my hand through my hair. Grateful was grateful, but this was something else entirely, and I needed to find a delicate way to fix it.

I got up and glanced at the clock. It was too late to call Aaron, but I needed to talk to someone. I could call Jane and let her see how she was coming between my wife and me. Maybe then she'd back off. Fuck, I couldn't call Jane. Despite my intentions for the call, Julia would go ballistic.

I went back into the bedroom and paced around, straining to hear something coming from Julia; but all that met my ears was silence. My hand hesitated over my phone and then I pulled it away.

"Damn it to hell!" I murmured in frustration. I reached for the phone again, and this time picked it up and punched Aaron's speed dial as I made my way back into the living room.

It rang three times before Aaron's groggy voice picked up. "What is it, Ryan? Is everything okay? It's the middle of the night!"

I sighed and sat down on the couch but leaned forward, resting my elbows on my knees and my head in my free hand. "Yeah. No…fuck, I don't know, Aaron!"

"Hold on… I need to go in the other room. I don't want to wake up Jenna," he said softly. I could hear the rustling of the bed covers and then a door open and shut before he spoke again. "Okay. Talk."

"Julia and I had a big blow up a couple of hours ago. Now she's locked in the spare room, and I can't get her to answer me."

"Christ. Is it about that woman?"

"What?" I asked, surprised. Then it dawned on me. Julia had talked to Jenna.

"What did Jenna tell you?"

"She wouldn't say much; said she promised Julia she'd keep their conversations secret, but she did mumble something about the woman who was hurt that same night you were."

"Yeah. Jane."

"Yes, that's her. Why would Jules be upset about her?"

"Jane called while we were decorating the tree. She was hysterical, crying about her boyfriend leaving her. I couldn't just hang up on her! I wanted to, but she's lost so much."

I heard Aaron expel his breath. "Explain it to Julia. She'll understand."

"Well, that's so easy! Why in hell didn't I think of that?" I spat sarcastically, and then continued. "Julia doesn't understand. Last night, we'd planned the tree thing, but Jane was crying about that asshole at work, and I invited them to dinner."

"So, two nights in a row? Are you crazy?"

"Yesterday, I only asked her because I thought if we could get her man to spend time with her, he'd pay her some attention, and she'd stop being so needy. But tonight, I didn't know who was on the phone. All this shit doesn't even matter. She interrupted our evening, and the next thing I knew, Julia was cleaning up the boxes and turning her back on me in bed."

"Shit, Ryan. I know you feel grateful, I would too, but for fuck's sake, don't let it mess with your marriage."

I shoved back until I was slouched against the back of the couch. "It isn't like that. Jane's a friend, and that's it. She's a good person who saved my life, and yeah, I feel that I owe her."

"Ryan, you just said she was needy. You have to stop and consider how this looks to your wife. I'm sure Jules is grateful, too, man, but she probably feels isolated and shut out from this thing you've got going with this Jane chick."

I flushed, instantly stood up angrily and walked to the window again. "I don't have any type of *thing* going with Jane, Aaron! I would never screw around on Julia! I thought I made that point when I beat the shit out of you at the gym. You know how much she means to me." My throat constricted and my lungs wouldn't expand.

Aaron's voice was calm and still low. "I'm not accusing you of fucking Jane, Ryan, but the two of you shared this near-death experience, and it would be natural to bond over it. That being said, you need to keep it in perspective. It's always been you and Julia and it may be hard for her to see you get close to someone else."

"But, I'm not *trying* to be close to Jane. I'm just helping her right now. She doesn't have anyone else. Her boyfriend is a dick. Jesus Christ, she got disfigured, and her life changed forever because of me. She can't have kids, Aaron. What the fuck am I supposed to do? Abandon her? I'm sure Julia knows it, but she's pulling away from me anyway and I..." I sighed deeply, feeling defensive. Hadn't I just told myself I had to man-up with Jane? "I am not dealing with it well. She doesn't trust me, which pisses me off. After everything we've been through, she has to know that I'd never let anyone come between us. Yet, here we sit in this shit storm."

"Just cool it with Jane, and try to make sure Julia knows she's the most important woman in your life."

"I do already. Jesus."

"Listen, you hard-headed son-of-a bitch," Aaron rasped out. "Don't forget what Julia went through when you were on lock-down in the hospital that night. She thought you might have been killed. She's the one who loves you, and has the most to lose if something happened to you. So wise the fuck up, Ryan. Julia went through it too. Just in a different way. She needs you. Jane may have saved you, but Julia almost lost you, and she's proba-bly afraid she's losing you all over again."

I stood there, stone still and listened to my brother's wise words. Words that ate away like acid in my gut. My heart broke that Julia could doubt my love or devotion for a single minute, but maybe he was right. "Fuck, when did you turn into a woman?" I tried to smile but didn't quite get the job done. I was tired, and my chest ached.

Aaron chuckled. "Just think about what I said."

I ran my hand through my hair, and heard the door to the spare room open slowly.

"Um, Aaron, I need to go. I'll call you tomorrow. I think I hear Jules."

"Okay, man. Don't fuck this up, Ryan. I won't be able to live with your sorry ass if she leaves you."

"I won't. Thanks, man. Bye." My heart thudded in my chest as I watched Julia walk slowly toward me, still dressed in one of my T-shirts. It hung loosely over her small form, leaving a long expanse of her legs completely bare. Her eyes were dark and sad as she looked up at me, leaving me aching to touch her and pull her close. I threw the phone down on the couch not caring where it landed.

"That was just Aaron." I said quickly, making sure she knew I wasn't speaking to Jane again. She nodded but didn't say anything. Still, I waited.

Finally, she reached for my hand and our fingers threaded together. I let my other one move up to cup her face in a gentle caress. Her cheek and the hair around her face were still damp, but this time from her tears, not her shower.

"I can't sleep without you," she whispered softly. Instantly, I enfolded her in a tight embrace and my lips came down on the top of her head as her arms wound around my waist. I was shirtless and her hands moved up my back as she pressed her cheek to my chest.

"Oh, babe, me either." I turned her back toward our bedroom.

We walked, arms wrapped around each other, down the hallway to our room and wordlessly moved to the edge of the bed. She crawled in ahead of me, and I dropped my pajama bottoms before lying down and pulling her next to me. She snuggled in close, our legs entwining. I had one arm around her back, and Julia rested her head in the crook of my shoulder, her fingers softly rubbing my chest. I reached up and grabbed her hand, pressing it down over my heart. I hoped she could feel it beating and know that, without her, it would surely stop. I held onto her for dear life and turned my face into her sweet smelling hair. "I can't stand it when you pull away from me..."

"It... *hurts*. I know what's going on with Jane, but I just... I can't help it," she said into the darkness. The ache in her voice was unmistakable and it weighed heavily on my heart. I couldn't see her face because it was nestled into the curve of my neck, but I knew her brow would be furrowed and exactly the pain I would find on her features. "And then I feel ashamed."

"Julia. You know that nothing will come between us. I just feel sorry for this girl, and grateful. She bought us some time during a scary situation, and I feel responsible, that's all."

"I know... me, too."

I could feel her nod slightly against my chest.

"But it still hurts that you give so much of your time to her. Hearing the tender tone in your voice when you speak to her," Julia's voice thickened. "That's how you speak to me. And I hardly see you now. She talks to you more than I do, and I guess... it's just, we get so little time together; I wanted tonight. I know it's selfish, but I'm jealous. I don't mean to be, but it hurts so much that she gets so much of you."

My arms tightened around her and I rolled us over until she was beneath me, so I could look into her face. I wanted her to feel engulfed by me, to physically feel the weight of my words and the love behind them. I studied her shadowed features and then smoothed the frown from between her brows with my thumb.

"Hey, she gets my friendship and that's it." I looked seriously into the green depths that were glistening as she fought back the tears. Her throat moved as she swallowed. "I can't believe you don't know that *nothing* will ever come between us. I love you more than life, and I know you *feel* that," I whispered against her skin and kissed her cheekbone with gentle lips. I tasted the salt of her silent tears on my tongue. I could feel her nod against me. "Then what's this all about?" My mouth found hers softly, and it sprung to life underneath mine, opening, seeking more pressure, which I was only too happy to give her.

"You're *it* for me," I said breathlessly between the kisses that were growing deeper and more and more passionate. "I don't ever want to be without you, and I never want a locked door between us again," I groaned into her mouth as she sucked my tongue in and surged her hips against mine. I was rock hard and ready, just as I was each time we touched. I moved against her, creating the delicious friction we both craved. If I just moved a fraction of an inch, I could be deep inside her. "Not being able to get to you is the worst thing you can do to me. Nothing can sepa-rate us, Julia. Ever."

My hands were holding both sides of her head, and her fin-gers were wound in my hair as we kissed hungrily, the passion between us was palpable. Part of me wanted to remove my shirt from her body, to kiss all over her, and another part of me was so damn hungry and desperate to claim her and reassure myself that she belonged to me, that I needed to be inside her immediately.

"Ugnnhhhh..." she moaned, when I could hold back no longer, I slid deeply into her. She was hot and wet as I pushed into her, hard. Over and over, I thrust into her as I continued to kiss her hungrily. Our mouths were mating like our bodies, a hot mash-up of frenzy and reverent worship. I would never get enough of her love. Her jealousy made my heart tighten and fill. If I didn't already know she loved me beyond possibility, she showed me over and over. I moved my hips in circles, pressing into her pubic bone to stimulate her clitoris and when I felt her clenching around me each time I pounded into her, I knew I was hitting the mark. I wanted to see her come. The little mewling sounds she was making deep within her throat were driving me wild with desire.

"Oh God, Julia." I punctuated my words with my hard thrusts into her. "You're all I want. You're all I ever need." We were both frantic in our lovemaking; her tears were still on my tongue as I kissed her over and over. "Tell me you know that. Tell me that you know how much I fucking love you."

"I know it, Ryan," she gasped against my mouth, "Uhh, uhh, uhh," her breath rushed out each time I pushed into her, filling her to the hilt. "Uhh, I love you, too. So much."

"Baby, I know. I know, Julia." She was clenching and releasing each time I moved in her, and it was killing me. "Julia, baby, I need to hear you. Jesus, I can feel you getting close," I said just before I crushed her mouth beneath mine, hungry to taste her again, to be completely lost in her. All of my senses were overwhelmed.

She whimpered into me as I felt the trembles start to overtake her, and I let myself explode into her little body. Thrusting in as deep as I could, and deeper as she raised her knees even higher around my waist. "Uhhhhhhh.... Julia, uhhhhhh," I grunted as I came hard, pushing in as deep as I could get.

We lay entwined like that, my face buried in her hair as we both struggled for breath. Her hands were gentle now as she stroked my back, over my neck, and up in my hair. She sent little tingles down my spine as her fingers stroked over and over. I couldn't help but hope we'd conceived.

"So incredible," I whispered against her mouth and then licked her upper lip with my tongue before she tilted her head and sucked my top lip in to nibble at it softly. I felt my heart squeeze in my chest as I pushed her damp hair off of her beautiful face and nuzzled against her cheek, very softly. "You're so beautiful, and I love you. There is no way I'll ever let anything destroy this."

"I know you love me, Ryan. But every minute you spend with her is a minute you're not with me. I know it's selfish, and I feel shitty about it, but it feels like you're giving her something that belongs to me, and I don't have anything to say about it. I don't want to lose any part of you." Her eyes closed and tears squeezed out from under her lids, and I sucked in air until my lungs couldn't hold anymore. How could she think that there would ever be anyone that could touch the way I felt about her? "What we have is so special, Ryan."

"So, why are you worried? You have every right to feel that way, but it's needless. Whenever you have these doubts, please remember that you are everything to me. *Everything.* If I had to die to prove it to you, I'd die."

Her arms tightened, her fingers pulled at my flesh, and she gasped. Her voice was full of tears. "Don't say that," she begged. "Please don't say that."

"It's the truth. Nothing matters more than you."

*****

On Monday morning, I went into the hospital with purpose. I would find Jane and try to explain the situation with Julia. Saturday had been an amazing, slow-paced day spent grocery shopping, working out, and making Christmas cookies. It re-minded me of the more carefree time at Stanford, when we were inseparable, and I enjoyed every minute of it. Julia carefully packed up boxes for both sets of parents, Aaron and Jenna, and of course, Ellie. Her face showed her sadness as she made a separate package for Harris. I knew what she was thinking and simply wrapped my arms around her from behind and rested my head on her shoulder while she wrote the address on the box with a Sharpie marker.

"I think this is fun. Who needs to spend loads of money on Christmas? It's been a great day." I cocked my head to kiss the skin behind her ear, and she sighed softly, pushing the box away and turning in my arms. What began as a soft kiss, turned into a

passionate lovemaking session that lasted the rest of the afternoon and on into the evening. Afterward, we were both starving,
so I started a fire while Julia ordered Chinese delivery. We
planned to wrap up together on the couch and watch a movie for
the rest of the night.

The day had been perfect except for three awkward moments. My pager went of twice, and then Jane called my personal cell. In light of what happened on Friday night, Julia visibly stiffened when it rang around 9 PM. My parents had called
earlier, and I'd answered, so when I shut it down instead of
picking up, the reason was obvious. I hadn't done anything to
cross the line with Jane anyway, but still, I felt guilty, and that
pissed me off. The day had been close to perfect, although I
pushed down the part of me that was still mad that Julia would
feel even the least bit insecure. As far as I was concerned, nothing had changed between us, and she needed to just see my
friendship with Jane for what it was.

After the call, something shifted, and the closeness of the
day disappeared in a puff of smoke. We went to bed in an uncomfortable silence, both of us hardly speaking. I was torn between not wanting to make things worse and shouting that she
was crazy to feel insecure at all. In the end, I shut my mouth,
because the night before, she'd asked me to keep the topic of
Jane out of our bedroom, but not being able to talk to Julia about
anything and everything did not sit well. I could feel her mind
working, even in the dark, wondering why Jane had my personal
number. I didn't sleep very well, to say the least.

This morning, Julia left early, leaving me a note that she
had a breakfast meeting with Meredith, who was in New York
for the week. My anger softened when I saw the plate of treats
she'd left for me to share at the hospital. It was an obvious white
flag. I huffed in amusement. I shouldn't have been surprised by

the gesture. At heart, Julia was the most generous and giving person I'd ever known.

I pulled one of my favorite cranberry cookies from underneath the cellophane before dropping the plate off at the ER desk and heading down to the lounge to lock up my coat and phone. I nodded to Caleb and two of the other nurses. One of them was new and I hadn't met her yet. She was standing next to Kari, but there was no sign of Jane. I felt slightly relieved for the brief reprieve from the conversation I dreaded. I stuffed the whole cookie in my mouth and chewed. It had to happen sooner than later because nothing made me more miserable than being at odds with Julia. There was an envelope taped to my locker from the Chief of Staff's office. My request for New Year's Eve off had been accepted, and I was pleased to see my shift on Christmas Eve ended at 7. Ideally, I would have liked the entire day off so Julia and I could have driven up to Boston, but it was already more than I'd hoped for.

The ER was quiet when I returned, and I was resolved to get things with Jane ironed out. She was behind the nurses' station, entering information into one of the patient's computer files. When she saw me, she stood and rushed over, her expression lighting up. "Hi, Ryan," she said brightly. No sign of the hysterics that I'd dealt with during our last phone call. Now that Julia opened my eyes, I could see what she saw, I had to be honest. Jane was a little over-enthusiastic to see me.

"Hey," I tried to dismiss her, walking behind the desk and shoving my ID card into the computer to look over the cases. Still, Jane hovered near. I needed to be brought up to speed for the shift change, so I turned my attention to the computer and to Caleb.

"It's been pretty quiet, Ryan," Caleb said, glancing behind me at Jane. His discomfort at her attention to me was clear.

"Who's the most critical?" I asked, still ignoring the woman behind me.

"Room three. The patient is complaining of a migraine headache, severe body pain, and lethargy."

"Is the pain manifesting in a specific region of the body?"

"Pretty much radiating everywhere, even in her bones. I ordered the standard blood work-up, but the results aren't back yet. I haven't prescribed anything for pain because I wanted to try and figure out what caused it first."

The woman must have been in misery because I could hear the moans from the other side of the ER. "I understand, but I think a small does of morphine in the IV is called for by the sound of things. Have you looked for parasites or viruses?" I typed the orders in, with the attending physician, Dr. Jameson looking on. I glanced his way. He was giving me the nod with a small smile, so I typed in the orders.

"No, that's a good idea. There is also an elderly man in room 7. Chest film showed pneumonia. He's being admitted."

"Obviously, IV antibiotics are already ordered?" I asked, and Caleb nodded. There wasn't more we could do in the ER. When he nodded, I continued. "How is he breathing?"

"Not great. His blood pressure is a little lower than we'd like. We're sending him to ICU."

"Ryan," Jane interrupted.

I turned abruptly and met her eyes. "Jane, if this isn't about the patients, we'll talk later."

"But I…"

"Later," I said firmly. The last thing I needed was the attending and the rest of the staff looking on to a personal conversation when I had work to be done. "As you can see, I'm in the middle of a brief. Please go draw another vile of blood from the patient in room three, and send it to the lab. Have it tested for viruses and organisms. I'm particularly looking for Lyme disease. And administer 10 mils of morphine into her IV."

Her eyes took on a wounded look, but she nodded and turned to do what I'd asked. "Yes, doctor."

"You make me look bad, Ryan," Caleb mused.

"I haven't examined her, so it's a guess at this point," I admitted. "But, I remember a case I studied in med school where the patient had chronic pain all over her body and initial tests showed nothing wrong. Plus, Lyme is more prevalent in the northeastern part of the country."

"She doesn't have any rashes, which would be a sign of the disease."

"She could have contracted it months ago, and it's just now showing symptoms. She may be beyond the rash."

We entered the room, and I proceeded to examine the patient after Jane was finished. The medication took the edge off, but the poor woman still winced continually as pain wracked her body. If it turned out that the Lyme tests were positive, I'd prescribed three days of IV antibiotics and if all went well, the patient would leave with oral hydrocodone for pain and see her primary doctor once a month. I didn't envy her. If it is Lyme's, it could hang on for months or more and a strong antibiotic course could create residual problems over time.

The afternoon progressed with Jane respecting the boundaries I'd set. At around six, I planned on a break and asked Jane to join me for dinner so we could talk. She was smiling happily, but I was filled with apprehension as we sat down across from each other.

"You seem to be in a better mood. Did you work things out with Daniel?" I asked, winding some leftover chicken lo-mein over my fork and shoving it into my mouth.

She shook her head. "No. He's still leaving, but I decided that you are right, Ryan. I deserve more."

It escaped my notice earlier, but she'd cut her hair to shoulder length and it hung loose around her face. It suited her.

"I'm glad you finally see that. Are you doing okay?"

She reached across the table for my hand, but I pulled it back, reaching for the can of soda in front of me. Jane hesitated and awkwardly picked up her fork.

"You're sweet to ask. I wanted to talk to you about it yesterday. That's why I called. Where were you?"

"Spending the day with Julia." I pointed to the Ziplock bag of sweets lying on the table at my side. "We made Christmas cookies."

"Yes, I saw the ones you brought in earlier."

I sat back in my chair, struggling to find words that would accomplish what I needed without hurting the woman in front of me. "Jane, I have to ask a favor of you. As my friend," I began.

Instantly, her blue eyes widened. "Anything, Ryan. You know that."

"I'm here and I can be a sounding board if you need to talk, but when I have a day off..." My voice trailed off when Jane's breath left in a small huff, and her demeanor became more closed off. *Shit!* "Julia and I are newlyweds, and we don't see each other enough, so on the few days we do get together, I just need to focus on her." *So please don't call.* I left the unsaid words hanging.

I lifted my eyes, and Jane's locked on. I hoped I didn't sound like too much of an asshole. I could keep talking, but I decided to shut the hell up and wait for her response.

"I understand, Ryan. I'm sorry." She sounded contrite and I could see that she was hurt. "I didn't mean to intrude or make Julia feel bad. When Daniel told me he was leaving, I needed a man to talk to. And I knew you'd make me feel less... worthless."

Jane was picking at her food, and I wasn't feeling all that hungry either, but if I didn't eat, I'd pay later. I decided to be more typical. I rolled my eyes and offered a wry expression. "I told you, he's a dick. Caleb is interested in you, Jane. He has a lot more to offer a woman."

She shrugged. "I know he likes me. I've known for a few months."

"He's a good guy. You should give him a chance."

"He's not... I mean the way you came in and knew what was wrong with Mrs. Roseman when he had no clue? That was..." She threw up her hands. "He's not half the doctor you are."

"Thanks, but he's a good doctor and a great guy. You should give him a chance."

Jane shook her head and shifted the subject away from Caleb.

"So, I thought of it first? So what? You can't judge Caleb by my actions. I just studied it 5 months ago."

"I suppose. Should I call Julia and apologize?" she asked sweetly. I felt relieved that she understood my situation so readily and was willing to mend any misunderstandings.

"No, that's okay. We'll work it out."

"Are you two fighting?"

"Not exactly. She was upset on Friday night, but yesterday was good."

Jane leaned her elbows on the table and slid her chair slightly closer to the table. "What are you getting her for Christmas? She mentioned it was a lean year."

A smile lifted the corner of my mouth. "Yeah. We're looking at houses in Brooklyn. I wish I could buy her something amazing, but we did promise each other we wouldn't go crazy."

"And you and Julia are all about keeping promises," Jane stated simply, and I felt she really understood our relationship.

"Yeah. We are."

"So you aren't getting her anything at all?"

I scooped up the last of my meal and hesitated before I took the last bite. "She's out of perfume. I was going to pick it up on my way home the other night, but traffic was insane."

"Traffic is one thing I don't envy about living in the city. Would it help if I pick it up for you? There's a Macy's in Douglaston. Would they have it?"

"I can't ask you to do that."

"Ryan, come on. It's no trouble." We threw our plates in the trash, and I opened the bag of cookies, and she took one. "I'm offering."

"Okay, yeah. If you really don't mind."

As we began the walk between the cafeteria and the ER, I felt a much more at ease.

"No. Just tell me what kind it is and give me the money."

"It's Christian Dior. Je Dur or something." I grinned in bemusement and Jane laughed.

"J'Adore," she corrected. "Do you want just the perfume? Sometimes at Christmas, they have gift sets."

"The most you can get for a couple hundred dollars."

"My cousin has some of that. It's pretty."

"Yeah." I grinned. "That shit drives me crazy."

The perfume wasn't all I planned on giving Julia. I was also writing something to have framed for the baby's room. I'd get home late and Julia would be sleeping, so I'd finish it and tomorrow send it off to Jenna, who'd agreed to take it to the frame shop near the Harvard Campus I'd used four years earlier. It was cutting it close and I'd have to pay extra to rush it and ship it back, but I wasn't finished with it yet because I wanted it to be perfect. The tension between us kept me from working on it, but now I could do it justice.

Walking back to the ER with Jane and no longer hearing what she was saying, my thoughts filled with how close Julia and I would feel when she opened it. I couldn't wait to see the look on her face; surely tears would shimmer in her beautiful eyes as she raised them to mine. My heart swelled to bursting in anticipation. I was certain she'd melt into me and we'd once again be *us*. She was my truth; my safest place on earth.

*****

Once again, it was after midnight when I arrived home and as usual, I was beat. My back ached. After Jane and I returned from our dinner break, we had an automobile accident and five victims, three of them critical, one a three-year-old boy. He made it, but his mother did not. I'd worked on her tirelessly for twenty-five minutes when she flat-lined, but it was useless. She wasn't wearing a seat belt, and her frontal lobe was mashed into the windshield at fifty miles per hour.

Julia stirred when I moved around the dark bedroom. "Ryan, are you here?" Her voice was soft and laced with sleep.

"Yes, baby," I answered, reaching out to rub her back gently through the blanket. We kept it cool in the bedroom; cooler than the rest of the apartment. Julia liked the thick comforter and snuggling close to me, but I was always warm, "Don't wake up. I'll come to bed soon." My fingers played in the dark strands of her hair.

She was on her stomach and turned her face toward me on her pillow. "How was your night?"

"Busy. Not great. Had a car accident victim that didn't make it."

"Oh... I'm sorry, honey." Julia's eyes glittered in the dark and her hair was all messy. She reached for me and I took her hand in mine, bringing it to my lips. She was so soft and alluring, and dead tired or not, my dick stiffened and started to throb. I was sitting on the bed now and hoped Julia didn't notice. It had been my plan to finish the note and then sleep, but my body had other ideas.

"I need to take a shower, babe."

"No, you don't." Julia moved up onto her knees and sat on her heels. One hand held the comforter to her breasts, but her shoulders were bare. I wanted to reach out and yank it from her, exposing the beauty I knew lay beneath. I leaned in to kiss the one closest to me. Her hand wound in my hair and began to gently scratch my scalp. It felt amazing and I let my forehead drop into the curve of her neck. "I can give you a massage."

"Mmm..." I moaned. "That sounds like heaven, but if you touch me, I'll wanna make love."

"I won't be provocative, Ryan. I just want to help you relax."

I huffed against the soft column of her neck. "You can't help it. You provoke me without trying."

"It's not time right now."

I smiled. She was keeping track, just as I was.

"I know."

"You do?" Her lips were so close to mine and I could feel them move against my cheek. My hands began to roam over her shoulders and up around both sides of her face. That beautiful face I adored.

"Of course."

"I didn't think you'd remember because our schedules are so screwy."

I chuckled softly and pulled back to look into her face. A small smile lifted one corner of her mouth, and she nuzzled her nose gently with mine.

"It's baby-time over New Year's." I was probably stinky with bad breath, but I wanted to kiss her more than I wanted to breathe. "Why do I always miss you so much?"

"Because I'm so adorable... and yes, it is over New Years."

My thumb moved across her cheek, and then my mouth followed the path.

"You know I always want to make love to you," I whispered. "When I'm near you, and when I'm not. Every minute; it doesn't matter." I placed a soft kiss on her parted lips, and her chin rose for more, but I climbed from the bed, not even bothering to hide my giant erection. "But I smell like the hospital."

"We don't need to make love... Just let me rub you down and relax you so you can sleep."

"We'll see. You have to work early."

"I don't care. And, I don't care what you smell like," Julia murmured as I walked into the bathroom and began stripping off my scrubs. "Ryan?"

"Just rest, baby. I'll be there soon," I called.

I lingered a little in the shower, allowing the hot water to rush over my skin and pound into my muscles, hoping it would be enough time for my wife to fall back to sleep. I almost fell asleep myself, leaning against the ceramic tile of the stall but then shook my head briskly and turned my face into the water, reaching out to crank it over to cold. The shock certainly did the trick.

Minutes later, I walked back out into the living room, with one towel slung low on my hips and using another to roughly dry my hair. I threw the one aside and rummaged through Julia's art table for a nice piece of paper and one of the ultra-fine markers she used to sign her drawings, before sitting down at the table with my thoughts. The tree lights cast a low glow through the small apartment, and it was enough to see what I was doing.

When I put the pen to paper, I was more concerned with how neatly I was writing than the words that just flew from my heart onto the page.

This Mad, Mad Love... I began. I never seemed at a loss for words to tell Julia what she meant to me, though I didn't think any could do her justice. I crumpled first one and then another sheet until, reading it back, I was satisfied. I tucked the paper away inside her desk, hidden under several of the magazine boards from past issues, and quietly made my way back to the bedroom.

The room was dark except from the residual filtering in from the other rooms. Julia was on her back, lying diagonally on the bed, her hair strewn like a dark halo around her head. I smiled as I dropped my towel and pulled back the cover. I'd have to move her over so I could slide in beside her. I hesitated only seconds before falling to my knees beside the bed.

I wanted to give her pleasure, after the past few days, and to reinforce my devotion and unselfishness in my love for her and to totally obliterate any doubt. The delicious ache began to build at my intention, while I reached beneath the edge of the sheet. Her body heat had warmed them, and the closer my hand got to her, the warmth intensified. My hand slid up her thigh to her hip then back down to curl around the back of her knee. I pulled Julia's lower body toward me and moaned softly.

I didn't want to talk. I didn't want to hear that I needed sleep or how I should let her take care of me. I wanted to taste her, to hear her moan my name as I made her come under my tongue.

Her head moved to one side as both hands slid up her smooth thighs. My hands closed around them and I slid her closer, bringing her horizontal on the bed and perpendicular to where I was at its side, pulling her closer and draping her legs over my shoulders. I turned my head, kissing the inside of her right knee with my open mouth, slightly sucking on her skin.

Julia lifted her head slightly, but she knew what I intended to do. "Ryan." She sighed softly, her legs stiffening as conflict crossed her beautiful features. I could almost hear the words telling me to stop and just hold her before she said them "You don't need..."

"Hush. I do need..." I murmured as I continued a delicious path of the same wet kisses up her leg and toward my goal. She knew how much going down on her excited me, and I knew I could make her writhe and moan within a couple of minutes, or I could take my time and draw it out. I moved, slowly repeating the kisses up her other leg, and she fell back, her legs falling open in surrender. I smiled against the tender flesh of her inner thigh, intoxicated by her scent as one hand flattened on her stomach and then slid up to fold around a full breast, kneading and then teasing the nipple with my fingers. It was already puck-ered, but it grew beneath my touch. I let her anticipation grow, kissing the flat plane of her abdomen below her navel and letting the warmth of my breath blow over her moist, tender flesh. She tensed, the fingers of both hands burying in my hair.

My cock was fully engorged, but her reaction caused my pounding heart to push in more blood until I thought the skin would split. It pulsed with aching need, but my purpose was Julia, not myself. I finally let my tongue lave her, and her breath drew in on a hiss followed by a soft moan, her fingers tugging at my hair. I was hungry and I let her know it, my hands clutching at her breasts and then one sliding down her body over her hip to hold the outside of her thigh. I licked and sucked, first teasing and then increasing the pressure with the flat of my tongue before finally sucking her clit into my mouth. I knew exactly how to pulse the suction to push her over the edge.

"Oh, God," Julia gasped. "Ryan, come inside me. I'm so close…"

I could feel the muscles in her legs begin to tighten and tremor around my head and didn't want to stop. When her back arched in orgasm, I moved up on the bed and dove into her. She was hot, wet, and slick, both from my saliva and her arousal. I thrust into her hard and fast, my fingers curling into the hair on both sides of her head as she rode out her orgasm. I took her mouth hungrily, and she parted her lips, her tongue and mine curling around each other's madly. Her body heaved beneath mine, her internal spasms sucking on my cock with amazing pull. She was tight, and I was so turned on that I couldn't go slow or hold back. The frantic way Julia kissed me and tugged at my hair told me she didn't want me to, and three forceful thrusts later, I came hard, pushing in to the hilt, pouring into her with a low groan. I turned my head to kiss the side of her face, wanting to kiss her mouth again. My body jerked and then stilled, my breath ragged and raspy and Julia's in soft little huffs. My nose traced her face, and then I kissed her deeply, my body pushing into hers, wanting her to feel the passion and love that she alone commanded. Her hands stroked my back and the hair at the nape of my neck. I was reluctant to break the connection, but we were cockeyed on the bed, and the covers were a tangled mess.

"Hold onto me, baby," I demanded softly, and Julia complied. My arm underneath her waist pulled her to me, as I crawled up the bed using one knee. I lowered her down, still beneath me; my eyes intent on hers. They sparkled in the darkness. It was unspoken intensity and love that poured between us, the closeness I depended on like air, once again, in place. I didn't need to say it, but I did anyway. "I love you, so much."

She nodded, the fingers of her right hand curled, and she ran her knuckles down my cheek, never looking away. I kissed her once more, softly; our lips and tongues gently tasting.

My heart filled as I rolled to my side, finally sliding out of her, but pulling her tight against my body, and fell into an exhausted sleep.

Julia ~

It was a week before Christmas, and Ryan and I hadn't seen each other much in the past few days. He worked late, and I left early, so we didn't have much time for conversations, and I had to be content with brief kisses and hugs when he left. He never left without kissing me goodbye, and he'd hold me close if we shared a few hours together in the middle of the night, almost always making love to me.

My body flushed as images of Ryan's lovemaking filled my mind. He was an amazing lover and knew just how to touch or kiss me to turn me into a quivering, helpless mass. Even when I was angry with him, my emotions betrayed me and I had absolutely no choice but to give him every piece of me. Body and soul. The pleasure he gave in the bedroom was insane, but I missed just talking to him; hearing about his day or sharing mine with him. It was like he didn't want to talk to me about the hospital and what went on there. The reason was obvious. Last weekend would have been nearly perfect if it weren't for those damn calls. After the last one, Ryan acted so guilty, and even though we cuddled on the couch, our hands entwined or traced lightly over each other, the conversation died.

Last night, Ryan mentioned, only briefly, that he'd asked Jane to be more judicious in her calls. I didn't question him further, instead choosing to trust that things would get better. It didn't. I could sense Ryan's discomfort every time his phone rang. When he did speak to her, his tone was more understanding than I would have liked. Given her persistence when he was home, I couldn't help but wonder how much she stalked him at the hospital. He barely mentioned her when we were together, throwing me an apologetic look on the two occasions he did pick up. Apparently, she and Daniel split, and she had to find a new place to live, and Ryan, Caleb and a few of the others were going to help her move, and they were all trying to coordinate schedules.

I tried not to let it bother me, but scowled despite my efforts. No doubt she would really turn her attention to Ryan. The hag would probably *accidentally* dump her lingerie drawers out in front of him *on purpose*, I thought bitchily, then felt bad that I would even think such a thing about a woman to whom I owed Ryan's life. It was exhausting fighting with myself all the time.

Snow was falling softly outside, and I had to admit that besides spring, winter was my favorite time in New York. I loved the lights making the snowflakes glisten as they fell and how Central Park was like a huge, sparkly white blanket in the center of the city. I gently pulled out the half-finished portrait from my portfolio, knowing that when Ryan saw it, any distance between us would melt away. I brought soft yellow matting board from work, and the new glass frame sat beside the table ready and waiting to receive its precious consignment. I brought out the portrait; ready to add just a touch of color to the soft lead pencil drawing. I wanted to use watercolors but it required taping the edges down and leaving it out to dry day after day as I slowly added subtle layers of color. That wasn't possible if I wanted to keep it a surprise, so I resorted to soft pastels. I placed soft pinks and yellows on the flesh, blending to create the slightest peachy hue, leaving a slight rosiness to the cheeks and nose.

I was careful not to smudge the delicate lines of the baby's face or muddy up the fine strokes of the hair as I worked to blend in the shades. I glanced down at my masterpiece; an infant version of Ryan's eyes, more rounded and shaded with a dark blue halo around the iris that faded through jade green to a light, faint yellow center surrounding the pupil, looked back at me. It was difficult to put much of myself into the drawing because I wanted so much for the baby to look like Ryan. So besides the blended eye color, I made the shape of the face and a bit of the nose like mine, but the mouth, dimples and eyes were all him.

I wondered if any of our parents suspected that we were trying. I could hear the question in Elyse's tone when I'd called and requested some of Ryan's baby pictures. She seemed only moderately satisfied when I told her that I only wanted some family pictures to make an album for Christmas, her tone brightening when she said she'd send several. My parents were like teenagers again, so caught up in rekindling their romance that they hardly noticed the rest of the world. My heart warmed, and a half smile lifted my lips.

I held the colored chalk between my thumb and index finger and used my ring finger of the same hand to carefully blend, blowing the excess dust off as I went. I concentrated hard on each feature individually, but when I finally lay the colors aside, I was able to look at it as a whole. The baby was breathtakingly beautiful, and my heart literally stopped as I wiped my stained fingers on a towel.

My heart filled with overwhelming love and longing for the baby yet to be conceived; remembering Ryan's words about his little soul waiting for us in heaven. Wow. I prayed I could give him a baby as beautiful as the one I'd created on paper. Excitement raced through me in anticipation of Ryan's reaction when he opened it. I imagined a Christmas as magical as the first one we spent in Estes Park when he'd given me the '*I Love You Because...*' poem. My intent was to hang it, right beside this portrait in the nursery. It seemed fitting, and I was certain Ryan would agree.

By the time I was ready for bed, the picture was framed and matted. Since I only had two gifts for him this year, I made sure this one was beautifully wrapped with gold foil paper and red gossamer ribbons.

Turning a small circle in the middle of the apartment, I looked for a place to hide it so Ryan wouldn't find it. Under the tree were the gifts the families had sent, along with the pair of shoes I bought Ryan, but this package would be recognizable as a framed picture, so it wanted to keep it out of site until the very last minute. A big smile slid across my mouth. I couldn't wait to give this to him.

Ryan would like the shoes, and he'd be disappointed at the impersonal nature of the gift. He'd conceal it well enough; but I knew him through and through. His eyes would flood with tears when he looked at the image of our future baby, not only because of the subject matter or that I'd drawn it, but because it would prove that I was ready and wanted a baby as much as he did. My throat tightened, and the back of my eyes burned at the thought. I didn't know how I could ever love him more, but every day that passed, I did.

Suddenly, it dawned on me where to hide the package.

~9~

Ryan ~

After my conversation with Jane, I felt better, confident there weren't any misunderstandings. Jane reinforced that belief five days later when she walked into the ER with a Macy's bag with Julia's perfume already wrapped inside. I was grateful for the help, and it was easy to slip the gift underneath the tree later that evening when Julia was working late.

I couldn't help digging around underneath and found a rectangular package with my name on it. It made a loud but dull thump when I shook it. After placing it back under the tree in exactly the place I found it, I brought out the padded envelope that Jenna had shipped by FedEx to the hospital. I opened it with rapt anticipation.

I let out my breath when I held it in my hands. Jenna had the framer shadow my writing with crimson so it looked like the red letters floated and my original writing was their shadow. The frame was muted gold, and the document was double-matted in the same shade of gold but with the crimson showing from the edge of the oval opening around the words. It turned out much better than I'd expected, and I couldn't stop grinning from ear to ear as I looked at it. Julia would probably bawl her eyes out, I thought happily with a low laugh. She'd love the shit out of it.

When Christmas Eve rolled around, I was jumping out of my skin to get home to her. She wasn't expecting me, so I'd screwed myself out of whatever meal she would have made if she'd known I was coming, but I didn't care. She worked hard and deserved to relax as much as I did.

The subway was crowded with people jostling packages as they made their way through the turnstiles and onto the trains. It was interesting to watch them and listen to the conversations of those near me, the expressions ranging from contented joy to weary skepticism. The movement of the train on the tracks and the many conversations was loud. A black woman was sitting across from me, her arm wrapped around a little boy about five or six. He was noticing my scrub pants beneath my parka, and when his eyes met mine, he shyly hid his face in his mother's side.

I smiled at the woman and she nodded in the boy's direction with a chuckle. "He's shy now, but when we get home, whoo-eee! Beneath that sweet face? He's a terror to behold."

My lips quirked. "But not tonight, though, right?" I directed my comment to the boy. He peeked out from his mother's side with one eye. "Santa Claus is coming."

He nodded and regarded me more openly. "You a doctor?" he asked bravely.

"I am. My name's Ryan. What's yours?" I held out my hand to shake his.

"Christopher." His dark eyes darted to his mother, and when she nodded her approval, he placed his little hand in mine.

"Nice to meet you, Christopher."

"Nice to meet you, Dr. Ryan." He shook my hand hard, and I couldn't help but laugh out loud at his serious expression, like he was trying to be so grown up. "Do you have kids?"

"Not yet, but I'd like to."

After that, he lost his shyness and spent the remainder of the trip next to me telling me about what he wanted from Santa and firing a hundred questions about the hospital and my job. His eyes lit up with exuberance up when he described a remote-control helicopter that he wanted. I glanced at his mom, and she nodded imperceptibly to the affirmative. *Santa* was going to deliver as hoped. The trip flew by and I found myself hoping I'd encounter them again. When I was about to leave, I shook his hand again.

"If I get sick, can you fix me?" Christopher asked.

"It would be my honor, Christopher." I patted the side of his cheek and told his mother the name of the hospital seconds before the train was pulling to a stop at my station. "Merry Christmas!"

Minutes later, I was rushing the last few blocks to our apartment building. It was snowing lightly. I felt great; excited to surprise Julia and anxious to give her the gifts. It didn't matter that we weren't having a huge Christmas, I was happy as hell. The only thing that could have made it better was seeing some of my family, but on the other hand, it was nice having this first Christmas as a married couple alone.

I didn't bother sneaking in, and burst loudly through the door, startling Julia in the kitchen. The apartment smelled wonderful, all ginger and some sort of roasting meat. The clatter of something dropping in the stainless steel sink interrupted White Christmas playing on the stereo.

"Ryan! You scared the crap out of me!"

I shrugged out of my coat and rushed to her, gathering her close. She had some sort of light green glop splattered on her face and in her hair. Her eyes were wide as I licked at a spot of the stuff on her cheek. It was sweet and hinted slightly of almonds.

"Yum," I said devilishly before my head swooped and I took her mouth in a deep kiss. She was still and slightly stiff in

my arms, frozen by the shock of seeing me, holding tight to a
wooden spoon filled with more green stuff. She relaxed instantly, her lips parting and coming alive with mine. I alternated
between hard kisses and light teasing ones, enjoying the luxury
of taking my time.

"As much as I want to," she said between kisses. "I can't
stand here and make out. I'm in the middle of something," she
protested, less than convincingly. A bright smile split her face.
"What are you doing home?"

I held her in the circle of my arms, unwilling to let her go.
Her green eyes sparkled up at me and her cheeks were flushed
nicely. "I begged to have part of the evening off to surprise you.
You look beautiful." My eyes roamed over her face and landed
on another big glop of the frosting in her hair. I smiled down at
her and squeezed her ass playfully. "Merry Christmas."

Julia giggled and hugged me back. I glanced over my
shoulder, looking for the spoon and wondering if she was going
to do something mean with it. "Don't even think about it," I
snorted.

She moved out of my arms reluctantly. "Come sit in here
with me while I finish. Unless you'd like to take a shower?"

I went behind her, sliding an arm under hers so I could stick
my finger in the bowl and get more of the sweet stuff. "I'll
shower later," I mumbled, putting my laden finger in my mouth.
"It tastes like almonds, so why is it green?"

"Duh! It's Christmas, right?" she scoffed, glancing up with
a smile. "I wanted to try something different. The frosting has
almond paste and I used a little Amaretto in the simple syrup.
I'm doing a slight variation on Red Velvet. Too bad my dad's
not here," she said with a sigh. "He'd love this."

I sat down on the stool nearest her and watched her deftly
slice the two deep red cake layers into four and pile the frosting

between them. "Yeah. Have you talked to your parents tonight?"
I watched her work to finish the cake, my hand reached out to
rub up and down her back.

Julia shook her head, and a lock of hair fell forward from
behind here ear. "Not yet. It's early there. I have plenty of time
to call, and I wanted to wait for you. Mom, especially, will want
to talk to her *son*."

I huffed softly, a half-smile lifting my lips slightly. "It's
really great that they're back together. You could have gone
home, you know. Just because my schedule is merciless, it's no
reason for you to miss your family."

She frowned and shook her head, not bothering to look up
from finishing the cake.

"You know I'd never leave on our first Christmas." Julia's
expression was wistful as she set the finished cake aside.

"But... it's not our first Christmas," I voiced her thoughts
aloud.

Julia turned toward me and laced her arms around my neck.
I pulled her closer between my knees and pushed the hair back
from her face, my fingers lingering in the soft strands.

"Right, it isn't, but we're married, and I wouldn't think of
leaving you on any Christmas." Her eyes were soft and full of
love. "Got it?"

I nodded and kissed her temple. Her skin was warm, the
scent of her shampoo and her skin filled my nostrils. "Yes,
ma'am." Her arms tightened and I allowed myself to just enjoy
holding her. "I'm sorry for all the shit with Jane." I felt it needed
to be said but wondered if this was the right time.

Julia's arms tightened and her lips found the pulse at the
base of my neck. I kissed the side of her face and then the top of
her head. No other words about the subject were necessary.
"When do I get my present?"

Instantly, she pulled back, her face full of amused skepticism, her eyebrow shooting up. "Have you been snooping under the tree, Matthews?"

I shook my head, my lips flattening together. "Who... What? Me?" I grinned, and she shoved my shoulder with her hand and moved away from me to open the oven. My stomach grumbled.

"Yes, *you*. You're worse than a kid."

I moved up behind her to look into the pan. It was a perfectly roasted beef tenderloin covered with some sort of herby crust and sitting in about an inch of dark au jus. "That looks amazing. I thought I'd show up unannounced and be faced with peanut butter and jelly sandwiches."

She lifted the beautiful roast onto a wooden cutting board, leaving it to rest. I started to pick at it, but she tapped the top of my knuckles with the metal tongs in her right hand.

"Hey!" I protested, pulling the stinging appendage back.

"I made this for the coming week. I will be busy with the last minute details of the gala and I don't want you to starve. I have several meals planned with the leftovers; stroganoff, barbeque sandwiches..." she paused and looked at me, waving the tongs around. "What will you survive on if I let you eat it all tonight?" Her voice was teasing.

"I can't have any of it?" I wrapped my arms around her from behind, blocking her from removing the potatoes from the oven. I moved the curtain of her hair to one side and nibbled on the cord of her neck. "Not even a little taste?" I smiled when she arched to allow more access to the skin I was kissing.

"Not until I finish the sauce. Open the wine, please." I ran my hands up and down her arms, not really wanting to stop touching her, but went to do her bidding.

Dinner was delicious. Julia made some sort of sauce with shallots, cognac and butter that oozed in rich goodness over the meat and the roasted potatoes were amazing. I wasn't a fan of spinach, but she did a quick sauté of some sort, and I had to admit, even that was delicious.

I was finishing a second helping of the beef. "So speaking of the gala... will Turner be there?"

Julia gave an amused snort. "Of course, do you really need to ask? We'll have a feature in the February issue, so he'll be taking pictures most of the evening. Why? Are you missing him?"

I rolled my eyes. "Oh, yes, definitely. Can't wait," I said dryly.

"He's really turned out to be a good guy, Ryan. You and Mike should be friends."

"Sure. I'd make time for a dude that's seen my wife almost naked, if I can work him in between the patients. Oh, wait, I'm already busy using those five minutes to make love to my wife. Sooorrrryyy, Turner!" I lifted my shoulders in an over-exaggerated shrug.

Julia removed my plate and took it along with hers to the kitchen, as I reached for the cabernet to refill our glasses. "You're impossible," she muttered. "Maybe we could introduce him to Jane, now that she's unattached."

I paused, mulling it over. She wasn't interested at all in Caleb, despite his crush on her. Maybe she'd be more receptive to someone flashier like Turner. I didn't comment because I thought the subject of Jane was taboo and was surprised that Julia would mention her.

"Come here," I called. Julia came to me and straddled my lap, her arms slid around my neck and her feet dangled on either side of my legs. I smiled wide as she wiggled on my lap.

"Time for dessert," she giggled. I pulled her hips flush with mine and wrapped my arms around her in a tight hug, turning my face into the curve between her shoulder and neck.

"You feel really good," I murmured, letting my hands lightly roam the contours of her hips and up her back. I stared into her face. She was glancing down, then lazily lifted her eyes to meet mine in a hooded gaze and all of the amusement vanished. Her teeth came out to bite her lower lip and she rubbed against me; my body sprang to life. My nose grazed the side of her face and I opened my lips over the fine bone in her cheek. "I can't even touch you without getting hard." I pulled her flush again and could feel her heat radiating through our clothes.

"I miss you… and hard works well for me right now," she whispered. I covered her mouth with a groan, letting my tongue dive in to taste her sweetness. I pressed her groin to mine, one hand behind her hips and one sliding up the center of her back to cup the back of her head under her hair. Julia responded by sucking on my tongue and rocking her hips into mine. My dick throbbed and pressed against her, seeking something to relieve the ache.

It felt like we were two kids in high school making out at the kitchen table between algebra and social studies homework, both of us trying to communicate all the frantic urgency we were feeling through our hands and mouths, and grinding of our hips. We took turns giving and receiving, something we'd become masters of. When I sucked on her top lip, she sucked gently on my bottom one. My heart rate increased, and I could feel Julia's pulse push against the soft skin at her throat. It didn't take long, and we were both panting. I sat up straighter and cradled both sides of her face in my hands. I didn't even care if we had sex. I just wanted to keep kissing her for hours.

A few minutes later, Julia lifted her head to rest her fore-head against mine, her breathing coming in soft, rapid pants. My mouth wandered along her jaw. "Is this my present? Because I love it."

"You know there's another one. It's not much. It was hard not buying you something big."

I pulled back then and looked up into her face. "This," I wrapped both of my hands around her butt cheeks and squeezed, "is my big present." Her eyes widened, and I laughed. "That's *not* what I meant. Your ass is perfect. Perfect fit for my hands. See?" I squeezed again, and Julia's expression softened into a smile but mine sobered. She was so beautiful in the soft glow illuminated from the combination of the fire, candles, and the tree. "I meant just being with you," I said seriously. "How about a game of Truth or Dare, later?"

"Why not now?" Julia asked before her mouth closed hotly over mine. She writhed against me again, and our kisses grew more heated. When her tongue swirled around mine in a passionate dance and she moved on me with practiced rhythm she knew drove me mad, I thought I'd come right there. I smoothed back her hair with both hands, my thumbs coming to tilt her mouth up so I could kiss her more deeply.

The doorman buzzed into the apartment and broke into our bubble. We were both startled, and Julia jumped in my arms. I let out a low groan in protest. "It's probably something from my folks. But the timing blows."

"I'll be right back." She dropped a brief kiss on my mouth. My head fell back as Julia jumped off my lap and ran to the door, pressing down the button and speaking into it.

"Yes?"

"Mrs. Matthews, you have a visitor, ma'am."

"Who is it, please?"

"Miss Cooper, ma'am."

Are you fucking kidding me! What was Jane doing here? I watched Julia's happy mood fall off her with the suddenness of an avalanche, and she turned a stony face toward me. Seconds later, her expression was an angry mask as she waited for me to say something.

"Ma'am?" the attendant asked again. Her finger let go of the intercom.

I took a breath and shook my head, getting up to walk over to stand beside Julia.

Her eyes shot daggers at me, but she didn't say a damn word and stomped away when I reached her. "Babe, I didn't invite her."

"It doesn't seem to matter, Ryan!" She turned back to me and hissed. "She takes too much for granted!" I opened my mouth to respond, but Julia cut me off. "Don't you dare say we owe her!"

"I was going to say… it's Christmas. And she has no one, now."

Julia laughed bitterly. "Wrong. Obviously, she has you!" she huffed and stormed off down the hall.

I stood there struggling with what to do next. It would be rude to ignore Jane now that she knew we were home. The door to the bedroom slammed with a resounding bang that shook the walls. I couldn't help the flinch it elicited.

I pushed the buzzer. "Okay. Please send her up."

I leaned against the door waiting the 45 seconds it would take Jane to ride up the elevator, pinching the bridge of my nose. I was fucked, either way. I'd be an asshole if I hadn't allowed her up, and I was an asshole if I did. Maybe whatever Jane's reason for stopping over would conclude quickly, and I could try to soothe Julia's ruffled feathers and salvage what I could of the evening. My thoughts turned to the framed poem under the tree.

"Goddamn it to Hell!" I muttered under my breath just before Jane knocked on the door. I ran a hand over my face and then through my hair, willing my face to be welcoming and not exuding the anger I was feeling. Fuck, I didn't know who I was mad at. Jane probably had good intentions, but I'd just explained things to her. And Julia... she was being ungracious as hell, everything considered.

I took a calming breath and opened the door. "Hi, Jane." She walked past me, scanning the inside of the apartment while carrying a green and red wrapped package and another bag that was obviously a bottle of wine.

"I'm sorry to stop by unannounced, Ryan. But, you left so fast, I didn't have an opportunity to give you the gift I have for you." Jane walked past me, and I was at a loss as to what to say. I didn't want the gift. I glanced nervously down the hall. No way in hell could I accept it, but Jane would be hurt if I refused.

I walked slowly behind her into the main part of the apartment, both of my hands lifting to fist in my hair. I quickly lowered them when she turned around. "Where is Julia?"

"She's... in the other room. Jane, we didn't talk about a gift exchange, and I feel bad cause..." I began.

She waved away my objection. "Oh, Ryan this is really nothing. You both mentioned that, well, I mean... I just wanted to contribute something to your Christmas. This is for you." She handed me the box, and my fingers automatically closed around it. "I brought Julia some wine. I didn't know what else to get her."

"It was unnecessary."

"I..." she looked up at me, and it occurred to me that I should take her coat and ask her to sit down. "I wanted to have a little piece of Christmas." My heart felt for her, and I glanced down briefly before meeting her eyes again.

"Jane, let me take your coat, and I'll go see what's keeping Julia." By the time I'd helped her out of her coat, Julia was leaning against the wall at the end of the hall, watching us. She wore a somewhat pinched expression; I could see the anger mixed with disappointment cross her features.

"Hello, Jane. Did you just leave the hospital?"

"A little while ago. I just wanted to stop by on my way home."

Julia nodded and came into the room. "Can I get you something to drink?"

"Oh!" Jane scrambled to retrieve the bag next to her. "I brought some wine, but I don't want to interrupt your evening."

"Don't be silly, it's sweet of you to stop by." A plastic smile pasted on Julia's face, then she disappeared into the kitchen with the wine. I stood there looking after my wife then back to Jane, who was now sitting in front of me.

"Excuse me a moment, won't you, Jane?" I found Julia pulling angrily at the foil around the neck of the bottle. "Honey, can I help you?"

Her eyes shot venom as she flashed the bottle so I could see the label. I flushed that it was my new cheap favorite merlot. I shrugged uncomfortably. "Coincidence."

Julia's lips pressed together in a firm line the entire time she worked the cork out of the bottle with the corkscrew and reached for three glasses.

"Oh, I'm sure the planets all aligned. I'm sure a choir of angels will begin their serenade momentarily." Her voice took on a sugary tone, yet sarcasm laced each word. She handed me two of the glasses and picked up the other with the bottle, motioning with her head that I should precede her into the other room. I started to get pissed myself. It wasn't like I'd planned this or asked Jane to be here, and Julia could damn well acknowledge that!

When I'd handed Jane the wine, Julia took a seat in the single chair at the end of the sofa, forcing me to take the end of the couch between her and Jane.

"Aren't you going to open your gift, hon?" Julia asked sweetly, wrinkling her nose at me. If the situation weren't so infuriating, I would have laughed my ass off.

As it was, the hair on the back of my neck stood up in agitation. Julia was leaving the door wide open, acting like she was fine, but I could see her seething. It was all I could do to sit there and not jump out of my skin. Jane picked the gift up off the coffee table and handed it to me.

I looked at it, concentrating on the holly pattern in the paper. *What the fuck?* All I knew was I wanted this over with. My hands began ripping at the wrapping.

Julia ~

I sat there watching Ryan accepting the gift from Jane, wanting to claw at her face the way Ryan was ripping at the wrapping paper. I took a long pull on my wine, emptying the glass and refilling it without taking my eyes off Jane. Couldn't she see that she was interrupting something? I could feel my heart beating; not in the excited, yummy way, but the sickening thud that felt like it was falling down a notch in your chest. My face must be red, because it felt like it was on fire. I could feel the heat moving up from my chest, over my cheeks, and toward my hairline. I inhaled until my lungs couldn't hold anymore.

Ryan's eyes touched mine briefly before he looked back down at the box in his hands. He was acting guilty as hell... I could see it all over him. And he could see I was fuming.

It was a shoebox. Perfect. I knew I shouldn't have told her what I was giving him. Lesson one when you know a woman was after your man: *Don't fucking talk to her about personal shit!* She came off so innocent and needy, but this was a calculated move to ruin Christmas between Ryan and me. *You little bitch! And why the hell is Ryan even accepting it?* My mind screamed.

When he opened the box, a pair of the ugliest shoes I'd ever seen lay inside. Ryan lifted one out and examined it. It looked like an old man's dress shoe crossed with a sneaker.

"They're Finns." Jane explained when Ryan didn't speak right away. She appeared to fidget a little when he wasn't all thankful and gushing, but if he knew what was good for him, he'd reign that shit in. "I... ugh, I didn't know the exact size, but the shoe salesman told me the average size for men was between eight and ten, so... I guessed, but you can exchange them if you need too. A lot of hospital personnel wear them."

Ryan's mouth opened, but I cut him off. "Ryan is anything but average," I snapped. Her eyes darted to mine and hardened. It was obvious she knew I was on to her not-so-covert ploy. I was sitting on the arm of the chair with one elbow on my knee and my wine glass in the other. I gulped it down and jumped up to refill it.

"They're too expensive, Jane. I can't..."

"Please don't say you can't accept them, Ryan. You've been so supportive, and I just wanted to say thank you." Her hand reached for Ryan's, and I wanted to rake my nails across her creamy skin hard enough to draw blood. When he didn't pull away immediately, my eyes widened and my head cocked slightly as his gaze met mine.

"I told you. I wanted to give someone something so it would at least seem like Christmas," Jane cooed. The expression she gave to Ryan was soft and pleading. I felt the bile rise up in my throat. I got up and almost vaulted into the kitchen trying to get my emotions under control. It wasn't his fault she showed up, but I was so mad at him. He had to know this was killing me! And, I felt venomous toward Jane. The bottle of wine Jane brought was near empty in the other room, so I opened the refrigerator and pulled out the half bottle of Chardonnay sitting on the shelf. I filled my glass to the rim and gulped half of it down in three big swallows. I was getting tipsy, and I was welcomed the slight buzz. I'd do anything to ease the painful black hole in my chest.

Maybe if I was numb, I wouldn't scream at Jane; or Ryan. Jealousy ate at me, sure, but I was disappointed in a huge way. Tonight started out so amazing but had turned to total crap. What could have been a beautiful, intimate experience was ruined. *Again.* I was through being gracious and understanding. Goddammit! Jane was out to get him, and I could see it clearly, even if Ryan couldn't. I glanced down at the counter and huffed. How could she weasel her way between us? If she was this blatant in front of me, what the hell was she like when I wasn't around? A shudder ran through me at the thought.

I set the glass down at a sound by the door. Ryan was helping Jane on with her coat. I walked over to lean on the doorjamb that connected the kitchen to the front entryway and watched Ryan hand Jane thirty dollars cash and give her a brief hug before opening the door. *What the fuck?*

"Goodbye, Jane." I forced myself to speak to her, but my words sounded a bit slurred. My head was starting to swim.

Jane offered me an acid smile that I could see right through. I returned it with equal venom. When did sweet little Jane turn into this? I laughed bitterly, my shoulder slipping off the wall. Ryan caught me, but I moved away, not wanting him to touch

me. His expression soured, his brow furrowing, and jaw hardening. *Well fuck him. Let him go play with Jane and his ugly damn
shoes!*

"Merry Christmas, Julia. I hope you enjoy the perfume."

Wait, what? My chin jutted out and I glanced between Ryan
and Jane as he opened the door, carefully watching Ryan's reac-
tions. He looked pissed.

"Jane, seriously?" Ryan motioned to the wrapped packages
under the tree.

"Oh, sorry." Her cloying response didn't fool either one of
us.

Ryan opened the door. "Make sure to get a cab, Jane. No
subway tonight." Ryan's voice was tight.

She reached out to touch the front of his shirt, her fingers
lingering on the fabric a little too long. I watched it happen in
slow motion. She nodded and murmured something I couldn't
hear past the blood rushing in my ears. When the door closed
behind her, I turned abruptly to go find more wine.

"Julia, you've had enough." Ryan's voice was soft but firm
behind me.

I finished the wine and reached for the bottle, laughing
lightly. "Oh, you can say that again."

Ryan came forward and roughly yanked the bottle from my
fingers. "You're drunk."

I scowled at him. "What do you care?" I huffed angrily.

"I want to give you your gifts. Come on." He sounded stiff,
and I couldn't decide if I wanted to scream furiously at him or
fall down crying. Tonight was ruined. Did he think I wanted to
exchange the gifts now? His hand closed around my wrist, and I
pulled it away like his touch burned.

"I don't feel like it, Ryan!"

"You know I didn't invite her here."

"So what? I don't feel like celebrating anymore." My answer was abrupt. I pushed away from the counter and went to sit next to the tree. I pulled the presents out one by one, sorting the ones from our parents and friends into two piles, leaving two under the tree. I put a hand to my head, feeling a little dizzy. Ryan came to sit on the couch near me, leaning forward, his elbows on his knees, watching.

I shoved one pile at him. "You want presents? Here ya go." My eyes finally filled with frustrated tears. I felt sorry for myself, sorry for the loss of the evening, sorry that I couldn't control this horrible jealousy or how angry I was.

Ryan scooted off the couch to sit Indian-style on the floor next to me and pointed to one of the two gifts left under the tree. "I want that one." He was trying to move past the last hour and a half, but I was still defensive and upset.

My chin quivered and two tears tumbled down my face as it crumpled. "No, you don't!"

"Yes, I do." His fingers reached out to graze my forearm in a peace offering.

I sniffed and sat up straighter, pushing the tears off my face with both hands. "Really? Okay." I reached for the gift, childishly ripping off the wrapping and dumping the contents of the Nike box in his lap.

"Another coincidence, right?" I sat back on my heels and stared at him, tears blurring my vision. "Right? Only these aren't four hundred dollars, and they'll fit."

Ryan pushed the shoes to the floor, and his fingers curled around my wrist, pulling me toward him. The lights were still low, but the votive candles were mostly burned out and all that was left was the soft glow from the tree. Despite my anger, I couldn't help notice the way the lights cast shadows on the perfect planes of his face, emphasizing the strength in his jaw and brow.

"They're perfect. Honey, I said I'm sorry she showed up." He tugged on my arm again. I wanted to go to him, my heart needed the comfort of his arms, but my brain was still defiant and angry. "Please don't let her ruin tonight."

"You said you talked to her!" My eyes flashed. "I'm sick of this, Ryan."

"I did, but it's Christmas, and she's alone."

"Yeah! It's OUR Christmas! Instead of lecturing me on how she's all alone, how 'bout you understand how invaded and cheated I feel!" I stood up and walked away then turned back and looked down at him, still on the floor in front of the tree and piles of gifts. "We should be making love right now, but instead, I don't think I can stand it if you touch me tonight." I overlapped both hands on my forehead and closed my eyes, swallowing the lump in my throat and willing myself not to cry.

When I looked down, Ryan's head bowed, and he ran one hand through his hair. My heart squeezed; he was tired and looked defeated when he finally looked up at me. "After everything we've been through together, you don't trust me?"

"This has nothing to do with trust."

"It has Goddamn *everything* to do with it!" He didn't shout, but his voice was loaded with anger and he quickly rose to his feet. His expression was pained and pissed. I threw up my hands.

"As amazing as you can be, Ryan, I sometimes forget that you're just a man. Instead of trying to turn this around on me, why don't you see it for what it is? You let her ruin this for us!"

"I haven't done one damn thing to encourage her, Julia!"

"Well, apparently you aren't great at discouraging her, either."

"I don't treat her any Goddamn different than I do any of the people I work with!" Ryan was yelling now.

"Are you sure about that? I don't see any of them showing up unannounced."

"This is bullshit, Julia! We could pick up right where we left off if you weren't so…" The muscle in Ryan's jaw was twitching and his fists were clenched.

"If I wasn't what? Right?" I waited for him to rail back at me, but he just glared at me, seething, his chest visibly rising and falling. Well, it served him right!

"Truth or Dare, Ryan?"

He didn't answer. "You said you wanted to play, so I'll start. I dare you to make it one damn day without letting that woman come between us." His eyes filled with something closer to hatred than I'd ever seen. "Don't want to do that? Okay." I taunted when he wouldn't answer. "Truth. Do I have to run out in the middle of the night and get myself raped or hurt to put me back on an even playing field with that bitch?"

"Shut the fuck up! I won't hear more of that crap!" He rushed at me and grabbed both of my arms and shook me roughly. His fingers dug into my flesh painfully. "Just stop it!"

I went limp in his arms, staring blankly up at him. He looked shocked that he'd touched me in anger and his hold loosened. "You're hurting me," I said stoically. "Let go." When Ryan's hands fell away, I turned my back on him. "I'm done fighting about this," I said weakly. "I gather that gift under the tree is perfume?"

He nodded wearily and bent to retrieve it, fingering the bow on the top without looking at me. I couldn't see his eyes, but his throat was working overtime.

"You told her what you were getting me for Christmas?" I huffed, "I did too, and she totally fucked me."

He seemed as defeated as I felt. "Jane picked it up for me. I couldn't seem to find the time, and she offered. I was talking to her about you and I..."

My throat constricted painfully, and I licked my lips, hurt that this woman was infiltrating us so deeply that she was even buying my Christmas gifts in Ryan's stead.

"Why don't you give it to your girlfriend?" I asked softly, leaving Ryan holding the gift before disappearing down the hall and closing my bedroom door softly behind me. I didn't have the energy to slam it.

*****

The week between Christmas and New Years was bearable, because between the gala and working on the mock-up for the March issue, I was completely immersed in work. Meredith came into town a few days early for meetings with my boss and the big bosses upstairs.

She popped into my office on Tuesday, unexpectedly asking me to lunch. I looked up from my piles of work and welcomed the reprieve, though I still had to come up with layouts for three feature articles. She looked amazing and chic, as usual, in a black suit and vibrant orange blouse; finished off by chunky costume jewelry that probably cost as much as the real stuff. Her hair was cut in a modern short style.

I rose from the desk to hug her. I was acutely aware of the bags under my eyes and the locks of hair that had worked their way loose from my up-do. Messy buns were in, but this was a case of not giving a shit after a sleepless night.

"Wow! What the hell happened to you?" Meredith asked. "Is that sorry excuse for a publisher, John, working you too hard? I'll go back upstairs and beat his ass!"

I couldn't help but smile as I hugged the smaller woman. I was small, but she was waif-thin.

"I'm working hard, sure, but not because of John. You look fantastic! I love your hair cut!"

Meredith patted the back of her head. "I finally caved. When you get to a certain age, I guess you have to chop it all off."

I rolled my eyes. "You're not of that age. Give me a break!"

"Thank you, darling! There are so many reasons I love you. Get your coat. I'm taking you to lunch at Butter."

"Meredith, that's so far from the office," I protested. "I have too much to do."

"Nonsense. I have a car waiting. Come on." She waved me toward the door, and less than half an hour later, we were being seated in the posh restaurant.

"I make it a point to come here every time I'm in New York."

We both ordered iced tea, and as I was glancing at the menu trying to determine what I could order that would allow me to take half home to Ryan, Meredith cleared her throat.

She set her menu aside. "Are you going to tell me what's up?"

I met her eyes, lifting my brows, and shaking my head. "Nothing. The event will go off without a hitch. We've got it all organized. Andrea will have the final head count to the caterer tomorrow."

Meredith sighed and rolled her eyes. "Julia," she said, exasperated, "I've worked with you for years. I know a little thing like a Lincoln Center party wouldn't give you sleepless nights."

I flushed guiltily but shook my head and lifted my shoulders in a way that said 'I don't know what you're talking about.' "I'm fine."

"Fine?" she said, disbelieving. "That's a four letter word, if I ever heard one."

"Yes." Things between Ryan and I were the worst they'd ever been, and I didn't want to get into it. I was almost thankful he had to work Christmas Day because it allowed me to call my mom and cry my eyes out. Ryan slept on the couch for three nights without a word of discussion, and I hadn't seen much of him. I missed him, but I wasn't sure how to heal the wound.

The waiter came and I ordered the rack of lamb and Meredith—the seared shrimp.

As soon as we were alone again, Meredith leaned back in her chair and eyed me skeptically. "I know that is all bullshit, Julia. But, if you insist you're fine, then it's the perfect time for me to tell you that I still want you to go to Paris. I still need you over there. I'm not happy with the team we have in place. I know you could do so much better, and God knows, we need higher circulation numbers."

I carefully set down my glass of iced tea and contemplated what to say. "Are you asking me to go help out on an issue or two or what?"

She looked at me like I was crazy. "No. I'm asking you to go over there and take over."

"Meredith… maybe if it were for a month or so, but not for longer."

She signed deeply. "Why?"

"Because, Ryan and I are trying to have a baby."

"Oh, Jesus! Then now is the time to go. You won't once you're pregnant, Julia."

"I know, I just… I don't know…" I stammered. "We're having problems, and now isn't a good time to leave."

"For God's sake, Julia! Why are you trying to start a family when you're not getting along with Ryan? A kid isn't going to fix it."

My fingers wadded up the napkin in my lap. "I don't know. When we decided to have a baby, we weren't having problems. Besides that, my best friend is going through a lot, and she needs me, too."

"This is your job and your future."

"Ryan is my future."

"I never will understand you. I'm handing you what you said you wanted since the day I hired you."

I knew I'd have to tell her everything. "It is. And I appreciate it, I really do. But..."

By the time we were through lunch and the waiter was boxing up the majority of my entrée, Meredith knew the entire story of Jane, from the gang incident all the way through Christmas Eve. Somehow, I manage to keep my voice fairly even and the tears at bay.

"Men can be blind, but given Ryan's looks, you'd think his eyes would be open." She threw her napkin on the table. "Maybe he's a little too secure, Julia. Maybe you leaving for Paris is what he needs; a wake-up call of sorts. And you could use the time to get your head on straight. If you're not going to tell that bitch off, I might do it for you."

"We'll see how it goes."

"I can't wait forever. If the current team doesn't turn things around, I'll have to get someone else in there. If that someone isn't going to be you, it will be someone. This opportunity has a shelf-life, just so you know, Julia."

"Okay, that's fair."

"It would be terrible if you lost this chance and yet you and Ryan still didn't make it."

My stomach lurched. She was right. Despite my declaration that my future was with Ryan, this was the first time ever that separation seemed like a real possibility. The thought dug away at my insides and I thought I might get physically ill. I couldn't take much more of the current situation. I wasn't sleeping or eating well, when I was eating at all. Work was the only thing that helped at all. Something had to give.

Ryan ~

My wife and I were barely speaking, and it was driving me insane. Christmas Eve was the worst night of my life, left frozen next to the tree, anger and resentment nailing me to the floor. I just couldn't beg forgiveness when I didn't do anything wrong. As the week progressed, I felt listless and empty; completely miserable. I was still pissed, but I wasn't sure at whom or what exactly; there were so many choices. I wanted to fucking kill something. I was snappy at work, practically snarling at Jane when I returned the shoes.

"I can't accept these, Jane. Thank you for the gesture."

"But, Ryan," she began, but I cut her off abruptly and was oblivious to the pain on her face.

"I said I can't take them, Jane."

"I want you to have them..."

"I don't want them! You're not my wife!" I shouted angrily, surprised at my own outburst.

I left Jane standing in the middle of the ER amid all the rest of the staff looking on in shock. Later, I felt bad about it, but I was suffocating when I was around her, like she was sucking the life right out of me. If I was honest with myself, I'd admit that she was. If I lost Julia over this, I might as well have died at the hands of those thugs. I wanted to call my dad, but my mood was so waspish, I'd probably come off pissy, and I didn't really feel like regurgitating the entire fucking mess, nor did I need to dump my problems in his lap. He'd probably just tell me to man up and deal, and I'd be even more pissed. Caleb tried to ask me about it, but he shut up when I told him I didn't want to discuss my personal life at the hospital.

The past week, Julia still made sure I was fed, even packed my lunch, but I was sleeping on the couch, and when we did happen to be home at the same time, I hated the haunted look in her eyes. Our conversations were uncomfortable and stilted. I felt alienated from her, and it made my heart hurt. She stayed far enough away from me that I couldn't pull her into my arms and erase all of this shit. We didn't touch at all, and it was killing me. This was the worst fight we'd ever had. These were the only nights she hadn't been next to me since the two weeks right before our wedding when she went to New York and I stayed in Boston; or, when she had a trip for work.

I hadn't given her the poem. Everyday I wanted to, but I needed it to mean as much to her as it did to me, and I just couldn't give it to her when we were fighting. I'd opened the perfume and left it on her dresser in place of the empty bottle. She used it, because I could smell it lingering in the house when I came home and she was still at work. I missed her more than I could stand.

It was New Year's Eve and Julia's gala was tonight. I hoped I could make tonight as spectacular as I wanted it to be. Julia was required to stay until the party was almost over, but the plan was to make the most of the rest of the evening. I'd been unable to take Julia on a honeymoon, and since we were trying to conceive, I made reservations at the Waldorf Astoria over two months ago. The room had a Jacuzzi and a big king bed, and I'd arranged for champagne and strawberries to be waiting just after midnight, the room filled with candlelight, roses, and our favorite sexy playlist playing on the stereo. It was meant to be perfect and magically romantic.

When my dad asked me what I wanted for Christmas and I told him I didn't need anything, he sent a check. I could think of nothing I'd rather use it on, and it helped me keep my plans a secret from Julia. To throw her off the scent, Mom sent gifts as well, not the least of which was the incredible gown hanging on the back of the bedroom door.

My hand reached out to touch the silk. It was a beautiful dark green that matched her eyes, with the slightest silver shimmer dusting the fabric, fitted through the top but with some sort of floaty skirt. I could only imagine how breathtaking she'd look. I took it from the door and laid it carefully across the made bed, placing her present next to it with a lone white rose.

Julia was in the bathtub, in our room. I wasn't even sure if she wanted me to accompany her tonight, but it was a public fundraiser and I had a ticket. I could go alone if I needed to, but I'd be damned if the evening would end without make-up sex.

I used the other bathroom to shower and change into my tuxedo. I hadn't worn it since our wedding. I took my time shaving and combing my hair before I put on the pristine white shirt without buttoning it. I felt a mixture of anxious anticipation and sadness at the possibility that Julia wouldn't want to reconcile. I splashed a little aftershave on my face, and it stung. I strung the bow tie around my neck, leaving it untied, the top few buttons of the shirt open, and slipped my feet in my polished black dress shoes.

I looked at myself in the mirror and decided, determined, I was going to arrive at the gala with my beautiful wife on my arm.

"Go get her," I told myself. My heart pounded. I'd never felt so at a loss to know what Julia's reaction would be. I knew her better than I knew myself, but this shit with Jane was new territory, and while I was angry, too, I had to put that aside. Doors or pride had no place between us.

Determined to put an end to this misery, I turned out of the bathroom at the same moment that our bedroom door burst open, and Julia appeared. In what seemed like a fraction of a second, she rushed to me and wrapped her arms around my waist burying her face in my naked chest. She still had her robe on, but her hair was done up in one of those fancy styles I couldn't remember the name of, and smelled like heaven. My arms closed around her shoulders.

"Baby, what?" I asked, thankful just to touch her again. Her fingers curled against the muscles of my back underneath my shirt, and her forehead still rested against me.

"I'm sorry, Ryan. I was so stupid."

"Me, too. It got way out of hand." Her hold around my waist tightened, but she still refused to look up, only nodding against me.

"Hey. I'll take care of everything. You'll see." A finger under her chin lifted her face so I could see her. There were tears in her eyes, threatening to fall. Her face was luminous perfection; silver and green shadow making her eyes glow; her eyes lined and lashes lush. I wanted to drown in them. I slid my arms underneath hers and hoisted her off the floor so our mouths were at the same level. I brushed my nose with hers, closing my eyes and breathing her in. Her hands wound in my hair on both sides of my head. "There never was, nor will there ever be... a love like this. You kill me when you don't trust that."

She nodded, her mouth reaching for mine. "That was the most beautiful thing I've ever read," she breathed against my lips. "Kiss me."

"You're so beautiful. I'm afraid I'll mess you up." Having her this close, breathing in her breath, it was extremely difficult not to crush her to me and do as she asked.

"I don't care." Her tongue darted out to lick inside my upper lip. "Please, Ryan. I missed you so much. I've been so unhappy."

Julia's words were my very thoughts, and I needed to kiss her as much as she needed me to. With a groan, I let myself fall into it like it was the last kiss we'd ever share. My mouth plundered hers, hungry for the taste and feel of her. Julia's response was explosive, and she met me kiss for fiery kiss. Our tongues made love to each other in reverence and urgency. My hand curved around the back of her neck, but my other arm still held her tight against me. My heart hammered against hers, and I slowed our kisses to gentle tasting. "I don't want to let you go, but we gotta go, babe." I set her gently down and kissed her one last time on the mouth then the tip of her nose. Joy filled me up as I looked down at her brilliant smile. I caught a tear before it rolled down her face to mar her make-up. "You look... stunning."

Her hand ran down my bare chest. "You don't look so bad yourself, but now you have lipstick on your face." Julia reached up to wipe some of the edge of my mouth with her thumb. I felt so relieved. "Thank you for still wanting to be with me tonight."

"Where else would I want to be but with you? Ever."

"Don't make me cry again. I already cried my eyes out when I read the poem. It literally stopped my heart."

"I meant every word." And just like that, we were Ryan and Julia again. I breathed a sigh of relief.

I took her hand and led her back into the bedroom. Her eyes were teasing when she dropped the robe and underneath had sexy black silk and lace lingerie. It was a strapless corset, matching lace panties, and stockings held in place by the garters on the corset. I could see everything through the lace, but the subtle covering made her body all the more delicious.

"Are you trying to kill me?" I groaned. She reached for the dress and I bent to kiss the back of her shoulder. I wanted nothing more than to make love to her, but instead, I helped her into her dress, zipping it up and sliding my hands down her bare arms. The diamond hairpins from our wedding sparkled in her hair. I was speechless when she turned to me and started to button up my shirt and then tied the bow tie. The entire time, I stood mesmerized by the perfection of her features, now glowing, and her eyes full of love. I stood motionless under her ministrations. I thought I'd lost that light in her eyes.

My knuckles brushed the back of her cheek. "Don't forget to remember... how much I love you."

Her face got serious and she cupped my jaw as she nodded. "I love you more."

"Do you wanna fight about it?" I chuckled, but love squeezed my heart. I shrugged into the jacket of my tux.

"I'm done fighting. I'm in the mood for love."

"There is a God after all." My tone was teasing but my intentions were right on point. The evening would begin for me when the gala ended.

She took the rose that I'd given her and broke it off, firmly placing the stem through the boutonniere hole in my lapel, smoothing the material when she was done. "You look perfect."

"I know you'll be busy tonight, but I want to dance with my beautiful girl."

Her white teeth flashed and a low laugh left her when she threaded her fingers through mine.

~10~

Ryan ~

Lincoln Center was buzzing. Julia was spectacular. I stood and watched her cool composure with a sort of awe. This was a public event to benefit AIDS research, but many very important people were attending; powerful business leaders, famous fashion designers, celebrities, musicians, the mayor of New York, and several of the big wigs from Condé Nast from all over the world. She looked elegant and so stunning; simply breathtaking. I swirled the scotch around my glass and the ice clinked on the side of the crystal.

The food was incredible; catered by a famous chef whose name I couldn't remember. I reached for one of the stuffed shrimp the waiter proffered and popped it in my mouth. The concert—a melding of several of the world's most accomplished classical ensembles—went off without a hitch. I was amazed that six separate groups could practice in different parts of the globe and then come together and be so magnificent. Julia had done her due diligence, introducing me to everyone, but the names started to become lost to me. I didn't know how she remembered them all, but she did. I made small talk with Meredith and John, sent Andrea a smile and wave from a few feet away, and avoided Turner as much as I could. He was busy snapping photographs. I'd have to make sure Julia got copies of the one of the two of us.

Everything was perfect. I'd never been more proud of her as I stood beside her and listened to her words. Being so close to her over the years had made me take for granted how well read and educated she was, and how well she carried herself. Maybe taking her for granted was the wrong word, but this certainly reminded me how amazing she was.

She looked so stunning that I found my eyes locked on her constantly, sometimes forgetting to breathe. Pride swelled my chest like a peacock's. This was her party, this was her world, and she handled it with calm, elegant precision. Later, with me, she'd alternate between lascivious and loving, tender and taking, but always passionate. She spoke to me without words, when our eyes would connect and the edges of that gorgeous mouth would lift in a sly smile, flirting and letting the tip of her tender, pink tongue peak out to lick her lip or bite her lower one. I was rock hard just looking at her, and I needed to adjust myself badly. I hoped no one noticed.

Julia was holding an almost-empty glass of white wine in her right hand. She leaned in to excuse herself from the matronly woman she was speaking to and glided toward me. I couldn't help it, my arm snaked around her waist and pulled her close enough that she could feel the effect she had on me. My open lips found the pulse at her temple and lingered on the warm skin and she sighed. I could feel her breath rush over the skin of my neck, and my arm tightened.

"When can you leave? I can't wait to get you alone."

"Mmmm..." her fingers curled into the front of my shirt and pressed into my abdomen. I could hear the desire in her purr. "Just after midnight. What time is it?"

"11:40." The music playing throughout the room was classical but the din of voices was constant. I longed for when the only sound in my ears was her breathing and soft moans. "We're almost there."

She looked up into my face with lazy, hooded eyes. "Are we?" she teased softly and pressed her hip into my erection.

"Soon," I said with a smile and bent to kiss her mouth. I didn't care if she spilled her wine, or if I happened to drop the glass in my hand; I didn't care that there were 400 people around us. My tongue pushed hungrily into her mouth, and though our surroundings gave her a second's hesitation, soon she was returning the kiss in full measure. I pulled her tighter, kissing her deeply. She reluctantly pulled her mouth away, but mine wanted to cling to hers.

"Ryan. I'm working."

"I know. I can't help it. You're so beautiful tonight."

I scanned the room over her head as her lips brushed my jaw, and my eyes locked with a pair of blue ones not twelve feet in front of us. My heart stopped. *What the fuck was Jane doing here?* Anger exploded, and my eyes saw red while heat infused beneath my skin like fire.

I couldn't believe my eyes. All I could think about as Jane continued to stare at me was that I had to get her out of here before Julia saw her. My heart felt like a tennis ball ricocheting uncontrollably around inside my chest. My jaw clenched and I held up a hand behind Julia's back, silently communicating to Jane that she shouldn't approach us. Even if I snubbed Jane in front of Julia, her wall would slam down between us and would ruin the rest of the night. *Goddamn it to hell!*

I tried to keep the panic out of my voice. "Baby, why don't you go finish up what you need to do so we can go? I have a surprise."

"Really?" Julia's face lit up. "But, what about our kiss at midnight?"

I nodded and kissed her once on the lips. "I'll meet you back here at midnight, okay?"

Her fingers wrapped around the sleeve of my tux. "I don't want to leave you. I've spent most of the night doing that."

"It's okay. It's only for a few minutes. We have all night." I tried to reassure her, but I needed her to leave me alone so I could deal with Jane. Panic welled up in my chest. Jane was out of line.

"Okay. Love you." Her eyes were big and round and full of love. I touched her chin.

"Love you. Go on."

After Julia left, I turned abruptly and rushed to where Jane was waiting. "What are you doing here?"

She huffed but her eyes looked hurt. She swallowed hard. "Thanks a lot. It's a free country."

I sighed, running a hand through my hair. I was agitated. "Look, I didn't mean it that way. It's just... I didn't expect you to be here."

"I haven't been here long. I was in the city with some friends and Caleb told me you'd be here. I wanted to wish you Happy New Year. That's all." She was dressed in some sort of pale blue dress, but I barely noticed.

I flushed guiltily, glancing over my shoulder to see if Julia was anywhere near us. I couldn't see her, so I relaxed a little. "Okay, Happy New Year." My voice was stilted, but I'd be damned if I could do anything about it.

"Where's Julia? I should say hello."

No! I wanted to shout at her. "She's busy working. We should let her be."

"She was just here."

"Yes, but she has to wrap things up."

Jane was fidgeting in front of me; unable to meet my eyes and staring off over my left shoulder. "Okay, well... I guess I'll see you at the hospital." I could see the hurt in her eyes, but I couldn't bring myself to comfort her. I needed her to leave. Now. She stood on her tiptoes and slid her arms up mine until they rested behind my neck.

It was uncomfortable, but I leaned in to hug her briefly, compassion for her loneliness wheedling its way to chip away at my anger.

"Happy New Year," I said gently and pulled back. Her arms tightened when she leaned up to place a kiss on my mouth, and my hands fell to her waist in shock. I was motionless; stone-still in disbelief that she'd just done that. I gently pulled her arms away from me, letting them drop to her side.

I had to make these words count without hurting her too badly. "Jane, this has to stop. Julia means everything to me. If I've done anything to give you the wrong impression, I'm sorry, but nothing will ever happen between us." I tried to keep my voice gentle but firm. "I like working with you and you're my friend."

Something in Jane's expression hardened but her voice was meek. "I know Ryan. Like I said, I just wanted to wish you well tonight. Bye."

I felt like a heel, but there was no way in hell I would let anything cause more of a chasm between Julia and I. After the past few days, I was done letting my guilt about Jane threaten my marriage. I watched her walk a few feet then returned to meet Julia as planned.

Julia ~

I raced to the bathroom to calm down, weaving and pushing past elegantly clad women and dozens of men in tuxedos. My heart felt ready to implode because of what I'd just seen. *Why was Jane here and why was she draped all over my husband? Why had Ryan allowed it?* I leaned on the ceramic vanity in the posh bathroom. The toilets were separate from the washroom, and my eyes locked onto my image in the mirror. My face was so red, when combined with the brilliant emerald green dress I looked like a poster-child for Christmas. My head throbbed with each beat of my heart and I was sure I'd have to scream in frustration or I'd literally burst.

I turned on the cold water and used my hand to scoop some up on the back of my neck. I tried to calm my breathing, but my whole body was shaking. I wasn't sure if I was just mad as hell or if I was falling apart.

The door opened, and a brush of light blue fabric passed through my periphery but then I closed my eyes, concentrating on getting my breathing under control so I didn't hyperventilate. A sob tried to well in my chest and I pushed it down, willing the tears away. I would not let that bitch make me fall apart and look like a fool in front of all my coworkers and guests. Not in a million years. I inhaled again.

"Why don't you just let him go, Julia?" Jane's voice bit into my thoughts and my eyes shot open. If looks could kill, she would've been gutted. My eyes met hers in the mirror when I straightened. I wanted to tell her to go fuck herself, but I wouldn't give her the satisfaction. I reached forward and took a tissue, my back as ridged as my resolve. The person who speaks first, loses. *I wasn't going to fucking lose to this...* For the first time in my life, my mind wanted to use the 'c' word.

"He belongs with me. We share the same work, he can talk to me about medicine and I get it. Ryan is brilliant and he deserves someone who does more than make cheesecake and arrange parties."

I glared at her in the mirror, wiping my hands on one of the plush towels provided before tossing it in the hamper to one side. I tried to walk around her, but she moved to block my passage, her eye full of hate.

"Does the truth make you speechless? I saved his life. He saved mine. That's a bond you can know nothing about, Julia. His blood flowed into me and mixed with mine. He reached inside my body and held my life in his hands. He belongs with me."

My heart pounded in my ears and throat. I could barely breathe. My mind insisted that she was a lying bitch, but I'd seen Ryan's arms around her and the kiss they shared, the soft expression on his face. I whirled on her and slapped her as hard as I could across the face, snapping her neck back. I hoped it hurt like hell!

"RYAN IS MINE!" I screamed at her. "He'll always be mine!"

I ran from the room as if hell were on my heels, gasping for air and feeling faint. I pressed a hand to my head. I could scream that Ryan was mine all night, but my heart was cracked open and bleeding like it had never been. I wasn't able to breathe as my eyes searched for Andrea through the crowd. I had to be pale; the glances that were cast in my direction were concerned. I was stopped twice, first by the mayor's wife and then by one of our assistants, to ask me if I was all right. My throat was tight with the effort not to fall apart, and all I could do was nod and keep moving.

I never thought Ryan would allow another woman to kiss him. Not that kind of kiss and not at my work function. Especially when he knew Jane wanted to take him away from me, and after everything that we'd fought about. I intentionally avoided the area of the room where I knew Ryan would be waiting and then scoffed at myself. Maybe he wouldn't be waiting at all.

I told Andrea I had to go and ripped the bracelet off my arm with trembling fingers. *R & J. How fucking ironic.*

"Julia, what?" She shook her head in protest. "You want me to what?"

Mike Turner burst into the room. "What's wrong?" He was genuinely concerned.

"Just please, take it to Ryan." We were in the coatroom, and I struggled to throw mine on. I was finally beginning to lose my carefully constructed façade. My eyes pleaded with her, and the first tears fell. "Please." I begged. "I can't face him right now."

"Julia... he's your husband."

"I have to leave before I completely lose it, Andrea. I'm sorry."

"I'll take you home. Come on," Mike said gently, his fingers closing around my elbow. "Its okay, come on. Let Ryan know," he instructed Andrea.

"No! I need time alone."

Mike and Andrea talked softly together but I didn't hear a word they said. I ran out of the venue crying, Mike chasing behind me with my coat. It was storming, mostly icy rain mixed with sleet. In the end, I didn't have the strength to protest when Mike threw his jacket over my shoulders and ushered me into a cab. I no longer cared if Ryan would be pissed at my choice of escort. I prayed Mike would get me home before I turned into a sobbing mess.

*****

My heart was aching and my face was covered in a deluge of silent tears. I'd left Mike dumbfounded in the lobby without so much as a thank you and now slammed my apartment door behind me. It didn't matter what Jane said to me, I had to believe

what I'd seen myself; the image of Jane clinging to Ryan still
burned behind my eyes. I felt sick to my stomach. Could it
have really happened? I knew that tender look on his face. I'd
seen it directed at me more times than I could count. His eyes
were so soft and gentle as he looked at her, and jealousy turned
my soul to ashes. I gasped and clawed at my chest as my lungs
constricted. I was suffocating. My heartbeat thundered in my
ears until I finally let go of the torrent of tears that had been
threatening for the past thirty minute trip from Midtown
Manhattan.

I stopped in the middle of our living room, turning around
in circles, clenching and unclenching my fists in desperation,
unsure of what to do with myself. I was transported back to the
many nights in college when I'd been alone while Ryan was out
with some faceless woman. All the torment I felt then was mag-
nified a hundred times, because this time, it wasn't in my imagination; I'd seen it with my own eyes. Finally, a broken sob
erupted from my chest as my shaking legs refused to hold me up.
I slowly sank to the floor.

I wrapped my right hand around my now empty left wrist.
Herculean sobs racked through me, and I fell to the carpet in
front of the sofa. This couldn't be happening. He said they were
only friends, but I knew too well what friendship with Ryan
meant.

"Oh, God! Wha... what am I... g... onna do?" I cried brokenly into the darkness, uncaring of whether the water or
makeup would seep into the rug or if the beautiful designer dress
was now completely ruined from the storm raging outside. I felt
embarrassed by Jane's confrontation. I'd been so sure of Ryan
and of us. I wanted to rewind the world two months; to scream,
to pull my hair out... *to die.*

I curled into myself, praying for the pain to end. I couldn't die, but I could scream, and I did—as loud and long as I could. The sound split the air, high-pitched, screeching and shrill; shattering the air like an angry siren. My hands wrapped in my wet hair and pulled until my scalp burned. Some of Elyse's pins landed with a barely perceptible thud next to me. The pain in my heart was unfathomable—unimaginable—even worse than when I'd remembered losing our baby. At least then, I'd had Ryan to hold onto. I needed him. Even though he was the source of the horrible pain, he was also the only one who could take it away. "Please..." I wasn't sure if I was begging or praying, but all I wanted was to feel nothing. "If this is real, I don't want to love him anymore..."

"Julia!" The voice on the other side of the door was frantic. The key rattled in the lock, and the door flew open with a bang against the opposite wall. I scrambled in the opposite direction as quickly as I could, panicked at the potential confrontation with Ryan. My pulse raced as I tried to run down the hall and put a locked door between us.

"Julia!" Ryan bellowed behind me in the hall, his voice frantic. "For God's sake! Are you all right? Is Turner in there with you?"

"Shut up, Ryan!" Fuck him for asking that after what I'd just witnessed! I tried to slam the door behind me, but he stopped it with a muscled forearm. "Just leave me alone!" Ryan grunted in pain as the wood slammed into his flesh, and I pushed on the door with all I had. He used his weight to force his way into the room, and I stumbled back, helpless to stop him despite using all my effort to close the door.

"What in the hell?" he railed. His hair and clothes were wet like mine, the tuxedo jacket and bow tie were missing, and two buttons undone; the fine white linen was plastered to his body and ruined.

"Why the fuck did you leave?" His eyes showed a mixture of anger, pain, and confusion. "And, would you mind explaining this?" His arm bent at the elbow, he held the bracelet in his clenched fist.

I turned, like a cornered rabbit, waiting to be eaten by my predator. My eyes widened and I stared at my husband. I was still shaking and my throat ached. Everything hurt.

When I didn't answer, he took a step toward me. I couldn't help flinching away, which only pissed him off more.

"Julia, answer me!" he yelled, the outburst making me flinch again. "Jesus Christ!" he muttered. "You're acting like I'm going to hurt you."

"You have hurt me! So much, I can't see straight! I can't breathe! I saw you with Jane, and you're accusing me of shit with Mike?"

His handsome face flashed recognition and then quickly hardened again. "You saw me comforting a friend! Andrea told me you left with Turner." The volume of his voice was lower now, but the tone still hard. "I'm so Goddamn sick of you not trusting me!"

"Well, I'm sick of you choosing that bitch over me! I never see you! You spend all of your time with that woman!"

Ryan ran a hand through his wet hair with a huff; I wasn't sure if it was disbelief or disgust. "It's fucking New Year's Eve, Julia! I had something special planned for us, and now it's completely fucked! Why didn't you talk to me about what you saw? Instead, you run to Andrea and ask her to give me the bracelet? To give to Jane?" he railed. "Is that what you're implying? And, then you run out into a storm like a child? You're acting insane!"

His expression was incredulous, but surely he knew what Jane was up to.

My face crumpled again as tears continued to flood my eyes, and I began to cry in earnest. "You don't know her like you think! She's nuh... not all unicorns and ruh... rainbows. I won't let you tuh... turn me into the bad guy on this, Ryan! She's truh... trying to break us up!"

"No, she isn't!" he said in disgust. "She felt bad tonight. She's alone. She knows I'm committed to you!"

"Then she's one up on me!" I put both hands over my face and fell against the wall with a painful bang, my shoulders shaking with the effort of my sobs. I wanted to tell him about the conversation in the bathroom, but I was so angry that doing so was even necessary; the words couldn't get past the ache. "Talk about not trusting someone! A year ago," I cried, defeated, "you would have believed me."

"Oh, fuck this!" Ryan rushed toward me and grabbed both of my wrists, prying my hands away from my face, his fingers pressing hard into my flesh as he yanked me toward him roughly. "What do I have to do? This is bullshit!" I struggled against him as he pushed me to the wall with his body, struggling to force the bracelet back on my left wrist. "This is *us*! Not me and Jane! *Us,* Julia! It makes me fucking sick that you could think I'd take it from your wrist and put it on hers! Or anyone else's!" He shouted in my face, his chest heaved against mine.

When Ryan had the bracelet once again ensconced on my wrist, he angrily shoved a knee between my legs and lifted me off the floor with it, both hands now pinning my arms to the wall over my head. My feet were left dangling off of the floor and one of the high-heeled pumps dropped off and smacked against the wall before landing with a soft thud on the carpet.

"This is madness!"

We were both furious, and the heat between our bodies began to seep steamily through our wet clothes. The smooth wool
crepe covering Ryan's hips brushed the of inside my thighs. I
began to struggle and pushed against his hands with all my might,
but he held me still as if I lay docile in his arms. Frustration
welled up in my chest. I was conflicted; part of me didn't want
Ryan touching me when he'd just touched her and part of me
needed the affirmation that he was still mine. He smelled like
cologne and the gel he used on his hair. I fought inhaling deeper,
silently praying not to find any traces of Jane's perfume lingering.

Despite my tears, my jaw jutted out in defiance, and my
eyes flashed angrily at my husband. I was helpless physically,
but I wouldn't let him break me.

"I didn't get a New Year's kiss from my wife." Ryan's
voice had dropped to the low, sexy tones he used when he made
love to me, but somehow it hurt this time. How could he act like
touching me would make the last two hours disappear?

"No... no, noooo!" My struggle renewed as I frantically
turned my face away; the vision of the kiss he'd given Jane reap-
peared in my mind, kissing Ryan. Kissing my husband, on this,
the first New Year's Eve of our married life. He rested his forehead on the side of my face, and I could feel the warmth of
breath rush over me, the scent of expensive scotch wafting into
my nostrils.

"I don't want to kiss you. I don't want you to touch me right
now." The words weren't true, but my pride insisted I say them.
I tried to hide the pain in my eyes, but knew I wouldn't succeed
because my brow was rumpled and my chin trembled. I'd never
been able to hide anything from the man who knew me better
than I knew myself.

His anger was tangible, his breathing heavy, his expression enraged. I could feel it, but his lips were gentle as they moved across my cheek toward my mouth, leaving a trail of fire that weakened my resolve. "Liar," he almost whispered.

When he felt the fight drain out of me, his hands released my wrists and strong fingers circled around my thighs, pulling my sex flush with his throbbing erection. Ryan groaned against the curve of my shoulder as my hands wound in his hair, and I wondered if he tasted the salt from my tears on his tongue. My heart was broken, and still, I couldn't deny him.

"I know you love me, so stop this," he demanded. I started to sob, hating my weakness; hating that he was right. "Do you feel how I want you? How hot I am for you? Julia," he groaned. "Tonight was going to be glorious."

I closed my eyes again, the pain still so fresh. I tried to deny the desire Ryan stirred within me. "All I can see is you kissing her."

He pulled back, and his frenzied blue eyes locked with mine and hardened. "I can't believe you're doing this," he spat out. "Happy *fucking* New Year! She kissed me! Barely! If you'd bothered to wait ten seconds..." Ryan paused and huffed. "Fuck this! Actions speak louder than words."

Exactly, my mind cried.

Strong fingers closed around my chin and forced my face to his, his tongue parting my lips and plundering my mouth in a thunderous kiss as he ground his pelvis into mine in a series of thrusts to show me his arousal. I hated my weakness, but my mouth finally responded to the fiery kiss, my hands tugging at his hair to bring his tongue in even deeper. When Ryan groaned into my mouth, the air left my lungs and I gasped for breath. His lips ripped from mine to let me breathe, his hands frantically ripping at my already ruined dress, his hands greedily seeking my breasts.

"*That* was a kiss," he said as his lips dragged across my cheek and to my temple, one hand moving between us to open his pants and push down his boxer briefs to expose himself. "What you saw meant nothing. *This*," he pushed his engorged cock against me again, the thick shaft pressing against my damp flesh through the silk panties, and rubbing in a slow, methodical rhythm, "belongs to you." Ryan's fingers kneaded and rolled my left nipple painfully. Still, it puckered and grew in his hand. His hips held me up as he reached down and roughly ripped the crotch of my panties away. I gasped in surprise when his fingers parted me, feeling the dampness of my desire. He sighed heavily, closing his eyes. "We fucking own each other, and you know it. Nothing or no one can *ever* change it." Two fingers sank inside me and I instinctively arched into them. "I know you know it, baby, so stop this."

"Ryan..." I whispered achingly. My heart still hurt, but I needed him desperately. His body, his mouth, his love... would take away all of the aches he created in me if I let it happen. I didn't want to think about tomorrow or if Jane would still be between us, I just wanted to drown in his love and his words and never let go. I wanted to let him mend the break in my heart and fill me with his body and his love.

"Say it!" Ryan commanded. My eyes snapped to his. "Tell me that you know," he said more softly.

"I know, Ryan." His mouth crashed into mine once again, our tongues tangling and laving deeply with each other; roughly, but deep and with purpose. He was showing me he loved me, making me acknowledge it. My heart swelled with love. He groaned when the thick head of his cock probed my entrance and he started to enter, stretching me wide as he pushed in deep. I arched, aching to take his thick length inside me inch by glorious inch.

"Uhhhh," I sighed in pleasure and squeezed around him when he was fully inside. Ryan stiffened against me, feeling my muscles milk at him. I wanted to burn my presence into his mind and onto his body; make him come harder and in ways no one else ever could. I loved him beyond reason, and I needed him to know no one could ever make him feel like I could.

"Fuck, you feel good," he murmured before his mouth took mine again. We were angry and hungry and ardent in our passion for each other. I clung to him, ripping at his shirt, my fingers parting the material and splaying out over his chest. He began to thrust, long and deep, each one punctuated roughly enough to bounce me against the wall, my breasts swelled in his hands as he teased and tugged at the nipples then letting the fullness fill his hand. His fingers closed around the mounds of flesh and he began to knead gently. The kisses softened, our lips lifting and feasting with determination as our bodies moved together. Ryan pulled at my bottom lip and licked at my top one before his tongue entered again. I sucked it deeper into my mouth.

My legs began to tingle as Ryan used his leverage to find my G-spot with the head of his dick. My breath hitched, and I squeezed around him and held it.

"That's it, baby," he encouraged softly between breathless kisses. "I can feel you starting… come for me, Julia."

"Ryan, I want you," I breathed. "Come with me." I concentrated hard, biting my lip, wanting it to last longer, but my fragile emotions and Ryan's urgency made it impossible.

"I love you, baby. Just let it go." His guttural words pushed me over the edge, and the orgasm washed over me in delicious waves that left me jerking against him. He pulled me off the wall, and my legs wrapped around him. Ryan held me tightly to him as he carried me to the bed and laid me down. I knew he hadn't come and I didn't want him to leave my body.

"No, Ryan." My fingers curled into his shoulders and the hair at the back of his head when he began to pull out. "Don't!"

"I'll be back. Let's take off these wet clothes, sweetheart." He kissed my mouth in gentle reassurance that he'd come back to me. The cold air that rushed over my damp skin caused goose bumps to pop out and made me shiver.

I watched him retreat in the dark, the white of his shirt a shadowy image as he peeled it off and stepped out of his pants and silk boxers before walking into the bathroom. A sloppy splat signaled he'd deposited the articles in a heap on the ceramic tile before returning to the bedroom completely naked, his erection still at full attention, to begin peeling my sodden dress, tattered panties, lace corset, and thigh high stockings from my body.

"It's a shame this dress is ruined. You were stunning in it." His voice was silken, but held a trace of sadness.

He was so beautiful; his hair still clung damply to his nape and forehead, and his muscles moved gracefully beneath his smooth skin. He was a trace thinner than he was a year ago; the lifestyle and rough hours of a medical resident clearly taking its toll.

I lifted my hand and ran it down his arm from his shoulder to his hand, tenderness flooded through me. I sucked in my breath. I loved this man beyond words, and suddenly, I regretted the loss of whatever he had planned for the remainder of the evening.

Ryan's deep blue eyes turned black in the darkness but glittered as he paused and studied my body, now left naked and vulnerable to his gaze. He ran a hand through his hair and sighed as the remnants of my clothes were tossed into the bathroom with his. I could sense his immense sorrow at the emotional barrier between us. Even when we were making love and we were locked together in our desperate closeness, there was melancholy beneath it. Suddenly, I was overwrought with the need to make sure he knew I loved him as much as I ever did and that I trusted him. I could see his pain, and I hated it.

"Ryan," I called softly.

"Mmm, huh?" he answered. He was standing at the foot of the bed, and I raised my arms, beckoning him to me. Thankfully, he didn't hesitate and crawled up the bed on his hands and knees toward me. One knee parted mine, and he settled into the cradle of my body in one fluid motion, his hands framing my face, thumbs tracing my temples at the same time as he came inside my body again. My leg hitched and curled around his hips, the heel of my foot pressed into his firm ass and my arms sliding up his muscled back.

"God," he groaned, his lids dropping slowly over his eyes. He dipped his head to kiss me softly, then with increasing ardor. Where our coupling had been hard and frenzied minutes before, it was now unhurried with tender urgency, the point this time to prove depth of love, not mutual ownership.

Ryan pushed into me with a steady and deep rhythm, our mouths giving and taking, licking, hovering, and then sucking madly on each other's. My fingers curled into the silken strands at the nape of his neck, and cupping his head possessively, I pulled his mouth closer to mine.

Ryan's breathing and low moans told me he was getting close, and he slowed and then stilled inside me. I could feel him fighting for control.

"Baby, don't stop," I whispered.

"If I don't, I'll come."

I didn't speak, but squeezed around him and arched my hips, pulling and then pushing on his body with mine, determined to do the work he refused to do and take him over the edge.

"Jesus," Ryan gasped, and then his body arched as he succumbed, thrusting into me again deeply and spilling hotly inside my body. I kissed his shoulder several times—my lips moving softly over his flesh; my legs and arms holding him tightly to me as he rode it out and groaned my name into my neck.

When it was over, Ryan pulled back and held my gaze, his breathing heavy as he pushed the hair away from my face, but he didn't say anything. His face looked pained, and it hurt me in ways I couldn't articulate. Neither one of us spoke. When he finally pulled out of me and moved to my side, he gathered me back against him. We both lay on our sides, his breath softly brushing my skin. My hand lay on the pillow beside my head and his slid up to thread tightly through mine. Ryan used the leverage to pull me back tighter, and I brought the top of his hand to my mouth at the same time as his lips tenderly brushed a trail across my shoulder. I trembled despite being held in the iron vice of his arms, and our hands were still locked together. His fingers tightened in silent command that I understood, without words, all he needed to say.

We owned each other, yes, but we loved more than anything. A love like this was once in ten thousand lifetimes, and despite Jane and the pain she'd caused, I was sure of two things: Ryan meant everything; he was my beginning and my end.

*****

I woke as the sun cast a rosy glow over the room. I was sprawled on my stomach across Ryan's naked body, his warmth seeping into me everywhere our skin touched. His knuckles traced lightly over my shoulder blade, just above the sheet and comforter that rested just across us both. The feather-light stroking sent tingles of contented peace through me. I could hear his heartbeat beneath my ear, his skin smooth under my cheek. I didn't want to wake up. I wanted more of his arms and to pretend everything since Christmas Eve hadn't happened; except that amazing poem. I'd keep that. I tightened my arms around him. Last night was the worst fight we'd ever had, but my heart was still so full of him; like I could eat him alive and still not be close enough.

"Baby, you awake?"

I closed my eyes tighter in protest, but I gave a barely perceptible nod. "I'm sorry about last night. Sorry I ruined the plans, whatever they were." I prepared myself for feeling like utter crap the minute he told me.

"We had a Jacuzzi suite at the Waldorf. Roses, champagne and strawberries."

My heart fell. "I'm sorry," I murmured sadly.

"It's just money, Julia. But, we do need to talk about why you left the gala without me." He rolled over on top of me and caged me in with his arms, his body pressing me down into the mattress. He could trap me all day long if he wanted, but I sure as hell didn't want to talk about *her*.

"I don't want to talk right now." I blinked several times as my chest tightened. "Please, Ryan. Not right now." I tried to nuzzle into his neck and reached up to kiss him, but my lips could only graze his jaw. "Can't you just hold me?"

Our angry and desperate lovemaking last night had at least convinced me he loved me, and he was at my mercy in that regard at least; as much as I was to him. Couldn't we just be together without rehashing it all? I wasn't ready to ruin the reprieve. "You promised we wouldn't talk about her in bed."

"We always talk about everything. What does it matter where?" He softened and kissed the side of my cheek, sliding his

lips warmly up to my temple. His hips probed mine. I didn't
even think he meant to, but our bodies had a mind of their own.
Too bad my heart was bleeding, once again. I closed my eyes,
willing my face not to crumple and my voice not to break, but
only partially succeeding.

"But... we don't anymore." I missed him so much. I missed
the hours we used to lay in each other's arms, gently touching
and telling each other everything, the Sundays over coffee,
shopping for nothing at all, and the piggyback walks we used to
take back in Boston. I missed just having him in the next room,
even if he was studying or I was working, and when he sat on a
kitchen stool and watched me cook. I felt lost when I thought
about it too much. I didn't want to think. I just wanted to soak
him up and believe that we'd be okay.

His mouth pulled gently from my lips, and his eyes bore
into mine; daring me to say the words as if they were untrue, as
if I'd imagined it all. "We..." he stopped, obviously trying to
articulate it in a way that would convince me. "I realize we don't
have as much time together as we had in Boston. But we knew
this was going to be tough. I'm with you as much as I can be
right now."

When he put it that way it sounded completely logical, and
to any other couple, maybe it was acceptable, but not for Ryan
and me. We revolved around each other. Like planets or solar
systems or something equally epic, but when the center of the
universe explodes, everything vaporizes like it never existed. I
felt stupid and ashamed to even have those thoughts, but jealousy is a selfish bitch that makes you do, say, and think things
you never thought yourself capable of. It makes you hurt people
you never wanted to hurt.

"I can't do this anymore. I can't ignore how much she hurts
me... But, I don't want to fight anymore."

Ryan's hands moved up to cup my face as his hips pressed into mine again, as if he had a point to make. My heart squeezed as my arms slid around him of their own accord, and I rested my forehead on the solid muscle of his shoulder, wanting to hide and forget the last few months.

"If you trusted me, you wouldn't be hurting," Ryan growled. I looked up to find his eyes flashing angrily in accusation; as if I were the one who'd done something wrong or maybe I was delusional and made up the entire thing in my head. Maybe he could make it into nothing, but I couldn't. My brow creased, and I pushed at his chest. Suddenly, I wanted him off of me.

"It has nothing to do with trust, Ryan."

"The hell it doesn't!" His eyes hardened. I pushed until he finally moved, but the fact that I wanted to break our contact clearly pissed him off more. I sat up on the side of the bed, pulling the sheet around my naked form.

"I trust you, but I don't trust her."

"Who cares about her? Where is Julia? I don't even know you right now."

"How dare you say that to me when you're the one who's changed? You're the one who *cares about her*! You're letting someone else pull you away from me!" I stood, dragging the sheet with me into the bathroom, but he followed closely on my heels, uncaring that he was naked. I began loudly opening and closing drawers, digging in each one, trying to make it look like I was searching for something when what I was really doing was trying not to show how much it hurt. I wanted to scream at the injustice of it all, to ask him why he couldn't see what she was doing to us? But what would it accomplish besides reducing me to a hot mess?

"Like hell! That's bullshit and you know it!" he railed, something thick and disgusted lacing his voice.

My back stiffened and my chin jutted out in defiance. "That's not how it feels." My words were soft and matter-of-fact. And, since Ryan seemed intent on digging this shit up and ruining what little we'd salvaged of last night, I let out words I knew would cut him to the bone. "I feel abandoned and alone. Even when you're fucking me, I'm alone."

"What did you just say?" Ryan visibly recoiled as if I'd slapped him, his jaw hardening and the muscle starting to twitch relentlessly as his eyes sliced me in half. He huffed and shook his head, then turned abruptly and left the bathroom. I followed as if in a trance, as if I couldn't stop myself. When he began to rapidly, but methodically, throw on his clothes, I sank to the bed again, my legs unable to hold me up. He finally paused to glare down at me, more livid than last night after he'd chased me through a storm. His eyes got dangerously dark, and his breath rushed out like someone stomped on his chest. Maybe that's what I did, but it hurt me to say it as much as it hurt him to hear.

"Is that what I've been doing? *Fucking you*?" The words ripped through his clenched teeth, and his voice cracked. I could see his throat constrict. "Is that how you feel when I touch you? When have I *ever* fucked you? Do you think my feelings have changed?"

I wanted to reach out to him and beg him not to go to work, to hold on for dear life and pretend nothing between us had changed. But, I couldn't. Even if he wrapped me in his arms and made me forget about Jane, I knew she'd still be intruding on our lives when my eyes opened. I'd suffer more for the momentary lapse into our love because still nothing would have changed. No matter how close we'd been last night, here she was, as if she were standing in the room between us. If I gave in to my heart and tried to take away the pain in his eyes, it would only be replaced by my own... and it would be like ripping open a half-healed wound.

Each time we fought about Jane, a teeny shard of her was left to fester and increase the chasm. Even when we made up, made love, professed how much we meant to each other, still... she'd always be there digging at me like slow poison. I didn't know how to stop feeling this way, and I didn't know how to stop it, but if one of us didn't do something, it would become an infection big enough to rip us apart forever. The thought left me cold, with a gaping hole cracking open my chest. My breath left in a quiet rush.

"Answer me!" Ryan shouted, red-faced, and teary, a vein in his forehead swollen and pushing purple against his skin.

I flinched so bad, my whole body jerked. I just looked up at him, my own eyes starting to flood. I pulled the sheet tighter around my chest as if it could protect my heart with it. The last was a lie, but this was the truth. "I don't know what to say that will make a difference."

He angrily dashed a tear away with his thumb, before both hands landed at his hips. "Just answer me, Julia! I deserve a fucking answer!" He was yelling, and I finally snapped.

"I just make cheesecake!" I screamed back. "She told me I just... she said she shares more with you than I do. She can talk to you about things that I can't! She's better for you than I am!"

"What *the hell* are you talking about?"

"You're both in medicine! You share blood and a life-altering experience! She's shared more with you than me!" I was still shouting, and he looked at me as if he'd never seen me before. "She can give you more!"

"I don't care if she said elephants shit marshmallows and ate one to prove it, Julia! How can you doubt me? All I fucking think about is you, but all you think about is Jane!"

"I don't..." I began but Ryan cut me off.

"The hell you don't! How in the hell did we get to this place?" Sorrow shone through his anger.

I swallowed hard, the lump in my throat hurt like hell. I silently begged myself not to fall into a sobbing mess. Why was he still yelling at me? Why wasn't he furious with *fucking Jane*?

One shoulder lifted in a half-assed shrug. "You're asking the wrong person."

"I guess if I'm already judged, I should just act out your little fantasy!"

It was my turn to be taken aback, bitch-slapped by his words; my eyes widened like saucers.

"Tell Ellie I said thanks for planting this shit in your head! Now I know why Harris left!" Ryan turned and stalked from the bedroom, leaving me stunned and frozen, still sitting on the bed. I should have shouted and told him Ellie wasn't responsible, he and Jane were, but I simply didn't have the energy.

I listened to him take his coat from the closet and slam out of the apartment. Finally, the tears rained down my cheeks and heaving pain racked through me. I fell onto the mattress crying so hard I couldn't talk, I couldn't cry out loud... only gasp for air when I absolutely had no choice but to breathe. I'd never felt more alone or hopeless than I did in that moment; the suffocating silence closing in on me like it would stamp out my existence if I didn't get out. I hated Jane. I hated New York... I hated Ryan for not believing me, and I hated myself because, despite everything, I still loved him so much I wanted to die.

I don't know how long I laid there, but I finally pulled myself up, took a shower and picked up my phone.

"Hi, Doll! Happy New Year!" Meredith's exuberance made it clear she was still imbibing from the celebration of the Holiday. "What are you up to?"

I took a deep breath and let the words rush out. "I've reconsidered. I'd like to go to Paris."

"Really? Wonderful! When can you go? John said February is almost wrapped. If you leave soon, you can work on the March issue."

"Yes. February is done, and goes to press Friday. Except I need to come up with a little two-page fill. I can come up with something, and then Andrea can facilitate it before she joins me. Or we can finish it there and just send it camera ready online. Would that work?"

"Hell, yes! When do you want to go?"

"I thought today."

"Wow! When you make up your mind, you really make up your mind."

I scratched the towel across the back of my neck. I felt sick to my stomach, but now I was committed to the job and committed to the break I needed from my life. Running away was never my idea of integrity, but sometimes you just have to do it to gain perspective. "Yeah. I just thought the sooner I go, the sooner I can come home. I'll just get a ticket and then submit with expenses. Okay?"

"Sure. Tomorrow, I'll let the staff know that you'll be in charge."

"I'll need to update my phone for international use, so I'd like to expense that as well." It would be easier than getting a new one.

"Of course. Not to look a gift-horse in the mouth, but why the sudden change of heart? Are you and Ryan squabbling?"

I hesitated, but what was the use in lying. "We both need a little clarity and we aren't seeing eye-to-eye."

"I'm sorry to hear that, sweetie. Never thought I'd see the day that you and doc-hottie had problems." She cleared her

throat lightly. "Does he know where you're going? Am I supposed to cover your tracks?"

"For now, I think that would be best, but I don't want to
think about it or I'm going to change my mind about going."

"Enough said. I'll have someone line up a hotel and text you
details. Call me once you get settled."

I should have felt exhilarated, but all I felt was deep sorrow.
I hung up the phone, got online, and booked a flight. Two hours
later, I was in a cab on my way to JFK. I couldn't afford to think
anymore. I needed to bury myself in work. I needed time and
distance to come to terms with seeing Jane's blatant attempt for
Ryan. But, I had to be honest; the reason I was leaving had less
to do with Jane, and more to do with Ryan. He needed to miss
me, like he'd never missed me, and hurt like I was hurting. Obviously, neither one of us was sexually deprived, but I missed
my best friend. It ripped my guts out to intentionally hurt him,
but maybe he'd understand why I had to leave. I really had no
idea what I was going to do once I got there, but in New York, I
was too close to the fire... and it would leave me in ashes.

~11~

Ryan ~

It was hard avoiding Jane, but I did my damnedest. My eyes landed on her, and of course, she was watching me like a hawk. I wanted to go off on her for the shit she said to Julia, but part of me, the regular guy part, wanted to just blow her off until she disappeared. I'd done it often enough in college, and I wasn't proud of it, but it was easier than dealing with female hysterics. I'd had enough of those from Julia.

The fucking thing was, I shouldn't have to go through this shit with Jane. We weren't lovers. We weren't even good friends. I mean, sure, she knew me better than anyone else I worked with, but that was to be expected after that night. How she got from there to trying to kiss me was beyond me. I wracked my brain for what the hell I did to give her the wrong impression, and I couldn't come up with one Goddamn thing. I treated her with respect and as a friend. Sure, I'd visited her quite a bit when she was recovering, but I would have done that for any of my colleagues. And I felt responsible. Part of me still did, but she was making it difficult to really care for her. What kind of a friend tries to tear apart your life? Resentment surged inside me.

She set whatever she was holding on the desk of the nurse's station and started walking toward me, her eyes never leaving mine. I inhaled and turned away, ready to duck into the bathroom, just to put a door between us. I was concerned I'd fucking lose it, and I didn't need to air my personal problems at work, especially not in front of the senior attending. I didn't get more than five steps when a hand tentatively touched my shoulder.

"Ryan."

I stopped abruptly and turned on my heel. I physically felt my guard go up, as if a solid steel gate just slammed down between us. Both my hands perched on my hips as I glared down at her. I knew I looked pissed and I didn't try to hide it. I *was* pissed!

"What is it?" I spat out impatiently.

Jane had the grace to flush. Her face was getting red and sort of blending in with the bright pink scrubs she was wearing. "I…" she stopped and looked away then back again. "Can we talk about what happened last night?"

I stared down at her, unmoving. "There's nothing to talk about. I've asked you nicely to respect my time with Julia, and last night I laid it out as clearly as I can. There's nothing else I can say to you. This is my life you're fucking with, not only with Julia but with my career. It has to stop."

She nodded weakly, wringing her hands in front of her, now unable to meet my gaze. "I know. I wanted to apologize. I didn't mean to… care about you, but you're just… you're just so…"

I put my hand up to stop her. "Stop. I'm just *so married,* Jane. Julia is the one who deserves an apology. I don't know the whole story about what you said to her last night, but I heard enough to know you were way out of line. Julia has been nothing but nice to you. I don't care what you've done for me, you had no right to deliberately hurt and belittle her like that." My voice was quiet but firm and insistent. I had a hard time keeping my voice free of loathing. "And just to be clear, she does a hell of a lot more for me than you can ever know."

Her eyes began to glisten, and she swallowed hard enough for me to see her throat working. "Okay. But, did she tell you she slapped me?"

I was momentarily stunned that Julia would do that, and I knew her well enough to know that she had to really be hurting to lash out like that. I wondered if she'd seen Jane kiss me before or after their confrontation, but I'd be damned if I'd ask Jane to clarify. The situation was beyond awkward.

"That's not like her, Jane. You must have said something ugly. Nevertheless, I'm shocked she would do something like that."

"I had too much to drink last night, and my emotions got the better of me. I can't help how I feel, but I'm really sorry. If you want me to call Julia, I will."

"No. Just leave her alone. I'll take care of Julia." I wanted to get to the bottom of exactly what Jane said to my wife, but that was on the bottom of my list of priorities. I turned and walked away, relieved that this confrontation was over. One down; one to go.

*****

It was midnight again, and I didn't have a clue what I would face on the other side of the apartment door. I pinched the bridge of my nose and paused for a beat before I shoved the key into the lock. My mind wore me out thinking of this shit all day long, and it was made worse when Julia didn't return any of my texts or the two phone calls I'd attempted. I was met by darkness when I pushed through the door, with only the lights flickering in from the windows to cast everything into varying shades of grey and black. It was barely enough to see clearly. Julia usually left the light over the stove on so I could find my way around the kitchen, but not so tonight. I walked in and flipped on the kitchen light, shrugging out of my leather jacket and hanging it over the back of one of the chairs at the same time.

My brow furrowed. The quiet was eerie, and something in the air felt weird. That steel wall I'd placed between me and Jane paled in comparison to the one I felt between Julia and I. I opened the refrigerator, but there wasn't a plate waiting. My eyebrow shot up. *Hmmm... she really must be pissed.*

I grabbed a bottle of water, opened it, and chugged half of it down before shutting the door harder than I needed to. Frustration made my muscles tight and my neck ache. I reached up to knead the offending flesh. *Screw eating,* I thought as I ignored the low rumble in my stomach. *Whatever.* Maybe things would look brighter in the light of day. I wasn't looking forward to another fight with Julia and longed for the nights when I would slide into bed and pull her close to me, without worry that she'd pull away. These past few weeks had been the most hellish that I could ever remember in our relationship, and I couldn't fucking stand it. I wanted a hot shower and sleep, but I didn't have a day off until Friday. I didn't think I could live with things the way they were until that evening when Julia came home from work. I meandered lethargically down the hall, running both hands through my hair.

Our bedroom felt as unwelcoming as the rest of the apartment, once again shrouded in darkness. No small light on in the bathroom; confirmation that she hadn't softened at all. Just fucking great! I sighed heavily as I kicked off the new shoes she'd given me and left them on the floor near the foot of the bed. I barely glanced at it before heading in and stepping under the hottest water I could stand. I didn't stay in there long, just a quick rinse of my body and fast shampoo of my hair. Briskly toweling dry, I didn't even bother wrapping one around me. I dropped it in a damp heap on the floor and turned off the light, looking forward to closing my eyes but not to another fight with my wife.

Today had been particularly brutal. Besides the torrent of my thoughts and the uncomfortable shit hanging between Jane and me, the team had a really bad burn victim—he fell asleep smoking in a recliner and lit up like a candle. I'd never seen anything like it, and medical school didn't prepare me for the horror of seeing someone's skin slide off and hang in sheets off his arms, legs, torso, and around his fingers. Eighty percent of his body was covered in third degree burns, and he literally wept body fluid onto the ER floor. It was unreal and just... unspeakable.

I bent to pull the covers down and noticed for the first time that the bed was empty. My hand pushed through the covers to smooth across the cold sheets. I closed my eyes and fell onto the bed, not bothering to cover up. Defeated, I flung an arm tiredly over my eyes. It wasn't the first time she had to work into the morning hours on some late deadline or Mike Turner fuck-up. I was too tired to be angry that she didn't call, but I wouldn't be able to sleep if I didn't know what was going on. I inhaled deeply and got up, grabbing my phone from the belt of the scrubs I'd left on the floor of the walk-in closet. I went back in and turned on the lamp on the nightstand closest to me. I scanned my phone. I had a missed call from my dad, a text from Caleb, and one from Aaron. Nothing from Julia. Panic seized my entire body.

I grabbed a pair of sweats from the third drawer of our dresser and pulled them on with one hand, the other pressing Julia on speed dial. It went immediately to voice mail. Her phone must be off. My heart rate sped up, and my chest tightened painfully. We were fighting, sure, but it wasn't like her to not let me know where she was at all times. I wondered if something happened. It was Sunday, and even if she were working, I'd normally be able to reach her, but it was too late to call the office. I ran out of the apartment and took the stairs, racing down to the garage. Both hands slammed into the heavy door to swing it open. I ran the few feet needed to see her car sitting next to my CRV.

"Fuck!" I inhaled and stood there with both hands threaded over the top of my head. I turned, scanning the entire garage. Nothing looked out of sort. My stomach ached by the time I got back to the apartment. I stalked around the living room, unsure what to fucking do with myself. I flipped on the TV then flipped if off again. I called Aaron, but it was Jenna who answered.

"Hello?" She sounded half-asleep.

"Hey, Jen. It's me. Have you guys heard from Julia? She wasn't here when I got home, and there isn't a note." I swallowed and ran a nervous hand through my hair.

"That's not like her." Her voice became more alert. "Have you tried to call?"

"No," I said, irritated. "I thought I'd wait for hell to freeze over before I did the first obvious fucking thing."

"I can hear you're upset, but you can stop taking it out on me, asshole!"

My breath rushed out. "I know. Sorry. I'm just... worried sick."

Jenna's voice softened. "We haven't heard from her. The last time I talked to her was on Christmas Day. If I were her, I'd bitch slap that Jane. Maybe she had something to do for her job."

"No," I returned abruptly. "She would have called or left me a message. This is completely out of character." My voice elevated with anxiety. I walked from the bedroom through the rest of the apartment, finally rummaging around Julia's art table for a clue that might tell me where she was.

I flung myself down on the couch, one hand covering my eyes and my stomach twisting in knots.

"Was something going on between you two?"

"Obviously you know what's going on, or you wouldn't have mentioned Jane, right?"

"Yeah, so fix it, dickhead."

Anger exploded behind my eyes, and I bolted upright. "What the hell do you know about what I've been doing?" I railed at her. "I'm freaking the fuck out, Jenna!"

"Calm down, Ryan. I only said that because you guys can work out anything."

I leaned against the wall in the hallway, my legs straight, propping me up. "I don't know. Maybe," I murmured more softly, fear skittering across my skin like electricity. "Maybe something happened. I can't call the cops until tomorrow night. She has to be gone for twenty-four hours before they'll do anything."

"Julia isn't stupid. She wouldn't put herself in danger."

"Neither one of us are thinking clearly right now, Jen," I said tiredly.

"I'll try to call her, Ryan, okay? If she's just pissed at you, maybe she'll talk to me."

My head fell forward, and I slid down the wall to the floor, resting the arm not holding the phone across my bent knee. "Thanks. I think I'll call her parents. It's earlier on the West Coast."

"Let me know if you hear something, and I'll do the same."

I called her dad first. I hesitated to talk to her mom, because I didn't want to worry them needlessly, but who the hell knew what was going on?

An hour later, I'd spoken to both of her parents and only succeeded in making her mother hysterical. Neither of them had heard from her since Christmas, either. What the hell was going on? I poured three fingers of scotch into a glass and slammed it and then refilled the glass.

It had been two hours since I'd found her gone. It finally dawned on me to check to see if any of her clothes were missing. At least, if she took some of her things, I could be more certain that she wasn't hurt or worse.

I flipped on the light in the closet. Julia had a lot of clothes, and it was difficult to notice any difference. I looked on the top shelves where the suitcases were stored. Mine was there, hers wasn't. *She left me.* My mind couldn't wrap around the concept. It just wasn't possible, but it was better than the alternative that she was raped, or worse, lying in some alley somewhere. If it were work-related she would tell me so; there really was only one other possibility.

It really hit me. *Julia left me.* Something I never even considered possible.

I stopped and ran a hand over my face, scrubbing at the stubble on my jaw with my fingers. It felt like my heart had fallen out of my chest and was lying at my feet, but at the same time, like it would explode and blow my whole body apart. I struggled to breathe as iron bands tightened around my chest. For five seconds, I hesitated, then I kicked into overdrive, pulling on a sweatshirt and shoving my feet in my Nikes without socks. I grabbed my keys and pulled on my coat, rushing from the apartment, phone in hand. I didn't know where I was going, but I knew I had to look for her. The next thing I knew, I was driving aimlessly around the city, racking up a hundred and fifty dollars of 411 calls for the numbers of every hotel I could think of. I went into four that were closest to her office, but each time the staff looked at me as if I was crazy and shook their heads when I gave them Julia's name.

"I'm sorry sir, we aren't at liberty to share personal information of our guests." They all had the same answer.

"Look, I can't find my wife. You don't have to tell me which room number. I just want to know she's safe," I told the last one, desperation lacing my voice. I could feel my eyes burning and my throat constricting as I pleaded with him. "*Please.*"

He looked nervously around the lush lobby to see who was watching him. Under normal circumstances, she'd never choose this hotel given our budget, but if she was upset enough to leave me, then all bets were off. The man nodded, his face sympathetic. "We don't have any Julia Matthews staying with us, sir. I'm sorry."

"What about Abbott? Julia Abbott?"

He punched a few keys on his computer and sadly shook his head. "No, I'm sorry."

My heart fell and I patted the marble on top of the concierge counter once.

"Okay, thanks, man." There was a parking ticket stuck to the window of my CRV, and I ripped it from under the windshield and shoved it in my pocket.

"Really? In the middle of the fucking night?" I murmured, but this wasn't Boston. It was Manhattan and everything was different here. Suddenly, I hated New York; hated what being here had done to us.

I got back in the car and headed toward Brooklyn. Maybe she'd gone there since it was where we were thinking of buying a house. As the night faded into the pinkish purple morning, I'd made no more progress. I almost fell asleep at the wheel. I finally pulled over when I swerved into another lane and the honking of the oncoming cars jerked me alert.

I parked in the small parking lot of a 7-11 and started making calls instead. My eyes burned and my head throbbed like a son-of-a-bitch. Two hours later, I couldn't think of any more hotels and had called Julia twenty more times with the same results: voicemail.

I hammered the steering wheel five times; so hard that the heel of my hand started to burn as blood rushed under my skin forming a deep purple bruise. I felt completely helpless not being able to reach Julia and know she was safe. It didn't matter that we were fighting. She could yell and scream or give me the cold shoulder, but I would have bet my life that she'd never leave me. I wrapped my arms around the steering wheel and closed my eyes, unable to hold it in anymore. The first tear or two squeezed silently from my closed eyes, and then I started to sob quietly. This whole thing was so fucking unreal. It couldn't be happening.

My left hand was still clutching my phone so tightly that my knuckles turned white. I pushed at the tears on my face with my injured right one. I dialed the hospital HR and told them I was sick. There was no fucking way I could work today. I was so physically and mentally exhausted. I wondered if I'd even be able to drive home. I dragged myself out of the car and bought an energy drink and breakfast burrito, chugging the drink down, hoping it would wake me up. The burrito tasted like ass, but I forced myself to swallow half of it before wrapping the rest up and tossing it on the passenger side floorboard. I started the car, put on a heavy metal station and cranked it.

I'd shoved my phone in my coat pocket, and when it rang, for a moment, my heart leapt in hope it was Julia, until I recognized my mother's ring tone. Jenna or Aaron must have called them. I put the car back in park and shut off the radio, not sure I wanted to get into it with my mom. I should just get my ass home before I killed myself. Talking would only make me lose it again. I hated feeling so fucking weak. I had less power now than when she didn't remember me. At least then, I had a choice to tell her or not. And, she was with me and I knew she was safe. I could take care of her then. Now, I couldn't do a Goddamned thing about any of it.

"Hello?" I cleared my throat and tried to keep it even. I was starting to get jittery from the lack of sleep and the energy drink.

"Honey, it's Mom."

"I know. I saw the caller I.D."

"Are you okay? Jenna and Aaron called and told me you don't know where Julia is."

"Yeah, and?"

"Have you heard from her? I hope she's okay."

So did I. "I think she left me. Her suitcase is gone. I drove around all night looking for her."

"Maybe she'll be at home when you get back, honey." I could hear the tears in my mother's voice.

"No. I don't think so. If she's left, it's worse than I thought."

"I can't believe that she'd ever leave you, baby. She loves you so much."

I felt disgust well up and lodge in my throat even as my eyes blurred. It was hard to push the next words out. "Well, sometimes, I guess, love isn't enough."

"Oh, Honey. Aaron's coming down. He's getting time off from the hospital and should be there by noon."

"For what? What's Aaron gonna do, Mom?" I leaned my head against the side window and closed my eyes.

"He's going to be with you, Ryan. You don't need to be alone right now."

"Is he going to uproot his life to babysit me if she never comes back? Screw that."

"Ryan! Stop talking that way."

I swallowed at the tightness in my throat, but nothing helped. I sucked in air until my lungs hurt, willing myself not to break down. I felt like such a pussy.

"I'm not going to sugarcoat it. It's bad. She doesn't trust me, and even though I'm fucking breaking in two that she left, we don't have shit if we don't have trust." Tears started to seep slowly from my eyes and I sniffed. "I'm so pissed at her! I do everything I can to show her how much she means to me, but if none of it matters, then fuck it! She won't even answer the phone!"

My mom sighed heavily on the other end of the line. "Ryan. It's gonna be okay. No one loves each other more than you two."

The pain in my chest increased and my shoulders started to shake in agony. "I... used to think so."

"Ryan, just go home, baby. Wait for Aaron. She'll call you."

I looked at my phone and still nothing from her. "I haven't heard from her in twenty-four hours."

"She'll call, Ryan. Do you really think Julia would throw your marriage away like this? Come on, honey. You know she'll call."

I didn't want to tell my mom the details about Jane, the gala and all the shit over Christmas. "Have you talked to her?" I asked hopefully.

"No. Do you want me to call her?"

"Jenna was going to try, but I haven't heard from her, so I doubt she'll talk to any of us. I'll call you later, Mom, okay? I want to get home in case she shows up."

"Okay, honey. Keep me posted. Your father said to tell you he loves you and we're here, Ryan. If you need us to come..."

"Mom, honestly, no. Don't take that wrong. I just... I'm a mess right now, and this is between Julia and me."

"Okay, son. Love you."

"You, too." I ended the call and put the car in gear.

*****

When the doorman buzzed that my brother was downstairs, I dragged myself off the couch and pushed the button by the door. "Send him up."

I unlocked the door and left it open a crack, then threw myself back down on the couch. There was a hockey game on ESPN but I wasn't really watching it. It was just the white noise I needed to keep my brain busy enough so I could doze. Aaron came through the door.

"Hey, brother," he said. His eyes were concerned when he came into the living room and shed his coat. He'd dropped his duffle bag by the door. "How you doing?" He sat down in the chair at the end of the couch and reached over to squeeze my shoulder.

I stared at the TV, not even looking at him. "I've been better."

"Haven't heard from Jules, yet, huh?" Aaron's voice was cautious.

I grabbed the phone from the coffee table in front of me and tossed it at him. "See for yourself. I've sent more than a hundred text messages. She's killing me. I can't fucking breathe, I'm so worried."

Aaron picked up the phone just as it jingled with an incoming message. After all the messages that weren't Julia, I didn't even flinch at the sound.

I slid my eyes to Aaron as he looked at the phone before setting it back on the table. "It's from Jane."

I shook my head and huffed. She'd texted and called several times, and each time my resentment of her grew. "She needs to disappear. I swear to fucking God, Aaron, I wish I'd been the one to take that knife in the gut that night. Everything is so fucked up because of it."

"Is it really due to that, or was this Jane woman warm for your form before all this happened? Maybe this was just the catalyst."

I lifted a shoulder in a half shrug. "No clue. Don't really give a shit, either." I slowly rose and walked into the kitchen. "You want a beer? As soon as I hear she's safe, I plan on switching to scotch. Passing out is the only way I can stop thinking about this shit."

"Yeah," he called back. "If that's what it takes to sleep, I think you should."

I walked back with two open beer bottles and handed one to Aaron, who was now flipping through the channels. "Do you mind?" he asked.

I shook my head and sat back down, taking a long pull on the beer. "The last text I sent to her was that I was calling the cops if I didn't hear from her, but I have to wait until tonight. Of course, it is so fucking wrong that they won't do anything. They wait until enough time has passed that if she was hurt or ab-ducted she could be dead before they do anything. I can't stand not knowing, Aaron." My throat was so tight it throbbed.

"Do you really think it might be foul play?"

"I don't think it started out that way. I think she's upset and left me, but she'd just tell me she left; she wouldn't put me through the hell of not knowing she's okay. It's been 42 hours since I left her yesterday morning. I hate this fucking town, Aaron."

My phone jingled again and I cringed. *Would Jane just leave me the hell alone already?*

"Aren't you going to check that?"

I shook my head. "I'm sure it's Jane again."

Aaron reached for the phone and then handed it to me. "It's from Julia, Ryan."

I bolted up and grabbed the phone, my heart beating like hell.

~R, I wanted to let you know I'm safe.
I just need some time alone. ~J

My thumbs flew over the keys as I returned her text.

Where are you?

It doesn't matter, Ryan.

"Goddammit!" I said aloud as I punched the keys again.

TELL ME where you are!

I can't. Just trust me that I'm okay and
I'll be in touch.

Yeah, right. You mean, the way you trust me?

I threw the phone on the couch next to me knowing she wouldn't return the text and got up to get the scotch.

"What's going on, Ryan?" Aaron asked.

"I'm getting shitfaced, that's what. She won't tell me where she is."

"At least you know she's safe."

I couldn't argue his logic, but still, my heart constricted so much it felt like it would implode. "Want scotch?" I asked.

"I'm good with beer."

"Okay, then," I muttered and took a swig from the bottle without bothering with a glass. The amber liquid burned all the way down. I wanted to sleep, to calm down, and to lose the sickening feeling that had taken root in my chest since the night before. I was so tired now; I couldn't fall asleep unaided and I needed it. I stood there and downed three more big swigs before taking it with me into the living room. I sprawled out on the couch and flung my arm over my eyes, trying to concentrate on the commentary from the game on television and praying for the solace of sleep.

Julia ~

I felt like a walking zombie. Two days. 48 hours. That's how long it'd been since I'd left New York, and slightly longer since I'd seen Ryan. My heart and head ached as I dropped my carry-on in the lavish hotel room. I had to hand it to Meredith. She didn't do anything half-assed. I fell on the bed in exhaustion. I'd cried practically the entire flight, and now I was completely spent. Thank God for the first class seat that meant more privacy. I was grateful for the flight attendant's discretion when she brought me two glasses of white wine and a hot towel. I refused the meal, my appetite completely nonexistent.

I felt empty and utterly alone. It was self-imposed isolation, but it still hurt like hell. Ryan's text made it worse and broke my heart, but I guess I shouldn't expect his understanding when I left without even a note.

During the flight, my phone had to be off, but after the last message, I deliberately turned it back off before listening to the many voicemails he'd left. I didn't want to face the anger I was sure to hear in his tone, or the scathing words of his messages. I'd left knowing full well it would hurt him deeply, and he'd be mad as hell. Guilt, and something that hurt so bad I couldn't articulate it, filled my entire being. The pain was soul-deep, physical, and debilitating. For the first time in forever, I couldn't reach for Ryan or call him and expect the comfort I needed. I blamed myself for leaving, but I blamed him for making it necessary.

My face crumpled and my chest seized as the tears began again. I rolled onto my side and drew my knees up, curling into a ball in hope to ease some of the pain, but it was hopeless. "Oh, Ryan. Please, forgive me," I cried, the sobs starting to shake my shoulders. I let myself drown in my grief, my right hand wrapped around the bracelet on my left wrist. I'd considered leaving it behind, but I couldn't make myself take it off again. After Ryan's impassioned forcing of it back in place, there was no way I'd ever take it off again. I was mad at him and hurt, but our souls were furled around each other as much as the letters on the bracelet. It was a tangible link to him; a part of both of us.

A few minutes later, I gathered the strength to pull out the phone and turned it on, scared shitless of what I would find, but desperate to hear his voice. There were 20 calls from Ryan, three from my dad, two from my mom, four from Jenna, one from Elyse and one from Ellie. Apparently, the cavalry was out in force.

I was a coward. I snuck away without talking to Ryan, knowing I wouldn't be able to leave if I did. I needed to clear my head, and get away from everything that brought Jane to mind. Now, I was avoiding his calls. He would be hurt, pissed and probably frantic. I knew my leaving would devastate him, and *still*, I left. The pain of living through more of that crap seemed more unthinkable in that moment than hurting him. I was going out of my mind.

My phone rang in my hand and I almost dropped it, my heart beginning to pound so furiously I could feel my pulse throbbing in my neck and ears.

My fingers trembled as I pushed connect. "Hello?"

"Thank God, you finally answered! Julia! Darling, we're all so worried about you! Ryan is out of his mind." Elyse's voice shook.

I closed my eyes against her words, against the burning behind my already swollen eyes. "I'm sorry," I said weakly, trying hard not to let my voice crack. My stuffy nose would give away that I'd been crying. "I just needed to get away for a little while."

"But, darling, without telling Ryan? This isn't like you." Her voice was filled with understanding that I didn't deserve.

The tears spilled and rolled in fat drops, one by one down my cheeks. "I knew I wouldn't be able to leave if I saw him first. He…" I tried to clear my throat, "he wouldn't have let me. I wouldn't have been strong enough to walk away from him."

"Oh, honey. You need to call him. He's so upset. What's this all about?"

"Didn't he…" I stopped to clear my throat "Didn't he tell you?"

"Yes, but I want to hear your side of it."

I tried to breathe evenly; to calm the erratic palpitation of my heart. "Ever since that night in the ER, the woman that saved him... she's chasing after Ryan with stars in her eyes. She doesn't give us a moment's peace. She calls in the middle of the night, pages him ten times a day, shows up at our apartment unannounced, and then stays all evening!" My voice broke on the words. "She's like a cancer seeping into my life, and he's letting her, Elyse. I saw them kiss on New Year's Eve at the Aids Gala."

She sighed heavily. "Yes, Ryan told me there were issues, but he said it was nothing, and you're making more of it than it is."

"It wasn't nothing. She's in love with him. She told me afterward that she wanted him. She cornered me in the bathroom when I went to get myself together."

Elyse gasped. "What? Did you tell Ryan?"

"It doesn't matter."

"I can't believe that anything you say wouldn't hold weight with my son, Julia."

"He knows she talked to me, but he never asked for details. He closes his eyes when it comes to her. He won't see her as anything other than this saint who sacrificed herself for him."

"I know he feels grateful, Julia, but that is all there is to it. You know how much he loves you."

"I'm not saying that he's cheating, but I still feel betrayed and resentful. Then after, I feel guilty and angry at myself because I owe Ryan's life to her! I can't stand watching it, Elyse! I just needed a break so I can breathe again and re-group. It wasn't Ryan that I was trying to get away from. But..." My voice broke on a sob. "I don't see him much. He's either working or constantly dealing with her. When we are together, we're either making love or screaming at each other." I flushed at my confession.

"You have to call him, Julia. It's not fair to put Ryan through not knowing where you are." She was soothing, but I could hear that she was anxious and upset. "To let him believe you've left him. You should have heard him when I called him yesterday."

"I texted that I was safe and I'd call soon. He knows I could never leave him. Not really, Elyse." I couldn't tell her that I couldn't call during the hours I was in the air.

Elyse's voice took on a harder, motherly tone. "Julia, how would you like it if he did this to you? Imagine how you'd feel. All he knows is that you aren't acting like yourself, and he doesn't have anything to hold on to. You need to call him this instant!"

"Is he okay?" I choked out, pressing my wrist to my mouth, tears rolling fatly down my cheeks.

"You know the answer to that. He's insane with worry, Julia, and it's not fair."

"Is it fair that he doesn't set up any boundaries with Jane? I feel like I'm the intruder, like I'm interrupting *them*. How am I supposed to feel, for God's sake? He's the only one that can fix it, and he just... won't." I wiped at the hot tears streaming down my face again.

"I understand why you might feel that way, but it's unfair to say he hasn't done anything about it. He said he's talked to her. You and Ryan will work this out. He loves you more than any-thing, and I know you feel the same way."

"Yes. I wouldn't be dying inside if I didn't love him so much." The words were soft, but with conviction.

"Ryan is dying with this, too. So, call him, baby. Please."

"When was the last time you spoke with him?"

"Just the one time. He's not answering anymore, but Aaron is in New York with him, and he said Ryan's a mess."

My hand clutched the material of my blouse over my heart. "He's probably so mad at me. It already hurts so bad, I just..."

"Just call him."

"Mmmm, huh," I sniffed.

We talked for a few more minutes, and I promised that I'd call Ryan as soon as I hung up the phone. I pushed one on speed dial before I could change my mind. My heart hammered so sickeningly, I felt it would burst out of my chest. Ryan picked up after two rings.

"Julia?" I could hear the panic in his voice, and it hurt. And he sounded utterly exhausted. "Where are you?" he demanded. "Jesus, are you okay?"

"I'm fine," I lied. I wasn't fine. I hadn't been fine for weeks. "I texted hours ago."

"Anyone could have sent a text from your phone. How was I to know someone hadn't hurt you and had your phone? I needed to hear your voice!"

My heart squeezed inside my chest and plummeted to the pit of my stomach. I'd never thought of that. "I'm sorry. From your response, it seemed you knew it was me. I didn't think you'd believe something bad happened to me."

"No shit, you didn't *think*!" he spat angrily, and I winced.

"Look, I don't want to talk if you're just going to yell at me." I was exhausted and emotionally drained.

"What did you expect me to do?" he yelled again. "Agghhhh! Tell me where you are! I'll come to get you." His voice was thick, throbbing with anger and something else completely indefinable.

"You can't come. Just... I need some time. Ryan, please. Just give me a little time," I said again, praying he would accept my plea and not press me. It was too much to hope for.

"Why are you doing this to me? To us?" Anguish practically dripped from his voice, and it killed me. It was more than anger; he was hurt.

"I didn't mean to hurt you." The words ripped from me. Physically, my throat was aching, and emotionally, I knew I was done.

He huffed into the phone. "Yeah, *right*! That's why you ran off without a fucking word? Don't ask me to believe you give a flying fuck what you'd put me through!" he ground out.

Tears squeezed from my closed eyes as I struggled not to let out the sobs building up inside. "I told you I didn't think. I just had to get away. I can't be in New York right now. I'm sorry you're hurting, but no more than me!"

"You left town? Are you in California with Ellie?"

"I'm not in California."

"Then, where are you? How in the hell am I supposed to keep my head in the job like this?" Ryan demanded. I pictured him pacing angrily around the apartment, just back from the hospital, still in his scrubs. I was certain he was exhausted.

My throat was swollen and I felt sick inside. "*Your* job. *Your* life. *Your friend.* Your everything, right? I'm just an observer. Stuck on the outside looking in." I hated the crack in my voice, the weakness and helplessness that held me prisoner.

"What exactly are you saying, Julia? Tell me where the hell you are! *Right now!*" His breathing was hard; I could hear the refrigerator door open and then slam over the phone, with the clink of glass bottles hitting each other echoing in the background.

I sucked in my breath and let my fury fly. It wasn't as if he didn't already know why I left. "I'm saying that while that woman is invading your every waking moment, as long as you *let her*, I'm not coming home, Ryan, okay?" I yelled into the phone, panting, my face crumpling in pain. "I can't take it anymore!" My chest was heaving, and I was shaking so much I almost dropped the phone.

He sighed heavily. "This is getting so fucking old. You know I was only trying to be a good friend and nothing more! We talked about this!"

I rolled over again; a new wave of pain threatening to drown me like the deepest ocean. That name was like nails on a chalkboard. I was so fucking sick of hearing it. Jane this, Jane that, poor Jane... *blah, blah, blah*! Maybe I was being a bitch, but at that point, the pain overtook caring.

"Barely, and so what? Nothing has changed! When you're done letting your *friend* suck up all your free time and remember you're married, give me a call."

"It isn't like that! I told her to back off, but I owe her! Don't we both owe her?"

I was so friggin' tired of hearing Ryan take her side over mine; tired of fighting with him over her, and tired of feeling upset that his words made me feel guilty about my own pain.

"I won't let you turn me into the bad guy over this, Ryan! I will not stay and watch while you let her drive a wedge between us. We never see each other, so I'm surprised you even notice I'm gone! Did you let Jane know you were calling me?" I asked bitterly. "I mean, could she spare you for a moment?" I sniffed. I knew I sounded like a petulant child and truly didn't care. "How generous. Remind me to thank her," I said sarcastically.

Ryan sucked in his breath harshly and paused. "This isn't you, Julia. Where is the generous, giving woman I know?" he asked quietly. "You're not being fair."

The air left my lungs in a whoosh as the pain replaced the anger instantly. My voice was quiet and raspy, my throat raw from crying. I felt numb.

"I can't believe you just said that to me." He was doing it again; taking her side over mine. Maybe that wasn't even what was happening, but resentment welled up inside me like a dam ready to burst. She was taking him away from me and he was letting her, he was *helping* her. *"I'm* not being fair?"

"It's not that Goddamned easy and you know it! I can't be an out-and-out bastard to her. She sacrificed a lot."

So did I, Ryan! I suffered your absence for years while we built this life!

"Yeah, I know the feeling. I guess she wins though, since she bled real blood," I said miserably. I flushed at the jab, but I was hurting so Goddamned bad, I couldn't help but lash out.

I could hear his breathing get shorter. He knew how much his words stung. "You know what we have is sacred. Please, just stop this." His voice was raw and urgent.

"Then why have I felt so alone? It feels like you've completely abandoned me."

"You know how much I love you and I'm sorry. I just ..."

"No," I begged. "Please don't say anymore. Every word... *hurts.* I can't take it. Just give me some time. Don't call me. Let me...figure things out." I felt like I was drowning, clawing for the surface and Ryan could save me, but he didn't.

"Julia... please..." I could hear his voice shaking, cracking; husky from tears. "Don't do this. We figure shit out together. So, tell me where you are so I can come to you. I need to come get you! I'm going crazy. For the past eight and a half years, I've always known where you are. This is killing me."

I closed my eyes, and my heart began to ache again when my Ryan finally showed up. That was the voice of the man who loved me, and I wanted nothing more than to be in his arms.

"I'm safe, and I'll call. I promise." My voice broke again.

"Are you... Is it... I mean, are we over?" Each word was dripping in emotion, anguish, and panic.

Pain sliced through me. A month ago those words would never have come out of his mouth. *Why didn't he know that nothing could ever make me leave him?*

"I just can't deal with it right now. I need a little break. Jane is taking a part of you that used to be mine, and I can't stand by and watch."

"For Christ's sake! No one has the part of me that belongs to you."

All of you used to belong to me. My heart was pounding. I wanted to claw the skin off of my body.

I know. I tried to force the words out, but they stuck in my throat because they felt like a lie. But, I *didn't* know. Not anymore. And, it was killing me.

The seconds ticked by while we both cried, both of us waiting for the other to say something and neither willing to end the call. I knew he could hear the tears and the sniffles, even though I kept the sobs confined to the silent shaking of my shoulders as I pressed the heel of my hand to my mouth. Somehow, I had to keep him from hearing how broken I really was.

"Just tell me that you still love me," he begged raggedly. "God, Julia, please."

That was the end of me, and the sobs finally erupted into the silent room. "You know..." I gasped. "You know how I feel, Ryan. Nothing will change that."

"The why didn't you come talk to me?" The words sounded like they were pulled from him, but they still sliced through my soul. "And why won't you *say it*?"

This was the second time he'd questioned me about loving him. The first time being when Meredith offered me the first promotion on his visit to New York for Valentine's Day when he proposed. I tried to swallow the pain so I could speak, but it still crept into my shaky voice. "Just a little time, okay? Try to under-stand how it's been for me." *I love you, but it hurts too much to be with you right now.* "I just really need your understanding. Just for a little while."

He sighed heavily. His voice was low and thick, laced with his own tears. "Okay. God, I'll try. When we got married, some-times you wondered if a love like this even exists, remember?" I remembered clearly; those words were part of my wedding vows. "It exists, or it wouldn't hurt so fucking bad. But, only for us, Julia." Ryan's voice was deep, but thick with tears. "Believe that and... don't forget to remember me."

I gasped as Ryan said the words that connected us for the past five years. My heart broke anew, shattering instantly into a million pieces that ripped me to shreds. He knew those words would yank my heart right from my chest. And, they did. It was pure manipulation, pure guilt, pure heaven, and pure hell. Two could play at that game.

As if I could ever forget him. My eyes squeezed shut and pushed more tears down my cheeks.

"*You forgot to remember me,*" I said weakly.

I quickly hung up the phone right before I pushed my face into one of the plush white pillows and screamed. I needed him like he used to be. I needed the brilliance of us, like we were, or it would never be good enough. I cried and cried into the pillow, praying for the strength to get my head on straight.

I needed time without suffering Jane's continued presence and the guilt I felt over being so angry. I needed sanity and peace and rational thought. I needed to be able to function and heal. But, I also knew that I'd never be able to breathe without him. Lately, I hadn't been able to breathe either way. Yes, I owed Jane everything... but until Ryan could put things into perspec-tive and take back our lives, I was out.

I got up and went to the suitcase, unzipping it, and pulling out the T-shirt I'd stashed there. I pulled it to my face and inhaled his scent as I went back to the bed. Still fully-clothed, I crawled under the covers, not caring if the sun ever came up again. I curled up and brought the shirt to my face, clutching it to me as I cried into the darkness. How quickly our lives had changed; the neat, perfect package was now so fucked up. Only one thing remained...the insane love. It was crippling in its intensity.

My fingers curled into the pillows and the fabric of the shirt as I sobbed softly into the darkness, aching for the arms that would ease the hurt, and the words that would assure me we'd be okay. I'd left him, but it felt like he'd left me. Like I was the one without the choice.

My broken words echoed around the room like they were coming from someone else.

"I just want you back, Ryan," I said into the darkness. "I want *us* back."

Half a world separated us, and I'd just severed my only connection to the one person I never thought I could live without. I'd walked away from the love of my life, in the desperate hope that my best friend would find his way back to me.

~12~

Julia ~

I'd finally fallen asleep after another two hours of crying, but it was the fitful, twilight-type that only made me feel even more exhausted. In the morning, I stood looking out the window over Paris with bloodshot eyes. The river looked dark sapphire, and the Eiffel Tower lifted against a bright azure sky. It was an artist's dream to be here, and I'd always wanted to come. I'd just never imagined it would be without Ryan. At least, not after I'd gotten in the accident and missed the opportunity last year.

Ryan talked of coming here and Italy to tour the many landmarks and museums so central to my art education. I felt numb; as if I were having some out of body experience, an elaborate nightmare that I would soon awake from.

The plush terry of the hotel robe that wrapped my body felt real enough, and my wet head was wrapped in a matching towel. I sniffed in regret, willing myself not to allow a new torrent of tears. My phone was conspicuously silent this morning, but he was only doing as I asked. It had only been twelve hours since we spoke, but there was that part of me that was surprised, and if I were honest, disappointed. My feelings were all screwed up, and I did need to sort stuff out, but my needy, sore heart longed for affirmation that he wanted me back.

I huffed, chastising myself and sat down on the edge of the bed. What did I expect? How many times had my father told me that guys are literal and will take spoken words for gospel. *'Men are easy, just don't say anything you don't mean,'* he'd told me once in high school when I had a fight with my boyfriend. *'You're confusing the poor kid, sweet pea.'*

I never confused Ryan and he never confused me. That was part of the reason we were connected from the hip from day one, but things were so screwed up now. My own conflicted feelings for Jane held me back from telling Ryan how much she was bothering me when she first started getting under my skin. That was my big mistake. But... normally, he would have just known without my having to say a word. I pulled the towel loose from my still-damp hair, and it fell heavily around my face. I pushed it behind my ears and dialed Meredith.

"How's Paris?" She was exuberant when she answered.

"I haven't seen much of it yet. I thought I'd give some thought to that fill before I go into the office."

"It's Sunday, anyway, hon."

"Oh, sorry, it's all sort of a blur. Does the Paris staff know about the hostile takeover?" I asked, only half kidding. "I wouldn't like it if someone showed up on my turf unannounced ready to rearrange everything."

Meredith laughed. "They expected you six months ago, babes. But don't worry, I told them it's temporary and that you're there because you're an ace. You'll show them how to get things done and that will be that. Unless... you decide you want to stay for good. In which case, Monique will be fired."

My face screwed up at her nonchalant dismissal of another person's worth. "No, Meredith. I promise... that won't be the case." Without giving her room to form an argument toward her cause, I asked when I could expect Andrea and Mike.

"Flying out tomorrow. John was sure pissed that I'm taking all of you. It's beyond me why he's scrambling. He knew it was coming."

I wasn't sure my New York publisher did, considering I had no intention of taking this job, given Ryan's and my plans. I could understand how he would be put out, and I felt a flash of guilt for the short notice. "I'll call him. That's the beauty of wireless. I can still do my job from here, if I need to."

"Honey, that's admirable, but concentrate on the job at hand."

"I want to be busy, so I don't mind working for both of you."

"Me first, John second. Got it?"

"Got it, but he would disagree. I did promise to do the fill for February. Two pages shouldn't be difficult. How is that issue stacking up here?"

"Shitty, I'm sure."

"Your confidence is overwhelming."

"You have no idea," she answered blandly. I could hear her pulling on a cigarette then blowing it all out.

"I'll try to think of a feature we can use in both. That way, I can ease into it and, hopefully, not piss anyone off over here."

"Who cares? Piss off whoever you need to, as long as you get the job done."

After I hung up, I returned the call from my parents. I'd planned to make light of it all and just say I had an emergency fire, but when my dad told me Ryan called him, I had to come clean. Thank God I didn't have to speak to my mother, but he made me promise to call her later in the week.

I dressed in jeans, a heavy wool sweater, and kept the make-up to a minimum. I didn't feel like taking the time, and I didn't really care what I looked like. I hoped getting out and exploring Paris, most specifically the Louvre, would lighten my mood and spark my creative juices for the magazine article. My stomach felt empty, but somehow not hungry, so I didn't bother with breakfast. I donned knee-high black leather walking boots and pulled on my long wool coat and mittens, shoving my phone into my purse and heading out of the hotel into the biting cold January air.

The city was far less bustling than New York, filled with sidewalk cafés and a lazy atmosphere that I welcomed. The street seating was, of course, abandoned for the warmth inside. It would be nice to visit again in the spring. Meredith said there was no place on earth like springtime in Paris. Again, my thoughts landed on Ryan and our plans to come together. Loneliness out-shadowed any wonder that I'd momentarily been able to conjure for my day's adventure.

The bitter wind whipped my hair into my eyes, and my gloved finger curled around a piece that found its way into the corner of my mouth. I pulled up my GPS app on my phone and entered the current address and that of the Louvre. It was northeast of my hotel and across the Seine River, but less than a mile. The wind would make my ears ache, but I chose not to hail a cab. My time in New York conditioned me to walk blocks and blocks without hesitation, so I didn't give it a second thought. I passed the French Institute, admiring the architecture, and promising myself to visit before I left the city. Today, though, my heart needed the more direct diversion that the Louvre and its magnificent contents would provide. I could just wander and keep to myself, which was all my fragile state could handle.

I hoped getting lost in the works of Michelangelo, da Vinci, Degas, and Monet would occupy my mind and ease the ache in my heart. I felt sick inside. Leaving just made a tough situation worse. I knew it even before I left, but I just couldn't stay. The abyss between Ryan and I made it difficult for me to tell him where I was, and I would be no better off than when I left. I sighed, telling myself that he needed the distance to gain perspective as much as I did.

I wasn't even sure what I expected Ryan to say to Jane, but after the bathroom scene at the gala. I was done with her. I couldn't feel sorry or empathetic anymore. The conflict I felt was now centered around Ryan, alone.

Despite my whole self-talk about perspective, I did want him to come after me to miss so much he wouldn't rest until he found me. Making him work for it was selfish, it would be detrimental to his residency, and there was no way I'd want his career to suffer, no matter what was going on between us. Ever. Even if I lost him completely, I'd never wish him anything but the very best. In that moment, I made the decision to call him later that night and tell him where I was. I had so much weakness where he was concerned, yet when we were together, he gave me so much strength. Longing just to talk to him became overwhelming.

My eyes filled with tears, and as quickly as one fat drop fell onto my cheek, I hastily brushed it away. I turned onto the bridge that would take me across the Seine and to the museum sitting at the end of it. I could see it from here, and its magnificence was nothing less than I expected.

I drew a deep breath, trying to calm my nerves. I'd never questioned that Ryan and I would be together forever, and I wanted to trust that. Except, this shit with Jane was the first time he'd chosen not to be available to me. Even in college when we were friends, and his girlfriends came and went, I knew that if I needed him, he'd drop everything in a heartbeat. That knowledge and my sketchpad were the only two things that held my heart together on those long, solitary evenings. Now, here I was again, with my art and uncertainty. I felt sad because I had to do something this drastic to motivate that kind of devotion.

I couldn't begin to guess what he'd do now. Had I done enough damage to make him walk away from me? I didn't want to consider it, but my heart sank to the pit of my stomach. My brain reeled so much I felt dizzy with it.

Seriously, I shouldn't have been surprised when he didn't call me this morning. Isn't that what I'd asked of him? It wasn't like him to give up all control and accept it without a fight, so doubt dug away at me. Would he throw it all back in my face? Ryan was proud and stubborn, but we'd always been connected on some celestial level that was a force stronger than either one of us. I closed my eyes, my throat beginning to tighten. I clung desperately to that connection, praying it would be strong enough to get us through it all. I stopped and grabbed the metal railing on the bridge for support as regret washed through me. I shouldn't have left.

I wanted to turn right around and go home, but Meredith would be angry that I started something I wasn't prepared to finish. It would certainly put my job in jeopardy, and if God forbid, Ryan and I did break up, work was all I'd have to get me through it.

The cold wind once again whipped my hair back and pushed the remnants of my tears back toward my ears. Angry at the mess I'd created for myself, I wiped them away with my cashmere glove and straightened my spine.

I continued on my way, noticing many couples on the bridge despite the icy temperature. Some passionately kissing, some talking or laughing, but all wrapped up lovingly in each other's arms. As I drew closer to the center of the river, I noticed the railing and fence were covered from top to bottom with all shapes and sizes of padlocks. Glancing around, I watched the couples and lifted a few of the locks to inspect them one by one. Some were expensive and some the dime store variety. All of them had two names and a date written with marker or scratched into the metal; some adorned with ribbons, yarn, or charms. I placed my elbows on the top of the fence and leaned over to look down at the murky water.

The couple standing next to me were obviously tourists, speaking in German. I observed them in my peripheral vision without looking at them directly. The young man put the padlock onto the fence, kissed the key then offered it to his girlfriend. She took it in her hand and gave it her own kiss. In a romantic gesture, the man placed his hand over hers, and laughing, they flung the key into the Seine. I'd never felt more alone than I did in that moment. I literally ached for Ryan to be beside me; to slide my hand around his bicep and lean my head on his strong shoulder. I swallowed back the lump of emotion in my throat. It should be us throwing our own key into the river below.

It was obvious from the expanse of locks on both sides of the bridge, and the many couples adding to it, that this was a long-standing lover's tradition. I wondered about the details of how it originated, whether it was connected to some mythical legend, and if the city would let them remain in place. Obviously, it was a pledge of unbreakable bonds symbolized by a lock that could never be undone since it was nearly impossible to recover the key. It would be so easy to burst into tears and sob my heart out. I didn't want to draw attention to myself or impact the happiness of these couples. I left the happy couples behind me and hurried on to the museum, the whole time fighting the emotions trying to erupt from within.

Two hours later, the gravity of what'd I'd done to Ryan by leaving without telling him, was still too fresh to allow thoughts of anything else. The subject of Jane seemed impossible for Ryan and I to discuss without blowing up at each other. The pain of not being able to talk to him, with the same ease that we communicated about everything else was the root of the problem. More than Jane's blatant attempts to take him; I was completely devastated that the intimate closeness we shared did not apply to this.

I was tired, and longed for a coffee shop that would allow me the Sunday ritual that had always made me feel close, despite the distance. I found one close by and ordered Ryan's soy cappuccino double shot instead of the iced coffee that was my usual. It was a small comfort, but it was something.

It was much stronger than I was used to, but I sat with my hands wrapped around the cup, gazing into the blazing fire from the central, stand-alone fireplace. The pipe that served as makeshift chimney ran directly up to the vaulted ceiling. How ironic that our choice of drink mirrored each of us so well: Ryan's so much stronger than mine. At least, that's how I felt sitting here, uneager to return to my empty hotel room and the even emptier bed. At least here, I could imagine he was also having coffee at the Hill of Beans near our house or even in the hospital cafeteria. My mind couldn't help reminding me that Jane was, no doubt, at the hospital tagging along after Ryan like a dog. I deeply resented how she invaded my thoughts of him, as she invaded our life together.

It began to get darker, the sun dropping to a place low in the sky and shone pink and orange in the violet sky below the edge of the clouds that were moving to the east. I looked forward to seeing the blue sky again tomorrow. In New York when you looked up, the sky got lost in the metal, bricks, and glass of the towering mass of buildings. The big expanse of sky and the art were my two favorite things about Paris so far.

I pulled out my phone, and though it was almost seven in the evening, it would be two o'clock on Sunday afternoon in New York. I was unsure if Ryan would get the message, but I had to send it anyway.

Having coffee and thinking of you.
I know things are messed up, but I miss you...

I waited for twenty minutes for a response that never came and finished Ryan's cappuccino, feeling bereft.

"Mon belle... Pourquoi avez-vous l'air si triste?"

I looked up to find a very finely dressed gentleman bending slightly at the waist as he inquired of me. I could tell by the inflection in his voice he was asking me something but I had no idea what. I took in the fine wool material of his black suit and the silk of his sienna tie, just the briefest shade darker than his shirt. I scrambled to pull up the English/French dictionary on my iPhone. I only knew a few basic phrases and had no idea what he'd just asked.

"Um..." I beseeched him with my eyes. "Pardonnez-moi. Could you repeat that?" I asked, stupidly mixing French and English. I ended up shaking my head in wry amusement. "Je ne parle pas Français." I grimaced at my horrible accent. I shrugged apologetically and shook my head. "I'm sorry."

"May I sit with you, mademoiselle?" He asked in perfect English, his accent impeccable. "I have been admiring you for quite some time as you sat here with your thoughts and felt I had to ask why you appear so sad."

The man was handsome, with salt and pepper hair, cut short, and he had an immaculately groomed goatee, his clothing and shoes as expensive as his carriage demanded they be. I sat in silence as he sat down before I had the chance to answer.

"It's *Madame* and I'm simply missing my husband, but thank you." I grabbed for my coat but the man put up his hand to stop me.

"Ah, he is a lucky man. There is no need to run away," he began with a charming smile. "You are quite beautiful. Your husband is insane to leave you to wander cafés alone."

"I'm meeting up with him for dinner soon. He had to work today, and I wanted to visit the Louvre," I lied, completely unprepared for such a situation.

"Ah, yes. It is amazing, is it not? It should not be missed while in Paris. You are American?" he asked, lifting his arm and signaling for the waiter. "Can I get you another café?"

"No, thank you." I studied his clear eyes with their light laugh lines. He had a fatherliness about him that settled me. It would be nice to lose a little time before facing my lonely hotel room. "But, if you don't mind... I am interested in the locks on the bridge. Will you tell me about them?"

He flashed a brilliant smile. "But, of course! First, I insist on introducing myself. My name is Étienne Lemieux. And, you are?" He proffered his hand. I marveled at the French language that made mere names sound like poetry.

"Julia Matthews." I took his hand, and he gently raised it to his lips for a soft kiss.

"The pleasure is mine, Julia. Americans are always fascinated by our customs of love."

My fingers fiddled with the napkin in my lap.

"Before I get into the story, what brings you to Paris?" His accent curled around each word like a lover.

"Work, I'm afraid. I'm a creative director for Vogue."

"Ah. Very impressive. So is that your interest in the locks? A story for your magazine?"

I stopped and met his eyes, as the first smile in what felt like forever lifted the corners of my mouth. "You know what? That's a fantastic idea." I chuckled.

"Most Parisians know about the locks, so how will you make interesting, eh?"

Étienne lifted his hand again and a waiter promptly appeared. He ordered for both of us and soon more coffee, sparkling water, and an assortment of fancy little sandwiches and pastries appeared on the table.

"Personally, I would choose a different venue for dinner, but you look like if you don't eat you'll blow away," he teased. "S'il vous plait." He offered the sandwiches. I'd just told him I was meeting Ryan, and though my stomach rumbled painfully, I shook my head. I'd order something from room service.

"No, thank you." I felt at a loss not knowing the language. I had the translator app on the phone but had yet to use it, except in the cab from the airport. "Forgive me. I always feel visitors should use the language of the country they are visiting, but I've only just arrived. I haven't quite gotten the hang of things."

Étienne took three sandwiches for himself, setting them on the small lunch plate in front of him. "Nonsense. Europe is a close community. We know many languages here. Come. You must at least try a sweet. We have the best pâtisseries in our city."

I obliged, choosing a fresh fruit tart, and using my fork, cut into it for a small bite. It was extremely delicious.

"I've always wanted to learn French and Spanish, since both of those languages are used on my continent, but I never seem to have the opportunity," I admitted sheepishly.

"The best way is to simply immerse yourself in the culture." He waved away my apology. "You are here now, and you will learn quickly. Now, for the story about the locks. You know Paris is the city of love, yes?"

"I've heard that, yes." I smiled and took another small bite of the decadent dessert.

"Are you a romantic at heart, Julia?"

"Yes, I suppose I am."

"And, your husband? Does he lavish you with romance? All women are beautiful and deserve to be worshiped."

I let out an embarrassed giggle. "Ryan is romantic, yes." The day was turning out to be much better than I'd thought it would. Ryan would be horrified that I was sharing dessert and coffee with a complete stranger, but we were in a public place, and I didn't feel the least bit threatened. It was so much more appealing than sitting here alone.

"Yes, well, lovers from around the world come to Paris and go to the bridges to pledge and seal their love for all eternity. They write their names or other words of love on the lock, place it on the fence, and then fling the key into the river."

"I did see some of them doing that."

"Well, it's said that the only way to break the seal of love pledged this way is to retrieve the key to unlock it. Nearly, if not absolutely, impossible."

"I thought so," I admitted. "Bridges? There is more than one?"

He nodded. "Ah, yes. Two. One, *Pont de l'Archevêché* is for lovers, and the other, the one across from the Museum, *Pont des Arts,* is for committed love." He laughed gently. "I'm sure you can guess that one is much more crowded than the other."

My heart warmed at the story, but I cast my eyes downward to hide the pain behind them. "Yes. There can be many lovers, but only one true love."

His icy eyes widened, slightly. "Ahhhh. I can see you have found him, already. There is no mistaking the soft glow about you. Whoever he is, he is very lucky, indeed."

"My husband, of course."

"Then, you are doubly lucky. So many of us do not ever find such a love, and the blessing of marriage with the same person, eh?" He lifted his demitasse to his lips.

"I can't imagine marrying someone I didn't love with all my heart." My emotions surely flowed over my face, and I hated that I had no ability to hide the expressiveness of my features.

He set his espresso back down on the saucer. "Sadly, this life is filled with many intrusions, and the road to love is not always a clear one. Quoi qu'il en soit, il serait beaucoup moins excitant..." he stopped himself and laid a hand on the front of his suit jacket. "Forgive me. I said it would be so much less exciting if it were so. Don't you agree?"

Heat seeped into my cheeks. I could use a little less excitement at the moment, I thought silently. "Maybe you will place a lock on *both* bridges before you leave the city?"

I smiled but took a sip of my coffee instead of answering, and cringed at its bitterness. The man took note of my sour face.

"My dear, why do you order this if you do not enjoy it?"

"I was trying something different, but it's much too strong for my liking."

He began to lift his hand once again. "Can I get you something else?"

"Thank you, no. I really enjoyed meeting you, monsieur, but I really must be going."

"Perhaps we will bump into each other again one day, madame," he said pleasantly.

"I'd like that. I'm sure I will visit the Louvre again."

"Be sure to visit the other obvious attractions: the Champs Elysées, Arch of Triumph, Eiffel Tower, and the Left Bank. The city has so much beauty to behold."

I stood and the gentleman followed, taking my coat and holding it while I slid my arms in the sleeves, then he settled it on my shoulders.

"I won't. Thank you."

"A bientôt, ma belle Julia. Au revoir." He lifted my hand to his mouth again.

"It's been a pleasure. Au revoir." I offered a smile and small wave and left the little café. My hotel wasn't far, but it was colder now that the sun had set. I hailed a passing taxi, suddenly anxious to get behind closed doors where I could take a bath and work out my article. And, despite my protests the night before, I wanted to try calling Ryan again. The melancholy ache returned, and climbing in the back seat, I dialed his number, hoping he'd be at lunch and able to talk, but it went straight to voicemail. His smooth voice rushed through the line, his message recorded before this mess held a lilt that was missing the last time we spoke. It sent a shiver racing across my skin. My heart fell when I wasn't able to speak to him.

"I know I asked you not to call... but I'm thinking about you, and I just wanted to hear your voice..." a few seconds ticked off as I struggled with what to say. *"Call me back."*

I sighed heavily as I finally gave the hotel address to the driver and sank back in the seat.

Ryan ~

"I know I asked you not to call... but I'm thinking about you and I just wanted to hear your voice... Call me back."

I checked the time stamp on Julia's message, proud of myself that I hadn't touched my phone in a day and a half. Dawn was breaking and she'd sent this yesterday afternoon. It took everything I had but I respected her request for no contact, yet she called *me!* A mixture of anger, conflict, and agony thundered through me. I wanted to throw my fucking phone through the wall just so I wouldn't call her back. I was trying to give her what she wanted, and now she was the one caving in, after I poured my guts out, and she wouldn't say she loved me back? She still wasn't saying it, and that was killing me. Didn't she know I needed those words? *She was missing me when she's the one who left? Fuck that.*

I closed my eyes and swallowed hard at the sudden tightness in my throat. I tried to clear it but it wouldn't budge. Kari and Caleb's eyes followed me as I passed them, walking behind the station to make notes on a computer file from my last patient. My brain wouldn't shut off. Every time a date or time appeared on the screen, on the wall clock, on the calendar... Each tick screamed that it was one more hour gone; one more day between me and Julia... one more second closer to the end of us. I was convinced that the longer she was gone, the less likely she'd be to ever come back to me. It seemed fucking unreal that this could even be happening. We were supposed to be invincible.

When she finally called a day and half after she disappeared, I'd forgotten my brother was listening and made an ass of myself, crying my eyes out and literally begging her not to throw us away. I could barely face him at the end of it, even though he respected me by not mentioning how I fell apart. Afterward, I closed myself in the bathroom because I wanted to be alone with my misery, and memories of Julia were on every surface of the bedroom. I sat on the cold tile for hours nursing the bottle of scotch until I passed out. I avoided alcohol poisoning by unspeakable puking in the early morning hours. I fell asleep hanging onto the toilet for dear life after the dry heaves had left my abdominals aching and eyes tearing. I felt like hell, and I looked even worse as I left for the hospital after I told Aaron to go back to Boston. I didn't need anyone witnessing this bullshit. My head pounded like a motherfucker, and I had a hard time giving a shit about anything.

Caleb came out of one of the examining rooms and put his hand on my shoulder in concern. "It's about time for a break, Ryan. You've been at it for almost twenty-four hours, man. Go home."

I nodded and shrugged away from his touch. It wasn't personal, but I just couldn't stand to be around anyone other than patients, and anyone touching me had me feeling claustrophobic. When he asked me if I needed to talk, I simply shook my head and walked away. I relived every second of the last few weeks in my head, again and again, so I sure as hell didn't need to do it in stereo surround sound.

I avoided Jane like the plague, scowling whenever she made eye contact. Something akin to hatred had taken root deep in my gut. Probably, the whole thing was my own fault, but she seriously hurt Julia, and I'd never forgive her for that. The protectiveness that I'd always felt reared, even though I played a big part in what happened. I vacillated between regret, wanting to call and beg forgiveness, and raging anger that she could ever leave me like that. Underneath it all was a deep-seated sadness that closed around my very soul and haunted every moment.

I took Dr. Jameson, the attending physician, aside and requested that he not schedule me with Jane. I didn't care if I had to work 72 hours straight; I needed to stay as far away from that woman as possible. I laughed bitterly when he asked if I wanted to file a harassment suit. That was too fucking funny, and I just shook my head and went back to work amid a bunch of hushed whispers between the nurses. I was this close to standing in the middle of the ER and explaining the entire fucking mess. At least then I wouldn't have to suffer their speculation, and one aspect of my life could return to normal. I needed something normal in this cluster fuck; one thing to hang onto.

I tried really hard to maintain my anger because it was easier to deal with than the pain. I wanted to hate Julia, but it was all I could do not to call her back the minute I heard her voice. My back and my resolve stiffened as I grabbed my stuff and headed home for the night. The last place I wanted to be was in that empty apartment.

I stared, unseeing, on the subway and somehow pushed through the door an hour later. Julia's absence was tangible; like the breath was gone from my life. I couldn't stand being here. At least at work, I had something to concentrate on other than the giant hole in my chest. I dropped my coat on the floor near my shoes, not bothering to eat. I resisted the urge to call the magazine to see if Andrea would give the information that would save my life. I fell heavily onto the couch, turning my face into the cushion. The morning sun shone in brightly through the open blinds, but I didn't have the energy to get up and shut them. I took the phone off of the waist of my scrub pants and roughly shoved it away. I don't know why I expected her to call when I'd ignored two messages. My heart seized and my eyes burned like a son-of-a-bitch. I closed them, but all I saw in my mind was Julia.

After a few minutes ticked by with each sickening thud of my heart, I made a decision. I'd be damned if I was going to lie here all day and fall to pieces. I summoned the strength to get up and go to the bedroom. Our wedding picture confronted me on the dresser, and her scent assaulted my nostrils. I sucked it in before I could stop myself, and it only made her absence more concrete. There was no way I'd be able to sleep in this room. I pulled three drawers open and dumped the contents on the bed, and filling my arms with the pile of boxers, socks, scrubs, sweats, and T-shirts, I carried everything into the spare room and dumped it on the floor in the corner of room.

I quickly changed into grey sweat pants, one of my Harvard T-shirts and an old Stanford hoodie. I shoved my feet in my Nikes and fingered the ear buds of my iPod in my ears, cranking the heavy metal playlist up. I pulled up the hood of the sweat-shirt, banged out of the apartment, and rushed out of the build-ing, heading toward Central Park at a jog. My goal was to push myself to the limit, sweat and burn until I couldn't run one more step, and I'd forced my resistant lungs to expand. When my legs were so spent they were shaking, I went to the gym to lift and box. I found someone to spot me, and I relentlessly hit and kicked the bag until I couldn't breathe and my muscles shook with exhaustion. I wanted physical pain, as bad as I could stand it. I wanted exhaustion so I could sleep. Anything was better than the ache in my chest.

Julia ~

"Are you sure you're up to this?" Mike asked loudly. The wind off of the river was chilly, and it was whipping the hair into my face. "You don't seem as psyched about this gig as I expected you to be!"

"I'm fine!" I was annoyed. I'd repeated the lie so many times over the past week that it was starting to become second nature. I might not be all sunshine and roses, but I'd gotten good at keeping the dam at bay until I was alone at night in my room. The change of scenery helped me get through the days; there were no memories of Ryan in Paris, no pictures of us strewn about my office. This assignment was changing that. No getting around it.

The sun was up, but it was freezing, the sky overcast and dreary, which would mean retouching these shots with Photoshop when we returned to the office. I shivered and bit my lip to try to keep my teeth from chattering. Ryan hadn't called me back and a week had passed since I'd arrived. I was sad, but doing the best I could for the magazine.

Andrea and Mike had arrived a day after me, and I told them about my idea for the New York edition for February. Instead of bulldozing the staff, we worked alongside them. My strategy was to bring our ideas and combine them with theirs, and grease the cogs with some of our practiced efficiency, rather than change the entire set-up. I wanted to create a working relationship between the two magazines so, in the future, we could share editorial and story ideas that could run in both editions simultaneously. It made sense and the transition would be easier. Besides, even if I aspired to be the hard-nosed-shark type, emotionally, I just wasn't up to it.

"We don't have time to waste, Mike. We need to email everything camera-ready today by 11 PM Paris time to meet New York's press deadline!"

He looked at me deadpan and rolled his eyes. "Who the hell do you think you're talking to? I know this, Julia."

Andrea was just arriving back from an engraver, and she rushed up to us at a trot. "Sorry I'm late! It turned out amazing!" Her pink-cheeked face lit up, eyes dancing and hair blowing around her head like a red halo.

I took the box and opened it, anxious about the contents. The heart-shaped lock and key had a gold tone overlaid on silver so the engraving shone silver on the gold surface. My heart stopped as I lifted it from the white tissue paper cradling it in the box and closely examined it. It was more beautiful than I expected it to be. I had to turn away from the other two as my eyes flooded with tears, the names and date turning blurry in my vision. I lifted a gloved hand under the edge of my sunglasses and brushed the telltale tear from under each eye. I blinked rapidly to stop more as my mouth lifted in a tremulous smile.

"It's perfect. I hesitate to leave it. Someone might try to cut it off and steal it." I glance up at Andrea, who reached out and hugged me. I was grateful for her silence or I would have turned into a crying mess. I tucked the key in the pocket of my coat. "Mike, have you found the place you want it?"

"Yeah." He pointed to an opening where the other locks were less decorative, so ours was the obvious focal point of the shot. He checked the light with his pocket meter. "Put it there."

I handed the box back to Andrea and went to do Mike's bidding. He came close to me as I carefully locked it in place. "Like this?"

He nodded and dropped his voice so only I could hear. "You're doing your job, but where's my snarky boss lady? Something going on?"

I nodded gently, carefully tying a small, perfect bow around one of the shanks at the top. The moss green satin was the perfect foil to the metal. My fingers lingered on the padlock before I backed away. "Yes." It was too much work to hide my emotions from my friends. No one from the office was with us, and I let my guard down. "Ryan and I are separated."

After a beat, he was incredulous. "You're kidding." His eyes bore into mine like he was having trouble believing me. "I figured something made you high-tail it to Paris after so many failed attempts by Meredith to get you here, but I never thought you'd say that." Mike slung an arm around my shoulders and pulled me to his side with a squeeze. "Believe me; he knows how good he's got it. It'll work out."

I lifted a shoulder in the start of a shrug. "I haven't talked to Ryan in a week. I didn't tell him where I was going… or even that I was leaving." I refused to look at Mike, both of us ignoring the milling crowds curiously looking at the tripod set up on the bridge.

"Holy shit. He's gotta be hot."

I sighed. "I know. My emotions were all over the place, and all I wanted to do was get away. So, I did."

"So what happens now? Will Meredith let you go home?"

"I haven't said anything. I told her I'd do the job, and it wouldn't be fair of me to leave yet. I figure I need at least three months to do it justice." I fiddled with the ribbon a little more, still shivering. "It isn't like he's beating down my inbox with love letters."

Mike moved away and opened the camera case sitting beside the tripod and placed it on top, tightening it securely. "Obviously, I don't know the story, but I'm sure he's wrecked. He's probably just being stubborn. You know what they say: all's fair in love and war."

My mind flashed to that first time Ryan made love to me and he'd said those very words. "Yeah. If this is war, I'll lose and lose huge," I repeated weakly, sadness swallowing me up. I drew in a painful breath, grateful that the sunglasses hid my eyes.

Mike waved Andrea into position with her silver reflector as he honed in on the lock I'd just put in place. He took a couple of shots with the mounted camera then removed it from the stand and held it up to his face, moving the focus on the lens slightly. The camera clicked off in a rapid succession as he moved a few feet left or right, closer or farther back. He stopped and took a few more steps back, eyeing the angles of the shot carefully. He was a talented photographer. I enjoyed watching him work, even though this was a still shoot.

"Julia, time for you. Take your gloves off and reach out with your left hand."

I did as I was told and held it while he took the photo.

"Now… Go over there and stand about five feet away, lean with your elbows on the rail, and look out over the river."

I followed the instruction, the wind blowing my dark hair off my face.

"Take off your sunglasses, honey," he instructed.

"Mike, I don't think…"

He interrupted me. "Julia, let me do my job. Please, take off your glasses."

"It's stupid to have me in the picture anyway, Mike. The story is about couples. It's one thing to have my hand in the pictures but…"

"I know what this is about." One eyebrow shot up, and he motioned for me to move with the camera. "So let's make sure we get the job done right, shall we?"

I was slightly put out that I was so transparent and to someone as inherently shallow as Mike Turner. Several clicks later,
we were finished, and I was removing the padlock and replacing
it in its box, overcome with how much my opinion of Mike had
changed over the years. "You're a really good friend."

We worked all evening, retouching photos and wrapping the
article around the pictures, adjusting font size and headline
depth, messing with color tones, until it was the best we could
get it. I pushed send on the file with an hour to spare.

*****

Four weeks later, after six more unanswered text attempts and
one unreturned phone call a week to Ryan, I was starting to lose
my last shred of hope. I was thinner and shaky; my appetite replaced with nausea. Not a day passed that I didn't cry my eyes
out at least once. Sometimes, I didn't even bother hiding it from
Andrea or Mike. Paris had lost what little luster it had, and I
wanted to go home more than anything.

When the Valentine's issue broke in New York, I held my
breath. My stomach fluttered and hope flickered every time my
office phone rang, but it was never Ryan. In all these weeks, he
hadn't answered once. I finally stopped trying, no longer willing
to make a fool of myself. I tried to put on a brave face and accept
the fact that it was over, but I was completely devastated and
unsure where my life would take me now. I felt desolate as the
holiday approached, eaten alive with thoughts of Jane worming
her way closer to Ryan while we were so broken. I walked
around like a bare shell of my former self as I retreated to my
room two days before Valentine's Day, barely making it behind
closed doors before my broken heart got the better of me, and I
fell to my knees in tears.

Andrea, Mike, and some of the staff asked me to go to dinner, but I wasn't up to it. I peeled off my suit and left it lying half-assed on the sofa in the other room of the suite and pulled on a pair of blue plaid flannel pajama bottoms and a long sleeved white Henley. My head throbbed. At 5:30 it was dark, but I still pulled the curtains closed on the window before grabbing my phone and crawling under the covers. I didn't bother with the TV, and the silence in the room boomed. I lay there missing Ryan and clutching my phone, willing it to ring. My face crumpled, and I rolled onto my side, tears streaming from my eyes. I let the sadness take over, crying harder than I had in weeks. I felt lost, alone... like my world was ending, and I only had myself to blame. Fighting with Ryan over Jane seemed better than the alternative.

I sobbed for long minutes, letting it all out until my nose was swollen closed. Still, I cried until I gagged, the combination of the snot running down my throat and my stomach heaving had me scrambling into the bathroom to throw up the entire contents of my stomach.

I sat there, panting, wiping off my face with a wad of toilet paper, and finally blowing my nose as hard as I could before pulling myself up and going back to bed.

I rubbed my nose with the back of my hand and turned on the phone. If Ryan had looked at the phone bill, he could tell I was in Paris, yet nothing. I sighed deeply. I could call him again, but I'd fall apart even worse if he didn't answer, and the days to come would be hell, always waiting. At least now, I didn't expect to hear from Ryan, and I didn't obsess over it like I did at the beginning. As much as I wanted to reach out to him, I didn't want to put myself back at square one.

I pressed 5, Aaron's speed dial. I fully expected voicemail and was surprised when he picked up.

"Yeah?" His deep voice bolted me upright. "Julia?"

"Yeah, Aaron."

I could hear him expel his breath in a huff, but he was quiet, waiting for me speak. My heart flipped uncomfortably as I struggled for what to say. "I've tried calling Ryan several times over the past month, and he hasn't returned any of them. I just wanted to ask… Is he… is he okay, Aaron?" My voice cracked and a tear tumbled down my cheek.

"No, he's fucked up, Julia."

My head fell forward and as much as I tried, I couldn't help crying harder.

"I've tried. I mean, I want to talk to him."

"He's on lockdown. He works doubles; barely calls any of us back. I've only heard from him twice, and I call him every other day. Mom is so worried, she's about ready to get on a plane, but he doesn't want to see any of us." When I didn't respond and continued to cry, he continued. "You know I love you, Julia, but I feel like an asshole talking to you when my brother is so destroyed."

My shoulders shook in silent sobs until I gasped for breath. "I'm… I'm so scared, Aaron."

Aaron said my name on a sigh. "Jules… I just… how could you leave him? I don't get any of this shit. I don't understand you leaving; I don't understand him refusing to talk to you."

"You haven't seen him, then?"

"I went down there right after you split. Where are you?"

"I'm on a job for the magazine. It just seemed like we both needed some time apart to think. We weren't communicating about the important stuff. Honestly, Aaron, I didn't think about what I was doing. I felt suffocated. Did Ryan tell you any of it?"

"Not a lot. *He needs you*, not me."

A small part of my heart leapt. "I've tried. I've even thought about going home, but I'm beginning to think he doesn't want me back."

"Come, on, for Christ's sake! Julia, listen to yourself! Do you honestly think Ryan wouldn't want you back? Ever in this fucking lifetime?" His voice thundered abruptly, and I flinched.

"A lot of things have changed, Aaron."

"Not. *That.* You should get your ass home."

I wanted nothing more, but I wanted Ryan—my Ryan—and the way we were before Jane. "I wish it were that easy. I'm sort of locked in here for a while."

"I guess it's a matter of priorities, huh? Look, I'm not going to tell Ryan we talked, because I'm not going to get his hopes up just to have you rip his guts out again. Just... get your shit together. If I gotta take sides on this, blood is thicker than water. I mean, he's not my real... you know what the hell I mean."

I nodded, even though he didn't see me. "I wouldn't expect anything else, Aaron. I'm glad he has you, and I'll try to get back to New York as soon as I can, I promise. Tell Jen hello. I love you guys."

I wiped my eyes with a tissue and turned on the light and my laptop, intent on searching for flights. I couldn't book it until I spoke with Meredith. She'd be so mad, she'd light up the sky, but I had to try to correct my mistake with Ryan. My phone started playing Ellie's ringtone, and I picked it up, happy to hear from her. I hadn't talked to her in over a month, so wrapped up in my own life that I didn't think much about her and Harris.

"Hi!"

"What's going on? I called your office and they said you didn't work there anymore? I mean, what the hell, Julia?"

"Sorry. I should have told you, but it was pretty sudden. I'm in Paris."

"Since when? This is just a short assignment, right?" Her voice was hesitant, and I imagined the cogs working in her head. She sounded happier, more like herself than I'd heard her in months.

"No, it's the job. Remember, the Paris edition? I've been here since the first of January."

"Holy shit! And you didn't bother telling me?" Hurt laced her tone.

"A lot has been going on, El. Ryan and I were fighting a lot, and I didn't want to burden you with it because you were dealing with your own stuff. Anyway, it just seemed like a good time."

She pulled in a sharp gasp. "Ryan isn't cheating, is he?"

I ran a shaky hand through my hair and crawled back into bed. "I don't think so. Not that way. It's about that woman he works with. She's just... he says they're friends, but she's in love with him and the situation became unbearable." Ellie knew the basic story surrounding that night in the ER, but we hadn't discussed it since right after I got back from L.A. I started to fill her in on Christmas and New Year's Eve, but left out a lot of the smaller details, trying to turn the conversation to her. "We don't need to talk about this. How are you and Harris doing?"

"Screw Harris and me, Julia! I've been a rotten friend. Shit, I'm so sorry! I'm sorta shocked by it all."

"It's okay. I should have called you, too. It's just been overwhelming, and it's all I can do to function."

"I remember how that feels."

"I know you do. I guess fairy tales don't exist."

"Julia." I could almost hear her shaking her head at me through the phone. "For you and Ryan... *they do*. No one is more perfect together than you two. He loves you more than anything, so what were you thinking running off to Paris?"

My chest tightened with emotion and my throat ached, making the words strained. One thing I knew for sure, Ryan was it for me. "I've been asking myself that a lot lately. I'm dying with how much I miss him."

"I've learned something and it took losing Harris to figure it out. Don't lose Ryan, Julia. My best friend told me to get my head out of my ass, and I ignored her. Don't make my mistake."

"Are you and Harris really over?"

"He's on a North American tour, and we're supposed to talk when he gets back in September. I'm still not sure I can handle that lifestyle. Being apart and worrying about the women. His band is a bunch of wild, single guys. I don't want to worry all the time."

"That's eight months, Ellie! He wanted to marry you."

"Look, Julia, I care about Harris a lot, but I don't want to be all tied up in knots all the time."

When I didn't hear her say she loved him, I wondered if maybe they weren't destined to be together. Even when I left New York and Ryan behind, there was never a doubt about us long-term, tied up in knots or not. I felt sad for them.

"I had high hopes for you two."

"Like I said, we'll hash it out eventually. We talk on the phone once a week or so, but the big talk is for later. Now enough with the bullshit; start packing, do you hear me?"

"I have to work it out with Meredith. She's coming this week to see how things are going. Maybe if I can show her our progress and how well the team here is catching on, it will be better than a phone call."

"She's going to be pissed, Jules. You have to prepare."

"That's putting it mildly, I'm afraid."

~13~

Ryan ~

Fucking Valentine's Day!

This wasn't at all how I'd anticipated this day to turn out. It grated on my nerves how much this particular holiday shoved how much I missed Julia down my Goddamned throat. The ER desk was awash with flowers and a couple of mylar balloons that said *'I Love You!'* and *'Be Mine'*. I wanted to be apathetic about it, but the truth was, I was dying inside. Loneliness had become like a sickness that had no cure. I knew I wouldn't see her, but that hadn't stopped me from buying *The Picture of Dorian Grey* when I'd seen it in the window of a collectable bookshop on my way to the gym last week. It was like it had some invisible hold on me, and I had to buy it. If she were here, I'd have given it to her today. I was such a sap, letting my emotions dictate my actions when my head screamed that I was a moron for buying it, and even more, when I'd written on the inside front cover.

The memory of last year when I surprised Julia in New York came to mind; sneaking in to her apartment, waking her up, and making love to her all night. I ran my hand over my jaw. If only something like that awaited me tonight. Incredible how twelve short months could change your life completely around. So much had happened in that time: Julia's accident and her memory loss, our wedding, moving to New York... all the shit with Jane. I groaned inwardly.

Kari stared at me.

"What? Do I have something on my face?" I asked, running my hand over my chin again.

She shook her head. "Are you okay, Ryan?"

Not at all, I wanted to answer. I knew I looked like shit. I was fit because working out passed time and kept me sane, but my heart was shattered, and my chest was a hallow void.

"Yeah, I'm good. A little tired, maybe." I tried to give her a half-smile but it didn't quite make it to my eyes. I could see the sympathy in her expression and the unspoken questions that she didn't ask.

"If you ever need to talk, I know about everything."

What? I frowned at her. *Sure, great! Just what I needed, people discussing my personal problems behind my back at my hospital.* I glanced angrily in Jane's direction, immediately believing she was the one who blabbed. For once, she wasn't watching me.

Kari put her hand on my arm. "Ryan, Caleb told me about what happened with Julia. If you ever need to talk, you know, get a woman's perspective, it might help to figure out what she's thinking."

I looked back at her and nodded slightly. I wanted to tell her that if anyone knew Julia and her fucked-up reasoning, it was me; except that I wasn't sure anymore. I didn't understand any of it.

She held up the open box of candy and offered me one. After Jane had no part of him, Caleb had turned his attention to Kari. He'd given her one of those obnoxious red velvet chocolate boxes that you get at the corner drug store. I wasn't a fan, but I humored her, hunting around in the box for one shaped like a square. Experience from childhood taught me that the square ones were more likely to be caramel. I couldn't stand the overly

sweet fillings that typically filled these things. I popped it in my
mouth. "Thanks. I don't like to talk about it anymore, Kari. But,
I appreciate the offer."

Jesus, I was tired. My feet felt like lead, and I could swear I
had a ten-pound brick on my forehead. I went to get a cup of coffee from the pot we kept in the alcove near the ER waiting room.
It was so strong it usually tasted like tar, but I didn't give a shit; I
needed strong. I just needed to stay awake. I scoffed at my train
of thought. At work, I did everything I could to stay awake, but
at home, I couldn't sleep if my life depended on it. The irony
was not lost on me.

The coffee didn't have the desired effect. In the past, I'd
tried stashing energy drinks in the refrigerator next to the coffee
pot, but someone always ripped them off. *Fucking people.*

I didn't have time to go to the lounge, so I found a corner of
the waiting room and sat down with my coffee, leaning my head
on the back of the chair and closing my eyes. I let myself listen
to the white noise sounds of the waiting room; people talking in
hushed tones, the admitting nurse asking for insurance information, a fussy baby. If I concentrated hard enough, my mind
would let me get in a little rest.

My life felt like a huge, black void, and though I had purpose in work, I hated everything else. I was a walking zombie,
unsure how I got through the days. It helped to work all night. I
hated the nights at home without her. My life stopped when she
said those five horrible words: "You forgot to remember me…"

Julia. My closed eyes squeezed tighter. She stopped calling
and texting, which, I admonished myself, was my own damn
fault. I would stop, too, if they were repeatedly unanswered. I
was still so angry, but more, I missed her like I'd lost half of myself. I gave a small huff. I guess that's what happened. I had to
stop and think how long she'd been in my life. Three and a half

years as my best friend, almost four as my long distance lover, the four months that we lived together during her recovery, six months married, and now six weeks since she'd left me. The longest six fucking weeks of my life, except for the week I didn't know if she'd live after her car accident. *Oh my God! Did we really go through all of that just to let it slip away now? And because of some twit interrupting our dinner a couple of times? Un-fucking-believable.*

Someone's hand slid up my thigh and I bolted upright, my eyes snapping open instantly and landing on Jane, perched on the edge of the chair next to mine, her hands now in her lap. My heart literally knocked against my ribs, and my hand landed on my chest with a thud.

"Jesus Christ, Jane! You scared the living shit out of me!" I relaxed back in the chair and closed my eyes again. I took another deep breath. "What is it?" I asked, annoyed that my thoughts had been interrupted, and I would now have to listen to what she said.

"Um... Ryan, I..."

My head snapped up again and I glared at her. "What?"

"I'm... I just wanted to apologize for everything again. I hate how strained we've become, and I just want to get back to normal."

I blinked and my jaw tightened. I considered her words for a minute. Could we ever go back, considering my world as I knew it was ruined, maybe beyond repair? "I don't know. I can't think about it right now. I'm too tired." I dismissed her hoping she would leave.

"Just think about it."

When I didn't answer, she finally rose and left the waiting area. The small bit of relaxation I had vanished, so I pushed up from the chair and decided to go for a walk around the hospital. I needed to wake up, so I choked down the now lukewarm coffee and started to move toward the hospital lobby, tossing the paper cup in the trash as I passed.

Louise was on desk duty. The old woman always had such a cheery smile, and I needed a little sunshine. She was talking to an elderly couple and pointing out directions, and I scooted past into the gift shop. There was always a nice assortment of fresh flowers in the cooler, and I reached in and pulled out a small arrangement of reds and pinks in a small, globular glass vase. There were some of those conversation hearts Julia hated at the register. I grabbed a box of those and then turned and reached for the latest edition of Vogue from the magazine rack. By the time I paid for the items, Louise was free. When she looked up at me, her blue eyes sparkled and a huge smile slid across her face. I smirked at the two bright pink splotches painted on her cheeks and the vivid red lipstick that wasn't quite staying within the outline of her lips.

"Happy Valentine's Day, Louie!" I said, mustering as much cheer as I could.

"Ryan, you handsome devil. Don't tease an old woman! It's hard on my heart."

I laughed out loud for the first time since I couldn't remember when.

"I'm not teasing." I grinned at her. "Look! I brought you presents." I set the flowers down on her desk and handed her the candy.

"Oh!" Her hand flew to her cheek. "You make an old woman blush! I'm so happy you stopped by! I've missed those dimples and sparkling blue eyes!"

"I've been really busy." I perched in the chair next to her desk. "Sorry."

She reminded me a lot of my grandmother on my father's side. Grandma Nettie. She had the same slight blue tint to her stark white hair and her make-up was exaggerated due, in part, to failing eyesight and the rest to exuberant personality. I sat beside her, reluctant to go back to the ER. Louise lifted the flowers and sniffed appreciatively as I flipped through the magazine.

"This is for you, too, of course, but I haven't looked at this issue yet. Do you mind?"

"Oh, goodness! Of course, not." She patted my hand as I turned the pages one by one. Julia's name was still on the mast-head page. I breathed a small sigh of relief and turned the page with shaky hands. Somehow, I'd managed to stop myself from calling or going over there to interrogate Andrea or her other staff. She said she'd left the city, but was she really that close all along? "What is that pretty wife of yours up to?"

"Working a lot." I tried to keep my voice even and not sound too sad. "We're both working a lot." I was at a loss for what to say. I didn't want to talk about it, but I didn't want to lie either.

"You do look very tired, dear. Are you eating right? You seem a little pale."

"I'm eating." I was living on meat sandwiches and the cafeteria salad bar.

My mouth quirked at her sweet concern, but then, as I casually glanced from Louie back to the page, I froze still as death, my breath leaving in a rush.

I couldn't tear my eyes away from the image in front of me. It was a bunch of locks on a fence over a river and at its center, and the camera zoomed in a particular one adorned with a light green ribbon. *Ryan & Julia* was engraved in cursive silver with *May 26* written in the same font, one line below it. It was our wedding date.

I sat up straighter in the chair and examined the picture more closely. The focus on the lock blurred the background, but a young woman, dark hair blowing in the wind was standing further down on the fence. I'd recognize that profile anywhere. The Eiffel Tower rose in the distance. Now I knew where she'd been all this time. My face turned hot as fire.

"Ryan, honey, are you all right?" Louie asked. "You're so flushed all of a sudden." She reached out and touched her cool, boney fingers to my forehead then my cheek.

I looked at her face briefly as I registered her voice, but didn't really hear what she said. My eyes returned to read the headline. *The Locks of Love by Julia Matthews.*

She'd never written for the magazine before, but that wasn't what shocked me. I snapped the issue shut and placed it on top of the desk, rising and shoving my hand around the back of my neck.

"I gotta go back to work," I said with an abruptness I couldn't quell, and jumped from the chair.

"Ryan, you look ill. Sit down."

I shook my head. "No, thank you, Louie. I really need to go. Have a good night."

She looked puzzled when I turned to leave and called after me. "Okay. Bye-bye, dear. Don't take so long to stop by next time."

I walked on unsteady legs as I made my way to the backside of the hospital, not sure why I hadn't thought of it before this. So that was that? Julia wasn't coming back? Not for months at least. Meredith had finally gotten her way and shipped her halfway around the world. Blood pounded in my veins so loud I could hear it rush in my ears, and it only made my head hurt worse. She used our problems to pick up where she left off last year. The bright lights down the long hallway I was striding through blurred, and looking at the floor, I walked faster, unsure what the fuck I was going to do next.

*****

Two days later, I'd done nothing but work straight through by choice. I didn't even care that Jane was there. I just didn't want to go home. I didn't want to stop and think. I felt betrayed and abandoned by the person who promised me forever, and now, I didn't give a rats ass if I had one more day, let alone forever. She didn't love me or she wouldn't have done what she did. The words bounded out in my head over and over again.

We were busy and I was thankful, but I was running on fumes. It was the weekend, and we had a lot of drunk driver accidents, more of the gang fights, and a guy who accidentally nailed his hand to a two by four. He was calmly sitting on the table telling us about how his brother-in-law took a jigsaw to the wall to cut out the chunk of wood he was nailed to. He sat in front of me with a nail through the back of his hand and the wood still attached. I ordered IV fluids just in case he went into shock. It would hurt like hell to remove it. I stared at it, carefully turning his hand trying to determine if it would hurt less to try and remove the wood first or see if I could push it up enough to cut off the head of the nail on the top of his hand. Either way, it had to be pulled through.

"I can take it, doc."

My eyes met his without wavering. "It's going to hurt like a mother when this comes out. I think we should sedate you."

The dude was huge; bald with long stringy sideburns and big beer gut. He was sweaty and smelled like dirty socks. "Look man," he protested, "I wasn't sedated when this fucker went in, I ain't gonna be sedated when it comes out."

This dickhead was a glutton for punishment, but whatever, I was too exhausted to argue. I put my hands up in resignation. *Whatever, asshole.* "Fine. I warned you."

Kari and another nurse, Nancy, assisted. While Nancy was unwrapping some of the surgical tools and assembling the materials for the sutures, I took Kari aside, whispering so only she heard me.

"Stinky over here will be squealing like a pig in about ten minutes, so have a syringe of morphine handy."

She held back a giggle and nodded her head. "Got it."

He was at least two hundred fifty pounds, and I doubted that Kari and Nancy together weighed that much. The brother-in-law was still in the room, and I asked him to help hold his friend down after we strapped his arms and legs on the table. I had him lean all his weight across sweaty guy's right shoulder while Nancy got the choice job of leaning across his thighs. I pushed on the wood side to see if I could ease it up enough to get the pliers around it and not pull out chunks of his skin.

"Doc, why don't you just saw off the wood? Take it off in pieces around the nail?"

"It isn't safe. I'm not going to risk cutting your hand in half. This is going to take a while."

I pushed hard on the wood and clamped around the nail head with the pliers, pulling on with subtle pressure. I needed to raise it up enough to get the cutters under it to remove the head. I'd then grab the wood and yank it out as fast as I could. The man hissed and bucked on the table as I worked to get enough space to slide the instrument in. Sweat started to bead on my forehead. We all had on gowns, gloves, and eye guards, making it hotter than a sauna. It was a tight fit, but I finally got the clamp on it and began to manually turn the small round blade, like cranking a can opener. Slowly, it began to grind through the metal shank of the nail.

"Fuckin' A! That hurts like a bitch!" The patient began a steady stream of cuss words. I kept cranking, the muscles in my arms straining with the pressure I had to use to help the blade go deeper into the metal, and my fingers getting numb from holding the instruments so tight for so long. Finally, the head of the nail popped off into the hand Kari had positioned to catch it.

I dropped the device on the metal table and tried to work the feeling back into my hands. "Are you okay?"

"I'm golden." I could see his bravado start to wan even if his words didn't.

"Last chance for juice." I looked blandly at the fat guy in front of me. His machismo act was just making my job harder. "If you thought that hurt, it was like a kiss compared to what's coming."

Sweat rolled down the man's face in rivers, and his shirt was wet with it.

Kari was washing his skin with iodine soap.

"There is no shame in taking the pain meds. This is a nasty injury."

"I said, no, doc."

"Okay, hold him down. Kari, help Nancy."

I made eye contact with the man still lying across his chest, letting him know this was it. I was through screwing with this guy. If he wanted to be tough, I might as well get it the hell over with. I was too tired and too hot to keep fucking around. I wrapped my gloved hands around the wood block with the nail embedded in the center.

"Okay, on three." My upper body and back muscles flexed. "One!" I yanked with all my might, and the man screamed like I

was sawing off his hand. The nail dragged through his flesh with
a sickening suction when it finally came out.

"You sorry fuck! You said on three! Son-of-a-bitch! Jesus!"

I moved away, peeling off my gloves, and putting on a new
pair. I was bored with this stupid jerk. Blood oozed from the
wound on both sides, and I examined it. It looked clean.

"My hand is on fire!"

I looked at him, expressionless, my tone brooking no argument when I addressed the nurses. "Kari, apply topical on both
wounds. Nancy, 100 mils morphine. The syringe is on the tray."

Her eyes got big and round. "What?"

"I said 100 milligrams of morphine. Put it in the IV."

Kari looked at me and held up a hand to Nancy. "Doctor,
may I speak with you for just a second before we get started?"

She placed some items in the trash and I joined her in the
corner of the room.

"Ryan. 100 will kill him. 15 maybe, because he's so big."

"Holy fuck," I murmured, the gravity of what I'd almost
done hitting me hard. "I meant 10 mils."

She turned and held up ten fingers to Nancy, who nodded
and placed the syringe in the IV port.

I didn't say another word as I sutured up the wound, and
though unknown by anyone but me, my hands were shaking.

Afterward, I ripped the gloves, mask, and eye guard off and
left the room in search of Jameson. He was my attending and
he'd decide if he'd take it to the chief of staff. I found him in his
office and knocked lightly on the glass.

He waved me in. I slumped into one of the chairs, my foot
bouncing nervously. I felt weird, my hands were numb, and I
was jittery like I'd just snorted a long line of cocaine and utterly
exhausted at the same time.

"Yes, Dr. Matthews? Still having trouble with Miss Cooper?"

I shook my head. "I almost overdosed a patient." I held up my hands and they shook like a leaf. "I can't feel my hands, I feel like I'm about to jump out of my skin."

Dr. Jameson put up a calming hand. "What was the drug?"

"IV morphine. I can't believe I just did that! I've never done anything close to that irresponsible before. Am I out of the program?"

"Does anyone else know about this?"

"Yes, two of the nurses. They caught it in time."

"So no one was hurt?"

"No." My knee continued to bounce rapidly.

"Ryan, calm down. You're overworked. How long have you been on?"

"I don't know. Since Tuesday evening?"

"It's Friday morning. So, no, you're not out of the program, but you are restricted from working more than twenty-four hours. It's irresponsible and the hospital would be liable. Are you on anything? Be straight with me."

"No! I don't sleep," I blurted. "I can't... seem to sleep."

"Like I said, you're overworked. I've seen it happen before. Your dedication is admirable, but go take a week off." He pulled out a prescription pad, wrote a scrip, and leaned forward to hand it to me. I reached for it, glancing down at the words. "That's an order."

"But..."

"Ryan, stop talking before I reconsider keeping you in the program. You have a brilliant future ahead of you. Don't screw it up. Fill that at the hospital pharmacy and go home." He turned back to the report he was working on. "That's all."

I felt like my ass was glued to the chair as I stared at him, stunned that I hadn't just ruined my entire career. I finally stood and walked slowly from the room. I'd go to the pharmacy for the meds, but then I was heading straight to one of the sleeping rooms. I was still reeling from the knowledge my wife was in Paris, and I didn't think I had enough physical stamina left for an hour on the subway.

Suddenly, it hit me that I had an entire week at my disposal. A week where I couldn't avoid the subject of Julia from bombarding my mind, and it all became so clear that I didn't want to avoid her anymore. A slow smile spread across my face. With the help of the sleeping pills Dr. Jameson prescribed and the knowledge that, when I woke, I would get on a plane and get my fucking life back; I was going to sleep like a baby.

*****

It felt so good. I was floating and warm, and Julia was with me. Nothing could be more perfect. I could see her face smiling down at me, her green eyes all soft and filled with love as she looked into mine. Her hair fell in a dark curtain around her face, tumbling over her shoulders; tickling my neck. Her fingers pushed my shirt up, and I reached up to tangle my fingers in the silky strands.

We were outside and the sun was shining; the vivid blue sky, dotted with fluffy cumulous clouds, created a brilliant backdrop. She was so beautiful and she smelled amazing. Her perfume wafted around me and I inhaled it deeper, wanting her very essence.

"Baby, we have to go to class," I murmured regretfully, sitting up slightly, my hand reaching out to pull on her shirt; only it was my T-shirt. It was almost summer vacation, and I'd be going

*home to Chicago and Julia to Kansas City. We'd fallen asleep in
my dorm room late last night after I'd finally caved and told her
I loved her. I'd wanted her for so long, and I regretted every
second I waited. Pretending to love someone you don't is hard,
but pretending not to love someone you do… is fucking torture.*

*She shook her head and bit her lip, grinding her hips down
against mine. I was already hard, and I wanted to move with her,
needing more pressure, my body craving hers. I sat up, my chin
tilting, reaching up for her mouth, and my fingers curled up her
thighs and then around her ass, pulling her tighter against me.*

*"I've dreamed of this forever…" I whispered with my eyes
closed. Her fingers slid up my arms and into my hair as our hips
ground together, the fabric separating our bodies not hiding her
heat or my raging erection. Julia moaned softly, and her breath
rushed out over my face, her mouth hovering over mine. Any
second now, I'd kiss her for the first time. "Since I first saw you,
I've wanted to touch you like this." I reached up to cup both
sides of her face, then combed my fingers through her hair. I
stopped moving when the hair in my hands was short; just hovering on her shoulders and thinner. Where was the luxurious,
thick hair I'd dreamed about raining over my body? My fingers
drew it out, mentally cataloging the differences.*

"Oh, yes Ryan… finally."

I sucked in my breath and pried my resistant eyes open. I
felt like they were glued shut, and it took three attempts. Fingers
pulled on the back of my head and wet lips slid over mine. It was
unfamiliar, the mouth too lax, too sloppy to be Julia's.

"Kiss me, Ryan. I want you so bad."

I struggled to focus in the dark room, and finally, the voice
registered in my sleepy mind.

"What the fuck? Did you think I wouldn't know you
weren't her?" I shoved the woman from my lap and scrambled

up from the bed. She reached for me, but I backed away, stumbling until I was leaning up against the opposite wall of the tiny room. "Get out." I put my hand over my eyes unable to stand looking at the woman I now loathed.

"Ryan," Jane began. "Just a second ago you wanted me."

"A second ago, I was dreaming about my *wife*!" I yelled at her. "What the fuck are you trying to do? Destroy my whole fucking life?" The sleeping pill was making my mind foggy and was hard to not fall on my ass. "I said, get out!" I hollered.

She stood and closed the space between us, her hand coming toward me. "Ryan, you told me that I deserved someone to love me." She started to cry in earnest. "You... said I was beautiful and desirable. I know you want me."

I flung her hand away in disgust and moved around behind her, opening the door to the room. "That's bullshit and you know it, Jane! I said that in a subjective way, as in there is someone out there for you, but I sure as hell didn't mean me! I don't even believe that Daniel was in a relationship with you. He sure as shit didn't act like it that one time I saw him in your room. You're delusional!"

She stared at me with wide, teary eyes, and I didn't feel one pang of sympathy. I couldn't stand the sight of her.

"Please go. I'm half asleep. I need you to leave. *Now!*" I waved through the open door.

She physically started when I shouted the word. "But you said... you said..." Tears tumbled down her face, the mixture of darkness and the light from the main room casting her face and body into shadows.

"*I said; I'm. Married*!" I grabbed her arm and yanked her out of the little room, letting go of her like her flesh burned mine and horrified about what almost happened. "Do you know the damage you've done to my life?"

"I saved you."

"Bullshit! You wrecked me, but I'll be damned if I let it happen anymore. Stay away from me; stay away from Julia!"

I went back in and slammed the door in her face, my chest heaving. I threw the lock in place and fell heavily on the edge of the bed, my elbows resting on my knees and both hands in my hair. I was physically exhausted and mentally shaken by what just happened, and the sleeping pill made my eyes heavy. My heart ached that I touched Jane at all, that she was on my lap, grinding on my dick; even if I wasn't conscious, I felt like hell about it. I hadn't touched anyone but Julia since before I'd almost kissed her on the dance floor the night I got accepted to Harvard. I felt sick to my stomach and all the more determined to bring her home. She belonged with me, and I was through playing these games. From now on, I was going to follow my gut and not let my stupid, misguided sense of duty fuck up what was important to me.

I moved to get up, anxious to get the hell out of there. However, my head was dizzy, and I helplessly sank back down. I wasn't going to be able to get home until I got the meds out of my system. I lay down on my back, pulling the blanket over me and flinging my arm over my eyes. I hated the drugged-induced stupor that took me out of control of my body, but I was just so damned tired. I had no choice but to sleep it off.

*****

I rushed up the stairs from the subway, taking them two at a time. Adrenaline surged through my veins as I took the last five blocks at a dead run. Once I'd woken up enough to remember that I was going to find Julia, I started to formulate a plan. I knew she was in Paris now, but how would I find her? The magazine was the obvious starting point. No doubt, it was the job she was offered last year, which worried me enough to give me pause. Maybe she wouldn't want to come home. I ran my hand through my hair and dug the key out of my pocket. I had to bring her home, no matter what her commitments were. Some things were more important than others.

There was no getting around calling the magazine at this point, and I dialed Julia's office phone on my way up the elevator. It went directly into voicemail, but it wasn't Julia's voice; it was Andrea, her assistant. My mind processed it. It meant it probably wasn't planned. Given everything that had happened, it was the only thing that made sense. She was running from me, not taking the job for the job's sake.

Thank you for calling the office of Julia Matthews, Creative Director for Vogue New York. Julia is on assignment out of the country until further notice. For magazine related business, please contact Denise Schrader at 718-586-705. If this is an emergency, please contact Andrea King via my cell, at 212-867-9388.

I ran the number over and over in my head as I ended the call and started another one. My thumb dialed the number as I pushed through the door of my apartment and headed to the bedroom.

"Andrea, this is Ryan Matthews. I know she's in Paris, and I'm on my way there. Can you please tell me where I can find her? I'd appreciate you keeping this between us. Thanks."

After I left the message, I shrugged out of my coat and left it on the couch. I'd peeled off the shirt to my scrubs before I'd reached the bedroom. Ten minutes and a quick shower later, I threw on my black silk boxers and sat down at the laptop to book my flight. I didn't dick around with Expedia or other fare fighter sites, I went directly to the airline and found the next available flight that still gave me enough time to get to the airport and through security. I'd set my wallet next to the computer and whipped out my American Express card. Before I could finish booking my flight, my phone buzzed. The number I'd called before flashed without a name. Andrea was texting.

OMG! I'm so glad to hear from you.

Fear closed in around my heart as my thumbs flew across the keys on my iPhone.

Is she okay?

Barely.

What's wrong?

Flu. And really down. When will you be here?

I sighed in relief.

*My plane leaves in about 3 hours. It's a direct flight,
but with the time difference, I land about 8 AM,
Paris time, Sunday morning. If the flight's on time.*

I finished my reservation while I waited for Andrea's response.

*We're staying at L'Empire Paris. Sunday morning,
she'll be at a café at 9 or 10... she always goes. I can't
remember the name, but I'll find out. Unless you want
to wait at the hotel? I'll get both addresses and text
you later. Have a safe flight!*

I wrote down the confirmation number for my flight on an old receipt I found stuffed in my wallet and noted I had about a hundred and twenty dollars cash. I'd most likely need more. Surely, they'd have currency exchange at the airport. Credit cards were always an option. I picked up the phone and slammed out my last response to Andrea.

Thanks. Pls send the name of the café when you can.
Don't tell her I'm coming. Pls.

Her response was fast.

I won't!

Thanks, again.

All that was left was to pack. Problem was, I hadn't done much laundry. I went into the closet and pulled down my suitcase. I didn't need this big damn thing, but my duffle was stored inside. I only planned on taking a couple of things. I threw it across the unmade bed and swiftly unzipped it, flinging open the top, and went to gather a couple pair of jeans, a handful of T-shirts, I pulled one button-down out of the closet—hanger and all, my black shoes, and a belt. I got dressed in a hurry, and sat on the bed next to the suitcase to pull on my white socks. The place was a mess, but given the events of the past few weeks, I hadn't cleaned a thing. Laundry piled up, dishes in the sink, a thick coating of dust on the furniture, and the trash overflowed. I'd have to take that out or the place would stink to high heaven when we got back.

I realized I was starting to think in 'we' again, but I was nervous. If I were honest with myself, I wasn't sure she'd come

home with me willingly. We hadn't talked since the night after
she left. I huffed. I had no one to blame but myself for not answering her calls and texts, but I was so damn angry and hurt. I'd
never wanted to hurt her before this, and the fact that I had deliberately cut her off, nagged at my gut. I'd most likely regret it;
however, I still struggled with her lack of trust.

I lifted the duffle out of the suitcase, ready to stuff the pile
of clothes waiting on the bed into it. Beneath it was a package;
glimmering gold wrapping paper and a filmy red ribbon with
gold sparkling edges. It was beautifully wrapped and had Julia's
stamp all over it. My focus shifted from packing as I lifted it out
of the suitcase. There wasn't a name on it, but then, we never put
names on the gifts we gave each other. My hand ran lightly over
the edges. Obviously, it was a frame.

I slid to the floor and leaned against the foot of the bed, the
package in my lap. My heart quickened and felt heavy in my
chest. I sat, realizing this was why Julia got so upset on
Christmas Eve. It was more than the shoes from Jane; it was
more than our interrupted evening. Tears burned the back of my
eyes before I even opened it. It was going to be something profound. I felt it in the depths of my soul. Something she'd drawn.
My hands were shaking. I was almost scared to open it, afraid it
would slice me open, but I had to know what was inside.

Slowly, I forced myself to pull off the ribbon. I leaned my
head back on the edge of the bed and closed my eyes. Not looking, I ripped through the center of the paper, so when I looked
down, I'd have no choice but to see what it was. I swallowed
hard and forced myself to look at what I held in my hands.

My breath stopped and tears started to roll as my hand
traced the little cherub face through the glass.

"Oh, my God." I could see us both in that face. My eyes,
but green, little dimples, the shape of her face... My heart

slammed against my ribs, and I felt like steel bands were wrapped around my lungs, preventing me from breathing. I pulled the picture to my chest and sobbed my heart out. She couldn't have given me anything that could mean more than this. Just as I'd written her that poem, she'd poured her heart into this knowing how much it would mean to me. I wiped my eyes and nose on a dirty T-shirt laying next to the bed, then rose to my feet, pushing the rest of the paper off the corners and letting it fall to the floor.

I set it on the bed, staring at it. I shook my head and blinked at the tears still clinging to my lashes. Then I shoved my clothes in the duffle and zipped it closed, flung it over my shoulder, and grabbed my coat, phone and keys. Stopping, I ran back into the bedroom and dug around in my underwear drawer until my hand landed on the passport shoved in the back.

"I would have been fucked if I'd forgotten you," I mumbled and jammed it in the inside breast pocket of my coat. I fumbled at the door, my shaking hands struggling to lock it. I flew down the stairs, not bothering with the elevator, and stood in the middle of the street so the cab coming at me had no choice but to stop.

"Hey, buddy, can't you see?" He pointed to the top of his cab where his light was off. "I'm not taking fares right now."

I opened the door anyway and slid in anyway. "This is an emergency. I'll give you a hundred bucks if you'll take me to JFK."

I held up the bill between two fingers and handed it to him through the small hole in the plexiglass divider. He took it and nodded. "International terminal. Air France."

Julia ~

I felt better after I'd made the decision to return to Ryan but my stomach fluttered in apprehension of my talk with Meredith.

She'd be furious, and I didn't know if the publisher in New York would give me my job back or if I'd even have a job. One thing my stupid little stint had proven was that Ryan was all that mattered. I knew it before, but the time apart hammered it into my heart like never before. I didn't care if we were homeless and starving, the only way I could be happy was if we were together. If that meant I had to suck up the crap with Jane, I'd learn to deal with it.

As I got closer to the office she was using, situated two floors above mine, my stomach heaved, and I had to duck into the bathroom. I looked in the mirror, telling myself to breath through my nose to quell the nausea. Breathe. Just Breathe.

I felt the bile rise up, and I bolted into one of the stalls to lurch into the toilet. I puked until I had nothing left inside and then pulled some toilet paper from the roll and wiped at my face. My eyes were watering slightly and my stomach felt better, but my skin felt clammy. I pressed the back of my hand to my cheek and went to the sink, turning on the water and scooping some up with my hand to rinse the sour taste out my mouth. "Gross."

When I straightened, I examined my sharp navy suit in the mirror to make sure I hadn't gotten vomit on it. I grimaced. My hair was up in a messy bun, and my face was pale, my eyes wider than normal. Well, it was now or never.

I walked on shaky legs to the mahogany door. It was cracked slightly, and when I peered in, Meredith waved me in.

"Where are you taking me for lunch?" she asked with a bright smile. "Things are going well, huh? I expected Monique to whine about you, but instead, she sings your praises."

I hovered just inside the door. "I like her. She's got good instincts, and she catches on quickly. I think the team has really come around."

Meredith bobbed her head, her hair sleek. She was perfection, as always. Her magenta lipstick perfectly matched the bright trim on her black suit.

"We can go to lunch, Mere, but I really need a minute."

She glanced up from the financial report on her desk. "Sure. What is it? You want a raise?" Her voice was amused, and she kept right on working.

I sat down, needing to get her attention. "Meredith." I smoothed the fabric of my navy wool skirt over my thighs and folded my hands in my lap. "I need to go back to New York."

She glanced up. "Okay. You can take a week off in about a month. That should be about the halfway point over here. I planned on suggesting it anyway."

I took a deep breath. "No. I need to go home."

She put her pen down and dropped the report. "What?"

"My place is in New York. I explained before, Ryan and I were fighting…"

"And you just thought you'd use me and this company as an excuse to save your little ass?"

"It wasn't saving my ass. I just thought we needed a little break."

"And now, you've had some epiphany, that your wonderful Ryan is perfect again?"

I was unnerved. I moved to the edge of the chair to stop my fidgeting. "No. Ryan isn't perfect. And it's no epiphany. You're right. I was wrong to take this job right now, but I've done my best here. They don't need me anymore."

"That's a load of crap!" Her lips pressed into a thin line and red splotches were cropping up around the neckline of her white blouse.

"Meredith, you just said that things were going well! I can help her from New York! Just like I did that assignment for John from here. Technology makes it completely doable."

She only heard the first sentence. "Yes, they're going well. But you've only just started over here, Julia. Who's to say what will happen if you bail now? I expect you to man up and finish what you started. You'll go home in a month. For a *visit*."

"Manning up means taking care of my marriage! That's the thing I need to finish. I'm going home, Meredith. With or without your blessing."

I pulled on the left sleeve of my jacket, my fingers coming into contact with the bracelet that I hadn't removed since the night Ryan forced it back on. "I'm leaving as soon as I can make arrangements. I suggest Mike and Andrea remain for another month."

"If you walk out that door, you'll be sorry, Julia! You're throwing away your career! Is he really worth that?"

I turned around to face her, a calmness spreading over me. "He's worth everything. I'm really sorry it has to come to this. I work my ass off for you and this company. I love my job... but not more than I love Ryan."

After I left Meredith, I spent the rest of the day going about business as usual even though I had effectively quit. I hadn't really considered how this would affect Mike or Andrea, but I wrote down ideas for the April and May issues and emailed it to Monique, copying Andrea and the other assistant. I sat back in the chair and looked out over the Paris landscape. It was beautiful, and I wanted to return with Ryan one day. I was still scared. Worried that now he might not want me. I considered calling him, but rather than second guess my decision and give him a chance to rant at me over the phone, I decided it was better to just go and face him. If he was in front of me, I'd be able to touch him, kiss him, and let him look in my eyes when I told him what an idiot I'd been. I'd do whatever it took to get his arms around me and know we were okay. I'd beg his forgiveness if I needed to.

Andrea came through my open door. "Is it true? You're leaving?"

"Yes. As soon as I can."

"But, it's Friday already."

"And?"

"Well, I mean... we have that meeting with Givenchy on Monday. You have to be there. And Mike told me he'd have those pictures mounted for you by Sunday. Can't you wait a couple of days? I mean, what's a couple of days?"

"You take the meeting. You'll be amazing. You have the proposal. We've gone over it ten times. Selling is the sales people's job. You just have to present the creative. You know that."

She stood looking at me, and I met her eyes. She was hiding something. "I'd feel better with you there. It's just a couple of days, Julia. Please. I can't take it. What if Meredith hate's it?"

"She basically fired me. I don't think I can go, even if I wanted to."

"Yeah, and she'll end up firing me, too. *Please*. What's a couple of days? I need you. I'll do everything else. I'll get your flight. I'll even help you pack."

I flushed, and pulled back from my desk.

"Julia, you look green. Are you okay?"

My stomach retched suddenly, and I barely had time to pull the trashcan from beneath the desk to heave into it. After our conversation, Meredith and I didn't keep our lunch plans, and I grabbed a tuna sandwich from the luncheonette on the lower level of the building. I felt horrible, not only for me but for Andrea having to witness it. When I was finished, I leaned back in the chair and reached for a Kleenex from the box on the credenza behind my desk.

Andrea's face was twisted in abhorrence. "Eewww... That's so nasty!"

"Sorry you had to see that. I think I have the flu. I was sick earlier, too."

"See? You can't leave this weekend. You need to go back to the hotel and rest for a couple of days. I'll book your flight for Monday night? You'll get everyone on the plane sick."

I nodded weakly. "You win."

"Do you need some water?" she asked gently.

"That would be great. Thanks." When she left, I tied the trash bag shut, cringing for the poor soul who had to empty it later.

Andrea returned with a bottle of Perrier, a glass of ice, and a lime wedge. "I thought it would be better than the alternative."

"Yeah." I took a careful sip. "I'm going to try a little, but I think I just need to go to bed."

"Okay. I'll check on you later. In case you need anything."

*****

Later that night, as I waited for Andrea to come to my room, I nibbled on saltine crackers and cream of chicken soup. The hotel food was good, but the room service menu was limited, and after almost six weeks of staying in alone more than going out, it was less appetizing. Coupled with my queasy stomach, it made it hard to eat much. I'd taken a hot shower and was dressed in Ryan's T-shirt and a pair of pink pajama pants. Now that I was going home, I ached to call him. I even picked up my phone twice to do it. But my heart was sore, and I didn't think I could take it if I called and it went straight to voicemail. I'd rather hold on to the little happiness that bloomed when I'd made the decision.

A knock at the door had me leaving the bedroom and going to answer it. Andrea sashayed into the room, dressed in an old grey sweat suit. She was carrying a small bag.

"What's your poison? Cookies, ice cream or popcorn?" She asked happily. The TV was on, but of course, it was in French, and though I knew a few words, six weeks wasn't enough to learn much.

"Ice cream, I think. What kind do you have?"

"Chocolate and cookies and cream."

"Chocolate?" I eyed her hopefully.

She handed me the pint of ice cream and a plastic spoon and plopped down on the end of the sofa, digging deep in the bag for the other one.

"You seem happier, Julia. It's been so hard to watch how sad you are."

"I shouldn't have come. I just… I miss him."

"We'll, he's definitely miss-able." She took a bite and then licked her spoon off upside down. Her eyes lit up as she dug out another bite. "And a lot of other 'ables'." She giggled and I laughed.

"Yes. He's all of that." I grinned at her. "Now that I've de-cided to go, I just want to go."

"I know. I talked to Mike. He's spending the weekend with some French chick, but he said he can meet you Sunday at that coffee shop you hang at, to give you the prints. I guess they're celebrating V-day late."

I watched her expression. "I'm sure it's not serious."

"It never is."

"Why don't you just tell him how you feel?"

Her head popped up and I regarded her steadily, challenging her to deny her feelings.

Her shoulder lifted in a shrug. "I don't know. We've known each other so long. We're friends."

"I know all about that."

"Are you sad you missed Valentine's Day with Ryan?"

I nodded. "Of course. It's our first since we've been married. But a lot of firsts got screwed this year." She knew about Jane. I'd broken down and told her right after we came to Paris.

"What do you think he got you?"

"Probably nothing."

"Isn't he into that sort of thing? From the flowers and stuff I've seen over the years, he seems very romantic. He's certainly gorgeous."

"So you've said. Repeatedly."

Her eyes got big and she grinned. "What? I'm not blind."

"Yes, he's romantic. But I'm not there, so... probably nothing. When I met him, he hated Valentine's Day. I remember the first time in college. His brother, Aaron, was stumbling all over himself for his girlfriend, and Ryan acted disgusted by it all. He was so cool. I mean, he acted like he was the shit." I lowered my voice in my best Ryan impression. "I don't fawn. I'm not the fawning type. I bask in the fawning!" A little giggle erupted in my chest as I remembered. "He was so ridiculous."

"Cause he *was*, right?"

I rolled my eyes at her exaggeration. "Whatever. That idiot attitude was what encouraged him. Basically, he was obnoxious. I had a date that year, he didn't." The chocolate ice cream was calming my stomach down. It tasted good, and I was almost finished with the entire pint. "I ended up blowing off my date to hangout with my best friend." I fell into my thoughts.

"Aaron. Chill, dude. Stop fidgeting, for Christ's sake! You'll scare the shit out of her."

"Shut up! It's only because you're never invested in your relationships that you can be so cool about women. I actually care about this girl." Aaron was agitated.

"You're right. I'm not the fawning type." Aaron seemed confused by Ryan's statement. *"I don't fawn. I* bask *in the fawning."* Ryan touted, grinning.

Aaron frowned blankly back as I watched the two of them. *"What the hell are you talking about?"*

"You! You're a mess. Get your balls back, man!"

"Well, some of us have to work at it, pretty boy."

"Yeah, Ryan, you have it easy! I mean, look at that mug!" I huffed, feeling sorry for Aaron. He was cute, but Ryan was... stunning. *"It's not as if you've ever had to work for it, so cut Aaron a break!"*

I was sitting on the chair at the other end of the sofa in the apartment Ryan shared with Aaron. I tried to concentrate on my calculus assignment.

"Shut up, Abbott." He nudged my shoulder and that familiar tingle ran through my entire body. *"You've probably got gaggles of poor assholes just waiting in line with hearts and flowers today. What happened to that sap making googly eyes at you in the library yesterday? Poor bastard!"* Ryan scoffed.

My eyes lifted from my assignment, and I scowled at him. *"Martin Frank? You've got to be kidding me!"*

One side of Ryan's mouth quirked in a smug smirk. The guy was a nerd, and I wasn't all that interested because I was in love with my best friend, and I had to cover however I could manage.

"Yeah, you guys could probably use the grease in his hair for lube." Ryan continued to goad and tried to smother a laugh.

I smiled and bit my lip, my eyes locked with Ryan's deep blue ones as I tried not to grin. *"Um, not all women need lube you know, Matthews. Maybe you aren't motivating enough."* I could hardly contain my laughter as I gave as good as I got. He turned the tables as usual.

"Humph!" He snorted in disgust. "That's not why they need it," he said dryly.

"Ugh," I moaned. My cheeks lit up like a firecracker. "Whatever. Your ego knows no bounds."

"It's part of my incredible charm."

Andrea shook her head. "You guys have a lot of great memories."

Her words brought me out of the past and into the present and the gravity of the situation. My expression sobered.

"I'm scared to go home. What if he doesn't want me anymore?"

"He wants you." She was so mater-of-fact, and I wanted to share her confidence. "You'll see. As soon as you get back, it will all be fixed, and you'll hop off into forever and have lots of babies. Looks like you're mostly packed."

My suitcase was open, sitting on the end of the bed and visible through the doorway. "Except a couple things." I stopped to consider her words, and my mind reverted to the past again to another time I was packing and feeling sick. A small smile lifted my mouth, and my hand wandered down to rest on my stomach. It was perfectly flat, but I'd only had one period since I'd been here and it was only just spotting.

"Andrea... I'm pregnant." Not... I could be, I might be... I knew when it happened; the night after the gala; that angry, passionate, amazing and horrible night. Right before I left him.

She flashed a bright smile and jumped up to hug me "That's why you puked! See? Ryan did give you something for Valentine's Day!"

~14~

Ryan ~

I had no idea what to expect when I found Julia. Physically, I felt strange, like I was out of my body or something. My arms had a weird tingling to them like they were asleep; sort of numb, except I could move them, but then again, I was exhausted from the flight. It was about six and half hours in the air, but the time on the plane and in the airports made it more like twelve. I tried to sleep on the plane, but couldn't. From the time I'd made the decision to go after Julia, until this minute, was only eighteen hours. *Eighteen hours?* I repeated the figure in my head. It felt like eighteen fucking years. The prior six weeks seemed like an eternity. It was like I hadn't seen her in forever. This separation was the worst of our lives; it had been the longest I'd ever gone without talking to Julia since we met. *Times forty*. But, who was keeping track?

I spent the whole flight thinking. I couldn't believe how blind I'd been about Jane. I began to see it clearly around Christmas, but before that, I had no clue what she was up to. Maybe my guilt just didn't want to see the way she was manipulating me. I still felt bad for her situation, but the episodes at Lincoln Center and in the doctors' lounge were big wake-up calls.

Julia and I were another story. I'd been wrong, but bottom line, she didn't trust me. It still ripped through my guts like a razor, and I couldn't reconcile any of it. How could she not trust me? How could she not understand that she was my entire reason for living? After everything we'd been through, and all the time that passed, hadn't I proven it a hundred times?

My heart hammered painfully. I was filled with worried anticipation, fear, and unadulterated resentment. Would she want to see me? I was still so damn mad that I couldn't see straight, even now, knowing why she left. She deserved to have me rail and scream at her, but maybe I needed her forgiveness as much as she needed mine. And what if she didn't even want to be with me anymore? That possibility scared the shit out of me and made my skin break out in goose bumps. Was she happy in Paris? It didn't matter. I'd say any Goddamn thing necessary to get her home where she belonged.

Even if I had to restart my residency at a new hospital, I'd separate myself from any contact with Jane. Whatever. I wanted my life back, but I needed Julia's trust; losing her was incomprehensible. I closed my eyes briefly to steady my nerves, before handing money to the cabbie and exiting the car. Unsure of the currency exchange rate, I shoved a wad of Euros in his hand. He looked at the bills and smiled with a nod. Apparently it was enough.

The cold February wind ripped cruelly through my jeans, whipping my hair into my eyes. It was the icy type that would your make ears ache and give you frostbite. I searched the street for the café name that was waiting in Andrea's long stream of texts when I landed and was completely disoriented in my direction in the unfamiliar landscape. The cloudy sky didn't help. I anxiously quickened my steps toward the end of the street.

I was frustrated with everyone involved. The whole fucking thing should never have happened. My eyes were hungry for the familiar curve of Julia's face and I wanted the hole in my chest to close. I was cold and shivering, but wasn't sure if it was the temperature or apprehension. I swallowed the tightening in my throat and tried to convince myself that our relationship would come out stronger, just like it always did when we had a hill to climb.

I pushed away thoughts of the angry exchanges and the long nights I'd suffered without her. My resolve strengthened, despite being uncertain how either of us would react when she finally stood in front of me.

I shoved my hands into the pockets of my leather coat and ducked my head against the cold, turning the corner on Saint-Germain Boulevard in search of the café de Flore. Andrea said Julia hadn't been to work in two days, except a couple of hours on Friday, but habitually visited there every Sunday. I'd wait all day if necessary. It was *Sunday*. My heart leapt hopefully.

Nerves made my stomach ache and my mind race back to the night I sped over to Julia's apartment all those years ago. I had a date with someone else, and felt suffocated. It was then that I'd finally been able to face that I was in love with my best friend. I felt the same now; jumping out of my skin at the uncertainty of how she'd respond. In the end, I'd chickened out of telling her I loved her, content to just be with her and grateful she wasn't with another guy. After that, we spent even more time together, and I only loved her more.

I inhaled deeply as my hand splayed out on the brass plate to push the front door open. She'd kept her feelings as hidden as I had yet we both felt the same overwhelming love. I prayed to God nothing had changed.

The welcome warmth of the restaurant engulfed me. It was a quaint little place filled with mahogany antiques, dark burgundy upholstery, and a lot of black and white framed art. Plush cushions were tied to the seats of the chairs surrounding each small, round table. Similar to coffeehouses in the United States, there was a roaring fire with some larger upholstered chairs and a sofa around it where patrons could cozy up for hours.

My breath caught as my eyes landed on Julia, fully ensconced in Mike Turner's embrace. My hands fisted at my sides and my heart dropped like a stone. Light exploded behind my eyes and fire ignited under the skin of my face and neck. A few seconds and a few quick strides later, I was standing above them, hovering over them. There were tears on Julia's cheeks. Her arms were around the other man's shoulders, her fingers curled tightly around a white handkerchief.

I huffed loudly enough to get their attention. "I came to remind you that I didn't forget you. That I could *never* forget you, but apparently I'm too late," I said as stoically as I could manage. I broke out in a cold sweat; I couldn't seem to move, though I was shaking violently. I wanted to rip Julia from Turner's arms and beat the living shit out of him.

Her eyes opened instantly at the sound of my voice and she gasped; scrambling away from Turner, toward me.

"Ryan!" The flash of happiness on her face was quickly replaced with panic as she took in the muscle working in my jaw and the anger surely burning in my eyes. I turned on my heel and strode quickly toward the door.

"Ryan!" she exclaimed painfully, hurrying after me. "It's not what it looks like, Ryan!"

Fire burned through my gut, my chest was aching and hollow, it hurt, and I couldn't breathe very well. The few people in the restaurant all stopped their conversations and watched my wife run after me as I made a hasty exit. My lips pressed together angrily, and I seemed lost for words though I wanted to shout at her. I wanted to get away, but I also wanted to take her in my arms and never let go for the rest of my life. Somehow, I kept walking, willing my legs to create distance as disbelief shattered through me like shards.

"Ryan, please!" Julia called after me again. The cold wind hit me in the face, the door banging loudly as my palms connected and it burst open.

"Ryan!" Julia's voice rose in desperation and her little hand closed around my wrist when she caught up to me... half-running beside me.

I stopped suddenly and faced her. "What?" I flung her hand away. Mike Turner emerged from the café half a block behind us, and his eyes met mine. "Is your boyfriend worried you might remember you're married? You seem to have forgotten easily enough!" I spat.

Both of our chests were heaving, our breaths mingling in a winter fog between us. Julia's teeth also began to chatter, which made me realize she'd chased me out of the restaurant without a coat. Her chin trembled as I glared at her, but still, she reached for me with both arms.

"Ryan, pl... please. You kn... know that's nuh... not true." Her green eyes, filling with fresh tears, implored me to have mercy on us both. "You're st... still the only one. Th... the only one who's tuh... touched me."

The tight knot in my gut loosened slightly as I glanced over her head at the other man, who turned away, heading the opposite direction down the block. Her fingers curled into my forearms as she shivered in front of me, her eyes pleading. She was suffering. I could feel it as if it were myself. I sucked in my breath and instantly pulled her into a tight embrace, holding her close to me.

Fuck it all! She was my wife, and no matter what, I loved her beyond how any normal man loved a woman. She owned me, and I knew it.

"I am so Goddammed mad at you right now, I can't even fucking breathe!" When she began to clutch at my shirt and sob into my chest, I almost broke. "I'm going to yell and scream at you until I'm hoarse, I swear to God!" My arms tightened as I wrapped her inside the opening of my coat, warm against me. My lips found her temple and then the side of her face, the salt of her tears on my tongue. My own eyes blurred. "Jesus, I was so worried about you. Right now, all I wanna do is make sure you're okay."

Julia's arms wrapped tightly around my waist under the jacket, her fingers fisting in the material of my shirt, and her head rested on my chest.

She clung to me, crying my name over and over, in the middle of the Paris street; the snow softly falling, the busy city noises fading into oblivion as the moment suffocated me. I wondered if she had an explanation to offer, and despite what she said, was Turner part of the reason she left me? The knot began to tighten again, the ache gnawing away at my insides.

"I thought... when you didn't call back... that you were done with me."

My jaw tensed, and I closed my eyes just before the words tore out through clenched teeth. "What do you think? That I could walk away from you even if I fucking wanted to?" I was furious that she'd even consider the possibility, but my heart squeezed as her little body shook with sobs in my arms. I couldn't know if we'd be able to get through all the mistrust, but I knew we loved each other so much I wanted to rip the heart from my chest, it hurt so bad.

My hands found her shoulders, and I pushed her back gently, my eyes seeking hers. The green orbs held the same loving expression I'd seen a million times, but deep sadness also. I fought the urge to brush my knuckles across her cheek when her foggy breath and chattering teeth reminded me how cold she must be.

"Come on." I shed my coat and wrapped it around her shoulders, leading her back to the café where we gathered up her coat, handbag, and briefcase. The waitress had it all waiting for us by the entrance.

"Merci." I thanked the woman quietly and helped Julia on with her long, black wool coat, cashmere scarf, and matching gloves and quickly shrugged back into mine. I tried hard to ignore the soft aroma of her perfume, which had wiggled its way into the lining of my coat in the mere moments she'd worn it. There were so many memories attached to that scent, and in this moment, it hurt too much to remember.

I hailed a taxi, and after joining me inside, Julia quietly murmured an address. I didn't ask her where we were going, and she didn't ask me if I wanted to go with her. Despite the tearful reunion, there was a lot of shit to clean up, and the invisible wall between us was awful. I wanted to hold her and forget everything that happened, but I knew we needed to hash everything out or we'd never recover.

Part of me was afraid to crack open the wound, terrified of the possibility we couldn't survive. Even when she couldn't remember me, I knew I'd be in her life, at least as her friend. Now, the future was uncertain; except that I'd love her until I died... no matter if we were together or not. We were both fragile, and I wasn't going to begin the conversation here. By New York time, it was the middle of the night and I was dead on my feet. There would be plenty of time to talk when my head was clear and sanity returned.

The fingers of one hand tried to rub away the burn in my eyes. I followed Julia into the lavish hotel wordlessly. I didn't take note of our surroundings. I didn't care where we were.

She dug in her purse for the key card and handed it over when we got to the door of the room. It was dark inside with the curtains pulled. Part of me hesitated, not wanting the lights on, not wanting to see the world she'd created in Paris without me.

"I just want to sleep." My voice sounded dead and distant, even to me. "I haven't slept in... Well, for a while."

"Don't you want to t ta—"

"We can talk later. I'm pissed and exhausted. It'll be easier later." I sensed, rather than saw, Julia nod. "I know it's morning for you, but I need to go to bed."

"Okay," she agreed, dropping her coat on a sofa and preceding me into another room, which had to be the bedroom of the suite. The light she switched on was low and filtered toward me enough to allow me to drop my bag on the couch, place my coat with hers, and follow.

The suite was elegant but lacked anything that would make it Julia's space. The low light was coming from the attached bathroom, and I could hear Julia moving around in there. When she came out, she looked ready for bed, too, which I didn't expect given the early morning hour. I cocked an eyebrow in question.

"I'm really tired, too. All the crying wipes me out," she offered in explanation. I didn't question it, just took it as a blessing, because maybe with her next to me, I'd finally be able to get the deep sleep I needed. I pulled off my shirt and kicked off my Nikes one by one. I inhaled and ran a hand through my hair. Then it occurred to me. Was I supposed to sleep in here with her? Should I go to the couch in the other room?

"Are you hungry? I don't have much food, but I have yogurt and fruit, and Pellegrino if you're thirsty. Or, I can call room service."

"I'm okay." The silence was awkward. It felt foreign, and I hated it.

"Do you need anything? You don't have much for bags," she asked quietly.

I shook my head, not knowing what the fuck I was doing. I shrugged in defeat. "Uh, toothpaste, and I don't have a toothbrush either." My mind flashed to all the times in college when we'd pulled all-nighters or I'd ended up crashed at her and Ellie's apartment after parties. She'd finally bought me my own toothbrush to have on hand.

"There's an extra one in the right hand drawer. I have a pair of your sweats and one of your T-shirts. Do you want them?"

I looked at her, finally taking in everything about her. She was thinner than I remembered, her cheeks slightly hollow, and dark shadows lurked under her eyes. The long sleeved thermal shirt she wore hung on her and her legs were bare beneath it, save for a pair of pink fuzzy socks. My mind briefly registered they were a stocking stuffer from a few Christmases back. I wanted to hold her and take away all the bullshit, but I couldn't let go of the fact she didn't trust me or that I'd found her in another man's arms thirty minutes before. Did she keep that toothbrush for him? My jaw tightened, but I mentally shook myself. She'd said no one touched her, but if she didn't trust me, could I believe her?

"Yeah, okay," I murmured softly. "Just the sweats."

"Obviously toiletries are provided here. That's where the extra tooth brush came from." She read my thoughts, and I flushed guiltily.

She walked forward and took some navy blue sweatpants from the open suitcase that rested on the only chair in the room, and laid them on the foot of the bed near me. I didn't ask her how or why they were with her in Paris. I didn't ask her why her suitcases were packed. Tonight was soon enough for questions and answers I might not be able to live with. In my haste, the sleeping pills were still in the pocket of my dirty scrubs laying in a pile on our bathroom floor in New York. Oh, well. Maybe with Julia finally in the same room, I'd be capable of sleep.

"Thanks. Where should I sleep?"

Julia's brow creased and pain registered on her beautiful features before she quickly masked it, and turned away. I knew her so well, yet the past six weeks made me feel like a stranger. I tried to shake it off, telling myself this was us and we'd always be us, but I didn't know where to begin. It hurt like hell. So much, it made me sick to my stomach.

"I thought..." she hesitated. "In the bed. Unless... you're not comfortable with that."

"No. I mean, it's fine," I said shortly, loudly clearing my throat, before heading into the bathroom and closing the door behind me.

When I'd finished, I turned out the light and made my way back to the bedroom. The bed was turned down and Julia lay on her side with her back to me. I could hear her breathing in the darkness. It was like a scene from a movie where the sounds are amplified obnoxiously, like the heartbeat from *A Tell Tale Heart* pounding harder and faster with each passing second. At least Julia was sleeping. I wondered if she'd recovered from her flu.

I hesitated a few seconds before dropping the sweats and crawling naked into bed. I was too exhausted not to get a good night's sleep, and the sweats would make me hot. *Sleep.* I drew the covers up to my waist, flung a bare arm over my eyes, and I willed the welcome oblivion to come quickly. I tried to ignore the delicious scent of my wife, now within arm's reach. She was close enough I could feel the heat radiating between our bodies; I could hear her soft intake of breath. I tried to ignore the emptiness in my arms and the soreness of my heart, and I wished to hell I'd remembered those fucking sleeping pills. You'd think that not sleeping for almost 24 hours, would have been enough.

Julia ~

Ryan tossed and turned next to me, and I started violently out of my fitful half-sleep when his hand flung heavily on my chest. My heart ached, and I longed to touch him. The wall between us was killing me. When he'd held me to him on the sidewalk, the big vacuum in my chest started to ease. But then, when he pushed me away and didn't hold me in the cab, it returned, more sickeningly than before.

Even with my husband beside me, I felt isolated; cut off from the one person I needed most in the world. I still didn't have him back. My best friend wasn't with me. I struggled with it, because, why was he here if he hadn't set things straight with Jane and finally understood how she made me feel? Would he fly all the way to Paris, just to fight with me? Was he here to end it? A bitter laugh bubbled up, and I held it in. Wouldn't that be unbelievable? After I'd decided I could put up with Jane as long as I knew Ryan was mine, maybe he didn't want me anymore. Maybe I'd pushed him too far. If I could, I'd rewind the world five plus years and just be his friend rather than not have him at all.

Tears stung at my eyes and bitterness threatened to choke me. I turned toward him in time to see him flop onto his stomach and push his pillow roughly to the floor. I put a trembling hand to my mouth to stop myself from calling out to him. I wanted his arms to cage me in and pull me to his chest. I wanted Ryan—my Ryan—to take all of this misery away. I wanted his passionate whispers and hungry kisses. I wanted to know he loved me. I needed it like I needed air.

I tried to inhale, but a sob rose up in my throat, so I turned my face into my pillow to smother it. I cried hard, my body shaking and my heart breaking, as I struggled to remain silent.

"Julia." Ryan called softly.

I gasped at the sound of his sleepy, velvet voice and turned, my hand reaching through the darkness for his. He rolled toward me and loomed above me as our hands threaded together.

"Are we together? Is this real?"

"Yes," I breathed, and an instant later, his mouth was hungrily latched onto mine. He kissed me like it was the first and last kiss we'd ever have. Not a minute passed and he had my shirt off, and we were skin on skin, both frantic in our efforts to get closer. My hands squeezed around his butt cheeks as I pulled his hips toward me, and he parted my legs with his knee.

We kissed again and again. Deep, aching kisses, full of passion and sorrow, want and need. But the need felt deeper than physical, even more than emotional. There was a desperateness born of uncertainty and urgency in each and every touch. Our fingers pulled at each other's flesh and then softened to reverent caresses, hands wound in each other's hair as we pulled each other closer still.

Neither of us uttered a word as our bodies came together in long slow thrusts, our mouths fed on the other and hands stroked and pleasured. My fingers traced the strong muscles of Ryan's back, memorizing every single line, feeling every flex as he moved above and inside me. He was strong and tender, heartbreakingly loving and demanding in his need at the same time.

My breath rushed out and my back arched, the tension beginning to build, my body opening. I pulled my knees up to take him in deeper, my hips thrusting opposite his. He was big and wide, swollen and hard as steel. It felt incredible as my body stretched to remember his, only to contract around him. Ryan groaned against my neck, gently biting my shoulder before claiming my mouth once again. I sucked on his thrusting tongue, and my body milked his, my muscles begging him to come inside me.

When my breaths began to come in soft pants, Ryan pulled hard on one breast with his mouth, sucking and twirling his tongue around the nipple before grazing it with his teeth. His breath was hot against me, and when his hand reached between us to stroke the sensitive flesh crying out for his attention, my head fell back in helpless abandon. His name left my mouth in a breathless rush, and he took me over the edge in a powerful climax. Ryan's thrusts slowed as I rode out my orgasm, his kisses became less demanding and tender until his movements stilled.

Even as my hips surged against him, urging him to continue and find his own release, he was motionless, still embedded deep within me but no longer kissing me. My eyes opened to find him staring down into my face, his expression pained, his brow furrowed in confusion and anger, his breathing ragged, and the low light making the light layer of perspiration on his skin glow. He'd just made such passionate love to me, but he was angry, and my heart crumbled to dust.

"How could you leave me without a Goddamn word?" he asked, sorrow dripping from his words. "Can't you *feel* how much I love you?" I was still gasping, my body twitching. I reached up to touch his face with gentle fingers, aching to take the pain from his eyes, praying for his understanding. "You knew what it would do to me!" he said brokenly. "I told you in Boston last year. It would fucking kill me if you left me!"

Ryan pulled out abruptly and moved to the edge of the bed, leaving my arms empty, my body bereft, and my heart breaking for both of us. I was still quaking with the aftershocks of my climax, and the air around me felt arctic at his absence. I rolled nearer, my eyes searching for his face, needing to read his expression, but his back was to me, his head dropped into his hands, his elbows on his knees. His body shook violently with the force of his pain, and I could almost smell his tears mixed in with the scent of our sex and his cologne. His quiet sobs were left alone in the silence; sorrow flowing and thundering around me like a violent storm.

He hadn't let himself come. This wasn't about sex. It was about love.

Nothing had changed the love; sometimes suffocating, sometimes debilitating, sometimes so joyous and incredible, but always overwhelming and utterly amazing. The mad, mad love remained, maybe stronger and more than it had ever been. Always growing, no matter what we faced. It had always been unconditional, and nothing could ever change it. Not in this lifetime or a thousand more. No matter how much we hurt each other, the love was still strong enough to make us invincible, or kill us both.

Crawling up behind him, I wordlessly slid my arms around his waist, one hand reaching out to wrap around one of his forearms. He didn't resist or pull from me, but his body was ridged. Tears spilled from my eyes as I tried to find a way to take away the pain I myself had caused. More than anything, I needed to heal the abyss between us, but I felt more helpless than I'd ever been.

"I'm so sorry, baby," I whispered, leaning into him and resting my cheek on the hard muscles of his bare back. His sobs shook us both, and my heart broke all over again.

"I wanted to make sure you were real, and not just another fucking dream that turns into a nightmare the minute my eyes open. I wanted..." his whisper broke raggedly. "No, I *needed* to be close to you... but even making love can't do it until we get this shit resolved between us."

"Ryan, I'm sorry..." I said again in a whisper, my mouth beginning to trace circles on his skin. "So sorry. I was wrong to leave you."

Tears dropped on the arm that I'd wrapped around him, and yet he said nothing. I kissed his back in a series of soft caresses while my fingers squeezed his arm and the other hand splayed open on his stomach moving upward. I paused when it rested over his heart. I could feel it pounding, feel his chest heaving in his anguish.

"I never should have left, but I was in so much pain. After I saw her in your arms and what she said to me..."

Ryan tensed even more. "She wasn't in my fucking arms, Julia!"

"Okay..." I soothed. "Maybe it wasn't what I thought, but it hurt more than anything has ever hurt me. And, after I left, I knew I'd hurt you, but I was in so much pain, I couldn't face yours, too. I was selfish. Please..." my voice broke on what seemed like a hallow explanation, even though I'd suffered un-speakably myself. I realized no amount of suffering would jus-tify leaving him, *ever*. Nothing was more important to me than being with this man. My heart thundered painfully in my chest as I waited for some sign that Ryan felt the same way. "Ryan, please forgive me," I begged again.

He didn't move or say a word as the precious seconds ticked by, my hands kneading the firm flesh of his chest, my forehead resting on the hard muscle of his back. Until finally, I could bear it no longer and scrambled off the bed and around in front of him, kneeling, naked, on the floor and forcing him to really see me. His features contorted in agony, and he turned his face to the side, as if he couldn't bear to look at me. My heart exploded. I knew he loved me. Knew it like I knew my own name, but we'd hurt each other worse than we ever had.

"Do you have any concept of what you put me through? Any fucking idea?" His voice was low and harsh, thick with pain. "Hearing you say I forgot to remember you—I can't believe you'd think that was ever a possibility. To use those words against me..."

"I felt like I was losing you," I said softly. My hands slid up from his knees to his thighs, up over his arms and then around his neck, my body hovering between his legs, yet he was still. I pressed my mouth to the curve between his neck and shoulder lovingly. Somehow, I had to make him understand. "I guess, I wanted you to feel the possibility of that loss, too. But, I love you, Ryan. I never stopped. Please..."

I didn't know what I was doing. I felt desperate for his forgiveness, for his arms around me, holding and cherishing, like I needed from him. I pressed more kisses to the side of his face, praying he'd turn and find my mouth. "Please, hold me, Ryan, and don't let go," I begged as I began crying in earnest. "I need to know you still love me. I need to know we'll *always be us*."

Instantly his arms locked around me in a tight embrace and his chest filled, pressing against mine. His face turned into the curve of my neck and stayed there for a good five minutes, one hand clutched into the hair at the back of my head and the other flat between my shoulder blades. My eyes closed in relief as I stroked the silk of his hair back and ran kisses across his shoulder and up his neck over and over again. My hammering heart slammed into his.

His hand closed around my upper arms and held me away so he could look at me. His blue eyes swam with tears, but they burned with fury.

"That's just it! You know how much I love you, Julia! You *know* you'll never lose me. Unless you want to kill me," he ground out, his voice thick and hard. "If you didn't know it, I wouldn't be breathing. That's why I'm so pissed! How can you not trust that?" I could physically feel his anger, but I also felt the magnitude of the love he couldn't deny. My heart swelled with hope.

My chin trembled and fat tears tumbled from my eyes. I reached for his face and nodded.

"Yes, I do. I know you didn't sleep with Jane."

"Would you still love me, even if I had?"

I gasped loudly. It never occurred to me that he might actually cheat. My face crumpled, and my shoulders shook. I cried harder, but still, I couldn't lie to him. I dug my fingers into the nape of his neck, and I held onto Ryan as if my life depended on it; because it did. I nodded as the truth rocketed through me. I loved him unconditionally, and I would never stop. No matter what. Forever.

"Yes. Even then."

"Really? Because you gutted me and still I love you! I fucking hate you right now, but I love you so Goddamn much it's killing me!" The words ripped from him even as his hands pulled me tightly against him again, his fingers digging into the flesh of my back painfully as he buried his face in my neck and shoulder sobbing with me. "It hurts so much! How could you doubt me? Did you really think I could touch anyone after you?"

"It wasn't about that. It was about..." my voice cracked as emotions choked off my words. God, my chest hurt!

"You don't have to say it. I know what it was about!" His voice was muffled against me.

"No!" I pushed back, and his dark eyes burned into mine. His face was damp with tears, the remnants clinging to his lashes. I reached out to brush them away with both hands. "No, obviously you don't. I..." The loss I felt, even as I held him in my arms, threatened to overwhelm me. "I just... I missed you. I felt pushed aside."

Ryan's face twisted. "But, we made love all the time. I thought you knew. When I touch you... I can't get closer to you than that. Our time was so limited, I tried to show you every minute we were together. Making love... it's like a religious experience!" He huffed in anguish. "At least, it is to me."

Panic seized my chest. How was I going to make him understand? "It is, Ryan. It means everything, but remember you used to tell me that as long as you had my words, you didn't need my body? Remember? In Estes Park that first Christmas?"

"Yeah, but what does that have to do with this? I was joking around!"

"That didn't make it less true, did it?" I pulled back. This time it was me who needed to see his face.

"No." He shook his head. "It's true."

"Right. I needed you! Just *you*. The talks, the coffee dates... just hanging out."

Realization flooded his beautiful face, and we came together almost violently, desperation filling our embrace. His hand threaded through the hair at the back of my head as my arms wrapped around his waist.

"I missed you," I whispered against him. "I needed my best friend."

"Oh, Jesus! I'm so fucking stupid." His soft lips rained kisses all over my face, at first quickly and then more slowly, becoming caressing in the way he savored my skin. My mouth ached for his; my heart ached for his love. "I'm sorry, baby," Ryan whispered against my lips. "You should know I'd never

put anyone before you. I'm sorry I made you feel that way. I'm
the one that needs forgiving."

He pushed back and cupped both sides of my face with his
hands; his thumbs brushed my cheekbones, and then one raked
over my lower lip. His eyes glistened with tears that still clung to
his lashes and left trails down his face, but his expression was
searching.

"Only if you forgive me too. I'm so sorry."

We were both laughing and crying at the same time as we
hugged and kissed over and over. Relief washed over me and I
could finally breathe again.

His strong arms tightened around my body and lifted me ef-
fortlessly onto the bed. Somehow, we ended up wound around
each other under the covers, my head resting on Ryan's chest as
his fingers traced delicate patterns on my shoulders and back.
My hand wandered down over his iron flat stomach to grasp
around him. He began to swell and harden instantly.

"Mmmmm..." he sighed.

I ached to tell him about the baby, but the moment seemed
to be just about us, and I wanted to bask in it for a few minutes.
The weeks apart seemed endless, and now, with his arms around
me, I felt safe and relaxed; finally happy. The last thing I wanted
was for Ryan to believe that the baby was the only reason I was
going back to him.

Suddenly, Ryan rolled over and pinned me down, cupping
both sides of my face with his hands, his thumbs brushing my
cheekbones roughly, and then one raked over my lower lip. His
eyes were still teary, but his expression was stern.

"When were you planning to tell me you were pregnant?"

My mouth fell open in a surprised gasp, and Ryan's eyes
widened with mine.

"Was that the only reason you were coming home?" he asked sadly. "How long have you known?"

"Ryan, no! I was coming home because I couldn't stand another minute away from you." My fingers traced down his cheek to the stubble on his chin. "I can't breathe when we're apart." My eyes searched his for some spark of belief, the blue depths as deep and dark as the ocean. "I was packing, yes, but I only just discovered it Friday evening. I've been throwing up, but I thought it was just because I've been so miserable and crying so much. I'd already made the decision to come home. Everything hurt, and I didn't want you to suffer anymore."

Ryan scowled down at me, but happiness shone in his eyes, his mouth twitched on one corner.

"Don't be mad." I pouted playfully, running a finger down the side of his face and then his lower lip. "I'm very happy about the baby, but it wasn't the reason I was coming home. You're the only reason I do anything." A tremulous smile tugged at my lips as I watched love soften his handsome features. I moved my hand up to brush the soft stubble that darkened his strong jaw. "I love you so much."

Ryan's big hand continued to stroke my cheek and brow as I waited for his response. Emotions flowed over his beautiful face: love, pride, pain. "I love you, too. I can't stand it if you don't know how much."

Ryan's mouth finally found mine in a tender kiss, his open mouth playing with mine. I lifted my face to his, hungry and wanting his tongue to pillage and plunder, to take what I wanted so much to give. His hands grazed the sides of my breasts, then one went around my back and the other slid to my abdomen, just below my waist. A shuddering sigh left him, and I threaded the fingers of both hands at his nape.

"Promise me you know," he demanded softly.

"I promise." My heart constricted and then exploded. "How did you know about the baby? I haven't told a single person... except Andrea."

Ryan's lips lifted in a half smile. "She didn't tell me. I know you; every nuance of your body. Your breasts were firm before but now they're like bouncy balls. And your nipples are slightly bigger and more plumped up." He grinned and moved to my side, letting his hand brush down my stomach, below my navel, before tenderly splaying his hand as I burst out laughing at his words.

He bent his head and kissed the top swell of one breast, brushing his chin over the nipple playfully, the soft bristles puckering the tender flesh. "I can't wait to watch you bloom with our baby. You're so beautiful," he whispered the worshiping words, and I'd never felt more cherished.

My fingers wound in his hair as I arched beneath his mouth, wanting more, wanting to show him how much he meant to me. "I should have known I couldn't fool you, Matthews," I teased. My expression sobered. "But I wasn't really trying to."

"I know. I saw the picture in the magazine when I bought it for Louie, but I refused to read the article. I thought you'd taken that job for God knew how long." Ryan brushed his nose against mine. "I was afraid to hope it was for me."

"Ryan," I said softly. "I thought my reason was transparent. Even Mike, figured out that it was to let you know where I was. It was the first thing we did here. I hoped... you'd come after me."

"That's nuts! I told you I'd come for you the day you left. You said you didn't want me!"

"I didn't then. I was trying to figure out a way to accept Jane. But two days later, I was taking that photo on the bridge,

Ryan. Because, I couldn't bear to be away from you and I wanted you to find me. But, you waited for weeks. Why didn't you talk to me?"

Ryan studied me, his beautiful smile fading to a serious look as the seconds ticked by. "I was pissed as hell and hurting. I wanted to punish you back, but then something happened that made me realize I was taking the biggest risk of my life by not coming after you." I cocked my head to look up at him and his fingers brushed my cheek. "I need to tell you this, baby." His fingers threaded through mine as he looked down into my face.

I frowned. "Is it going to hurt me? If so, I don't want to know. It doesn't matter."

"I don't want it to hurt, but I have to tell you, even if it does, sweetheart. We can't have any secrets between us."

"Okay," I sighed, bracing myself for what was to come. Ryan's hand tightened on mine.

"I was going crazy, and I was so pissed because you left and wouldn't tell me where you were. When I figured it out, I was pissed that you took the job, and that would probably mean we were over. I couldn't sleep, and I was eating like shit. I was living on energy drinks to keep me awake at work, but I was starting to lose it. I was shaky and snapping at everyone; I could barely function. When I almost dosed someone the wrong meds, Dr. Jameson finally prescribed sleeping pills and insisted I go home and take a few days off. He could have kicked me out of the program."

I turned my face into his neck and leaned my forehead on his shoulder. "Ryan," I breathed. "I'm sorry. Oh, my God!"

Ryan's lips brushed my temple. "Babe, let me get this out."

I lifted up on my elbows just enough to look into his eyes and frowned. Anxiety forced my heart to thud painfully, and the trepidation in Ryan's expression didn't help.

"I hated the apartment," he pressed on. "You were everywhere, and I couldn't stand being there without you. I could still smell you in the bedroom. I could smell us together, and I couldn't take it. So, I took the pills at the hospital and went to one of the on-call rooms."

I remembered that room well and could see where this was going. I struggled to get up, suddenly wanting to be free, but Ryan refused to let me escape.

"Jane came to you." It was statement. I knew it already.

"Yes. You were right about her. I'm sorry I didn't realize what she was capable of."

"I told you!"

"I know. I should've listened."

My throat tightened up again and my eyes burned, anger and jealousy turning me inside out. "What did she do?" I demanded.

"I thought I was dreaming. We were still at Stanford, I told you how I really felt, and we made love. I was aching for you and so desperate to believe that you were with me. I needed just a moment without the constant ache I'd been feeling for weeks. She wore your perfume... I thought she was you."

"Oh, God!" I struggled more forcefully as the pictures of Jane making love to my husband started playing in my head. I felt claustrophobic, like an animal clawing to be free of a trap. "Let me up, Ryan!"

"No!"

"Please, don't tell me anymore," I begged and gave up fighting, turning my face away and struggling not to cry. I didn't want this to matter, but it did. So much. "Please, I don't want the picture painted in my head." But it was too late.

"Julia. For God's sake! Look at me."

"How far did she go?" I demanded. I didn't want to know, but now, I had to.

"I was half asleep, babe."

"Did she get you off? Did she get off on you?"

"Honey, stop."

"Did she?" I asked painfully.

"No, I didn't come. I don't know if she did or not! We were fully clothed, honey. She kissed me, but that's all that happened. I told you, I was half asleep, and it doesn't even matter!" His voice was low and urgent, laced with desperation of its own. "The minute I realized she wasn't you, I stopped her, Julia! I shoved her to the floor and told her to get the fuck away from me! She knows we can't even be friends, now."

I couldn't move, but I tried. All I could think about was Jane on top of my husband, rubbing all over him, and moaning his name. Even if they had clothes on, it wasn't something I could bear thinking about. I pushed against him again, but Ryan still had my arms pinned down and his leg flung over both of mine.

"No! You will stay still and listen!" He shook me gently. "*You are my life*! Look into my eyes! You know it's always been you since the moment we met! It will always be *you*!"

My chest was heaving and tears burned the back of my eyes, my whole body shaking with my grief. He didn't deserve my anger. I was to blame for leaving him, but still it hurt like hell to hear that another woman tried to seduce my husband. I struggled to push the words out. "It's all... muh... my fault! It happened because I left."

Gentle fingers pushed my hair back and traced the side of my face, and Ryan kissed me gently as I tried not to cry. "Oh, baby, no, it isn't. It's mine, too. You shouldn't have left without talking to me, but I shouldn't have let Jane come between us in the first place. I let my guilt get out of hand. I didn't want to believe anything bad about her, and I closed my eyes to what it was doing to you because I assumed you'd know we were solid. It never crossed my mind you'd actually think I could want anyone else. You were laughing just a second ago, so stop crying, baby. It's over."

He kissed me harder, his tongue invading my mouth and teasing mine into play. I wound my arms tightly around his shoulders, and pulled his mouth closer. "I'm still sorry," I whispered against his mouth.

"Me, too. I went home, determined to find you. I stopped being a stubborn ass and called your office. Andrea texted back and I told her I was coming to Paris. Then, she told me about the café' and how you'd probably be there on Sunday."

I closed my eyes and turned my face into the strong column of Ryan's neck. "I went every Sunday." I couldn't seem to stop the stupid tears, and Ryan's arms tightened in understanding. His hand stroked down my back, smoothing my hair over my skin.

"I love you, baby. I did that on Sundays too. But, why was Turner with you?"

"We were meeting for coffee to say goodbye, and I wanted the finals from the bridge shoot. I wanted a close-up of our lock so I could frame it and keep it forever." Talking about it made me relive the emotions of the day I'd placed it on the bridge and the pain I felt not having him with me. "But I left it there."

Ryan's eyes were glassy when he nodded. "It's okay. We'll fix it. He can send another one."

"Did you read the article?"

"Yeah. I bought another copy and read it on the subway. I couldn't reconcile how you could do that for us, when you believed I was letting Jane get between us."

"Because, even if she separated us… in my heart, you were still mine."

"We're so fucked up, baby girl. All this could have been avoided."

All I could do was nod.

"When I pulled that suitcase down and found that picture… I cried like a baby. It's incredible." His hand smoothed over my stomach again. "And, here he is, like a miracle. We're going to be okay, my love. We're going to be better than okay, I promise. This shit is never going to happen again, okay?"

"Okay." I blinked and reached up to flutter my fingers along his jaw. "Ryan, make love to me again and this time… I want you to come."

He smirked and rolled onto his back, pulling me with him so I straddled him, my legs resting outside his thighs. "Yes, ma'am."

My fingers wound in his hair and our mouths hovered together, now so serious. His hand pulled my hips against his, and I could feel his hardness.

"I don't want to wait," I breathed.

He slid into me, pulling me flush against him so he was buried to the hilt inside me. "Then don't wait."

His delicious breath brushed my face, and his lower lip bumped and nudged the top one of mine, until finally, after what felt like eternity, his mouth crashed over mine. The kisses were passionate, giving and taking, as our hips rocked together.

I gasped, feeling my entire body start to tingle. "Ryan, I love you."

"I love you, and you're mine. You belong with me."

Ryan ~

She was so damn beautiful. I watched Julia from the next seat, my hand resting warmly on her leg beneath the blanket. She was sleeping peacefully, leaning on the closed window shade with her Stanford hoodie bunched up behind her head. I yawned, covering my mouth with my hand. I was looking forward to our bed. I hadn't wanted to be there in six weeks but now the proposition was glorious.

Julia and I had been exhausted from the days and nights apart, but our lovemaking couldn't be denied after our reunion. We stayed a few days in Paris, running around the city, putting the lock on the fence and leaving it there, Julia running around the Louvre to show me all the great works that mattered to her. Last night, we went up the Eiffel Tower. As glorious as the days had been, the nights were even better. We couldn't get enough of each other and made love several times a night. We were paying for it now, but it was so worth it.

Undoubtedly, she had to feel exhausted all the time now anyway. Growing a baby surely had to take a lot out of her, and I should have been more considerate by making sure she rested more. But, it was technically our honeymoon, and once we touched, there was no holding back.

I sucked in a deep breath, filling my lungs to capacity. I was finally whole now that I had Julia beside me again, and the prospect of our baby was a bonus. I could, literally, feel tenderness fill me up as I looked upon the woman next to me. I was truly blessed.

The flight attendant paused on her way past and laughed at my expression. My smile widened. I didn't give a fuck what she thought about the sappy look on my face; I was happy as hell!

"Do you need anything? Perhaps some wine?"

"Sure. Red, please. Do you have Merlot?"

"What about your companion?" she nodded in my wife's direction.

"My wife can't have alcohol; we're expecting our first baby," I announced happily. It was the first time I'd said it out loud to someone else, and it felt miraculous.

"Congratulations. How about some apple juice?"

"She prefers orange, if you have it."

By the time I'd placed the juice on her tray table, Julia began to stir. Her eyes fluttered open slowly.

"Flight attendants drooling all over you, hmmm?"

I glanced over and was met with bright green eyes and a brilliant smile.

I grinned again. "Who?"

"Uh huh, whatever," Julia grunted as she pushed herself into a sitting position and picked up her juice.

She was so cute. I chuckled and squeezed her thigh, leaning over to place an open-mouthed kiss on her lips. "Mmm, you taste so good."

"Flattery will get you everywhere." She smiled and nudged my shoulder with hers.

"I'm counting on it." I leaned into her and took her hand in mine, bringing it up to brush my lips against her knuckles, and she laid her head on my shoulder. We couldn't stop touching each other, but I wasn't complaining. Julia put on a brave face about Jane, but it would kill her to think of me working beside her day after day. I knew that I couldn't stand it if Turner had really tried to have her. If he'd touched her in the way Jane had touched me, I'd want to kill him. There was no way in hell I'd stand by quietly while Julia saw him every day after something like that.

"Turner didn't try anything while you were in Paris, did he?" My eyes met hers and didn't flinch. After what I'd shared our first night back together, I hardly had the right to ask, but I had to know.

She shook her head slowly. "No. He, um… he's actually become a good friend. He admitted to me that he had hopes in my direction in the past, but after photographing our wedding, he knew it was a lost cause. He told me to get my ass back where I belonged. He's got his eye on Andrea. She can't see it. It's sort of hilarious."

My eyebrows shot up. I was skeptical. "Really?"

"Yeah, really." She scrunched her nose at me. "What brought that on?"

"This whole thing. I emailed Dr. Jameson this morning and told him I was leaving St. Vincent's."

Julia's back stiffened as she sat up straighter. "What? Why? Ryan, you'll have to start your residency all over again!"

"So what? I refuse to put you through the pain of having me around Jane every day."

Her head cocked to one side, and she relaxed, her expression filling with love and incredulousness. "Are you certain?"

"Yes. You," I rubbed my thumb over the back of her hand over and over in a gentle caress and reached over with my other hand to press it to her still flat tummy, "and, this, are all that matter to me now."

"I already love you more than I can stand. You have to stop or I'll explode."

I leaned back in the leather seat. "Yeah, I know." I flashed a brilliant smile and winked at her. She giggled and smoothed the blanket on her lap.

"I will explode." She laughed softly and put a hand on her belly. "Literally."

"You'll be gorgeous." I reached out and brushed her chin with my index finger.

She'd taken the week off to play in Paris, except for Monday afternoon, and I hadn't questioned her. She was coming home with me, and I just figured she would resume her old position. If not, plenty of magazines would want to hire her. I wasn't sweating it.

"So, I guess we're both unemployed."

"What?" I asked in surprise.

"Yeah. I quit Vogue." She seemed at ease with what would have been a major crisis a few weeks ago.

"You did? Why didn't you tell me before?"

"I was afraid you'd feel like it was your fault."

"When did this happen?"

"When I wanted to come home. I told Meredith that I couldn't stand being away from you. Even though she saw how it was killing me, she refused to let me go home. She laughed it off and said she'd have me home before for a measly visit in a month and that was the end of the discussion. So I quit. This whole fucked-up mess has taught me that no job is worth being away from you or risking what's between us. It looks like we both made the same call."

I looked at her and felt my heart expand painfully. Incredibly, my love for my amazing wife grew yet again. She was amazing. "I thought we decided we're indestructible."

"Yes, but we don't need to antagonize each other, right?" Julia smiled softly and leaned toward me for a soft kiss. "We're going to be poor, so it's a good thing we can live on love... *and sex*." Julia smirked at me and waggled her sculpted eyebrows.

I laughed out loud. "We'll manage somehow."

"Should we go back to Boston? Being there with you after the accident meant so much to me. I bet Mass General would love to get you back."

I watched her closely as the enormity of her words sank in. "Wow. Really?" I missed Boston.

She lifted her shoulder in a half-shrug. "Yes." I fell into the soft green orbs of her eyes as the softly spoken word left her mouth.

"I want to have the baby with Aaron and Jenna close by anyway."

"That's a very sweet thought."

Her eyes connected and stayed on mine. "Ryan..." Julia reached out and threaded her fingers to mine; lifting my hand, she bent to brush her lips across the top of it. "I'd like you to deliver the baby; just you and me. We're so close, and this is such an intimate thing, I don't want to share it with anyone else. Do you think that would be okay?"

My throat started to close before she was finished speaking, and my eyes burned with emotion. I was overwhelmed. "I think... that would be... unbelievably... *perfect*. If there are no complications, and I feel it's safe, I would really love that, babe." An incredulous laugh burst out. "How did I ever get so lucky? You're so *fucking amazing*."

Happiness filled her beautiful green eyes, and the music of her laughter filled my soul with joy. "Takes one to know one, Matthews."

Happiness and contentment settled over me like a thick, fluffy blanket. I flashed my wife a brilliant smile and squeezed her hand. "Yeah. I guess it does."

~Epilogue~

Ryan ~

I drew my hand down over the swollen curve of Julia's pregnant belly, spreading my fingers wide to hold as much of it as I could in my hand; always waiting for the miracle of a flutter or kick. We sat in the freshly finished nursery, snuggled up together in the plush chaise lounge. Julia's hand was wrapped around my bicep, and her forehead rested against it, her back against my chest as she sat between my legs. I leaned in to press my lips to the top of her head. She was so beautiful to me as her body changed before my eyes. She sighed with satisfaction, and I had no desire to move, just enjoying Julia's scent and the feeling of holding her close. My lips remained against her skin.

After two months of hunting around different parts of the city, we found a modest home in an older neighborhood. Julia liked the architecture and character much more than newer, more modern, cookie-cutter types; the landscaping was more detailed and the trees taller and more luxurious. Being an artist, she obviously translated individuality into beauty. She loved the hardwood floors and deep woodwork, arched entryways, and the quaint little touches. It was the window seat in this room that had sold us the house. It was the perfect place for our family to grow.

Of course, it wasn't so perfect when we bought it and it needed quite a bit of work, but the price was right. The budget was tighter than tight, but somehow, we made it work. Julia did a lot of the painting, but we hired a contractor for the rework of the kitchen and bathroom. I helped as much as possible when I was home, but she seemed to enjoy putting her stamp on it. We saved decorating the nursery until after the first ultrasound and didn't begin until the first of May. I didn't really want to know the sex of the baby, but Julia argued that we could get to know the baby and also personalize the space. And, she glowed like a light bulb the entire time we worked on it. My mom sent a fifteen hundred dollar gift certificate from Babies "R" Us to make sure we had everything we needed. The kid was going to be spoiled rotten.

I glanced around the now perfectly appointed room. Ellie and both of our mothers had flown in for the baby shower Jenna had thrown last month, and now, the room was a baby paradise. Instead of the typical light blue, the room was done in eggshell with touches of dark teals and browns. Julia had a specific name for each one of the colors, but I didn't bog my brain down with that crap. It looked good;—not all frou-frou—and that's what mattered to me.

Julia's mom handmade a quilt in the same color scheme; you could visibly see all the love she poured into it. Ellie and my mom sent packages almost weekly with baby clothes and stuffed animals. My father commissioned a wood carver in Chicago to create the mobile hanging over the crib; and the hand carved toy trucks, sailboats, and teddy bears exactly matched the images on Marin's quilt. The music box at the center of it played row *Row, Row, Row Your Boat.*

There was a dresser full of diapers, blankets, onesies, and footed pajamas, a bookshelf already filled with children's classics, a chaise and rocking chair, and a dark mahogany crib and changing table. It looked like an ad out of Vogue Baby. I huffed out a small laugh. I wasn't sure why I expected anything less.

We'd moved to Boston as soon as we could break our lease in New York. Meredith called ten times, begging Julia to reconsider leaving Condé Nast, and I was proud of her steadfastness that initiated the move. I was extremely proud when I listened to her on the phone, only two days after we'd returned to New York, telling her ex-boss that she wouldn't choose her job over her family ever again. It turned out Meredith was the one who caved and made an offer for Julia to work on the magazine, freelance, from Boston. We moved her art table and bought an old desk at a flea market, and both now sat in her new office in the other spare bedroom. It was all coming together like perfect pieces of a puzzle.

My place in the residency program at Mass General was secured before we'd packed one box. I was happy as hell to be back in familiar surroundings, working closely with some of my friends, and mostly, to have Aaron and Jenna near. It was like stepping back into the most comfortable pair of jeans I ever had.

Aaron was focusing on internal medicine, so he wasn't working in the ER with me, but I still had Jenna. The hours were grueling, and I was still away from Julia more than either of us liked, but the two women spent a lot of time together. Somehow, it made my time away easier. I felt safer, more at ease.

Now all that was left to do was have the baby. I'd never forget how I felt when I looked at the ultrasound screen, holding Julia's hand. *She looked up at me with expectant eyes, waiting for me to tell her if our baby was a boy or a girl. My heart almost flew out of my chest as the nurse rolled the instrument around in the goo on Julia's rounded stomach. When that little profile showed up on the screen, my eyes blurred, and I squeezed her hand so hard she had to tell me to loosen my grip. A few more turns and we made sure the baby was healthy, and the sex became clear. I puffed up like a peacock, bending down to kiss my wife happily.*

"Ryan? Well, what?" She'd been so anxious, pulling at my shirt with her free hand. "Ryan!"

"It's a boy." Her face lit up, and she cried, all at the same time. I grinned so hard, my face hurt. I smiled softly now, remembering.

Julia sat back with a satisfied expression. "I told you."

The baby was measured to make sure he was developing on schedule, and he was perfect.

When we left the appointment, I hoisted her up on my back for a piggyback ride to the car.

The fingers of Julia's other hand traced delicate lines in the hair on my forearm that held her close. "What are you thinking about?"

"Well…" I murmured softly, enjoying the feeling of having her enfolded against me. "I'm thinking that the baby is due in a week, and we still have to choose his name."

Her arms rested over mine and tightened, bringing mine closer around her. "I know. Jenna said we should combine our names. She suggested Julian."

My face screwed up in protest. "Uh… no. My son isn't going to have a pussy name like that!" I insisted.

Julia giggled happily. "I told her you'd say that."

I huffed, grinning. "No shit."

"Zane?" she asked softly.

I didn't hesitate. "What? So he can get his ass teased off. 'Hey! Insane Zane!' No, thanks."

"Elliott?"

"No."

"Jason? Or Jace for short?"

I grimaced again. I liked Jace, but Jason, no way in hell. "Jason reminds me of that ass-wipe who followed you around like a dog junior year."

Julia snorted softly and looked up at me, her expression amused. "Jason Milner?" she asked incredulously.

I shook my head and screwed up my face. "See? Why'd ya have to go and remember that dickhead's name?"

She laughed out loud. "Why don't you come up with something since you hate all of my ideas? We could name him after your dad."

I lifted a shoulder. "Eh... I thought of that. But won't your dad be pissed?"

"I don't like my dad's name that much, but don't tell him I said that."

"This is a hell of a lot harder than I thought it would be."

"What about Aaron or Ryan? Or your middle name?"

I let that sit for a minute, contemplating the options. I was certain it would mean a lot to Aaron if I named my son after him, and at the same time, I'd be proud as hell if my little boy had my name.

"Aaron Mitchell or Ryan Aaron?" Julia asked, still stroking her fingers up and down my arm.

"I don't know. Ryan Aaron feels goofy."

"That's because you're used to Ryan Mitchell. So, what about a derivative name? One we make out of Ryan and Aaron?"

"You mean like Ry-ron?" I thought it sounded completely ludicrous and the tone in my voice said so. "You want me to name my son *Ry-ron*? That's... Uh, when hell freezes over."

Julia burst out laughing. "No, not like Ry-ron. Oh, my God, Ryan! It doesn't have to be so literal!"

I couldn't help the deep chuckle that rumbled through my chest. "Then, what? Ay-on?"

She reached around and punched me playfully in the arm, still laughing. "No! What about Aiden, only we spell it with an A N at the end or Y after A? Like A I D A N, A Y D A N or A Y D E N? That way, he'll have some letters from each of your names? I like that a lot."

"Yeah, I can see that."

"Which one do you like the most?"

I mulled it over, trying to think of any stupid nicknames that could be made out of it and then whether it was dignified enough for him as a man. It had to fit him all his life. "I think A I D A N is nice."

She nodded. "Okay, then Aidan it is."

"Aidan Aaron?" I asked.

Julia shrugged against me. "That could work. But, see, I have this mad crush on the baby's daddy, so I'd really love to see my son carry some part of your name in a real way, Ryan. So, Aidan Mitchell is my favorite."

My mouth lifted in a slow smile, and love for the woman in my arms once again lurched in my chest. I pulled her closer, kissing the side of her face. "I love you, you know."

Julia turned in my arms, and I moved to let her adjust. She turned sideways and draped both legs over the top of my left thigh. She settled against my chest and wrapped her arms around my waist. Her nose brushed against my jaw, and then she kissed along its line. Her lips were warm and coaxing.

"Yes, I know," she whispered against my jaw. My body reacted automatically. "Ryan…"

I knew she wanted to make love. Our mothers were coming, and this would be the last day we had to ourselves. "Baby…"

I'd long since convinced her that I found her pregnant body as arousing as ever, but we were getting so close to the due date, and though my body was aching with want, I thought we should hold off.

"What? You know it won't hurt the baby." Her hand trailed down my chest and pushed up under the edge of my T-shirt to slide along the top of my jeans and over the bulge underneath the denim. Her fingers closed around my length, and I closed my eyes as she moved her hand up and down, pressing her fingers in small circles when she got to the head. "You want me," she whispered against my mouth. I wanted to let loose on her, but I just couldn't.

I let out a small groan, willing my hips to keep from thrusting against her hands. "I do, but babe... the baby's turned, and there's something so wrong about jabbing my cock in close to his little head. Especially, now that he has a name," I lamented regretfully. Shit, was it ever regretfully.

Instantly, Julia's hand stopped, and she pulled back to raise an eyebrow at me. "Are you serious?"

I inhaled deeply. "Unfortunately, yes." My mouth twisted in a wry smile. "I just can't poke at my son like this."

"Ryan, you're a doctor. You know it won't hurt him."

I moved my head in a small circle that was neither positive nor negative. "Mmmm, my head knows, but I still worry. These are my babies right here," I pointed between her heart and her tummy, "not just random patients." I reached up to cup her face, my thumb brushing her cheekbone. "We're getting so close. Let's not take any unnecessary risks."

I kissed her lips softly, my mouth savoring hers. It was mean, but something devious drove me on. I knew that kiss was more arousing, but I couldn't help it. I lifted her so she was straddling my lap. Despite her pregnancy, she was still small, and I lifted her easily, pulling her closer. Her body was much the same as before; her back and hips still slim, except for the baby bump in front, perfectly round, and her breasts being slightly larger and heavier.

"We can still play," I said softly, kissing the underside of her jaw and leaving a fiery trail down the column of her neck.

"This big belly gets in the way." I could hear the pout in her voice, and my mouth twitched in amusement. She really wanted me.

"Wanna bet?" I pushed her dress up over her thighs, sliding my hands around behind her to press her closer, groin against groin. Julia ground against me and wound her hands through my hair. I could feel her heat through her panties and my jeans, but I wanted to get even closer. I scooted forward on the chaise, lifting her with me, until I was able to plant my feet on the floor. I picked her up and carried her with me into the master bedroom.

As soon as I laid down flat on our bed, Julia's hands deftly opened the front of my jeans and pulled my boxers down. My full erection bobbed free. She licked her hand and then brought it around me, pulling and pushing, rubbing her thumb around the head with each stroke. It didn't take long until I was so turned on that a drop of clear liquid pearled on the tip.

"Uhhh..." My head fell back against the pillows, and I closed my eyes. Julia eased off me until she was on her knees between my spread legs. I lay there, helpless as she took me deep into her mouth. I wound my hands in her hair as she sucked hard, wrapping both hands around the shaft. She drove me crazy, teasing the head with her tongue, and then sliding her lips down and sucking on the way back out. It felt so good, and watching her was so sexy; it didn't take me long to come. I felt guilty coming in the mouth of my pregnant wife, but she got me so hot so fast, I lost control of what was happening.

Her eyes were smug and teasing as she crawled up on top of me. "Gotcha," she said, laying down and curling into me, yawning. My pants still hung open, my boxers pushed down and leaving me exposed. I reached down to pull them back in place.

My brow furrowed in confusion. I thought she'd still want to make love.

"Jules?"

"Hmmm?" She snuggled closer, hooking a leg over mine, and her belly resting against and on me.

"Don't you want me to take care of you? We don't have to be done."

"Let's take a nap."

I kicked at the throw at the foot of the bed until I could hoist it up with my toes and grab it with my free hand to pull it over her. When I was satisfied she was covered, I pulled her further into my embrace. She was already asleep.

Aaron was picking up our mothers at the airport later, and they'd be with us for dinner. Julia's rule of no clocks in the bedroom had me wondering how much time we had until they arrived, but it really didn't matter. Julia had a quick dinner planned, and the evening would be casual. No doubt the moms would pitch in.

I was torn between watching her sleep and holding her close, but in the end, I realized I was tired, too. Soon we'd be parents, and sleep would become scarce. I planted a lingering kiss on Julia's forehead. She sighed my name, and my eyes closed.

*****

"Julia, darling, do you need help?" my mother asked. Julia was chopping up various fresh vegetables and placing them in bowls next to one with hamburger and another with sliced chicken.

She looked up and smiled. "I'm good, Elyse."

"Ryan, you shouldn't allow her to work like this."

I sat on a stool next to my wife, unable to help myself, and ran a hand down the back of her head to tangle in the long hair at her nape. "You know she does what she wants."

Julia took a big chef's knife to three carrots she had lined up on the wooden chopping block. "Believe me, he spoils me."

Aaron was in the living room, and Jenna was setting the table in the dining room.

"What are you making, honey?" Marin asked.

"Well, it's sort of an 'assemble your own meal' thing. You put butter and meat in the bottom of a piece of foil, you add whatever vegetables you want, and then the seasoning you want. I have a variety of sauces and spices for the rest of you, but Ryan's boring. He likes just salt and pepper. You put everything you want in the foil and then fold it like a pocket. Throw it in the oven for an hour, and that's it. It's really easy. Dad used to make this when I was a kid and spent the summers in California. He's not that great of a cook, but this always turned out. Sometimes we threw it on coals or a campfire."

Marin smiled and glanced between us. "You guys look very happy."

Julia rubbed her lower back, and instantly, I perked up. "Baby, are you hurting?"

"My back's a little achy, that's all."

"What happened at the last doctor's appointment?" My mom asked, getting juice from the refrigerator and pouring a glass.

"She's about thirty percent effaced but no dilation yet. This backache could be something, though."

"Pfft. It would be too much to hope for." Julia began tearing pieces of foil off of the roll. "First babies are never on time."

"Make Aaron's a little bigger, Julia," Jenna said, taking a seat across from me. "I really love this house. Better than ours. I

wish you would have been in town when I was decorating."
Their house was about twenty minutes away and was more modern. "Our place feels like the hospital."

"We have time," Julia began, but then winced.

I reached out and placed a hand on her stomach. The baby
kicked hard. "He's getting busy."

"Aaron!" Jenna called. "Come in here and tell me what you
want to eat."

I studied Julia as she made my dinner and hers and helped
with the others until they were all in the oven and the timer was
set.

"Have you decided on a name?" Marin asked hopefully.

"Yes! Tell us! We've suffered long enough," my mom
added.

My eyes met Julia's and locked. We hadn't talked about
whether we'd share it, but I smiled at her. I knew what she was
thinking.

"Yep, we figured that out earlier today actually."

"Nothing like waiting until the last minute," Aaron muttered, grabbing a beer and going back in the other room.

"Well?"

"What did you decide?"

"Out with it!"

All the women talked at once.

"We're not telling. I didn't get my way about not knowing
the baby's sex, so, you'll know when you're introduced to the
little man."

Julia waddled a little when she walked from the island to
place the dishes in the sink, but other than her swollen stomach,
you wouldn't know she was pregnant. I thought she was cute.
Her face was still so beautiful, but I noticed sharp pain in her
eyes.

I took her arm and pulled her a little closer. "Baby, are you having contractions?" My hand splayed out on her stomach again.

She shook her head. "No, I don't think so, but I am going to take a bath while dinner's in the oven."

"Honey, are you okay?" Marin asked. "I bet the baby is ready. You are all belly."

"I'm fine, Mom. I'm glad you're all here, though." She kissed her mother's cheek and went to hug my mom.

"When I get pregnant, I bet I'll gain a hundred pounds," Jenna lamented. "Julia will probably be one of those who a week after the baby is born, you won't be able to tell she was ever pregnant."

"I'm careful. Not too much sugar or white flour. Ryan keeps pretty good track of me."

"Yeah, easy for the dudes. They get to imbibe and dole out orders while we have to suffer," Jenna retorted.

"How is that different from everyday life?" my mother asked.

"Ryan's good. He doesn't eat tempting things in front of me. I'll be back," Julia said, smiling and rubbing her tummy. She turned toward the stairs and I grabbed her hand.

"I'm coming with you." I stared into her green eyes and they softened. She touched my jaw and started to speak. "Don't argue."

She nodded, and we left the others downstairs to watch the food. Jenna and Aaron were tangled together on the couch watching CSI, and our moms were in the kitchen, happily chatting about the baby.

I soon had the water running but didn't add any bubble bath or bath salts just in case. My fingers tested the water, making sure it was warm and not too hot.

"Can I have it hot, honey?"

Julia was undressing behind me. When we had the bathroom redone, we picked a wider tub with Jacuzzi jets, big
enough for the two of us. I lit a candle and turned off the light.

"Not too hot, baby. It's not good for either of you."

"I know, but my back hurts so bad." Dropping her dress,
Julia grabbed the edge of the vanity and gasped, her whole body
tensing.

"Jules, honey, you're having contractions."

"Does that mean I can't have a bath? Labor will be long,
right?"

"Generally on first babies, it is." I picked her up in my arms
and gently lowered her into the tub. "Hold on." I shot into the
bedroom and pulled out the stopwatch I had hidden in my underwear drawer. Technology was great, but my iPhone would
time-out in between contractions, and I didn't want to mess with
it. "It's going to take some time, baby. I'll start timing the next
one. We don't have to go into the hospital until they're ten minutes apart."

She reached for my hand. "I trust you."

I sat on the floor next to the tub, holding her hand and cupping her face with the other. "It's finally happening. You're going to be the most amazing mother."

We sat there together, just gazing at each other, and her
eyes began to water. "Don't make me cry."

My own eyes started to burn and I blinked. "Nah, this is
going to be an incredible experience. It's going to be okay. I
wish I could take the pain for you, my love."

We'd talked about the baby's birth several times. Julia
reiterated how she wanted me to deliver him alone with her, but I
could tell she needed some reassurance. She told me she didn't
want an epidural or medications at all, but I'd seen women in
labor and knew how much it hurt.

"So, if you change your mind about the epidural, I'm on board."

"Ryan, no. Someone will have to come in then, and I don't want that. We agreed; it's only us from the minute we get me hooked up to the monitors until Aidan is out."

I smiled and my heart tightened. This was the first time she'd referred to him by name.

"Please. Just us, okay?"

"Unless something happens. But, that's my call, and you have to trust me on that." Our fingers moved and threaded together. I understood why she wanted us to be alone, and the thought of it filled me with emotions I couldn't put into words, but there was no way I'd take any chances with her safety. She nodded. "Is the water helping at all?"

"Maybe a little."

I reached in and tested it. It was a little cool so I turned on the hot faucet and moved the water around to blend it in.

"This baby is going to be amazing." I settled in to talk to her. The contractions would start slow and be short and most likely the baby wouldn't be born until well into the next day. "Is it selfish to hope he looks like the picture you drew?"

Her mouth curved in a loving smile. "No. I hope he does, too. There are worse things than looking like you."

My hand wound around hers again as I leaned against the side of the tub. "Have I told you how absolutely thankful I am for psych 101?"

Julia swallowed, and tears flooded her eyes.

"I have everything I could want, and it's all because you love me." I lifted the hand I held to my mouth and said the next words against it. "I'll never find the words to tell you how much you have meant to my life. I love you more every single day. You're so... precious to me. I never want to lose you."

Two tears tumbled down her face, and she sat up and opened her arms to me. I gathered her close, not caring if I'd get wet. "You're never going to."

I turned my head and kissed her cheek, then her temple; my throat beginning to ache. She tensed again, and I quickly grabbed the stopwatch, clicking it on. "Tell me when it's over."

"Okay. They're not too bad yet. Like really painful period cramps."

Her fingers curled around the edge of the tub, and her face grimaced. It was hurting worse than she let on. "Ugh...." She let out a little moan.

"Will it help to breathe?" We'd taken the natural childbirth classes three months prior, and I afterward, we'd joked about all the huffing and puffing.

"It's over now."

I stopped the watch. The contraction was 40 seconds. "They're not too long yet, sweetheart. Do you want to get out of the tub? I want to keep an eye on you, and we won't be able to tell if your water breaks in the tub."

She nodded, and after I noted the time and set the watch back down, I lifted her from the tub and wrapped her in a towel.

By the time she was dressed in a pair of old sweats and one of my T-shirts, Marin was calling up the stairs that dinner was done.

Jenna was putting the foil packets onto plates, and my mother was getting everyone drinks.

My hand stayed on the curve of Julia's lower back and rubbed back and forth.

"Everyone hungry?" Mom asked, smiling all the way to her eyes.

"I don't feel like eating much."

"You need to eat, honey. This might be the last time you'll get to for a while."

Jenna, Marin, and my mother stopped what they were doing and looked at us with wide eyes.

"Oh, my God!" Marin gushed and moved forward to put both hands on Julia's face. "Are you in labor?"

"Just barely," she answered with a smile.

"What?" Aaron rushed in from the other room. "Jules, seriously?"

She nodded. I was fucking jumping out of my skin, but I tried to appear calm. "Let's just keep our wits about us. Call the grandpas and tell them to get their asses on a couple of planes." I laughed. All three women went for their phones.

Jenna called Ellie. "Ellie! Julia's in labor!" They all scattered into other rooms for their respective calls.

"Let's eat!" Aaron picked up his plate, and I shook my head at him. "What? You said be normal." He grabbed a fresh beer and went into the other room.

I laughed happily and nodded. "I hope everyone makes it in time. Do you want to sit at the table or in the other room with everyone?"

The evening was spent watching TV with Julia curled on my lap in our big chair, my feet propped on the ottoman. I had the stopwatch and was timing her contractions. Sometimes no one knew but the two of us when she had one, but when I felt her tense, I automatically started timing. Her forehead rested against my jaw.

Every once in a while, one of the moms or Jenna would ask about Julia's progress; all of them anxious and concerned. About midnight, when the contractions were about twenty minutes apart, a hot wetness seeped between us, saturating her sweats and my jeans. Her head popped up instantly, her lush mouth forming a silent 'o'.

"Either you just peed on me, or we need to go to the hospital." My hand pushed her hair back from her surprised face. When her understanding dawned in her eyes, I leaned in and kissed her gently. "This is it. Ready to go have a baby, baby?" I asked. Her cheek was so soft under my fingers. I wanted to memorize every nuance of this moment.

Listening, Jenna jumped up from the floor in front of the couch. Aaron was asleep behind her and she smacked him on his shoulder. "Wake your ass up, Uncle Aaron! We gotta go!"

"Oh my God! Here we go!" Marin stood up at the same time as my mother, who put both hands to her mouth.

I took Julia upstairs to change while the others scrambled around like the three stooges, only there were four. We both changed our pants, and when we went back downstairs, they all stood waiting by the door.

"Jenna, can you drive our moms in your car?" I threw Aaron the keys to Julia's Mazda. "Aaron, you're with us."

Julia ~

Ryan was calm on the outside, but I could tell he was freaking out a little bit in the way he moved around the room, his eye always on the monitor, swiftly sitting beside me then jumping up again. After Jenna helped to hook me up on the monitor, everyone left Ryan and me alone. The pain was intense at times, and Ryan would hold my hand and help me concentrate on the breathing. I did it to give Ryan something to do, when I thought it was basically all bullshit. It didn't ease the pain at all.

We'd been here almost ten hours and the sun was up, but the window blinds were drawn and the lights low. Ryan had packed a portable stereo, and it played songs from our playlist softly in the background.

The last time he checked me, I was nine centimeters dilated and about ninety percent effaced. Ryan sat next to me and held my hand, studying my face. I just couldn't look away from him, even as the pain tore through me. I squeezed his hand tight and focused on his gorgeous eyes. I tried to think about us and not the pain, about holding the baby and not how my body would probably rip in half pushing him out.

"You're amazing. Why aren't you screaming? I know it hurts like a motherfucker." Ryan was in his scrubs, a gown sitting ready on the chair, the lower portion of the mask tied around his neck so he could tie it up easily. His hair was hidden beneath the blue surgical cap and a fine sheen of sweat beaded on his brow.

We were in a birthing room and would be able to stay in here unless there were complications. Aaron and Jenna waited just outside the door, while our parents, Ellie and Harris waited down the hall in the waiting room. I might be writhing in pain, but joy had a hold on my heart.

"He isn't coming into this world hearing his mother screaming." My body seized again, but I kept my eyes trained on my husband.

"You're so brave. Just breathe, baby. Just think of it as a little closer to having our son." His fingers brushed my hair back and wiped my forehead with a damp cloth. "Why aren't you cussing me out for getting you in this position?"

"I love you and…" Another contraction ripped through me. They were longer now and much harder. "You… you didn't… do it alone. I really want to push. Can I?"

Ryan moved quickly, pulling on some gloves. I bent my knees up, and when he put two fingers inside me and one on top of my stomach, it hurt like hell. My face crumpled and I bit my lip. "Jesus, it hurts, Ryan."

"I'm sorry, baby. You're dilated, and not quite a hundred percent effaced, but yes, we'll get you ready to push."

Ryan propped me up on four pillows and dropped the lower portion of the bed, pulling a chair in between my bent knees, and wrapping his hands around my thighs he scooted me gently to the end of the bed. He ripped off the gloves, tied the gown in place, and grabbed another pair.

"Honey, I want you to put your feet flat up against my shoulders and use me as leverage. I'm going to hold your hands and help you as much as I can. I'll pull you into a curled position to push during the contractions." I did as he asked and his hands wrapped around my wrists.

I nodded and bit my lip. Ryan's eyes were trained on the monitors. "Another one's coming, baby. Take a deep breath and hold it. One, Two..." I pushed so hard I thought the blood vessels in my face would burst. "Three... four..." He continued to count to ten, and then I let my breath out and sucked in another one. "Good job. Wait until the next one."

"Fuck, it hurts, Ryan!"

"I'm sorry, it's too late for meds, honey. You're doing amazing!"

Three more pushes and minutes that felt like hours later, sweat was starting to soak the forehead of his surgical cap.

"Aggggggggg...." I grunted as Ryan counted off again, my fingers biting into his, and my feet pushed against his chest so hard he'd probably have bruises.

"He's crowning, Julia! I can see him!" The excitement in Ryan's eyes distracted me from the burning I felt as my body opened. "Stop pushing, now. Stop, okay?" His pull on my hands relaxed and I gripped tighter, trying to pull my body up, but instead of pulling to help me, he reversed his pressure, making it difficult for me to continue. "Baby, I need you to stop!"

"I don't want to! I want him out! I want him out! I want him *out!*" I yelled at him.

"Julia, stop or you'll tear. Jesus!"

"What's wrong?" I asked, panicked, and lay back trying not to push. I looked up at the ceiling.

He unwound his hands from mine. "I can make this easier with an episiotomy, but I'm not sure I'll be able to cut you."

I was panting for breath. "Just do it, Ryan. If that's what we need to do… do it!"

Ryan nodded. "You've been pushing about 35 minutes. As soon as the next contraction starts, I'll do it, and you push through it. It will help you not feel it as much."

"Okay," I licked my lips and nodded rapidly.

"Jesus, Julia…" His eyes were tearing up. "I'm so sorry to put you through this."

"I wouldn't go through this for anyone else. But it's you and me, Matthews. He'll be worth it. You'll see."

A little cry broke from his chest. "I love you so fucking much!" His voice cracked just as my body contracted again.

"Okay, here we go," he said.

I took a deep breath and tried to use my elbows as leverage. My feet were still against him, but I no longer had his hands to pull me forward. I pushed with all my might, concentrating on getting the baby out. The muscles in my thighs and arms started to shake.

Ryan set the scalpel back on the metal tray. I vaguely registered the blood.

"Push, baby, here he comes. His head is almost out. Stop when I tell you, okay?"

"Ernnnnnn…." I pushed as hard as I could. My face felt like it was ready to explode with the effort.

"Okay, stop."

"What's happening?" I asked, panting.

"I'm making sure the cord isn't caught around his neck and clearing out his nose." He reached for something and I heard this sucking sound as he sucked out the baby's nose and mouth.

"What's he look like? Is he bald?"

"My son is not bald." Ryan's brilliant blue eyes locked with mine for a second. They were all I could see of his face. "He has lots of dark hair."

I smiled and started to cry.

"Okay, baby. One more big one."

I sniffed and sucked in my breath. It took just a second or two before the baby slid from my body, and Ryan was lifting him up to rest on my chest and stomach. I gazed at my baby. He wasn't making a sound. Ryan grabbed a towel and started to briskly rub the blood and white gunk from his skin. The baby sucked in his first breath and started to wail.

I was laughing and crying at the same time. "Oh my God. He's gorgeous."

Ryan came to me and kissed me, one arm behind me and the other around me and our baby. "He's a miracle. He's perfect. He has huge balls." He laughed happily, staring at Aidan.

I laughed out loud, tears raining from my eyes. I touched his downy cheek with my finger.

At the sound of the baby crying, Jenna burst through the door, fully dressed in a surgical gown. She looked at the three of us and smiled. "Time of birth?" Her eyes rolled as she waited for Ryan to tell her.

"Oh, shit." He looked at the clock. "About five minutes ago."

Jenna huffed, her smile hidden by her mask, but I could see it in her eyes. "Dickhead."

Ryan laughed, and she smiled at me and took a good look at her nephew, still crying in my arms. Jenna handed me a receiving blanket and helped me wrap it around Aidan's little pink body,

I snuggled him close to my chest, examining every perfect thing about him. "Hey..." I hushed him. "It's okay... You're okay." He stopped crying and looked up at me with dark eyes. It was hard to tell now, but I hoped with all my heart that his eyes would be as blue as his daddy's. I leaned in to kiss his little head. He was so tiny. Jenna moved away then came back and put a little hat on his head.

"Give me the little man. Time to weigh him and all that shit." Then she took Aidan from me.

Ryan changed gloves again. "Sorry, baby. We're not quite done. I'll need one more push to deliver the placenta then I'll need to stitch you up."

To say that was the grossest thing ever would have been an understatement and I was glad when it was over. When Ryan finally pulled the gloves and mask off, he stared into my eyes, both of us getting choked up as he gathered me close. He laid his head down on my chest and, I wrapped my arms around him. When he looked at me, we were both crying.

"Thank you. He's amazing. You're still everything. Only now, Aidan is part of us. It always amazes me how there is always more and more love... it blows my mind."

I nodded and kissed his mouth, clutching him close. Jenna was discrete, giving us some privacy with her back to us, cuddling our little son and speaking to him in hushed tones.

I was yearning to hold Aidan, so Jenna gave the baby back to me, and Ryan went to tell the others.

After everything was cleaned up and we were finally alone again, the baby suckling at my breast, Ryan went to the duffle bag setting in the chair. "I got you this for Valentine's Day before I came to Paris. But, after I found out about the baby, I decided this was the day to give it to you."

He handed me a book, and I looked at it, puzzled until it finally registered. It was a copy of Dorian Grey. I opened the front cover, and the words he'd written inside made my breath catch. My mind flew to the night we made love for the first time, when he woke to find me drawing his portrait.

~J
You'll always have my soul...
Forever,
~R

I couldn't help starting to cry and moved over in the bed so Ryan could crawl in with me. He gathered me close, and I held our son and love was like a tidal wave around us. His head rested against mine, and I stared into his eyes. The fingers of Ryan's other hand curled around my wrist on top of the bundle.

"Me, too. No getting around it. Even if I didn't want to love you, I would."

"That works, 'cause you're stuck with me." He smiled a soft, teary smile. "I mean, us."

Ryan ~

Julia was luminous and took to motherhood with an easy grace. Aidan would hush at the mere sound of her voice, and it filled me with so much pride and love, I thought I'd burst. I knew how he felt though. I was a slave to that voice, too. His hair was dark like hers, but he was the spitting image of me. The portrait that hung above the crib was an amazing likeness.

Our family and friends stayed in town until Julia had been home for more than a week. With all of our bedrooms spoken for, only Marin and Paul stayed with us and Ellie, Harris, and my parents at Aaron and Jenna's place. Everyone loved Aidan's name and the grandparents doted on him, even Aaron got a little sappy when I'd told him how we decided on it. Everyone was happy to see Ellie and Harris back together, especially Julia. Apparently, Harris would only reconcile when she finally agreed to marry him, and she was sporting a big rock.

About two weeks after the baby was born, Julia made a beautiful brunch before everyone left with tearful goodbyes and promises to come to visit soon. Our mothers were the worst, both of them bawling their eyes out. My dad rolled his eyes and smiled over my mother's head, and he almost dragged her out the door. Everyone planned on returning in December. Aidan would be four months old, and there was nothing that would keep those grandparents away from his first Christmas.

That was a month ago, and the time had flown by in a blur. I couldn't wait to get home from the hospital, anxious to get my hands on my son. He was growing so fast, everyday a little different, and I didn't want to miss a second of it. I glanced down at the baby in my wife's arms, and Julia handed him to me. "Time for bed, Daddy." She gave me a warmed bottle of breast milk and went to take a bath. I welcomed the task, because I loved time alone with him.

He was a good baby and hardly ever cried. I smiled down at the little face and patted his bottom. "You don't cry because Mommy and Daddy don't let you cry, do we, Aidan?" The baby version of my blue eyes looked up at me quietly, as if he understood everything I said. Julia was an amazing mother and my little man wanted for nothing. He was healthy as a horse and happy.

I settled in the rocking chair with just one small lamp casting a golden glow through the room. Aidan suckled away at the bottle, his little eyes were closed, his skin translucent, his tiny hand fisted and resting against mine. He was fresh from his bath and I inhaled the scent of baby powder. I kissed the top of his head, his mini-me dimples showing up as he sucked. I grinned from ear to ear at the wonder that was my son. Life was perfect. It wasn't long before he'd finished his bottle and was sleeping soundly all swaddled up in his crib.

I made sure the baby monitor was on and then went to find Julia. It would be about three hours until our son would need attention, but I'd take advantage of the time. It had been a long six weeks without making love to her, and I ached to have her. Our room had a soft glow of candles and smelled like vanilla. Julia was under the covers waiting and watching me as I wordlessly discarded my clothes, my eyes burning into hers.

The poem I'd written last Christmas hung centered above the headboard, and the words reverberated in my head as I peeled back the covers and gathered my naked wife close to me. She welcomed me into her embrace wordlessly, and I came to settle above her, into the cradle created by her body. I was hard before I'd undressed, realizing she had the same intentions for the evening as I did. I was hungry for her, but my movements were slow as I gazed deeply into her eyes and let my mouth roam over her cheekbone, her eyelids, and jaw. My need was great, but my love was greater and I wanted Julia to feel it in every breath.

She sighed as my mouth moved lower, and between kisses, I murmured the words that defined what she meant to me. But even these words, that hurt so much they could have been written in blood, could never be enough to describe how deeply she affected me, how she filled my heart, how she gave meaning to my very existence... and how every day, incredibly, impossibly, it was always more...

This Mad, Mad Love

Words cannot express...
All I feel for you.
As I search for explanation,
I am certain it is more than love...
A living thing,
Yet undefined by mere mortals...
Maybe even God,
You are my breath,
Yet you steal it away...
You are my heartbeat,
Yet you stop it with one brief glance...
Without you, I am lost.
I am nothing...
A bottomless abyss,
Empty and waiting
To be filled by you.
I ache to touch you,
To taste you,

To fulfill you,
To have you...
Our ecstasy is beyond imagining.
I consume you,
Yet am consumed by you...
Your beauty slays me.
Your touch unravels me.
I am humbled by these emotions,
Yet empowered, because you are mine.
I am you and you are me;
Never to be parted.
To lose you, would be to lose myself...
To cease to exist.
For there is nothing for me
Forever...
But you,
And this Mad, Mad Love...

CPSIA information can be obtained at www.ICGtesting.com
Printed in the USA
LVOW06s1052080414

380802LV00001B/13/P